ALSO BY ARI BARAN

The Penalty Box Series

Game Misconduct
Delay of Game
Home Ice Advantage
Goaltender Interference

Delay of Game contains descriptions of anxiety, body dysmorphia, and drug and alcohol use.

DELAY OF GAME

ARI BARAN

HARLEQUIN

HARLEQUIN®

Recycling programs for this product may not exist in your area.

ISBN-13: 978-1-335-00440-6

Delay of Game

First published in 2023. This edition published in 2026.

Harlequin Enterprises ULC
22 Adelaide St. West, 41st Floor
Toronto, Ontario M5H 4E3, Canada
Harlequin.com

HarperCollins Publishers
Macken House, 39/40 Mayor Street Upper,
Dublin 1, D01 C9W8, Ireland
www.HarperCollins.com

Printed in U.S.A.
1 2 3 4 5 6 7 8 9 10 HDC 29 28 27 26

DELAY OF
GAME

I.

TWO YEARS AGO

PROLOGUE

The Offseason

"You are *so* hot," the girl slurred, looking up at him from the floor of the bar's bathroom. She was probably pretty cute when she wasn't wasted. One of her tits was sort of falling out of her shirt. Her eye makeup was smudged and her hair was messy where he'd pulled it when she'd pushed him against the wall earlier, before they'd stumbled into the bathroom. She stared at his crotch like she wanted to devour it.

Zach really hoped she didn't. Or at least, like, that she didn't use teeth.

But what he said was, "Yeah, I know."

The bathrooms were disgusting, but at least the door locked. The night had been a blur, the kind of nirvana-level drunk where everything seemed like a good idea and it was impossible to say no. So far he had said yes to a lot of shots bought for him by fans in the bar, yes to the kind of ill-advised shirtless dancing that would make his agent scream at him once she saw the social media posts, yes to snorting some coke, and yes, apparently, to getting blown in a filthy bathroom.

He was just the right kind of fucked up for that, but at

least the sink was there to keep him from tipping sideways. His hands were white-knuckled where he gripped the porcelain for balance.

"Oh my goddd, I can't believe I'm doing this. I've, like, watched you play *forever*. I even saw a game in Vancouver—"

"Look, are you gonna like…uh, I really, really don't wanna talk hockey right now."

"Oh, yeah." She swayed a little. She hiccupped. "Gimme a sec, I'm not tryna puke on your dick."

"Thanks," he said. He had just enough hand-eye coordination to undo his belt buckle and zipper and pull it out, but anything beyond that was iffy.

She was sucking him off messily and enthusiastically and he was just starting to get into it when his phone vibrated against his ass. No one usually called him at this time of night unless it was a tier-three-to-four bro trying to party, or his agent trying to let him know that he'd fucked up. It was like Russian roulette, whether the night would continue, or whether he'd have to do damage control. Zach closed his eyes, enjoying the last few seconds of the high and getting his dick sucked, before it was time to face the music.

He pulled the phone out of his pocket while the girl was still working and saw *Kelly* flashing on the screen.

Shit. Agent.

Zach took a deep breath, answered the phone, and tried not to sound too fucked up when he answered. "Kellyyyyy… Kells…uhhh…hey."

So maybe a two on the one-to-ten scale of not sounding too fucked up.

He'd do better next time.

The girl started to pull away and Zach waved his hand like *shh, shh, no*, and, rolling her eyes, she went back down.

"Reed, what the *hell* are you—" Kelly was furious, but she was always angry with him. She was a great agent, and he was a nightmare client. There was a reason her contact photo was the frowny face emoji. "Well, never mind, don't tell me. It's this kind of behavior that *got* you traded."

Zach jerked backward, pulling his dick out of the chick's mouth, not even caring that he scraped himself on her teeth. *"Traded?"*

"To the Philadelphia *fucking* Constitution," Kelly said grimly. "You didn't *see*? They announced it on fucking Twitter before they even called me, for Chrissake."

"I'm—a little—fuck, fuck, a little busy—"

"*Are you fucking*—I told you to stop doing that when you answer the phone, for *fuck's sake*, Zachary, get your shit *together*!"

The girl, who'd gone back to sucking him off despite his best efforts, moved her head away from him but kept one hand curled around his erection. Like she wasn't quite ready to give up yet. "Bad time?"

"Hang on, I gotta take this," he whisper-shouted to Kelly, then looked down at the girl again. "That was great, but uh, yeah. A really bad time. Sorry, you were great. Like really great."

She rolled her eyes and hauled herself to her feet. "You're hot, but you're kind of an asshole, you know?"

"Yeah, I know," he said, with a deep sigh, and watched her go. She flounced a little bit as she slammed the door behind her, and he sighed again. Then it hit him. *"They traded me to Philly?"*

"That's what I've been *trying to tell you*, you fucking *moron*."

Zach suddenly felt like if he didn't sit down on the floor, he was gonna end up there anyway. He was too fucked up to really feel it, but he knew it was lurking around the corner. He sat down on the floor. It was wet and whatever he was sitting in soaked into his jeans.

They'd *traded* him?

"But I was—I was gonna buy a house."

"Well, clean up your goddamn act and talk to a Realtor in Philly, my boy, because you fucked this one up *royally*. I'm sure you're too fucked up to appreciate the elegance of that particular fucking pun, but also, fuck *you*, Zachary."

"Kells, I—I gotta go."

"Don't fucking hang up on me, Zachary—"

Zachary Reed, twenty-two years old and a Cup champion, formerly of Montreal, sat on the floor of a filthy bathroom with his dick out, completely fucked up, and thought, *Well, you* won't *feel it if you stay that way.*

Zach felt like he was sweating alcohol. It was probably a good thing that even when he was blacked out he could keep his shit together, for the most part, or he'd have to drink at home with no company.

The last two weeks were mostly wiped out of his memory, but the stuff he did remember pretty much sucked as much as anything he could remember sucking, even worse than the first time he'd left home for a billet and missed his mom so much that he'd cried silently into the pillow the first night but couldn't tell anyone, because you couldn't admit to shit like that.

Crying on some bar counters.

Throwing up in some bar bathrooms.

Telling a lot of bartenders exactly how the Royal had done him wrong.

He'd probably fucked some people in the middle of all of it, but the only concrete memory was boning some dude in an apartment he didn't recognize and then having to stop because he had gotten really emotional thinking about the trade and lost his erection, so...probably better not to remember any of that.

At some point he'd gotten a text message from some rando on the Cons but he'd ignored it, because fuck. *Philadelphia?*

"But like..." he said, lip trembling, "how could they *trade* me? I helped them win a Cup?"

"It's rough, bro," the bartender agreed.

Someone put a hand on his shoulder and Zach almost cried again, because he was completely alone in this world, and it was a comforting touch.

"Dude," Jamie Ayer, his now former teammate, said, "c'mon, let's get out of here."

"I'm not done, though."

Zach wasn't a small guy, but Jammer was bigger, and Zach was having a hard time coordinating his limbs to fight back. So he let Jammer half drag, half carry him out of there. He'd done the same for Jammer over the years, although probably Jammer hadn't ever been this embarrassing.

Zach was suddenly overcome by the fact that even if it had been years since they'd hooked up, Jammer was his best bro and they wouldn't ever play on the same team again, and his eyes welled up. "Jammer," he mumbled into one beefy shoulder, "this is *it* for us, you know?

We're…never…gonna play together *again.* This is the end of an *era.*"

"I know, bud," Jammer said, helping him into the car. "It sucks. But also, it's time to, you know…sober up a little. Or at least drink at home where people can't see you."

Zach stuck out his lower lip, mulish, and sank down farther into the seat. He felt dizzy and nauseous and probably looked like shit. He hadn't really gone home much over the last week or so and hadn't really remembered to eat. He knew it was bad, and he was overwhelmed with love for Jammer and hatred for Montreal's GM.

"I fucking *hate* Poulin," Zach said angrily. His body listed to the side. He tried to right himself, but it was too much effort.

Sleeping would be better.

Zach woke up in the shower, naked, water in his eyes and nose. He spluttered, "Jammer, what the *hell*?"

"Oh, you're awake," Jammer said cheerfully. He sat on the floor of the bathroom, his back propped up against the sink cabinet. He was holding a Kindle. Looked like he'd been there a while. "Wasn't sure if that would work."

Zach thought about getting up, but it seemed like a lot of effort. The floor was where he belonged.

"So you rejoining the world of the living, or what?"

"No," Zach said stubbornly.

"You can't stay in the shower forever."

"Watch me."

"Sure, dude. I'm gonna order us some pizza, see you downstairs."

Just to spite him, Zach stayed in the shower for another hour, until the water was freezing cold and *he* was freezing cold. His fingers were all pruny. So was his ass, probably. He tried to crane around to look at it, because when else would you see what you'd look like as an old man, but his head hurt too much, so he gave up and lay back down on the tiles.

Life was so unfair.

Hey, Nate had texted, this is Nate Singer, from the Cons. Just wanted to welcome you to the team and let you know that whatever happened in Montreal, it doesn't matter here.

It had been an olive branch of sorts, but Reed hadn't responded. Nate knew he shouldn't worry about it, but the sick feeling anchored firmly in the pit of his stomach. Had he phrased it badly? Offended Reed?

It wasn't every day that guys got traded in that kind of a situation, and the first thing he'd felt was sympathy. It probably wasn't easy to go from a Cup championship team to the worst team in the league, and under those circumstances. He tried not to think about it, but he was already worrying about training camp, so it was just one more thing to add to the list.

His fiancée, Rachel, was looking at her phone as she ate the dinner he'd made them. Probably scrolling through work emails; she had the kind of job where you were always on call even when you weren't, supply chain management for one of the big pharmaceutical companies down at the Navy Yard. He was proud of her, because she was brilliant, and if he sometimes wished she had a little more time for him during the summer, he couldn't judge because he was never around during the rest of the year.

She looked up midbite and saw him watching her. "What's wrong?"

"Just thinking about training camp. We don't have a captain and there are so many rookies, and now Reed..."

"You're going to be the captain," Rach said, looking back down at her phone.

"Rach, we've been through this, and I'm not."

"Yes, you are. You're the backbone of this team. You've been here the longest, through all the personnel changes. You're still young, so you can be a franchise face if Cote somehow manages to pull this team the fuck around. You're going to be it, Nate."

He looked down at his plate. He didn't want to be it. He really hoped she wasn't right, even though she usually was. Captain was a lot of responsibility, and he didn't think he was ready for that. Didn't think he'd ever be ready for it. You thought of the captains as the stars, the talent, and he had never been that. Sure, he worked hard, and he played his heart out every night, no one could deny that. But there was a reason the Cons had taken him in the fifth round, and it wasn't because he was captain material.

"Ugh, *stop* it."

"Stop what?"

"You're thinking about how you don't deserve it. Well, you know what, Nate? You do, and if they don't *make* you captain, you should talk to your agent and see what your options are looking like for next year. I know you have a few seasons left on your contract, but you could always demand a trade."

"Rach! I couldn't—even if I wanted to be captain, I could never leave Philly."

Rach's unreadable face was doing things. A twitch of her mouth and a tightening of her jaw. "I know. But maybe you should." She got up from the table abruptly and stalked over to the sink.

No one could do angry dishes like Rach, Nate thought, sad and fond.

Nate went out onto the roof deck after Rach went to bed, lay on his back on one of the reclining chairs, and stared up at the sky. You could barely see the Summer Triangle with all of the lights, but locating it made him feel better, somehow.

His phone buzzed.

Reed had responded, Thanks.

That wasn't much better than no response, and Nate sighed. He really, really hoped he wasn't given the captaincy.

Altair, Deneb, Vega, he repeated to himself, eyes tracking the stars in the sky as he did, until he felt less upset, if not necessarily less anxious.

"All I have to do is prove them wrong, right? That's the best revenge, right?"

"I'm not really sure if you should be looking at it as *revenge*, bro," Jammer said, because he was annoyingly reasonable these days.

"I absolutely should!"

"You're only gonna sabotage yourself if you're doing it to make these assholes sorry," Jammer said, and exhaled a cloud of smoke. He passed the bong to Zach. "You gotta do it for the *right* reasons, man. You gotta do it for *you*."

Zach inhaled, let it sit in his lungs, savoring the taste. He exhaled again, coughing a little. Jammer always had the best stuff. "When did you turn into a fucking philosopher, man?"

"Therapy, bro. Maybe you should, like, look into it?"

"You're *shitting* me."

"Nah," Jammer said, shrugging and making a sort of

grabby hand motion at the bong. "You're too high strung to fuck around with. Like kicking a puppy."

"Fuck *you,*" Zach growled, but passed it anyway. Jammer could be obnoxious as fuck, but he was still a tier one bro.

"So you write back to Singer yet?"

"Ugh, yes. That asshole."

"Thought that was nice of him, actually. Considering you're damaged goods and all now."

"It was so fucking *condescending*, Jams!"

"How was it condescending?"

"'It doesn't matter here,'" Zach said, with an exaggerated accent, like he imagined a Philadelphian must talk. He mostly only had *Rocky* to go on and he hadn't seen that in years. It probably didn't sound like someone from Philly at all, but he hoped that wherever Nate Singer was, he felt insulted, somehow.

Jammer looked at him pityingly.

Zach tried not to think about all of his broken promises: the team breakfasts he'd missed, the practices he'd been present but not-really-present for, constantly telling Kelly he'd clean up his act *next* time. Well. Kelly had dropped him, and so had the team, and now all he had to look forward to was Philadelphia and Nate fucking Singer.

"Besides. I'm just gonna go and I'm gonna play hockey and I'm *not* gonna get in any more trouble and it doesn't fucking matter what Captain America or the rest of the team thinks about me."

Jammer raised his eyebrows but said nothing.

"What?"

"I love you, bro, but you know..."

"What?"

"It was what the rest of the team thought about you that got you traded in the first place."

Zach reared back, like Jammer had punched him in the chest. That's what it felt like. It felt like betrayal. *"Jams?"*

"*I* didn't think that, obviously. But I'm not the whole team. And you're so fucking good, Zach, you could be like—legendary. If you'd just fucking get your shit together."

Zach put his head down in his lap and did not cry, but shit, his head was a fucking mess. "I just gotta go and I gotta prove them wrong."

"For *you*," Jammer said, patting his back.

Zach didn't know if doing it for himself was gonna be enough, but he didn't have the heart to tell Jammer that. "Pass it, bro. I got a week before I gotta start training again."

Jammer beamed at him. "That's what I like to hear."

The first thing Zach thought when he landed in Philly was that the city was a lot uglier than Montreal and it smelled like piss. That seemed appropriate, given his overall life experiences recently. He breathed it in deep, just to spite himself, and thought, *this is the first day of the rest of your life, buddy.*

The second thing he thought was that there was no way he was looking up anyone on the team before he had to. They might've been in the same city, but that didn't mean they had to be *friends*. He'd ignored friendly text messages from Nate Singer, who'd gotten his number from someone Zach was going to have to yell at later.

No. He was going to unpack his shit, figure out how to get around to the practice facility from his apartment, and work the fuck out at the gym until he could show everyone on the ice that even if he'd fucked up his life, he was still one of the best players out there.

The weird thing was that it felt like being in a billet again. Like he'd left home for the first time.

He'd really loved the guys on the Royal, with the exception of the Morin twins, who always looked at him like they'd look at some shit on their shoes, and although Zach tried to tell himself they looked that way at everyone, it was especially geared at him. He'd really loved Montreal. He'd really loved the house he'd been so close to buying. He'd put in the offer right before the trade and he had been ready to adopt a dog.

It was a whole life he'd never actually get to have, and Zach, for the first time he could remember, found out that it really fucking sucked not to get what you wanted.

He'd worked off the sadness fat, he'd worked himself into top beginning-of-the-season shape, he'd grown a beard, and he knew he looked good. The last few weeks in Montreal he'd looked and smelled like a hobo, which was the natural result of the amount of alcohol he'd drunk and the kind of food he'd been eating.

Now he was getting checked out at the gym again, and the grocery store, and when he walked down the street. Normally this would have cheered him up, but even the satisfaction of knowing that total strangers wanted to fuck him couldn't penetrate the fog.

So *what* if he was sad.

So what if he missed Jammer and Greenie and Legs and even Safy, the untouchable, responsible, self-sacrificing captain.

He was here to play hockey and he could *certainly*

fucking do that. He showed up for the first training camp early, and it was the first time he'd ever been early for anything in his entire life. This was a year of firsts.

He waited on the bench while he watched Group 1 skating. He *wasn't* nervous. The Cons were the worst team in the league, and he was definitely better than even their best player, probably. They were a mess on the ice; so what if he was a mess off of it?

He wasn't nervous, even though the Morin twins' little sister would be there, and he wasn't nervous, even though he was going to have to deal with that condescending fuckhead Singer without being a Problem. He wasn't nervous even *if* probably half of these guys he'd never met before had already seen embarrassing pictures of him on the internet.

The younger Morin had shown up early too. She was a big girl, taller than him even though she was a few years younger. Her brothers were big too. She was striking, in the sense that she looked like she'd punch you in the face. If he hadn't been in such a bad mood, that thought would have amused him. Striking and punching, you know?

"Morin, right?" he asked, glancing sideways at her. Her face was carefully blank, like she didn't want anyone to know a damn thing about what was going on in her head. "Tell your brothers I said bonjour. If you talk to them. I mean…of course you talk to them, but. You know, right?"

"Ouais," she said, and looked very steadily directly into his eyes. "I will…pass your regards." Her eyes flicked downward. She had the same heavy Quebecois accent as her brothers. On them, it sounded pretentious. On her, it just sounded a little awkward.

He sighed. She'd definitely seen pictures of his dick. "You googled me, didn't you?"

Morin's face looked like she was having an aneurysm, but she said, level as anything, "I prescout all potential teammates."

"Jesus fucking Christ."

So if Morin had seen it, they'd probably all seen it. He hadn't googled recently because he hadn't wanted to see what had come out of his posttrade mess, but he knew the third result pretrade had been an extremely ill-advised nude he'd sent to the girl he was seeing at the time. She'd promptly sold it to TMZ.

"Well, at least the team is so bad that you, ah, won't be the story for very long."

He knew. He looked back out at the ice, at the team of guys who hadn't made the playoffs in fucking *years*. His team. "All I wanna do is play hockey, Morin."

"Then we are on the same page, Reed."

"I'm turning over a new leaf. I'm not going to fuck it up here too."

"You are here early."

"I'm going to do a lot more than that."

Thankfully she stopped talking to him after that. Knowing the Morin brothers, he didn't think she'd feel sorry for him, which was fine. He didn't want pity. But he also didn't want to talk. In their own ways they were both gimmicks, except she was still on her entry-level contract, and they'd paid a lot more for him. That wouldn't stop them from trading him again, of course, if anyone would even want him after this.

Maybe it wasn't pity after all—maybe they were just in exactly the same boat.

Maybe she was nervous too?

"Hey," someone said, and Zach's head snapped up and his heart stopped.

Okay. So he'd caved. He'd looked Nate Singer up, so he knew about him vaguely, knew what he looked like in headshots. But Singer, it turned out, was one of those people whose photos didn't really look anything like them in motion. He was a tall, burly guy, but it was his face that caught Zach's attention. He was just kind of bland looking in pictures, like a caricature of a guy who spent all his time working on a farm, but there was something about him in person, something in his blue eyes and the way he held himself, about the firmness of his jaw and the almost nervous smile, that made him—

Jesus, he had to get it together. Singer was an overly friendly, condescending *problem* and also Zach definitely did *not* shit where he ate anymore.

He'd learned that lesson the hard way too.

"Hey, Singer," Morin said so casually that Zach almost rolled his eyes. If she was anything like her brothers, she was more than a little mercenary no matter her nerves.

The corner of Singer's mouth tipped up and Zach, even though he felt like puking all over his skates, almost felt the urge to smile back.

Singer was talking, in a voice that did have a distinct accent, one Zach couldn't place. Weird *a*'s, a little nasal. It was a good voice, though. A steady baritone. "I just wanted to check in with you both. I'm skating with your group, but if you've got some time I'd like to talk to both of you separately. Morin, I'll catch you after it's done, yeah?"

"Sure. I'll...catch you then." And she vaulted herself over the boards onto the ice.

Zach turned to Singer, who stared back at him, all serious business, no smiles. His head was very close to Zach's, leaning in. Zach realized too late that he had folded his arms extremely defensively, like Singer was gonna start lecturing him. For all Zach knew, he was.

"Look," Zach said, trying to head it off. "I know what you're probably thinking, but I promise you, I'm not going to cause any trouble for the team. I learned my lesson. All business now. I'm gonna stay away from alcohol and drugs for like, months, at least, you know...you don't have to keep an eye on me or anything."

"That's not why I wanted to talk to you," Singer said, taken aback. For such a big guy, he almost seemed to unconsciously try to make himself smaller, his shoulders hunched over. "I just wanted to make sure you were settling into the city okay, see if you needed anything?"

"I'm good."

"You sure?"

"Yes."

"Also, if anyone gives you a hard time about, uh, everything that happened, I just wanted you to know that I'm, uh, in your corner, and I'll put a stop to it. It's one thing to chirp, but that should, uh, be off-limits. I think."

Zach stared at him, trying to see if Singer was fucking with him, but his face was almost painfully earnest. Earnestness shone out of every all-American pore, shone out of his deep blue eyes and extremely white, even teeth. Zach couldn't even bring himself to hate the guy, because he was just so. Fucking. Earnest. It was impossible to be a dick in the face of all of that, and something in Zach surrendered before he'd even really tried to enter the battle.

"Uh, yeah, bro. Thanks. I got it, but thanks."

"Okay," Singer said, and clapped him on the shoulder. "See you out on the ice, huh?"

"Yeah," Zach said, and watched him skate away.

II.
SUMMER

CHAPTER ONE

July

Zachary Reed had a lot of obsessive thoughts about the captain of his hockey team, but one of the few G-rated ones was: *I need to win Nate a Cup.*

It was probably his least fun obsessive thought, but also the one he had the most. Or almost the most. It had come to him in his second season with the Cons and hadn't gone away.

If anything it had actually gotten worse the longer he knew Nate Singer.

He'd ended up thinking about it until it festered, and now here he was in Tulum, drunk off his ass at the pool of an all-inclusive resort with four of his tier one bros and a bunch of extremely hot strangers wearing next to nothing, and all he could think was: *I need to win Nate a Cup, how am I gonna win Nate a Cup, what will Nate's face look like when I win him a Cup?*

He wondered how it would feel to know that Nate knew that Zach had done it for *him*.

Like: Nate wanted to win, obviously. You didn't wear a C for a major league hockey team by not caring about winning. But he was noble about it. He had all kinds of ideas about the *team's* legacy and what the city deserved. Zach just wanted to make his best bro cry tears of joy, no matter how many people he had to flatten against the boards on the way.

Zach just wanted to give Nate something no one had ever given him before.

He shouldn't be thinking about this.

He was on vacation with the tier one bros, and vacation time with those dudes was all about drinking and dancing really badly and fucking their way through wherever they happened to be. Occasionally, in the past, hooking up with Jammer, who was at the very top tier of tier one bros. Blowing off steam and *not* thinking about hockey for at least a week or two and then crawling, feeling like the living dead, back to the airport to return to real life and training. Refreshed, recharged, whatever happened there stayed there.

Jammer handed him a Modelo Negra. "Dude…you've got that look on your face."

"I'm *thinking*."

"Since when do you do that?"

Zach didn't bother answering him. The pool was saltwater, painted so that the water looked like the crystal blue of the ocean when the light reflected through it. A deeply tanned girl in a barely-there string bikini jumped into the pool and emerged, glistening, to the surface. Jammer watched her intently. As she turned and flipped her hair, spraying droplets everywhere, she saw them looking and smiled; Jammer whistled. He still played for the Royal and was one of the few dudes from the team that Zach still saw on a regular basis. He was a connoisseur of women of all sorts, but he smiled a little ruefully now after looking from the woman to Zach and back.

"She's into *you*, bro."

Zach waved him away. It wasn't like hot people being into him was anything unusual. Generally, he was usually pretty enthusiastic about that. But today, it was just a distraction. "I told you, dude, I'm thinking. I've gotta like… I've gotta win Nate a Cup, you know? I've gotta just *do it*, man."

Jammer's sudden laughter startled him, even though it wasn't that loud over the noise of everyone else screaming and *whoo*ing. He laughed until he wheezed and coughed, and then said, "*Bro.* Oh, bro, you got it bad."

"How do you think I should do it?" Zach said, ignoring him. Not only was Jammer not helping, Zach couldn't let the idea go. And besides, he didn't have *anything* bad. In fact, he was excellent and had never been better. Unlike Jammer, who was content to sit here drinking and ogling pool-goers, Zach was being responsible and thinking about the future.

So really, he was great.

Fantastic.

The best.

He struggled into a sitting position. He was aware he probably looked insane. His hair had gotten long over the summer and he had it up in a miniature topknot, but he was drunk and disheveled enough that the overall effect was less hipster, more hobo. He knew he had that manic intensity you could only get when you were completely fucked up, but he couldn't do anything about that.

He felt slightly insane.

His skin felt hot and tight and uncomfortable, and it wasn't entirely due to the sun.

"Jammer, I gotta do it, I gotta get it for him, this is gonna be the year, but like…should I fight more? What about in the dressing room, should I like, step it up with the rooks? Bro, I gotta do *something*, we were so close last year. You should've seen his *face* when we lost, I can't let him go through that again…"

Jammer stopped laughing and started staring at him like he'd grown another head. "Who are you and what've you done with my Reedsy?"

Zach stared at the pool. The girl was smiling at them again. He thought about how much time he was wasting here in Mexico, when he could be at home, helping Nate achieve his dreams. Zach was gripped with the sudden need to see him, like, right now, even though he couldn't tell Nate about his grand ambitions. It wouldn't be until Nate handed him the Cup on the ice that he'd be able to say, *I did this for you, this was all for you.*

He staggered to his feet. "Bro, I gotta… I gotta go."

"What? Go *where*? Are you gonna puke or something?"

"I'm gonna… I gotta go back to Philly, like, right now, bro. I gotta change my flights. I gotta go, I gotta go."

"Wait a minute, Reeds—"

But Zach was already half running, half staggering to their suite, and he didn't hear whatever else Jammer had to say to him.

Nate walked briskly down the half block it took to get to his parents' house. As always, he greeted them with a new bottle of wine that they would end up storing in the basement and never using. As always, he let his mother hug him and plant an awkwardly wet kiss on his cheek. As always, his father clapped him on the back. His parents lived pretty much around the corner from him; the developers had started building new townhomes nearby, he had jumped at the chance to buy property close to them. It had its downsides, of course, but it was still by design.

The downsides became evident later on, after they'd sat down for dinner.

"You look like you're a million miles away, kid," his father said, from across the table. Dad was a big man, although he'd lost a couple of inches as he'd aged. Nate was taller than him for the first time he could remember, and the experience was disconcerting. His parents had been older when they'd had him, and it was weird being reminded that they were aging in *real* ways.

"I'm just thinking." Nate pushed the meat and potatoes around on his plate with the mismatched cutlery his mom put out when company wasn't there. Coming home always felt like this, on the defensive in case his parents were worrying about him again. It was funny: they were so fucking proud of him, but they also still talked to him like he was the shy, anxious teenager they had dragged to a therapist's office. Who'd refused to talk at all.

Nate had a lot of responsibilities resting on his shoulders. When the season ended those responsibilities, technically, evaporated. At least for a time. Once everyone packed up their lockers and went home to their respective states and provinces and countries, Nate was left alone in Philadelphia, the way he always was. The beginning of the offseason was a familiar routine. Rehab the injuries he inevitably played through by the end of the year. Take a couple of weeks to try to gain back some of the weight he'd lost. Start working out in the gym before eventually getting back on the ice. He usually spent some time at his parents' house, because they never got to see him as often as they would have liked during the season, and because he was a dutiful son.

None of those things helped him feel any better about the season ending. None of those things actually made him feel any kind of hope about the next season on the horizon, but he did them anyway, because that's what was expected of him.

"About what?" Mom asked, bringing another serving dish out of the kitchen.

It was always like this, too: too much food, too many things he shouldn't be eating, even though he did need to pack on some pounds before training seriously started. "The summer. Next season. If the front office is going to make any trades at the draft, or whether they're going to let us try again as a group next season. You know. The usual."

He hated talking about this shit with them: they didn't understand why he got like this in the offseason. They never had. It wasn't worth trying to explain either, because that just made it worse. They *wanted* to get it. But their jobs were so straightforward, with success measured in making a bus route on time or hitting your quotas at the shipyard. Not that either of his parents worked easy jobs. They'd labored hard to put food on the table when he was younger, to pay for his hockey fees and equipment. To make sure he was doing what he loved to do.

It just wasn't the same. He made more money now than they'd probably made in their entire working careers, and it didn't matter, because when it came down to it, he was a failure. He looked down at the brisket Mom had probably been cooking since earlier that afternoon and pushed at it with his fork again.

"Have you heard from Rachel at all?" Mom asked abruptly.

"What? No, why would she—why would you even ask?"

"I just worry that you're lonely, honey. And I thought

maybe… I don't know. Maybe she would have missed you too."

Nate could feel his face flushing, hot and red. Rachel was his ex-fiancée; they'd been together since high school. She had been planning their life together almost since that time. That hadn't stopped her from abruptly dumping him two seasons ago, right around when they were supposed to have started planning the wedding.

His parents still held out hope they would get back together because on paper, everything about Rachel was perfect. She was smart, she was ambitious and she was *beautiful*. She was Jewish. She had grown up on the Main Line and had those Main Line manners, the kind of girl who'd gone to Camp Ramah in the summers. But when her parents moved into the city when she was in high school, she had met Nate and had never looked back.

"I'm not lonely," he said. His mouth felt stuffed full of cotton balls. "I have Zach. I mean, I have the team and Zach. And Bee, I mean, and the rest of the guys. I'm really busy."

It was stupid, that his mind immediately jumped to Zach, when Mom was talking about *romance*. But Zach was the person in his life: the biggest and most important person in his life. Pretty much the only person he felt completely comfortable around.

"But don't you want to be able to come *home* to someone?" Mom asked, patting Dad on the hand. "When I came home from a rough night driving the 3, it helped to have your dad here to vent to."

"It's the last thing on my mind right now," Nate said. It wasn't a lie, exactly. He hated lying to his parents. It was easier just to omit things, the same way he'd done his whole life. To retreat into silence and let their well-meaning worry wash over him. It was the same reason he kept coming back, dutiful and uncomfortable and awkward, even though he knew how the conversations would end.

"Okay," Mom said. "But just so you know, if you want to, we started paying membership dues at B'nai Abraham again, so we could always..."

"Mom! I don't have *time*." Nate exhaled. "Look, I'm sorry. I didn't mean to snap at you, I really didn't. I just have—uh, a lot on my mind. Could we please—could we please talk about something else?"

"Sure," Dad said, skeptical.

It was a quiet rest of the dinner. Nate's hands and back felt clammy and sweaty as he kept his mouth shut during it. The only comfort was knowing what he'd planned next. He just had to make it through another few hours.

Nate exhaled a smoke ring. It was almost a perfect night, now that he'd made his escape from his parents' house. He couldn't really see the stars through the glare of the city lights below and all around him, but sprawled on his back in a chair on his roof deck and staring up at the night sky with the moon lazily traversing across his field of vision, it didn't matter. His body felt relaxed and heavy in a way it never did when he was playing.

It was a risk, taking a week after the Cons either failed to make the playoffs or their postseason ended, to get very drunk and smoke a lot of weed without talking to another living soul, but he did it anyway.

Marijuana wasn't a performance-enhancing drug. It technically wasn't included on the list of banned substances, but even then, it would not look good if it showed up on a random test. He rarely did anything that would risk his career or captaincy. But this was the way he'd learned how to reset in juniors. The *only* way he could deal with the crushing anxiety and responsibility that weighed him down during the year. The only way to go into the grind of another season, knowing they were going to lose.

He'd been through eight years of losses, and each year it was harder to bear. It was even worse now that he was the captain, and in addition to being responsible for mediating with the refs and for the team's success on the ice, he was responsible for so much more off of it. It was Nate's job to do everything from making sure the guys knew when they needed to make it to the airport and the buses to mediating personal disputes between players to checking in and making sure that there weren't any issues with the coaching staff. And particularly because he didn't have a WAG to do it, Nate made sure he organized a lot of the social outings himself.

He was entitled to one week off per year. One week to get crossfaded and forget literally everything. The week helped.

At least, the week usually helped.

Except.

This summer he was having a hard time letting go the way he usually did. He *usually* let the phone die and limited his computer time. Became impossible to reach, completely disconnected. His friends didn't call him. His teammates didn't call him. His parents didn't call him. Even his agent knew not to call him.

This summer, he had his phone compulsively in hand.

Specifically, he looked at Zach's Snapchat and Instagram stories…well, a lot more than he should have. Even when he tried to ration himself (the rules: only check once a day, no repeat viewing allowed, no stalking any linked profiles) he found that promise impossible to keep.

Zach was the kind of guy who had bros in different area codes. A *lot* of bros in a lot of different area codes. This summer he'd already gone home to Vancouver and then to Miami and Tulum, bouncing around each city with separate groups of friends. Nate found himself stalking their profiles too. Sometimes he'd catch a glimpse of Zach in one of their videos, lurking in the background or front and center, and his attention would focus on that tiny sliver, the beacon that drew him.

Zach, drunk and cheerful, smiling that fucking smile that lit up his whole face. Zach in the background of a video in a nightclub, dancing extremely badly, completely unembarrassed. Zach trash talking one of the bros, imitating him with a painful accuracy. Zach doing body shots and having body shots done off of him on a private Instagram profile linked in one of the earlier stories that Nate had maybe requested to follow earlier that day. Zach with his arms thrown over the shoulders of two of his friends, the three of them beaming like they'd never had so much fun in their lives.

That was the one he kept coming back to, studying the faces of the other hockey players who had claimed parts of Zach's life that he couldn't access. They were probably perfectly nice dudes. Prominently featured was Jamie Ayer who, along with Matthew Safaryan, the Royal's captain, was one of the few guys from Montreal who had stood by Zach after the trade. Nate knew how hard the situation had been for Zach and *should* have been grateful to Jammer for making it easier.

But he found himself frowning anyway.

At Jammer's easy smile and thick torso and bare abs

and Zach's face, which was doing the twinkling thing it did that made Nate want to smile back no matter what kind of mood he was in. It was a weird feeling, twisting his stomach, looking at it. Those guys barely even saw Zach during the year, didn't know him the way Nate did. They probably thought partying *was* all there was to him.

They didn't know the guy who came to practice earlier than almost anyone on the team, who was always last on the ice after a game even when he had to play mind games with opponents. They didn't know the guy who came to dinner at his friends' parents' houses dressed up and made even Nate's taciturn father soften reflexively under the force of his megawatt grin.

This was supposed to be Nate's week to disconnect his brain, to be alone to recharge.

But here he was, alone and recharging, and all he could think was that he was really fucking lonely.

When he'd been with Rachel, even she avoided him when he got like this. He was so carefully in control of himself the rest of the year that the dark mood after the inevitable season's loss scared her, and when Rachel had been scared, she'd expressed it with annoyance. Even after she'd left, he hadn't wanted *anyone* there.

And now, after the worst loss he could ever remember, all he could think about was Zach.

And the worst thing about it was Nate knew what was going on.

He was *jealous*.

He was jealous and he didn't understand why. Of course it made sense that Zach should recover from the rough postseason in his own way. Of course it made sense that Zach would hang out with his friends during that time. Nate had chosen this week to be alone; he'd never told Zach what he did during that time because he didn't want Zach to think less of him.

He *shouldn't* be jealous. It was what Nate had wanted. It didn't make sense. It wasn't fair to Zach. He wanted Zach to be happy more than anything.

The real problem here was that he wasn't fucked up *enough.* His body was vibrating, but he was still thinking about this.

It was time to roll another joint and make another drink.

He was in the middle of an inhale when he heard noise from downstairs and choked, lurched to his feet. Almost lost his balance. Realized that maybe he was more fucked up than he'd thought a moment ago. If this was a break-in, he wasn't gonna be much use after all. But then he heard footsteps on the stairs, someone taking them two at a time at top speed.

He recognized the cadence of the steps, but his brain rejected the thought. It wasn't possible.

Zach pushed the roof deck door open and for a second, Nate thought, *did I go too far this time? Am I hallucinating?* There was no way that Zach, tanned and muscular and wearing a tank top that said *I PISS EXCELLENCE* could be here, in Nate's house. Zach had the door code, sure, but it was not possible. Because Zach was in Mexico until next week.

Nate's brain wasn't moving quickly enough to catch up with any of this.

But then Zach crossed the space between them in two very fast steps and threw his arms around Nate. They had hugged before, of course. You hugged a lot of dudes on the ice. After you scored a goal, after your teammate scored a goal, after a devastating loss at the end of the season. You hugged it out. Brief and manly and usually with a slap on the back.

This wasn't anything like that.

There were no jerseys or pads between them. Zach was wearing that stupid tank top. Nate wasn't wearing a shirt. The touch of Zach's skin hit him like an electric shock. He almost recoiled but Zach's grip crushed his ribs and Zach's head rested somewhere between his jaw and shoulder and for a minute Nate forgot to breathe. No air in his lungs and his heart stopped. Nate couldn't tell if it was a *really* long hug or if he was just really high and losing track of time. But he eventually remembered that he should do something instead of just standing there. He put his arms around Zach and patted him awkwardly on the back. It was half affectionate and half making sure Zach was really there.

After fifty years, Zach let go and immediately grabbed Nate by the shoulders to hold him at arm's length. He inhaled. His eyes went wide, and his mouth opened a little, and Nate thought, *his teeth are really white.* Then: *he looks so good.* Zach's beard wasn't as scruffy as it had gotten during the playoffs, but his messy brown curls were on the longer side, falling in his eyes, and he was glowing a little. Maybe that was just Nate's brain, but maybe it was one and a half weeks in the sun without a care in the world.

"Um," Nate said.

"Nathaniel David Singer," Zach whispered, scandalized.

"What? I mean, what? What are you doing—you're in Tulum?"

"I'm clearly not in Tulum and *you* are clearly *fucked up.*" It wasn't clear whether Zach was horrified, delighted, or both. His fingers dug into the muscle and tendon of Nate's shoulder and Nate shivered. "Look at your *eyes*, bro."

"I, uh… I can't look at my eyes, they're my eyes, they're in my head… I'm not that…"

Zach had never had much respect for anyone's personal space and inserted himself into it like you would welcome the intrusion. Because he was Zach, because he was terrible and wonderful, most people did. Zach was doing it to Nate right now, close enough to feel the warmth radiating from his body, peering up at Nate's face like if he looked at it long enough, he'd find some sort of secret. He was so close that Nate could feel the heat prickling his skin, like standing too near an open oven.

"You really are, dude. Holy shit, is *this* what you do every summer during the week you're gone?"

Nate's legs got shaky, and he sat down abruptly on the patio chair. His body weighed a million pounds but his head was floating. "I, uh…" His tongue moved thick and slow. His heart raced and sweat prickled on his back and stomach. "You can't tell anyone. Zach, you can't."

Zach sat down next to him and folded one leg up on the chair with no regard for the fact that he was wearing shoes. Well. Sandals. His tanned, muscular thighs peeked out from beneath what seemed like three-inch inseam shorts.

"Dude, of course I wouldn't tell anyone. I just didn't know *you…*" He stared at Nate like he was seeing him for the first time, and Nate withered under the attention. Like he didn't notice at all, Zach reached out and put his hand on Nate's knee.

Nate shivered again, but Zach was already asking, "Is this like that Amish teenagers gone wild thing or something? Look, if I do it too, will you stop freaking out? Like you can swear me to secrecy and shit, and I can't break the bond because I've *partook*?"

"No, that's a bad idea. A really bad idea. I wouldn't ask you to...not after what happened in Montreal."

"I had serious stuff I wanted to talk to you about, but that can wait. Bro, do you *know* how much I like getting fucked up with you and how *rarely* you do it?"

"I can't during the year," Nate said, feeling suddenly apologetic. It was hard to deny Zach anything, but this was his captain's responsibility. "Not like this. I don't..."

"Okay, shut up. It's just pot, come on. I'm *here*, and I'm *so in*, bro. Also, I wanna see you do this, it's like... dude, this is like Christmas *and* discovering a cryptid all at once. It's like someone gift wrapped Bigfoot for me. Except it's you." His eyes were fixed on Nate's face, and his voice, damn him, had that coaxing softness he used with his dogs mostly but sometimes on Nate, a voice that made it hard to refuse him. "C'mon, Nate, I wanna see you do it. Please?"

Nate looked down at the joint, burned out on the table. He looked at Zach, his face a picture of innocence and longing. He sighed. He picked up the joint and lighter, rolling the end of the paper gently in the flame until it glowed nice and red.

The whole time Zach stared at him, and Nate licked his lips a little nervously. He felt thirteen again, awkward and pimply and hoping desperately to impress the girl he'd had a crush on all year even though he knew she'd never look at him twice. He'd been young and hadn't known anything then, and he'd spent five minutes coughing and choking, but now he inhaled the smoke into his mouth and held it there. Drew in a breath of air on top of it. Let it sink down into his lungs.

Zach watched him still, and it was the steady, fascinated expression on his face that made Nate do it. That and the courage or the stupidity that came from this week and lowered inhibitions.

He leaned forward to close the distance between them, and Zach tipped forward too, magnetically drawn into it. Zach's lips under his were warm and soft, and they parted before Nate exhaled into his mouth. Nate opened his eyes and saw that Zach's were closed while he inhaled. His eyelashes were dark against his cheeks and his hand, groping around reflexively, closed on Nate's wrist.

Nate pulled away.

Zach exhaled and Nate watched the smoke curl from his lips and thought, *that was my breath, it was inside of him*. When Zach opened his eyes again, they were very wide and very dark. He looked stunned.

Well, it *was* really good weed.

It wasn't a kiss. It wasn't really a kiss. He never would have done that. It was just—

"Uh, I'm gonna go see what you've got in your kitchen before I smoke anything else," Zach said, voice bright and casual. He pulled away and slid off of the chair. "I think *you* should probably eat something. And drink some water. I'll be right back."

Nate watched his retreating back, a little stunned himself.

Maybe he was going to have to rethink his week.

Maybe Zach had changed that too, along with everything else in his life.

Nate decided he had to lie down to think about that one, and so he did.

im losing my fucking mind, Zach texted furiously, once he slammed the door behind him.

Jammer replied almost immediately, which, considering he was still in Tulum, would normally have warmed Zach's withered heart. As it was, it was kinda worrying. Like he'd been waiting by the phone for Zach to fuck it all up.

Told u it was a mistake.

ur almost never right about anything

Fuck u. Sup, tho?

Zach was about to type *kind of kissed the captain and im gonna set myself on fire about it* before he thought about it for longer than the panicked second it had taken him to send the first text. That would make at least two ways he could ruin Nate's life, even if Jammer remained a true bro and took those secrets to the grave. Even though he trusted Jammer with *his* life, or at least, with most life-adjacent things, he couldn't trust him with *Nate's*.

Instead, he frowned at his phone for a minute. i've made some bad life choices. some really bad life choices

That's not news, bro.

jammer for once in ur fucking life

Deep breaths, dude. Feel ur breath. Be present in ur body.

JAMMER NOW IS NOT THE TIME FOR MINDFULNESS

Bro, I'm just tryna help.

Zach took a deep breath and felt his breath be present in his body. Or tried to. His body still felt like screaming and maybe throwing the phone at the wall. Instead, he said, im gonna set myself on fire

Maaaaybe just work on healthy boundaries instead.

wtf jammer

Just sayin.

im EXTREMELY HEALTHY

Bro.

i am! don't send me thinking face emojis!!!

He's straight. Right?

Zach wasn't straight, of course. He'd known Nathaniel Singer going on three seasons now, and previously he would've said he knew the answer, and it wasn't one that was compatible with all of Zach's stupid daydreams. Of course Jammer had guessed what this was about. It was too late now. Zach thought about the way Nate's chapped lips had pressed softly against his mouth. The way they fit like they were meant to be there. The hungry look in his eyes as he watched the exhale.

Yesterday he would have said *of course*.

Today, he hesitated. It wasn't a kiss. It *wasn't* a kiss. It was just shotgunning. Zach had done that a million times before too. It hadn't meant anything then either. Right? Finally: he's fucked up

Healthy. Boundaries. Bro.

ughhhhhh i know im gonna get him some water and a sandwich

Attaboy. Deep breaths. I believe in u, buddy.

Instead of throwing his phone down the stairs, Zach took his feet carefully down them. Nate's house had a lot of stairs. It was four stories, not counting the roof deck. Zach was as familiar with every inch of it as he was with his own house, and lately he'd been spending significantly more time here. It was just—if they were hanging out late, and they both had to be at practice in the morning, it didn't always make sense for him to go home, unless he needed to feed Hank and Dolly. He didn't do it often, but he basically had his shit situated permanently in the guest room on the third floor anyway. That was just the kind of guy that Nate was. Just in case. Ready for any eventuality.

He knew every inch of the house, including the kitchen, although he usually wasn't allowed to do much down there. Nate was a fucking excellent cook, which was one of the benefits of having him as a best friend. Zach was mostly good at bringing beer or ordering shit off of Caviar.

Even without Rachel, Nate had probably the most adult kitchen of anyone Zach had ever known. He had fruit in bowls on the counters and the lemons weren't just for show. The lemons weren't even brown or moldy. Fresh bread that only sometimes came in a plastic bag. In the fridge, there were leftovers in little glass containers, labeled with the date and what was in them. He had, like, actual vegetables in the crisper.

Zach rooted through some of the leftovers and found grilled chicken breasts and sliced cheese (actually stored in the drawer, who even did that?) and made Nate a sandwich. Because he was a good bro and he knew Nate would appreciate appropriate condiments, he also put some mustard on it, and some of the spinach he'd found in the crisper. He went back up the stairs, with a cup of ice-cold water in one hand, another tucked in his arm, and the plate in the other.

When he managed to get the door open, he saw Nate was sitting on the chaise, his head down. For a second, Zach took the opportunity to stare at him. His blond hair was sweaty and tangled and hanging in his face, his clear blue eyes were still red-rimmed and distant. His distinctive, prominent nose was hidden, along with his full mouth, in the crook of his elbow. He hadn't put on his shirt, and Zach could see every single inch of his broad shoulders, his sturdy chest and barrel torso—the thick, soft blond hair on his chest.

Zach took a deep breath. "Hey, buddy."

Nate looked up, still fucked up but smiling when he saw it was Zach, and Zach thought about what Jammer had said.

Healthy boundaries.

Jammer didn't know what the fuck he was talking about.

CHAPTER TWO

August

Nate had been born and raised in Philly, so it wasn't unusual that he spent his offseason there too. Zach had his Philly residence, but usually returned to Surrey, BC, after the season ended and stayed there until camp started. The fact that he was back early was unusual, and Nate didn't know how to adjust to it. They normally spent most of their free time together during the season, but the way Zach had just shown up on his doorstep and his own stunningly poor, fucked-up decision-making had rattled him.

It wasn't that he was avoiding Zach, *per se*.

He was just…not answering his phone or texts.

It wasn't like it was that unusual. Nate was busy.

Rookie camp was gearing up to start in a few days. Older players didn't usually attend, but since Nate was always in Philly anyway, and because he was the captain, he usually stopped by and helped the coaches out on the ice. He liked to get to know the prospects, to have an idea of what their potential was and what their personalities were like. It was important to have a feel for what was going on with the team and in the room: if you didn't, you risked the kind of shit that had gone on there right under his nose a few years ago.

He still felt guilty thinking about how he'd missed one of the players trying to bully Bee off of the team. Nate hadn't been able to tell that Kyle Hill—now the Long Island Railers' problem—had that kind of a nasty streak in him. He had been too wrapped up in his own head about a captaincy he hadn't deserved to notice the rot in the locker room. A rot that was *his* responsibility to eradicate.

So Nate had a lot on his mind when he was meeting the rookies. He couldn't afford to miss anything like that again. So if Zach's calls and texts didn't get answered as immediately as they normally would have been, that was, like, not really Nate's fault.

After everything that had happened over the summer, it felt good to get onto the ice again around other people. Nate never felt like himself unless he was in skates, on the rink. Off the ice, he was huge and awkward, looming and lurking. On the ice he could fly; on the ice he was weightless.

On the ice, the nasty little voice in his head was too busy to speak up.

This year's crop of rookies was a motley bunch. Until about two seasons ago, the Cons had been a lottery team despite his best efforts, so they had a mix of head-scratchers from the previous regime mixed in with the kind of high-end prospects that had columnists on *The Athletic* salivating despite a historically bad track record when it came to development.

Nate watched them milling around by the boards, listened to the hum of nervous, excited chatter that melted into the other noises of the rink. The raised voices of the coaches and trainers, the swish of blades on the ice, the occasional bang of a shot hitting the boards, the hum of the crowd already in the stands. Only in cities like Montreal and Philly did you get crowds like this just for rookie camps. He remembered what it had felt like his first camp, the swell of pride knowing he'd be playing for his hometown team, the anxiety that had had him puking before each day, also because he'd be playing for his hometown team.

There was Joshua Gagnon, an undersized, redheaded monster of a puck hound, a fifth-round pick like Nate, already nicknamed Gags even though his name wasn't pronounced like that at all. There was Pavel Tarasov, a slick, puck-moving defenseman, really too old for rookie camp at twenty-four, but freshly freed from his contract with CSKA Moscow and technically still a rookie. Juha Korhonen, already six feet tall but with the kind of permanent baby face that made people assume he was shorter than he was. He'd put on quite a show at the World Juniors earlier in the summer and Nate would have to find the time to congratulate him personally for Finland's gold, since it had been almost entirely his personal accomplishment. Owen Lee, their most promising goalie prospect, freshly eighteen and so tightly wound the springs were about to snap.

Nate shuffled his mental rolodex around as he watched them interacting, and particularly made a note to talk to Lee, or have Sakari Mäkelä, the Cons' longtime goalie, reach out to him. He'd have to go and talk to them all eventually, but it always took him some time to work up to it. Nate knew it was dumb as hell to be so nervous about talking to *rookies*, especially when they all looked up to him because he was the captain of the team they all hoped they'd be playing for this season or next. But that was Nate's brain: he'd had to learn how to work around it.

A flash of red, white, and blue out of the corner of his eye.

Zach, on the ice, in his practice gear.

"You don't usually come to the rookie camp," Nate said, when Zach had skated over to him and bumped his shoulder against Nate's.

"I'm not usually in Philly this early," Zach said. His tone was light, joking. He was smiling his media smile, the one that didn't really reach his eyes.

Nate looked back out at the rookies, who were gathering at center ice for the inevitable speeches. He would have to give one himself. "Why did you come back so early, by the way?"

Zach didn't look at him either. His eyes were on Gagnon, jokingly shoving a hand at Korhonen's shoulder, shaking out his fist with an exaggerated wince like the kid's solid muscle had hurt him. "Oh, you know. Just had a few things I had to get done."

Nate took a deep breath. His face felt hot, the same way it had felt that night on his roof deck when he'd made some extremely stupid decisions. "Look, Zach, about the—about the roof. I'm sorry. I didn't mean to make things weird."

Zach exploded, suddenly, with laughter. When he laughed, his whole face crinkled up, his warm brown eyes almost shut. You could see his dimples when he did it, his white teeth, his red tongue. He laughed with his whole body. It sounded too loud in the low hum of the rink. The rookies all turned to stare at them, but Zach ignored them. "You thought *that* made things weird instead of ignoring—oh, Nathaniel, you are a piece of fuckin' work sometimes, you know?"

"Well, yeah. You know this about me, bud."

Zach looked fond as hell, and that made it a little easier to bear. "Well, stop making it weird and get back to being normal. I miss hanging out with you, Cap."

The tension in Nate's shoulders let out, infinitesimally. It felt like he could start breathing again. "I gotta go talk to them now, you know."

"Be right behind you."

One day, Nate knew he wouldn't have Zach to back him up, to make it easier. That day wasn't now. He nodded and skated, without another word, for the center dot.

Zach had only ever been to one rookie camp before this one. In Montreal, he'd made the team right out of his first training camp, and he'd never looked back. He'd been with the Cons for two full seasons now, and he'd worn the A for one of them, but he was still usually in BC at this point in the year. So it just hadn't been possible. They didn't really *need* him there either, because rookie camps were about the rookies and the staff, not the veteran players. But Nate always went, and Nate had been avoiding him, so the logical way to get past that was to show up too.

It turned out to be a good idea, so he stuck around even after he'd managed to convince Nate to stop being weird. It was fun to be out on the ice again. He never stopped skating very long, even in the offseason, but it was good to get back early. It was also fun to watch the prospects interacting with each other and with Nate.

The thing about Nate was that he was really good at what he did, but he never seemed to realize it. Zach had been his best friend going on three seasons now and had watched him from the moment that Coach Cote announced that he'd be wearing the C. Zach had been there to see his evolution from throwing up after every game, to barely being able to give a speech, to understanding when players were having a rough time—like Mike Sato had been last year—to now, checking in with each of the guys to see how they felt their camp was going and what their expectations were for the next year.

"He's really grown into it, huh?" Coach Ford asked. He was the assistant coach who worked with the forwards and on the power play; he was older than Cote and had survived from the last regime, but it was clear that there were no hard feelings about who'd ended up with the golden clipboard. Just like Zach would never have wanted to be captain, it was clear that Coach Ford was perfectly happy where he was.

"Yeah," Zach agreed. "But, you know. He works really hard at it."

They both watched Nate, who was demonstrating to Korhonen how to do one of the drills. It was deceptively difficult; a weight-shifting and stick-handling exercise with added crossovers that required precision and concentration to get right. The first time most of the rookies had skated it, they'd fallen out of formation easily. Nate did it as naturally as he breathed, but slowly, taking the time to explain.

"I had my doubts at first, but he's proven me wrong."

For a second Zach felt the prickly annoyance he always felt when someone insulted Nate, even though this wasn't an insult. Instead of giving in to it, he just nodded and turned his attention back to the kids. He was particularly interested in Gagnon, a prospect who hadn't been on the radar for the last few seasons but had a tenacity that Zach liked. There was promise there, even before he'd had his breakout season in the Quebec major junior league.

After the drills finished and the kids started to file off the ice for the locker rooms, Gagnon hesitated.

"Let me guess," Zach said. "You like to be the last one off the ice?"

"How'd you know?" Gagnon asked. He had a smattering of freckles across his nose, a narrow, pointed face and big brown eyes, almost the same color as his dark red hair. The effect reminded Zach a little bit of a dappled hound dog, the kind that you saw in old paintings of hunting unicorns in the forest. One specific painting that he and Nate had seen, the one time they went to the art museum.

"I do the same thing. My suggestion is don't let people know about it, if you can help it."

"Why not?"

"Guys on the other teams'll do their best to fuck with you, yeah? All kinds of mind games and waiting it out. And then it's just extra stress you don't need."

Gagnon's eyes widened again. "Thanks."

"Any time. How're you settling in?"

"Pretty good, I think. It's a way different pace from juniors. But I'm twenty, so I kinda have to pick up the pace this year, you know? Or I'm gonna either be an overager or putting in my time in the minors if they don't offer me an ELC."

"No shame in going to Allentown."

"Well, that's easy for *you* to say."

"I didn't spend any time in the A," Zach agreed, "but Nate did, and it didn't hurt him at all. Not to say you won't make it out of camp. I watched you today, and I think you've got a chance."

"Really?"

Gagnon's face was so young and hopeful at the offer that Zach had to keep himself from cringing, embarrassed by how earnest he had been. "Yeah, of course, bud. I wouldn't say it if I didn't mean it. You got good hands and good hustle. Hey, I'll tell you what. When we get back into the dressing room, gimme your number. You can text me with whatever questions you got, okay?"

Gagnon blinked. "Yeah, um, wow. Thanks, Reed."

Zach shrugged, rolling his shoulders. "Any time. Not a problem, Gagnon."

"Uh, you can call me Gags, if you want? All of the guys do."

Even now, it was still weird to realize that the kids looked up to him and valued his opinion. He clapped Gagnon on the back and said, "Got it, Gags."

III.
FALL

CHAPTER THREE

September

For all of the awkwardness Nate had agonized over the last few weeks, it was easy to forget once Zach had made it obvious they could pretend it hadn't happened. And Nate had really missed spending time with him, which was normal, because Zach was his best friend and they had always spent all of their free time together.

It was hard to imagine, sometimes, that when Zach had first gotten traded from Montreal he'd been so depressed about the trade and so on edge about being judged by his new teammates that he'd spent most of the first training camp alternately ignoring and making fun of Nate. Nate hadn't known how to feel about him at first either, because all of his usual gestures of friendship had been rebuffed and rejected and he was always hyperconscious of how his teammates felt about him. When Zach had teased him and needled him and been awkward and prickly, Nate had just...retreated.

Those two preseasons seemed like a lifetime ago, and since then Zach had become the person he spent the most time with, the person he talked to the most, and just generally, his most leaned-upon buddy. It was hard to imagine being able to handle the captaincy without Zach as his A. He'd done it one season, and he never wanted to do it again.

He didn't truly feel at ease again until Zach followed him home for dinner and a movie night after they were finished with the on-ice stuff. They might have lived around the corner from each other now, but Zach couldn't cook for shit and Nate enjoyed doing it, so they spent a good amount of time at each other's places for meals. Tonight, Zach had already fed the dogs, so he brought them over too; by the time he was finished helping Nate wash the dishes and clean up, it was already pretty late.

"Buddy, we don't have to watch the movie if you don't want to," Zach said.

Nate couldn't even remember what he'd agreed to watch. Zach was really into whatever comic book shit was out at that time and Nate preferred more original sci-fi or fantasy stuff. "No, it's cool, we agreed. I'll stay up for it."

"If you're sure," Zach said, skeptical.

Halfway through the movie, Nate was yawning, the kind of huge, face-splitting yawns that rebounded three times worse if you tried to choke them down.

He woke up disoriented and really warm. The TV still glowed, lighting up the dark room sickly purple and red. Nate realized he must have slid to the side on the couch while he was passed out. He was tucked underneath Zach's arm, face pressed against his ribs. Zach was asleep too, if his deep, even breathing was anything to go by.

At a certain point in their first season, the late-night chats in each other's hotel rooms had ended up with one of them passing out in the other one's bed. Nate always slept better those nights, like having another warm body around quelled all of the anxious, frenetic thoughts that ping-ponged around his brain when he was alone.

Or maybe it was just having Zach's warm body around.

Nate thought: *I should wake him up.*

He didn't.

Nate closed his eyes and drifted off again.

When Nate opened his eyes, he regretted all of his life decisions that had led him up to that point.

He always slept better than he usually did when Zach stayed over. That was exactly as to be expected. And he had slept soundly the rest of the night. As soon as he realized where he was and what was going on, any rested, calm feeling evaporated.

Nate had never woken up quite like this before.

They were still on the couch, and Zach was fast asleep, his deep and even breathing proof of that. During the night they had shifted around so that Nate was wedged in between the back of the couch cushions and Zach himself, and he was tucked up against the muscle of Zach's back. And he was embarrassingly, painfully hard, pressed so tightly in the small space against the curve of Zach's ass. The heat of Zach's body felt like it would burn him alive and part of Nate kind of wished that it would.

He was hyperaware of every little detail: the way Zach's hair curled against his neck. The little mole on his shoulder, exposed by the stretched-out neckline of his T-shirt. The familiar frame of his body, somehow lanky and muscular all at once. The way he smelled, the same familiar shampoo that he had been using since Nate had met him. And here Nate was, nose buried in Zach's hair like some kind of a serial killer or something.

He closed his eyes and wondered whether it was possible to sink into the floor. To will himself out of existence.

If Zach woke up, there was no way he wouldn't feel the way Nate's body had betrayed him. He was so close that Nate could feel every breath he took, every inhale, and he had to hold his own breath to keep a groan from escaping his lips. Even the tiniest hint of friction felt insane; and he could almost feel the sweat starting to bead at his neck, holding himself so still.

Nate had to think about this logically. Somehow, he had to get out of this without waking Zach up. Somehow he had to fix it. It had been one thing to almost kiss Zach while fucked up, but this? He'd never be able to explain *this* in a normal way.

Nate tried to put a little distance between himself and Zach's body but only found himself pressed against the cushions again. Zach made a small noise, a sleepy, satisfied little noise, and moved back into the half an inch of space that Nate had managed to open up. Nate couldn't help it: he managed to choke back the noise, but it was still—audible.

Zach went still. He was definitely not asleep anymore.

Fucking hell.

"Uh," Nate managed, "sorry. Sorry. Can you—"

Zach sat up in one easy movement, turned at an angle so he was looking down at Nate. His brown eyes were sleepy and hooded, and his mouth was tilted up in an amused smile. Things were happening to Nate: he was humiliated and embarrassed but he was also—for some reason, he couldn't look away from Zach's mouth.

"It happens to all of us, huh?" Zach said, and his hand twitched.

For a second, Nate thought he was going to lift it. To

do what? He couldn't even think about that. He could still feel the heat of Zach's body between them, like a tangible thing he could reach out to capture. His own body was just doing the weirdest fucking things. It felt like he was shaking, although whether it was nerves or humiliation at the betrayal, he couldn't tell.

"It never happened to me. Not when you've slept— I'm sorry, I didn't mean to make things weird again." He tried to laugh, but it was a miserable, choked-off sound. "This is just… I don't know what came over me."

"It's only gonna be weird if you avoid me at camp again."

"I won't," Nate said, "I promise." The words felt weird and thick on his tongue and he wondered why the erection wasn't going *away*. It should have been wilting, fading, with how fucking miserable he was. With even the dogs, still curled up together on the floor, staring at him. But under the force of Zach's amused examination, he was still…

"I, uh," Nate mumbled, "I gotta go to the bathroom."

"Sure," Zach said, and it was like his eyes were laughing. Practically twinkling, like he knew exactly how much pain Nate was in, but he wasn't disgusted by it; he was just…amused. "I'll be here when you're done."

Nate beat a hasty retreat upstairs and, safely in his own bedroom, resisted the urge to bang his head against the wall. The whole morning felt surreal, like a woozy dream that had suddenly turned into a nightmare. Usually, he didn't wake up like this, so horny he could have come just from another stray touch. Usually he was too busy worrying or planning or *thinking*, like his brain insisted on coming up with various ways to prevent him from relief. It almost felt like an illness, like his body was caught in the grip of a nauseous fever, and the only cure was—

He half collapsed on his bed, the untouched pillows cool against his overheated neck; shoved his hand down his boxers. His dick was still hard and felt almost hot in his hand, almost feverish, like he was burning up from the inside. Normally he would have used lube but today he found that he didn't need to; he was already leaking and wet. Nate closed his eyes as he rubbed his thumb through the dampness, dragged it down his length.

It felt so fucking good, just to touch himself, although relief remained out of reach. His breath hitched as he picked up the pace, fist flying. It was almost painful to do it, he was so fucking worked up, on the edge already but unable to let go.

He tried to conjure a mental image—anything—to help him along. Thinking of Rachel felt wrong and weird now, even though he could easily conjure up what her body looked like, tanned skin against the white sheets, her dark hair spread out against the pillow. He tensed up, picturing her frowning up at him in bed. Okay. Not Rachel.

A generic woman. That would be safe. He tried to imagine her breasts, her face, but he couldn't picture it. He tried to think of anyone, and he just—

His hand slowed.

Nate thought about Zach, tense against Nate's body, and he thought about Zach, almost laughing at him, about Zach's brown eyes and smile and the way he'd tilted his head to look down at Nate. He could feel his hand speeding up, like it had a mind of its own.

He couldn't think about Zach right now. He couldn't stop thinking about Zach right now. The chill swept through him, his whole body curled and tense.

The orgasm hit him suddenly, like a slapshot to the helmet, just as painfully intense. Sparks behind the eyes. The come hot and wet on his fingers. Nate shivered, gasping; he felt almost too sensitive and raw to even think about touching himself again. Or moving. Or doing anything else.

For a second, his brain was blissfully blank. No thoughts. No anxiety. And then he realized what he'd done and his face flushed hot and red again.

Okay. That was…weird.

Objectively, it was weird, to think about Zach while jerking off. Everything felt slow in his head, mixed up and muddy, and it wasn't just the postorgasm haze. Nate stared at the ceiling and thought, *well, that can never happen again.* The guilt of knowing it had happened at all curled through his stomach, an uneasy edge to something that should have felt satisfying.

Nate exhaled again. Sat up. Went to the bathroom to clean himself off.

He was going to be normal about this because he had to be normal about this. He had promised Zach, and he always kept his promises.

He didn't have a choice.

By the time training camp rolled around and the rest of the boys had come back from their vacations and offseason homes and training facilities, Zach was *ready* for it.

He'd been thinking about the shit that had driven him out of Tulum for the last couple of weeks and he hadn't come any closer to the answers. He needed to get Nate a Cup, but he didn't even know where to start. He'd written and crumpled up so many stupid lists in the privacy of his own home, where Nate couldn't see, and he wasn't any closer to the answers.

The team was mostly the same this season, with a few subtractions and graduations. They'd lost Parsons in free agency, and no one had really been too sad to see him go—for some reason, Detroit had signed him for a 4x4 AAV. And, like, good luck with that. If you needed a guy to cross-check someone into your own goalie, Parsons was your guy.

But the core of the roster had remained the same. The coaching staff was the same. Sakari Mäkelä, their goalie, was all healed up from the injury that had kept him out of most of their last round of the playoffs. Beatrice Morin, the first woman drafted into the league and their star forward, was back. Mike Sato, coming off of a ridiculous career year and an entirely changed play style, was back, and even weirder, he was happy and *smiling* and laughing, joking around with Bee as they shoved each other around the ice.

It felt like they were so close.

It had felt like that last year too. But for whatever reason, they just couldn't get over the hump.

Well, the one good thing was that the Hornets probably wouldn't make it to the finals again. Not after that last, long offseason and all the injuries they were probably still rehabbing.

Zach felt better while the team was actually doing the drills. Coach had them working on some of the same basics that the rookies had been doing, with a particular focus on the small game situations. His body felt good; he was always in *shape* and conditioned, but it was satisfying to, like, have it recognized.

When he was moving, he didn't have to think about

Nate. When he was moving, he didn't have to think about waking up with Nate hard against him, the promise of everything he couldn't have just barely within reach. He knew it hadn't *meant* anything. He knew it was probably just morning wood, like anyone else might have gotten. It was just inconvenient timing that Zach had happened to be sleeping there as close as he had been. But it had felt… Zach wanted to shiver, thinking about the way he could have shifted backward against Nate. Just an inch, just a shimmy. Nate's cock would've fit right up against the crease of his ass. It would have been so easy.

He knew what Nate had been doing in the bathroom after that.

He could have—

"Thinking, Zachary?" Netty asked him.

He had to get it together. He couldn't be thinking about this shit during camp. He had to concentrate. Whatever had happened at Nate's house, it wasn't like it was anything that would happen again.

Even if Netty probably would've been the one guy on the team who would've understood the kind of distraction you couldn't control, because he had cheerfully slept his way through half of Philadelphia. Netty was one of Zach's good friends on the team: they'd spent a lot of time together during Zach's first season, throwing parties and go-karting in Allentown. That didn't mean Zach could tell him any of what was bothering him *really*.

"What are we missing, Netty?"

"Missing? Don't follow," he said, scratching behind his ear.

"The *playoffs*, the *Cup*—"

"Well." Netty shrugged. "Probably would've helped if Mäkelä hadn't gotten injured last year. You know?"

"You're *right*, but..." Zach said, a little put out. "Even if Socks wasn't up to taking over the crease, there should've been enough offense to put us over the edge. And I just couldn't *score* in those last few games. What do you think—"

For a man who had described himself as pathological fun-haver, Netty looked surprisingly serious when he turned his dark eyes on Zach. "Too early to worry about this, I think," he said, and shrugged again. "We see how the season goes. We know what to expect in playoffs. Mäkelä has to stay healthy, but the rest? Granny said two things."

"Uh...what did she say?"

Netty laughed again. "It's just a saying, a proverb. You know, means like, no one can know for certain."

"That's the problem, though. I *need* to know. I need to—"

"Zachary. *You* need to chill. Come out and party with me again some time, we loosen you right up."

Zach thought about it. He had to watch his shit during the season. There was a time he hadn't cared about any of that. A time when he'd spent a good portion of the nights after games completely wasted. A time when doing lines in the bar bathroom afterward was just a way to keep the party going. A time when even if he woke up hungover in the morning, he rolled onto the ice like nothing was wrong. Hadn't realized at all that it wasn't normal to feel stretched thin and floppy like melting cheese. The worst part about that time was that he hadn't even realized how bad it had been getting until he got the rude awakening of the trade.

Netty knew what he was about—once Zach had been traded to Philly, he couldn't fuck around like that any longer—and he respected Zach's boundaries, even though they'd still partied a bit that first year. It wasn't like Zach was *sober*—he still went out with the boys as a team—but. There was a reason they didn't spend quite as much time together these days. He'd tried dipping his toe into that pond that first season, and afterward, looking at himself in the mirror, he hadn't liked what he'd seen. It just reminded him of the end in Montreal. The more responsibility that had been placed on Zach's shoulders, the more conscious he'd become of what that entailed. Zach wore the A and had his goals, and Netty still seemed inhuman and impervious, no matter what he put into his body or who he took home.

It had just occurred to Zach, one day, that he couldn't be that guy, even if Netty could.

"Not this close to the start of the season," he said, a little regretfully.

"All right." Netty shrugged. "No offense taken. But you should, like. Chill. Maybe do yoga with Mäkelä or something."

"Yoga with Mack," Zach said, a snort escaping his nose. "Great way to sprain an MCL."

"What's this about your MCL?" Nate asked, skating by, a worried frown creasing his forehead.

"Netty thinks I should start doing yoga."

Nate blinked. "*You?* Why?"

"He needs to chill out," Netty said.

"I'm not flexible," Zach pointed out. "Like, at all."

"You learn."

Nate, face still flushed from exertion, said, "Leave him alone, Netty."

"I go, I go." He held up his hands in surrender.

Zach exhaled, long and slow. He felt weirdly tense

almost all the time now, like his body was twisted up in knots about how much he needed this season to go well, how much he needed to distance himself from what he had been only three years ago.

Yoga. Hah.

Still. Maybe Netty did have a point.

CHAPTER FOUR

October

Nate always liked the preseason games, even though they didn't count. It was a chance to get back into the swing of things and especially to see which rookies were really pushing for the roster spots and what they could do.

He particularly loved the surprises, like when Bee had stormed onto the team straight out of camp. When the Cons had drafted her, there'd been a lot of talk about how it was a publicity stunt for a team perennially at the bottom of the standings, but it was with Bee's help that the Cons had finally turned their fortunes around. They'd made the playoffs two seasons in a row now after missing them for the five seasons before that, and Nate was stupid pumped to see what they could do this year.

Or when Mike suddenly went from a guy who either sat in the press box or played third pair minutes and spent most of his time in the penalty box to a legit puck-moving defenseman who could quarterback a power play or eat minutes on the penalty kill, and it was mostly because of his boyfriend, who was now an assistant coach in New Jersey.

Hockey was so fucking weird that way, and Nate loved it.

Even though the games were close in distance, they were far enough from Philly that the Cons had an overnight between the first game in Boston and the second one in Buffalo. Management was all about conserving costs and doing the right thing for the environment these days.

The Beacons had been a perennial playoff team for over a decade now, but during the offseason they'd lost Tyler Hamilton, their longtime 1C, and Kristian Rajala, their equally longtime goalie. They'd had their Cups, but by now, those wins were a long time ago. Hockey years were like dog years that way. With the mortgaging of the future they'd done and some poor drafting, the cupboards were pretty bare. So Nate wasn't surprised when the Cons' rookies and bubble roster curb-stomped them.

He and Zach sat that game out, even though they were in the press box watching and would travel for the rest of the games with the team.

"Gags has been on a tear, huh?" Zach asked.

Together, they watched the redheaded rookie shrug off a slightly-too-late hit from a Beacons forward and throw his gloves off. Before the linesman could get in the way, he was trading punches with the other guy, who had to be at least half a foot taller and twice his weight. Considering the size disparity, Nate thought Gags wasn't doing too badly.

Fighting was a funny thing in hockey. Nate had never actually gotten into one himself. Even though he was a big guy and people tried it all the time, he just never really felt the need to go. He'd been called a pussy, a little bitch, and worse. More than once. Nate just shrugged it off; he didn't have anything to prove.

He frowned. "We should have Mike talk to him. I don't want him to feel like he's got to fight to be noticed."

"I can do it," Zach said. "I've got his number already."

Nate was distracted by the fight again. The linesman had gotten in between the players, finally, and split it up. Gags spat some blood onto the ice and made a rude gesture at the Beacon and Nate sighed. "Yep. An extra two for unsportsmanlike."

"I'll talk to him."

"Don't be, like, too mean about it, okay? I don't wanna discourage him. I try to do a compliment and then what I'm concerned about and then a compliment." Zach started laughing, all of a sudden, and Nate could feel his ears turning red. "What? What's so funny?"

"Dude, that's a *strategy* you do on purpose? You did that to me, like, all the time my first season."

"Well, um. It worked, right?"

Zach shook his head, expression rueful. "I mean, I guess."

"You did a lot of it on your own," Nate blurted out, before he could stop it.

"Yeah, I know." Zach's brown eyes were dancing, like they always did when Nate was embarrassing himself. With anyone else it would have made it worse, but Nate didn't mind when Zach laughed at him, because it was never *mean*. It was like a secret joke that just the two of them were in on. "But thanks."

Their arms were close together on the armrest; Zach had never really cared much about personal space the way most players did. Even through the suit jacket sleeve, Nate could feel the hair on his wrist stand on end. He looked away.

Below them, the Beacons scored shorthanded. He could

see Bee on the bench, grimacing. Even though it was only a preseason game, she *hated* when the other team scored. Nate couldn't blame her; he hated it just as much, even if he was too even-keeled to let the rest of the team know. He could also see Antti Salonen, his other alternate captain, shaking his head at her. He was playing tonight, the veteran leadership the kids needed.

Even with the shitty goal, the Cons did manage to win the game by four. Nate spent a lot of time afterward talking to the rookies who hadn't had spectacular showings about not letting it get them down too much. About keeping their eyes on the prize. About the preseason being about showing the brass what they had and knowing where their development would be best spent in the future.

From the dejected frowns and sighs, Nate wasn't sure how much he was getting through to them. At least he had Zach there to make jokes and lighten the mood.

There weren't a lot of surprises this season: the roster spots were mostly secure. Gags made the team out of camp, which Nate felt had been earned despite the dumb fight. Tarasov made it, of course, a definite upgrade on Parsons. Owen Lee had been a bit of a revelation and made a serious push at consideration, but the Cons still had Ruslan Sokolov, their backup goalie, signed for another season and couldn't afford to lose him on waivers. The goalie depth wasn't that great, and if Lee ended up struggling, and Socks was gone…it would've been bad news. While he might have been gone at the trade deadline, it didn't make sense to disrupt Lee's development. Goalies were always tricky, and easier to ruin than skaters. So Lee would be going back to his junior team in Winnipeg.

There weren't any real surprises. That didn't mean he wasn't nervous anyway.

Heading into the regular season, Nate took stock of the roster. It was a good group, but he hadn't really allowed himself to have good feelings about the season in years. He'd been optimistic once, a hometown kid drafted in the fifth round, finally getting a chance to play for his childhood team. Years of crushing losses and last-place-in-the-division finishes had shown him the folly of his ways. He had always been told that you had to believe you could win it in order to win it, but that was easier said than done. Even though things were different now, there was a part of him that just always expected the worst, no matter what life actually had to show him, no matter the fact that you truly had to go into the season *expecting* to win if you wanted to have any actual, real hope of winning.

The first regular season game was also the home opener. Some teams made a big deal out of it, but the Cons never bothered. It was just nice to play at the Franklin, to hear the fans yelling *shoooooot* and the familiar boom of the announcer calling the PECO power play. It was nice to look up at the stands and see the seas of red and white and blue, thousands of individual people smudged into a faceless sea of jerseys. From this distance he couldn't make out any of the guys dressed up as Ben Franklin, drunk and waving their prop Constitutions, but he knew they were there anyway.

Nate could lose himself in the play, didn't have to say anything except *got time* or *change!* or if things were really going tits up, *I got it I got it I got it*. Didn't have to do anything except predict where Zach or Bee were going to be, didn't have to feel out of place or awkward or weird. Didn't have any responsibilities except talking to the refs, breathing hard, when Mike got called for cross-checking.

"Come on," Nate said to Harris Sheldon, a ref who'd become something of a cult figure online for his colorful phrasing and memeable facial expressions, "that was just a little tap."

"Singer," Sheldon said, rolling his eyes. "I was born at night, not last night."

They were playing the New Jersey Scouts. Before the game, Nate had asked Mike if he was going to be okay playing them with Daniel Garcia, his boyfriend, on the opposing bench. The whole thing still kind of boggled his mind: the two defensemen had fought almost every game they'd played together and somehow managed to fall in love in the middle of it. Even though neither of them was out publicly, both teams knew about the relationship. In addition to telling the players, it had to be disclosed to management, and the fact that everyone had been mostly chill about it was probably a sign that the league was changing, even at that glacial pace.

Mike had shrugged and said, "Easier than fighting him," and Nate shook his head, watching Mike playing now, sprinting up the ice to join the shorthanded rush.

In the locker room after the win, Netty's awful win song playlist blaring on the speakers, the team stripped down for the showers. Netty was already teasing Mike. "You gonna let Garcia forget it, Misha?"

"Not a chance," Mike said, a shark's grin on his face, his tattooed body already covered in darker splotches beneath the ink, bruises that would show up in full force and color tomorrow.

"Michael," Bee said severely in her thick Quebecois

accent. She changed in the locker rooms with the rest of them, efficient and unselfconscious. By this point, even though she had been a novelty when she'd been drafted, she was just one of the guys, and no one looked at her twice. "This is not the way to build a healthy relationship."

"You're one to talk, Ms. Ticket to Finland to Get My Ex-Boyfriend Back," Mike shot right back.

Behind them, Mäkelä rolled his ice-chip-blue eyes up at the ceiling—he was the boyfriend in question—and said, "I am staying out of this one."

At one point, Mike had been worried about telling the team that he was gay, but he had done it. Nate was proud of the guys, the group he had built: everyone had been cool about it. And now they were chirping Mike about his boyfriend the same way they would've chirped anyone about a wife or girlfriend, the same way they chirped Bee about Mack, teasing and needling, but with affection and camaraderie.

Hockey *was* fucking weird, and he loved it.

The worst part about hockey, Zach had always thought, was the constant traveling. If he could play eighty-two home games, he would. He usually tried to pass out on the planes if he could because he was so shit at cards. He had enough money at this point in his life to afford losing a few hands, but he'd grown up with a family that had to pinch every penny to afford his fees and equipment and some of that had just stuck with him.

It was part of the reason he and Nate had gotten along so well to start—they'd both been raised the same way, blue collar. They had a lot in common even if there were a lot of other differences, like the fact that Nate was Jewish and pretty serious about it and Zach had been raised lackadaisically Catholic and wasn't serious about it at all.

Nate couldn't miss games even if they fell on the important holidays, but he didn't eat pork or shellfish, and he had a number tattooed on the inside of his left forearm. Zach had asked him about it once, and Nate had explained about how his grandfather had survived Auschwitz and had been tattooed there against his will. Nate's parents had been *pissed* at him for getting it. Tattoos were apparently a big no-no with really traditional Jewish families, and *that* kind of tattoo even more so.

"So why'd you do it?" Zach had asked.

Nate had shrugged and said that his Zayde had never gotten the original removed because it was a reminder that he was still alive and the people who'd done it to him were dead. Zach could still remember the icy look in Nate's eyes when he'd said, "When he died, it felt like the right thing to do to keep him in the world, somehow. To keep remembering him. Because no one's remembering *those* bastards."

It was weird, how many memories of Nate Zach had collected in such a relatively short period of time. How much Zach thought about him, collected all of the little crumbs of information no one on the team knew like they were gold and hoarded in a dragon's lair.

He was in his usual seat in the plane, in the back, next to Nate. Nate, who had promptly put in his AirPods—whether he was listening to some weird Norwegian black metal band or a boring hockey stats podcast was anyone's best guess—and fell asleep. His head rested on Zach's shoulder, and Zach, as always, had to resist the urge to smooth his hair down, brush it away from his eyes.

Today Zach couldn't sleep for some reason, even though

it was early and a lot of the guys were passed out already. His brain kept churning over stuff, about Nate and the promise Zach had made that Nate didn't even know about. He didn't have any reason to be, like, anxious. They were doing pretty well to start the season and the rookies had slotted in without too much trouble, Tarasov especially picking up right where he'd left off at CSKA. Tarasov, who was snoring gently, body slumped against Mike's despite the armrest between them. The two of them didn't always play on a pair together because they had similar skill sets, and it made more sense to spread them out along the lineup. But when they did, they were lethal.

Gags had had a rough couple of games adjusting to the increased pace and physicality of the big leagues. He'd had to remember to keep his head up at all times, never give up on the play as long as he was still on the ice. He got blown up in the corners a few times, but popped right back up like a whack-a-mole. He wasn't playing badly, exactly, but he definitely stood out, and not in a good way. Zach could see him, getting up and down from his seat, pacing up the length of the aisle.

Zach shifted gently so that he wouldn't wake up Nate, tipping his head back into the space of his seat with two fingers. Nate stirred and made a soft noise that knocked the wind right out of Zach's gut, but didn't open his eyes. Zach thought, again, how Nate had felt tucked up against his back, how hard he'd been.

Okay. Jesus. Get it the fuck together, Zachary.

There wasn't a whole lot of room in the plane's aisle, even though he and Gags were nowhere near the biggest guys on the team. "Gags," he whispered, "everything cool?"

Gags turned those hound dog eyes on him. His hair

was a little disheveled, like he'd been pulling at it where Zach couldn't see. "Yeah, it's cool. I just, uh, get like… you know?"

Zach thought about three seasons with Nate, sitting outside the stall in the bathroom to keep anyone else from coming in while he puked, talking him down from panic attacks, being the only one on the team who knew how twisted up in knots he got before and after games. He didn't always understand it, but he probably knew better than a lot of the other dudes what was up. He said carefully, "Yeah, um. That's not super unusual, you know?"

"Do *you* ever feel like that?"

"I don't. But I have some really good friends who do. It's not weird."

"I *feel*—" Gags blew out his breath in a sharp huff, and his brilliant orange bangs flew up. "I *feel* frustrated."

"Don't fight it so much on the ice. You gotta let the game come to you sometimes. You're good at what you do, that's why you earned that spot out of camp. You just have to stop getting in your own way."

"Oh, when you say it like that, simple, mets-en."

Zach reached out and ruffled his hair. "I believe in you, bud. You just have to believe in yourself."

Gags erupted into choking little snickers that he tried desperately to swallow down so he didn't wake anyone up. "*Crisse*, who pissed a motivational video into *your* coffee?"

Zach turned wounded eyes on him. "Joshua Gagnon, do you talk to your mother with that mouth?"

Gags settled back down into his chair, but he was smiling. "*My* mama? You should fucking hear her talk, man. A hundred times worse than me."

"You good, though?"

"Yeah. Fine."

Zach ruffled his hair again and looped back up the aisle to where Nate was listing to one side without Zach's body to hold him up. He wasn't entirely sure if Gags was telling the truth, but at least he was talking about it. Zach hadn't had anyone to talk to when he was a rookie in Montreal. Safaryan had tried, but Zach hadn't taken the olive branch. The idea of needing to rely on anyone, even the captain who was probably going to be a Hall of Famer one day—it had felt like weakness. Zach had just been there, the number two overall pick in an Original Six franchise, with all of the expectations of an entire province on his shoulders. And he'd given them what they wanted—the Cup—but he'd also had to find ways to deal with the pressure. And ultimately, he'd paid the price.

Philly was a different kind of market and Gags was a different kind of kid. But Zach felt uneasy, remembering how close he'd come to losing everything. He wished Nate were awake so that he could talk to him about it, but Nate was still fast asleep, his eyelashes resting on his cheek. Instead, Zach tucked his shoulder back under Nate's chin. Felt Nate's breath hot against his neck. Closed his eyes and, finally, drifted off into an uneasy sleep.

Nate got a close and personal view of the smeared, dirty glass as Dylan Cameron, one of the Calgary Stampede's most annoying forwards, smashed him into it. Nate was a big guy at 220 pounds. Cameron was a little bigger, and he was *mean*. Last playoffs, when he'd been playing for Tampa, he'd ended Danny Garcia's playing career with a nasty hip check.

This time the boarding had been partially Nate's fault.

He'd had his head down, and he should have known better. But—

Nate picked himself up off the ice, wheezing. He could already hear what the announcers must have been saying: *bone-crushing hit; Singer slow to get up.* All of the pads in the world couldn't cushion the blow of over two hundred pounds of muscle slamming into you at twenty miles per hour. His head was spinning a little, but he didn't think it was a concussion. Just a bit of wooziness he'd have to shake off. He'd have to get it together. He could hear noise behind him and saw both Zach and Bee up in Cameron's face, with the linesman trying to get in between them before it got nasty.

"It was a clean hit!" Cameron yelled at them.

The ref sighed. "Come on, buddy. Who the fuck are you trying to kid? You know that was boarding."

"You're fucking kidding me!"

"Yeah, he's totally known for his sparkling sense of humor," Nate said. His voice still sounded a little tight. He had to get it together even if his chest felt like he'd bruised a rib. They would be on the power play, and Nate was on the first unit. They'd probably start with the second this time, but he'd only have a few seconds of respite on the bench before swinging into action again.

"Shut the fuck up, *Singer*," Cameron snarled.

Nate rolled his eyes at the tone; he'd heard it before. Often followed by a word that started with *K*. Even then, he'd never dropped the gloves. He wondered what Zayde would've thought about that. *He'd* been a fighter. Nate was a competitor, but fighting? It just wasn't in his temperament. He'd learned to shrug things off even if his friends didn't like to let them go.

Cameron skated to the box, Zach dogging his heels,

chirping him the whole way. Nate frowned as he dragged himself back to the bench. That wasn't like Zach. Zach was cheerful, Zach made lighthearted jokes, Zach was the life of the party, even when the party was on the ice. Right now, Zach looked like he would've ripped Cameron's throat out if it wouldn't have immediately negated the power play and put them back at four on four.

It was a very weird experience.

"You okay, Cap?" Bee asked, slowing her pace to match his.

"I'm fine," he assured her. "It's kind of sweet everyone's so worried about me, but I'm a big boy. I can handle it."

She patted him on the shoulder. "You shouldn't have to."

"Don't *you* go fighting him either." Bee could hold her own, but the last thing Nate wanted was more violence when his ribs still felt like they'd been run over by a tractor.

"Cross my heart and hope to die," she said solemnly.

"That's really not necessary—" Nate started, then stopped as Zach drifted back across the ice toward him. Circling the wagons, as it were. "Hey, bud. You good?"

"*I'm* fine, I just..."

"Hey," Nate said softly. "You're gonna have to go take that face-off. I'll be right behind you. You don't have to worry about me."

"You know I—"

"I know."

Zach clapped him on the back, and Nate wheezed again. "Jesus, Singer. Maybe you should get it looked at by the trainers?"

"I'm *fine*."

Zach won the face-off, swiped it clean back to Nate, ready to receive it, ready to sprint it up the ice and ignore the fact that every movement hurt. He thought about Cameron, the word that he hadn't articulated but that both of them had been thinking.

The goal light and the goal horn blaring. Zach screaming in his face after he'd roofed it top shelf over the Calgary goalie's shoulder. Zach's gloved hands gripping his shoulders. That was better than his fist in anyone's face. Nate exhaled, long and slow. It hurt to do it.

That was hockey.

CHAPTER FIVE

November

They went out after the game in Columbus to celebrate the win. Salonen—Sally—the ridiculous Finnish menace that he was, had already started buying drinks. Zach was always sure that Sally was drinking too, but no matter how deep into closing out the bar they got, he never seemed to show a single sign of intoxication.

Gags hadn't scored, but he'd had a solid game, and he was in the thick of it now, beaming and drunk and red-faced and wide-eyed, talking a mile a minute about a tricky play he'd broken up, batting a saucer pass right out of midair to cut the defenders off before they'd been able to complete the move. Zach watched him, frowning a little. Something about the way Gags was gesturing and laughing set him on edge. He made a mental note to keep an eye on him next time, but Nate had already begged off, so Zach made his way toward the door to start the walk back to the hotel, only a few blocks away.

Zach, are you alive? Mom texted him. He'd just been gearing up to go up to Nate's room to hang when he saw it. I know you're alive because I'm watching you on TV, but that's about it. Zach immediately regretted leaving the banner alerts up on his phone.

She picked up on the first ring, and he sighed. "Hi, Mom."

"Look, I didn't mean to be a jerk about it, but you've been even less communicative than usual, kiddo."

"You have Mark's kid and Catie and Carrie's games to keep you busy. You don't need to hear from me all the time too. And you know what the travel schedule's like."

Mom made a tutting noise low in the back of her throat, a noise that made her sound about fifty years older than she was. She might have been a grandmother before her fiftieth birthday, but she was also the kind of mom who made teammates take the piss out of him and whistle and say shit like, *damn, dude, your mom's hot as fuck*. He'd known even back then that saying anything would only have made it worse, so he'd rolled his eyes and ignored it, but. She wasn't like Nate's mom, even though they both had that kind of anxious mom energy that made you feel like shit when you didn't call.

"Of course we need to hear from you. You know we worry when we don't."

Zach sighed again, more explosive this time, because he knew exactly where this was coming from. Sure. He'd fucked up in Montreal. And he'd hidden exactly how much he was screwing up in Montreal from them until it had been too late. His parents hadn't known any of the details until they ended up on the internet. Videos of Zach on TikTok, naked and fucked up out of his mind in some random girl's hotel room. A picture of him doing lines in a bar bathroom. In and out of peoples' social media like some kind of particularly screwed-up cryptid. That kind of shit. He hadn't been careful once in his life, and people he'd partied with had taken full advantage.

But it had been a really long time since then, and things were different now. He'd worked hard to turn over a new leaf when he arrived in Philadelphia, as tough as it had been to resist temptation, and now, seasons later, he was busy mentoring rookies, not embarrassing the front office or his teammates.

The fact that Mom and Dad still saw him *this* way, even after years of working to show everyone they'd been wrong about him—it stung.

They chatted a little longer, about Catie's high school team and Carrie's tryout with the Montreal professional women's hockey team, but Zach couldn't shake the feeling that she was mostly keeping him on the phone to see if he sounded like he was wasted. He *wasn't*. He was just tired. From the game, and of this: of being treated like he was still an irresponsible child when he'd done the hard work of growing up all on his own.

"Hey, Mom, I gotta go," Zach said, and hung up abruptly before she could answer.

He couldn't really afford to spend too much time worrying about his parents. He had to check into his hotel room and get unpacked, handle all of the usual shit he had to handle on the road. With the last few versions of the collective bargaining agreement, players who weren't on their entry-level contracts didn't have to have roommates if they didn't want to. Some teams still asked their players to do it. Voluntarily of course. To be self-sacrificing and save money, *of course*. But the Cons had deep pockets for all the team had been scraping the bottom of the barrel of the standings for so long, and so the guys had been given a choice.

Nate chose to room by himself, which wasn't surprising. It wasn't because he was the captain or because he was full of himself, it was just, Zach thought fondly, that he was shy and really *needed* his quiet downtime after the games. He'd put in his appearances at the team hangouts, because he was the captain, but Zach was probably the only one on the team who knew how relieved he was to escape after.

Nate never seemed to mind when Zach showed up and knocked on the door, though. He opened it almost immediately, the same way he always did. Zach saw that he was already dressed for bed. He wore his ratty Cons playoff T-shirt and a pair of soft joggers that hung low on his hips, so old the elastic was shot, left nothing to the imagination. His feet were bare. He smiled when he saw who it was, and for a second Zach was punched in the stomach by just how fucking hot Nate was.

It wasn't just his body, huge and burly and with a solid core that sometimes Zach just had the urge to touch, it was everything about him. Individually it was like all of his features should have been too big for his face—the strong nose, hooked with the bump at the bridge where it had been broken, the full mouth, the huge blue eyes fringed with thick eyelashes, a few shades darker than his hair. He had light freckles, just a smattering of them on his nose and his shoulders and across his shoulder blades.

And when he smiled, it was like his whole solemn, worried face just lit up, like you could finally see what he was like inside. The way Zach knew him.

Zach had been doomed since the first training camp.

"Hey," Nate said, and blinked. "You okay, buddy?"

"Yeah, uh… My mom called. I just—you mind if I crash here with you tonight?"

"Of course not. Come on in."

"Thanks," Zach said. It was stupid, that his parents thinking about him like that upset him so much. *He* knew what he was about. Nate knew what he was about. The team knew what he was about. That was the important thing. It was so fucking dumb, that he was in his mid-twenties, and he still cared so much about what his parents thought about him.

"Do you...want to talk about it?" Nate asked, hesitant. He slanted a gaze sideways at Zach, always anxious about pushing too much.

"No," Zach interrupted. "God, no. Like, the last thing I wanna do is talk about it. I'd be down for just, uh. Watching a movie or something."

Nate was looking at him again, shrewd and worried and kind, and said, "Whatever you want, buddy."

With anyone else, the normal thing to do would have been to sit apart, each of them with a queen bed to themselves. That was what Zach did whenever he normally hung out with hockey buddies, even the hockey buddies he was hooking up with. That was—well, the normal thing to do. Two bros chilling two beds apart, because they weren't gay. Even if they *were* kind of gay. Or at least bi. Or even horny enough not to care about who was sucking whose dick.

He wasn't sure when things had shifted with Nate, but he didn't have to ask anymore, didn't have to question it.

He flopped down on the bed Nate had been sitting in, the blankets displaced by his body, wriggled around until he got comfortable. Nate sat down next to him, more deliberately, and flipped through the TV channels, looking for something both of them would like. They couldn't usually watch comedies because Nate got such awful second-hand embarrassment sometimes that he had to turn them off, so the options were limited.

"You know," Nate said, halfway through. Zach, who

hadn't even been watching the movie, was already half-asleep, his face smashed against Nate's bicep. "Your parents are gonna have to get over it sometime."

"Huh?" Zach mumbled.

"Never mind."

"Mmm. 'Kay."

At some point in the middle of the night Zach woke up, pressed against Nate's muscular back. His breathing was deep and even. Zach, like a fucking creep, sat up a little, peered over his shoulder. In sleep, Nate's anxious face smoothed out into something calmer, although Zach could still see the way that the dark circles under his eyes were carved in deep, the way his eyelids looked almost bruised. The captain was always tired. He often slept with one hand tucked underneath the pillow, a posture that almost reminded Zach of a little kid and gave him weird, protective urges.

Zach exhaled. It was pressing his luck every time he did this, every time Nate let him wake up in the same bed and smiled at him in the morning like what they were doing wasn't weird as hell. Like what had happened back in September, the thing they'd never talked about again, wasn't lurking in the back of his head every time.

He sighed. He should go back to his own room. He should really, really go back to his own room. In his sleep, Nate made a soft, quiet noise, and turned over toward Zach. His arm looped over Zach's waist, a heavy, comforting weight over Zach's body.

Zach should really, *really* go back to his own room.

He didn't.

By mid-November Nate felt like the team had started to get the hang of things and the new guys were all integrated in.

One of their longtime wingers, Clark, had gotten a necessary hernia surgery and would probably miss the rest of the season. They called up Adam Belsky, a defensively sound middle six kid who'd been playing the last two seasons in Allentown, to handle it. It had taken Belsky a few weeks to get into the rhythm of things, but now he fit in as seamlessly as you could hope. Gags had calmed down on the ice, although between him and Netty, the team hangs after games were dangerous places to be. At least, Nate thought a little doubtfully, he was fitting in.

They were in Boston again.

The Cons didn't have a real rivalry with the Beacons, not the way they did with Pittsburgh or even the New York Liberty, both of whom had recently won Cups, which always made it worse. Boston fans were annoying, but it was the same way there the way it was in any big hockey city like Montreal. It just made it more fun to win at home and shut them up. And it was way better than a place like Toronto, which had the history and the obsession, but where tickets were so expensive that it meant most of the attendees were corporate assholes who weren't paying attention to the game anyway. The Toronto crowds were always quiet, no matter who was winning.

Even on the bench, when Nate needed to keep half an ear out for line changes, he was always watching the play. He had been a fifth-round pick for a number of reasons—one of which was his weight and the fact that scouts had concerns about conditioning, which was just another way of saying he was fat—but the other was his hockey sense.

As a kid he'd always been forcing the play, so nervous about fucking up that he actually made it worse for himself. It had taken a few years in the minors, the seasons of experience, to understand how to leave some of that in the locker room. And despite what a lot of the scouts thought, you *could* learn how to improve your reads. He was a case in point. But it was an active thing, something he was always working on, and he felt like if he started slouching just a bit, he'd lose the ability he'd worked so hard to earn.

Coach Cote still ran the aggressive 2-1-2 forecheck that the Cons had been using since the '70s, back when they were more concerned about outmuscling the rest of the league than they were about skill. It wasn't a difficult system and it still worked for them. As Nate watched, Andersson and Gags moved across the blue line, pushing the Beacons' d-men back. As they moved forward, Netty swung across to cover the exits and behind them, Mike following close to pinch, Tarasov a few paces behind. Andersson managed to intercept a pass as Gags swept back across to prevent an odd man rush and managed to fire it through traffic to him. The pass quickly turned into another, and then a shot that landed, satisfyingly, into the back of the net.

Nate smiled as he watched them celly.

For a second, he allowed himself to think: *maybe this year will be a good one.*

IV.
WINTER

CHAPTER SIX

December

It was the third game they'd lost in a row and Nate was trying not to panic.

Each season since Coach Cote had taken over and Zach and Bee had joined the team, he'd had the secret thought, for brief, almost nonexistent instances: *maybe, maybe, we have a chance at the Cup*. He hadn't fully let himself form it even though Coach used to say that if you went into the season expecting anything other than the Cup you'd already lost it. He *knew* that. Nate also knew he would never be able to grow the kind of balls that let you believe it.

Still. Three losses in a row was worrying. He'd had hopes for this season after the crushing disappointment of the second round last year. But at this rate…

He'd already thrown up. His mouth tasted sour, like vomit and sweat and mucus, and his body felt shaky, the adrenaline of the game and the disappointment of the loss. The rest of the team had already gone, but he was still walking around the locker room, like if he paced enough, he'd be able to figure out the magic formula to get them back on track. Sometimes it was comforting to be in here, with the stalls arrayed around the circle of the room, the familiar faces in the same order every time. Even while he paced, he was careful not to step on the Cons' logo in the middle of the floor; it was bad fucking luck to do that, and Nate was superstitious as anyone.

It didn't ease his frustration.

He smacked his head against the wall.

"Whoa, buddy, buddy," Zach said from behind him, hand on his back. "Aren't you the one who's always like, *no head injuries*?"

"We lost *again*."

"So you're trying to give *yourself* a concussion?"

"It's my fault, Zach."

"Uh, dude, we've been through this like a million times over the last few years…our losses are everyone's fault, not just yours."

"That's not very encouraging," Nate said, with a noise that wasn't quite a laugh but wasn't quite a sob either. It sounded like the dying wheeze of a small animal run over by a car on the highway, which also accurately described what he felt like right now.

Zach was looking at him with his head cocked a little to the side. "We're just in a little rut. And *you*… Hey, when was the last time you got laid?"

"I—what?"

"You know, having *relations*, doing the hanky-panky, jamming the clam, torpedoing the eel, shucking the oyster—"

"Oh my *god*, fucking stop it—uh, why do most of those euphemisms have to do with fish?"

"Don't worry about it, man. But I mean, jokes aside, when *was* the last time?"

Nate could feel the tips of his ears getting hot. He

could remember exactly the last time, and it was last year. Zach had brought his girlfriend at the time—Alison—to practice. Nate had looked up into the bleachers, saw her sitting there cheering him on during the 5x5 drills, and felt shittier than he'd felt since Rachel had left him. That night he'd gone out to a bar and picked up the first cute, brown-eyed girl with a crooked smile who'd looked back at him twice, and gone back to her place.

It had been sex, all right.

"Uh..."

Zach was looking at him expectantly, then sympathetically. "Dude."

"Last season, okay? Before—" *you broke up with Alison* "—the playoffs."

"Oh my fucking god, bro. Dude! *Dude?* Dude. Like—what? *Bro.*" Nate's face must have reflected some of the horror he felt, because Zach's expression turned immediately solicitous. Instead of berating Nate further, he crossed the locker room to grab Nate's arm, fingers tightening around the bicep. "We're going out, and I'm *going* to get you laid, and we're *gonna* break this losing streak, okay?"

"I don't think—"

"Don't argue with me, bro. Like, just don't."

When it came to Zach, Nate sometimes felt like the man was a tsunami in the actual sense of what tsunamis were like. Not a sudden huge and rising wave, but the slow and inexorable crush of the water rising steadily and bearing away everything in its path, ripping it from its moorings and carrying it away. Nate was helpless in the face of it.

And that was how he found himself bullied into going home, brushing his teeth and getting changed into clothes that Zach deemed acceptable for a night out ("I'm not gonna be your wingman if you look like a fuckin' slob, bro") and dragged back out again, feeling like he was a million feet tall and completely out of place at the trendy rooftop bar Zach had chosen.

Nate was the sort of person who hadn't dated so much as he had been acquired by his first and only girlfriend. She'd decided that she wanted to date him, and she did. Before her, he'd been a greasy, chubby virgin who spent more time in the basement of his parents' house trying to Febreze away the smell of weed than he had going on dates. And after her, he'd been too depressed to try meeting anyone new on his own. Even if he had made a legitimate effort to rebound, that was his entire young adult dating life gone. Where most people developed skills by trial and error, Nate had nothing.

He'd tried to convey some of this to Zach, but Zach had only looked at him in confusion and said, "Bro, you don't have to *talk* to them. Just look hot and I'll do the rest, okay?"

"But I'm *not* hot?"

"Shh, shh, Nathaniel. What did I tell you about talking?"

Nate had shut his mouth, face burning, and let Zach bully him into the bar. It was a crisp December night. All Nate needed was a sweater and a light coat, and the city sparkled below them.

Zach bought them shots, and when Nate looked at him questioningly, said, "Liquid courage, bro," and so Nate did the shot. Zach bought another round and nudged the glass across the bar to him. "See, your problem is that you just think too much."

"I…can't really help it."

"But that's the thing, dude, right? Like what's the big deal if you embarrass yourself in front of some chick at a bar? You're never gonna see her again, probably, and you're the captain of a *professional hockey team*."

I don't deserve to be, he thought, but what he said was, "I don't see how they're connected—"

"The *point* I'm trying to make is like. Who cares if you embarrass yourself a little, because in the end, dude, you're like—you're doing pretty fucking good, right? One person's opinion don't mean shit."

Nate caught himself licking his lower lip, nervously. It bore the sharp sting of vodka. "I mean…when you put it that way…it makes sense? But like…my brain just… I *know* it's not a big deal, but it's like I can't stop thinking about it, and when I do I just feel sick, and…"

"See," Zach said fondly, "you just gotta listen to me instead of your brain."

The laugh escaped him like he'd been punched in the ribs—shocked out of him. "God, Zach," he said, helpless.

Zach patted him on the arm. He was smiling at Nate in the way that made his eyes crinkle up, made Nate smile back whether he felt like it or not. Zach's mouth tipped up at the corner and the dimple deepened the way it always did when they got caught up in the hall of mirrors of grinning at each other. "You keep drinking until your brain shuts up, and I'm gonna go find your first opportunity."

Nate took his advice, because there was no way he was going to get through the night if he didn't. He was a little buzzed by the time Zach brought the first girl over. She was pretty in a very girl-next-door kind of way, with curly brown hair, melting brown eyes, and a mischievous smile. He smiled awkwardly at her, and she smiled back, like she was amused at his incompetence.

"Eva, this is Nate," Zach was saying, "he's having a

pretty shitty night tonight, but I'm like 99% sure your smile could cheer *anyone* up."

She raised her eyebrows. "Only 99%?"

"He, uh, means I'm—uh—"

"Now, buddy, what'd we say about being down on yourself?"

The girl was laughing at them now. "You guys are cute."

In the end she didn't end up hanging out that long; Nate couldn't make himself open his goddamn mouth. It wasn't just that he was nervous, because he was, but he didn't—the more they talked and the more they drank, the more he knew he didn't want to go home with her even if *she* wanted to go home with him. He knew Zach was trying valiantly to keep the conversation going, kept elbowing him in the side when he gave monosyllable answers or couldn't quite look her in the eyes, but he just—he didn't want to do it.

Eventually, Eva smiled, bid them a cheerful good-night, and strolled away, hips swaying.

Zach looked at him, reproachful. "Okay, so you weren't into her, but there are a fuck-ton of girls here. I'm gonna find you *someone*."

Nate watched him walk away, striding confidently, purposefully, through the crowd. A man on a mission, secure in the fact that no one who'd ever seen him hadn't thought, *god, he's fucking hot*.

The same thing happened with Hailey, Madison, Taylor, and Emily. By the time Hannah walked away rolling her eyes, Nate was extremely drunk, and Zach was looking at him with a combination of pity and horror.

"My god, dude," he said, after they finished their latest round of shots.

Nate didn't want to think about the tab, between what

they'd drank between them and the drinks he'd bought the girls Zach had roped. Zach was drunk enough now that he was listing sideways a little, like a ship on a rough ocean. No—more accurately, like the Leaning Tower of Pisa, because neither the tower nor Zach were moving. Zach tilted against Nate, used Nate's body for support. And Nate let him do it, which the small part of his brain he usually ignored said was a bad idea, but the rest of him liked too much to stop.

"What?"

"Is this really how you are when you go out, like all the time?"

"I don't know, I don't like… I don't go out a lot."

"You go out with us all the time."

"Yeah, but that's with the boys, I'm not like—not like trying to pick up."

"Why not?" Zach said, looking up at Nate, his eyes wide, like he was seriously confused. "Anyone would like… Any girl would be like lucky to have you, you know?"

Nate thought, *I'm not drunk enough for this*. He said, "I, uh, I don't know about that."

Zach patted his forearm reassuringly. "Don't worry, bud. I promised I'd get you laid and New Zach keeps his fuckin' promises, all right?"

"I…" Nate's teeth worried his lower lip and he blinked when Zach's hazy eyes focused very sharply on his mouth. "I'd rather just go home."

"But—"

"I'm just… Can we just play video games or something? I'm not really—I don't really want to—" He could feel the frustration with himself rising hot and sick in his chest. If he did pick up a girl, he'd go home with her and he'd do or say something awkward and he'd hate himself in the morning and he wouldn't feel any better anyway. But if he went home and hung out with Zach, he wouldn't be embarrassed. It would just be—it would be like normal. "I just want to go home."

"Hey," Zach said, so reassuring that Nate almost melted with relief right then and there, "hey, buddy, 'course we can go home, okay?"

"Thanks," he said, voice rough, low. God, he was an embarrassing fucking mess, wasn't he? Amazing Zach still put up with him, really.

But Zach wasn't just putting up with Nate—Zach was leading him right back out of the bar and down the elevator and requesting a Lyft while they both lurched in place, too drunk to stand quite straight unless they were leaning against each other. Zach kept grabbing Nate's arm, like he wanted to make sure Nate didn't fall over without him, a curiously solicitous gesture that warmed the pit of Nate's stomach.

By the time they got back to Nate's place, he wasn't exactly sobering up, but the stress of the whole night buzzing through him still felt like being trashed twice as bad. He kicked off his shoes and dropped his keys on the little table by the door and started toward the kitchen. "You want anything to drink?"

"Sure," Zach said, using the toe of one shoe to step out of the other one, "whatever you got."

Nate poured them both the last of the Red Brick whiskey he had left, and said, "Cheers." He tried not to stare at Zach drinking, the way his throat bobbed when he swallowed. His head was going to weird fucking places these days. "So…video games?"

"Whatever you want, dude," Zach said, patting him on

the hand. "I made you go out, so you can pick the game, I guess?"

"I dunno," Nate said, and partially sat but mostly collapsed onto the couch, Zach following after him. He had most of the usual hockey player favorites, but he didn't really feel like *Call of Duty* or *Battlefield*. There were always the old standbys, though. "Chel?"

Of course. The old standby of hockey players everywhere: playing *more* hockey on a videogame console. "Hah. Sure. But I'm playing the Cons."

"Bastard," Nate said, without rancor, but it was actually difficult to choose a replacement team. He always played as the Cons when it was just him, or usually when the rest of the team was here. Only Zach was comfortable enough to insist. Nate would probably choose a Western Conference team because there were less built-in rivalries, like the Edmonton Skyhawks or the Calgary Stampede. Even the Winnipeg Falcons. A team that didn't matter at all.

Once they got settled, he let Zach pick first, but then stared at the screen for long enough that Zach started elbowing him in the side. The couch was big enough to seat four or six people, but they were sitting close enough that it was easy to reach, close enough that Nate could feel the warmth of Zach's body leaning into his entire side.

"Come on, dude, you gotta pick," Zach said, his bony elbow digging painfully into Nate's hip.

"Give me a sec—"

"No, come on, make up your mind—"

"Ow—"

Nate caught Zach's arm in his hand and pulled it back. Or tried to. Zach was strong enough that there wasn't a struggle exactly. Just an easy resistance. Nate looked down at his arm, feeling the muscle flex under his fingers, then up at his face, all of the familiar lines of it, the way his mouth parted, the way his eyes widened when he looked up and realized Nate was staring at him.

"What—" Zach started to say, but he didn't finish, because Nate lunged forward and kissed him, and Zach made a noise of surprise that sounded like Nate had punched him in the ribs instead.

His lips were warm and soft and at first, he seemed like he was too surprised to open his mouth. Nate's heart almost stopped, wrenched painfully tight in his chest, thinking, *oh no, oh god, oh no.* Then Zach's mouth *did* open, with a gasp of surprise, and Nate kept kissing him, desperately, tongue slipping into the space it was given. He could taste Zach, all of the shots they'd shared that night, that slight difference that was like, *oh, this is someone else's mouth.*

And then some ineffable balance shifted, and Zach's entire body melted against him, and he was kissing Nate back.

Nate hadn't really thought about what he was doing, hadn't thought about the consequences of his actions, but he was rapidly finding out that kissing Zachary Reed wasn't something that could be done by half measures, and he couldn't regret what he'd done.

Zach was wild, almost, his body shivering under Nate's hands. He shook like every stroke of his fingers down Zach's sides, even through his clothes, burned him. His mouth hot and wet and intense, his teeth digging into Nate's lip until Nate whimpered, not in a *stop that hurts* way but an *oh god keep doing it* way. His tongue fucking Nate's mouth, half teasing, half obscene.

Eventually Nate had to pull away, gasping for breath.

He opened his eyes and felt the bottom drop out of the world again.

Zach was panting too, his lips red and slick with spit, his eyes so fucking wide, a little crazy looking. He looked fucking amazing. He looked like he was about to say something, and Nate realized he couldn't bear it if Zach told him that he was making a mistake, or asked him to take a minute to think about it, so he kissed him again, one of his hands tangled in Zach's curly hair. He wasn't sure whether he wanted to pull it or stroke it, so he did both, alternating.

All he knew was he wanted Zach close and closer.

Somehow, they had shifted around so Zach was on top of him, straddling Nate's legs and pressing himself so close that Nate could feel Zach's cock grinding against the muscle of his stomach, his hands tugging Nate's shirt out of where it had been tucked into his belt. Hands dragging up Nate's ribs, he gasped a strangled, pained noise into Nate's mouth before pulling away. Just an inch, like it hurt him to do even that.

"Nate—"

"It's fine, please, it's fine, please don't—"

"Are you—"

"Zach—"

"Are you sure—what—"

"Please, don't stop, please," Nate said, helplessly, because he wanted this, *needed this*, and Zach said, *"Fuck,"* and went back to ruining him, his hands hot against Nate's back and ribs again. It already felt like he was burning and now just burned hotter. He could feel the imprints of Zach's fingers wherever they dragged, thinking in the dazed part of his brain that still had the power of conscious thought: *it feels like they should leave a mark.*

Nate knew he wasn't anywhere near as experienced as Zach. Somehow, it didn't matter. He was still trying to touch everything he could reach, his fingers exploring the ridges of muscle hidden underneath Zach's button-up shirt. He had seen them before, had even touched them before, but this was different, feeling the way they shifted as Zach shivered and groaned under Nate's hands, like every touch destroyed him just as much as he was destroying Nate. Learning every inch of his body. Like when Nate's fingers pinched his nipple, just testing, Zach made another one of those punched-in-the-ribs noises and pulled away again.

Nate stared at him and wondered how he hadn't thought to do this before and Zach stared back like Nate was someone he didn't know at all even though he'd thought he had, like Nate was someone he wanted to devour.

"Take off your shirt?" Nate asked, almost shocked by how needy he sounded, how rough his voice was already, but he couldn't be embarrassed by it. Couldn't even stop to think about how they'd gotten here, how much he needed—

Zach didn't even bother with the buttons, just yanked the entire thing over his head, like it was easy, but before Nate could even get the glimpse of him he wanted so badly, Zach's insistent hands were trying to get Nate's sweater and shirt off too. Nate wasn't as coordinated or used to undressing in a hurry as Zach was, so there were a few moments of fumbling that would have made him laugh in another less desperate, less charged time. As it was, his heart kept pounding, throwing itself against his ribs like it too wanted to escape.

Zach swore as he tried to get the sweater over Nate's head and when he finally managed it, dove forward and pressed a line of rough, sloppy kisses up the side of Nate's neck. Nate could hear himself, the noises he was making in response, the gasp when Zach dug his teeth into the skin right below Nate's jaw and sucked a mark there, like—

Zach pushed him down on the couch, still straddling him, and Nate found himself rolling his hips up into it, thoughtlessly at first but rewarded when Zach bit his lip and groaned and ground himself back down into it and the shock of the friction shivered through him.

This was—this wasn't like him, it was a risk, the whole thing was fucking stupid—making out with his best friend, risking the most important relationship in his life—but it was hard to listen to the darkest and most doubtful parts of his brain when Zach so clearly wanted him too, when Zach seemed almost as overwhelmed as he felt, when Zach's hands were tracing the lines of Nate's chest and abdomen like he was a rare and precious book that needed to be learned by heart.

They fumbled at each other's bodies and with each other's clothes until the tension was almost unbearable. Nate felt like he was going to jump out of his skin, felt like he was already out of it, every inch of him raw and exposed, just from making out on the couch like teenagers.

No. Not like teenagers. This was adult. This was something he hadn't felt in a long time, burning desperation building in the pit of his stomach, his skin hypersensitive everywhere Zach touched him, every time their lips met and Nate learned the shape and feel of his mouth.

Somewhere along the way he'd lost his pants and if three days ago someone had said, *Nate, in a couple days you're going to be on your couch in your boxers with Zach Reed on top of you with his dick out*, he would have laughed in their face. As it was, every part of him that was touching Zach, every place their bodies connected, felt like it was on fire. He struggled up onto his elbows so he could look at Zach's dick.

He'd seen it before. He'd seen all of the guys on the team naked, and Bee, and had never really thought about it beyond *these are my teammates and we're all going into the showers.* This was different. Like the rest of Zach's body, he'd seen it before, but it felt so different.

He'd never allowed himself to feel the shivery longing he felt now examining Zach, thinking, *I want to touch him, I* could *touch him,* allowing himself to look hungrily at the way Zach's body was a really beautiful thing by any metric you wanted to measure it by, the way it was a work of art on its own, the compact muscle and graceful lines of him, the way there wasn't a bit of him that wasn't made and shaped expressly for the game they loved.

And the way his cock was straining and damp at the tip of his foreskin, still untouched, the slight curve of it, the outline of the veins in the side.

Nate shocked himself by reaching out and wrapping his fingers around it, sliding up. It felt like touching his own dick when he was jerking off, in that the feeling of soft skin sliding over the hardness of the rest of it was the same, but it was so different. Zach wasn't cut and it was strangely, weirdly fascinating to feel the change that made. Learning the noises Zach couldn't choke back when Nate changed his tempo and his grip, when his hand sliding up caught some of the liquid at the tip and dragged it back down Zach's overheated skin.

His brain blanked out when Zach exhaled sharply and breathed, "God, Nate, god, you're so good," and leaned forward to kiss him, sloppy and desperate, mumbling into his mouth, "Take off your fucking boxers, baby, I wanna, *fuck*, I wanna—"

Nate shivered, hearing that, but he couldn't think about it too long.

"I want to blow you," he interrupted him, a little shocked at his own boldness, a little shocked that it was true. That it was really, *really* true. God, he wanted it. Zach's cock in his mouth, at the back of his throat, maybe—

Zach was very still on top of him even though Nate could feel his entire body trembling, and Nate's fingers tightened around his dick. "Nate—you don't have to—"

"I want to, I want you, I want—"

Zach didn't say anything, just leaned back down. Their mouths were so close, not kissing, not talking, and it was like when Nate breathed out Zach breathed in. He thought of the night Zach had come home early from Tulum, the way Nate had exhaled the smoke into his lungs and thought maybe he'd wanted this then too and just hadn't known. Had needed this and hadn't *known*. Had never even thought to hope Zach could want him like this. Had never even been able to conceptualize what it would mean.

"You," Zach mumbled, "are gonna *kill* me, dude."

"Please—"

"Have you ever done this—"

"I haven't, but I've—I mean, I've had my dick sucked, but I haven't—just tell me what to do and I'll—"

"Fuck," Zach groaned, and scrambled back down Nate's body.

It was what Nate had wanted but he still felt the absence of the weight, felt it like a loss. But then he was distracted by Zach, on his back at the other end of the couch. By the chance to see the muscled entirety of him, naked, waiting in anticipation. The tattoos that covered his arms, the blackwork Cup against the Montreal skyline marring the smooth expanse of his chest. It was kind of overwhelming, and he knew he was staring. Zach looked up at him, his eyes as dark as Nate had ever seen them, and licked his lips.

"Nate—"

"I'm just—I'm sorry, it's just, you're just..." He gestured helplessly at Zach's body. "You're *so*, you're really..."

He would have expected Zach to make a joke, like, *yeah, I know I'm hot*, because that would have been a pretty Zach thing to do. Instead, Zach said roughly, "Come here, baby," and reached up to slide his hand around the back of Nate's neck and pull him down into a messy kiss.

Nate only moved away so he could mouth his way down Zach's body, breath damp against his skin. He was still pretty drunk, but he could also feel every single thing with intense clarity. The way Zach's muscles shifted under his tongue, the way he held himself in check so carefully, the little noises of protest he made when Nate took too long to get where he needed to go. But he didn't say anything, didn't tell Nate to get on with it.

Whenever Nate dared to look up at him, Zach was staring down, propped up on his elbows to get a better view, his eyes so intense that Nate had to look away.

Finally he was staring directly at Zach's dick, an inch away from his face. Part of him felt like he should be more weirded out by this than he was. Mostly all he could think about was that he wanted to make Zach feel good, feel as good as he made Nate feel, and it was easier that way. He wrapped his hand around the base of Zach's cock again, then ran his tongue up the rest of the length, an experimental kind of taste. It just tasted like clean skin, but when he caught his tongue around the tip, he could taste the faint salt of the liquid beading there.

Zach was trembling again, breath ragged, his hands curled into fists at his sides, and Nate took pity on him and slid his mouth down. It was—kind of weird. It took him a minute to try to figure out how to hold his mouth so his teeth didn't scrape anything. Another minute to explore the shape with his tongue and see what he could handle. He chanced a look up at Zach through his eyelashes, saw him with his eyes screwed shut and his teeth pressed into his lower lip, heard him panting, and thought, *okay, I can do this.*

He knew he wasn't an expert or anything, but he tried to think about the things that felt good to him and to do *that.* It was different, though, drunkenly trying to suck Zach's cock and swirl his tongue around the head and breathe through his nose at the same time, uncoordinated but enthusiastic.

He let go of it and pressed his wet palms against Zach's trembling thighs, raked his fingers down them and listened to the way Zach's breath hitched, then leaned forward to take more of him in. Zach's hand was resting in his hair, stroking—*petting,* his brain supplied unhelpfully—without pushing him down and Nate could feel his own dick, straining painfully against the fabric of his underwear.

It wasn't easy. He choked a little and had to pull back, eyes watering.

"Easy," Zach said, still staring at him, "it's okay, you're—you're doing—really, you're good—"

His whole body buzzed with it. The sensations were overwhelming. How wet his face was, sloppy with spit and Zach; how Zach's abs felt, flexing where Nate's forehead was pressed against his stomach. Nate felt like he could do this forever, like he *wanted* to do this forever, to have Zach trapped under him and inside of him and needing him.

Zach, who was so carefully trying not to thrust into his mouth but whose fingers flexed against Nate's skull convulsively. Zach, who was murmuring a steady stream of instructions in a broken, overwhelmed voice that went straight to Nate's dick, "—yeah, like that, lick—no—a little deeper, oh—*oh*—you got it, you got it—easy, easy, breathe, baby—suck harder, god, yeah, like that, like that, yes—oh, fuck, fuck, I'm gonna—stop, Nate—"

Nate didn't stop, just looked up at Zach to see what he looked like when he was coming, what he looked like when his head fell back against the arm of the couch as he made a kind of punched-out whimper. He had an objectively stupid but also really sexy expression on his face, his eyes screwed shut and his mouth open, and then he came in Nate's mouth even while he was trying to push Nate's head away.

Nate swallowed. He hadn't known what to expect there either. It was a little salty, but not unbearable. He kept it up until Zach made a pained noise and said, "Stop, too much, too much, *ah*..."

Zach's hand on his chin, drawing him up and into another messy kiss, licking the taste of himself out of Nate's mouth. Oh, *shit*, he didn't know he was going to be into that, but he was. Nate felt dumb and needy and unbearably horny, dick just aching to be touched. He'd been so focused on Zach the whole time that he hadn't even thought to touch himself.

As far as drunken hookups went this was a really fucking weird one.

Zach, with the smoothness of someone who *was* used to hooking up, sat up and pushed Nate back down in the same motion, so he was bracketed underneath Zach's body. Looked down at Nate's boxers, the wet spot that revealed, embarrassingly, exactly what Nate needed.

"Why the fuck are you still wearing these?"

"I, uh, forgot to take them..." Nate said, his voice rubbed a little raw even though Zach had been unbearably gentle.

"C'mon, c'mon," Zach said, tugging them down so eagerly Nate forgot to be self-conscious about what he looked like, just hitched his hips up to help it along. Zach stared down at him with a weird, fierce expression that Nate couldn't interpret, one hand stroking across Nate's chest, thumb flicking over his nipple.

"Was it—was I okay?"

"Were you—Jesus, Nate, you were...*yes*."

"Okay, I just—"

"Nate? Baby? Shut up. Just let me do this."

"I—oh, fuck, Zach," he cried, the air punched out of the lungs when Zach, who'd been stroking his chest and abs soothingly, leaned forward and kissed the inside of his thigh, a shockingly sensitive spot, then sucked a harder, almost bruising bite against it. Kept doing it, his mouth attacking Nate's thighs and then the line where his leg met his hip, the V-line below his abs, and then his stomach, until Nate was writhing under him, his dick so hard it was almost painful, leaving a little glistening streak against his skin whenever it touched.

Relief—he needed some kind of—he was about to

wrap his hand around himself when Zach took his wrist gently in his fingers and said, "No."

"What?"

"I wanna do it, baby."

"Well, would you *please*—" He could feel Zach grinning against his stomach and yelped when Zach's tongue licked the sticky spot from his skin.

"Okay, okay."

He's done this before, Nate thought nonsensically, when Zach leaned forward and teased his tongue around the head of Nate's dick, pressed against the underside of the crown, before he took him down to the root in one smooth movement. It was almost too much. The wet suction was a lot, but seeing Zach's eyes, looking up at Nate through his eyelashes, feeling Zach's beard rub against his already sensitive thighs, it was too much. There was no way he was going to be able to last very long, even though he wanted to, even though he wanted to enjoy every second of it, he was already so—

Zach sucked really hard on the head and Nate felt the sensation like electric shocks all over his body.

"Fuck, Zach, *please*."

His hands fumbled over Zach's head, over his shoulders, over every part of him he could reach. His muscles, shifting to support his weight, warm under Nate's hands. The thick hair, easy to twist his fingers in and tug. And then all he could think about was the wet heat of Zach's mouth, how good it felt, how much he *wanted*—

It was almost a surprise when he came, shocked out of his body by Zach doing something particularly tricky with his tongue and pressing his thumb against the rim of Nate's hole, an orgasm that felt like it'd been punched out of him.

He lay there, panting, completely dumb and unable to recover the last shreds of conscious thought he'd had remaining, while Zach looked down at him with that strange mixture of fondness and worry.

Nate wanted to say something to him, wanted to tell him he wasn't gonna regret it in the morning, but before he could wrap his brain around the words, he fell asleep like that, lulled into it by the way Zach draped himself back over Nate's body, kissing him, murmuring almost wordlessly into his ear, hands soothing against his sweaty skin.

Three things occurred to Zach as he lurched into wakefulness.

First: he had the kind of headache that felt like someone jamming an ice pick into your ear.

Second: he was naked.

Third: he was definitely not in his own bed.

He sat up, or tried to, and ended up tumbling off the couch and onto the floor, tangled in a blanket.

"Uhh...dude, you okay?"

Nate. He was in Nate's house. It smelled like toast and butter frying, and someone had put a blanket over him in the middle of the night.

Just like that, everything that happened last night flashed behind his eyes like you usually only saw in movie montages. Going out with the intention of getting Nate laid. Well. He hadn't been lying about his intentions. New Zach did keep his promises, even if that wasn't the way he'd expected to do it.

He looked up from his vantage point on the hardwood floor. While Zach would normally have tried not to stare, things had taken an unpredictable turn. He'd woken up naked on a lot of peoples' floors, but none of them were Nate's.

Nate, who was in the kitchen, at the stove. He wasn't wearing a shirt, and Zach could see the flush that turned his entire face red on his neck and chest too. He wished he hadn't learned last night exactly how Nate looked when he blushed down his whole body. He wished he didn't still have the urge to darken it.

What did you say when you got drunk and accidentally fucked your best friend?

He could almost hear Jammer's voice drawling *accidentally, huh?* And thought, viciously, *shut up.*

"I, uh, sorry. Kinda disoriented."

Nate smiled, lopsided and awkward, and said, "Yeah, I figured. We were, uh, both pretty drunk last night. There's coffee. And, um, I'm making breakfast."

What did you say when you got drunk and accidentally fucked your best friend and then he made you breakfast in the morning?

What came out of Zach's mouth was: "Thank *fuck*."

Nate laughed and turned away from him to shake a pan on the stove.

Zach struggled to his feet and then stumbled across the room to the spot where his boxers had somehow ended up. This was probably a good thing. Nate didn't seem to be freaking out or anything, and that had been, like, a pretty real possibility.

Zach had never really had any particular angst about *anything* involving sex: he'd started early and continued often, indiscriminate about gender. If you'd asked him his body count, he wouldn't have been able to tell you. Nate, on the other hand, had *maybe* slept with two women.

And now, he'd also slept with Zach, who definitely wasn't a woman.

So if he *had* freaked out, a little bit, Zach wouldn't have blamed him.

Zach put on his boxers and stared at Nate's back, like if he did it long enough, Nate would turn around and look at him. He didn't, so Zach went to see what he was making.

It was eggs, exactly the way Zach liked them, scrambled and fluffy. There were even chives in there. There were blistered cherry tomatoes and chicken sausages, and bowls of yogurt with sliced-up strawberries and granola that Nate made himself in large batches. There was toast, a little scrape of butter already melting on it. Nate never had salted butter at home, but he'd put some flaky salt on the bread. Zach's chest felt like it was swelling, like it would explode. It was like...all of his favorite breakfast shit in one place. And Nate had *made* it for him.

Nate glanced sideways at him, and said, "Uh, hey. Good morning, buddy."

Zach stared back at him. Nate didn't seem to be panicking. His face was a little red, and his hair was still messy, and he had a hickey on his hip, right above the line of his sweatpants. But his blue eyes were wide open, innocent, and he didn't look freaked out. Like, that was good, right? That Nate wasn't panicking.

In fact, it didn't seem like his first gay experience had fazed him at all.

As Zach reached across the table to help himself to a piece of toast, a thought occurred to him that hit like a clenched fist against his chest.

What if Nate wasn't freaking out because he didn't care?

What if he wasn't freaking out because he didn't remember?

They *had* had a lot to drink. Just because Zach would remember every single second of the evening in photographic detail for the rest of his life didn't mean Nate would.

Oh, Jesus *Christ*.

"You okay, dude?" Nate asked, as he spooned the eggs onto plates. He was frowning, worried, and Zach contemplated how much he'd regret it if he slid around the side of the kitchen island and kissed him.

"Yeah, I… Head. It hurts."

"You definitely need some coffee. You're, like, barely coherent."

"That's normal, buddy. How many times do I gotta tell you I'm only half fluent in English?"

Nate was still watching him, with that half-worried, half-fond expression on his face. "It's way too early to be this self-deprecating. Just drink some coffee and eat something, all right?"

They ate in relative silence, and it was the most awkward period of not-talking Zach could remember between them since pretty much the beginning of his time in Philadelphia. The food was really fucking good and Zach wished he had pants because he kind of got a little hard every time Nate cooked for him lately, and it was even worse now that he'd sucked Nate's dick. Now that he knew the sounds Nate made when he was completely lost in the moment.

But if Nate didn't remember, Zach didn't want to ruin things, and he realized with a sinking kind of horror that now he was *really* going to have to keep it bros.

Except now whenever he tried to think *bros, it's just*

bros, nothing more than that, he could only picture Nate staring at Zach's naked body with something like awe; Nate asking, uncharacteristically short of breath, *was I okay?* Nate squirming underneath his mouth. Nate's hands twisting in his hair when he came.

Keep. It. Bros.

"So Jammer's new girlfriend is like an Instagram poet or something," he said, to break the silence, pushing some of the leftover eggs around on his plate.

"A what?"

"Like…she writes poetry, but it's all really short and it has illustrations, and she posts it on Instagram. I'll show you." Zach realized his phone was probably still in his jeans, which were nowhere in sight. "Anyway, it's like, *I struggled with the loneliness inside myself, before I let it blossom into a sunflower.*"

"I'm sorry, what?"

"It's poetry, dude, I dunno. It's kind of funny, you have to see the—here, give me your phone."

Nate handed it over without further argument, and Zach entered in Nate's passcode. Six digits; his number and the year the Cons had drafted him. The phone background was a fairly new picture. It was the first line—Nate, Zach, and Bee—sitting on the bench together at a game, staring out intently at the ice. Bee was whispering something to Zach, who had his arm slung over Nate's shoulders. Zach sucked in a breath and opened Instagram to show Nate exactly how bad the poetry was.

Nate leaned over the island to get a better look, close enough that Zach could see the freckles on his shoulders and the blond hair on his chest. Which, he now knew, was soft under his fingertips.

This was fine.

He'd kept it bros for three seasons so far. A drunken blowjob wasn't going to change that.

Especially if Nate didn't remember it.

Jesus *Christ*, Zach was fucked.

Somehow, Nate managed to keep it together until Zach had found his jeans—they had ended up wedged behind the couch—and gotten dressed to leave.

Zach had hesitated in the door for a second, like he'd wanted to say something, and Nate had a desperate, wild thought: *you could kiss him and see what happens*. But there was nothing artificially lowering his inhibitions like last night, so he'd swallowed hard and said, "See you at the rink, bud."

Zach stared at him for slightly too long, said, "Yeah," and let Nate shut the door behind him.

He stared at the door for a minute. He looked down at his bare feet on the wooden floor. He started to walk back toward the kitchen, but that required effort, so Nate sat down on the floor.

Then he lay down on the floor.

That seemed like a good way to handle things.

He wasn't entirely sure how he'd gotten through the entire morning without breaking, but he was getting better at controlling himself. That was a lie. He was getting better at controlling himself while sober. Drunk Nate was a complete and utter *disaster*. Hand over his eyes, he groaned in dismay, remembering far too clearly exactly how much of a disaster he'd been.

Like—in retrospect, there were probably a lot of things about last night that he could be freaking out about. Kissing a dude. Hooking up with a dude and enjoying it as much as he'd ever enjoyed being with Rachel.

Surprisingly, maybe, he wasn't that freaked out about that aspect of things. He'd never really thought about it before, but also…like…just in retrospect, a lot of things about his life made sense in a way that they hadn't necessarily made sense before.

Maybe there had been something more to his dumb, hormonal teen locker room angst, the detailed admiration of his teammates' bodies and his complete hatred of his own. The way he froze up talking to anyone, uncomfortable for reasons he couldn't even begin to describe. And as an adult, maybe there was a reason he had usually just kept his eyes level in the locker room as a rule.

It definitely was not a particularly heterosexual thing to kiss your best friend, and, well. Some of it had probably been percolating in the most secret parts of his brain, the parts that half of his conscious thought wouldn't even acknowledge, for longer than he'd realized. Maybe…he wasn't straight?

Maybe he would have figured it out sooner if Rachel hadn't swooped in to rescue him from his youthful flailing and he'd never had to think about it again after that, but who the hell knew? And he *was* really, really fucking dumb, no one would have ever said otherwise. It was absolutely in character to not even have a goddamn clue about this until his midtwenties.

So: a surprise to him but not, really, that surprising.

He wasn't freaking out about hooking up with a guy.

He *was* freaking out about hooking up with a teammate.

He was *absolutely* freaking out about hooking up with Zach.

Zach had seemed completely unfazed. He'd woken up, eaten the food Nate had made for them like he had done for years of their friendship; he'd invaded Nate's personal space like it was a concept he'd never heard of, like he'd done for years of their friendship; and he'd talked about stupid things and made Nate laugh, like he'd done for years of their friendship.

Not once had he mentioned anything that had happened the night before.

Which was completely fine because Nate didn't want to talk about it either.

It was so fucking obviously a huge mistake. It had seemed like a great idea at the time. Hell, it had *felt* like a great idea at the time.

But guys like Zach and guys like Nate, it just—it just didn't make sense. It was like a very bad teen movie where the jock had to date the nerd on a bet, and he knew how the bridge of those movies always went. Humiliation. And real life wasn't like the movies. There weren't happy endings waiting after a big apology.

It was really not any surprise that Zach hadn't wanted to talk about it. Even if he'd seemed pretty into it at the time, he was probably embarrassed to wake up and realize he'd hooked up with *Nate*. It was one thing to be best friends with a guy, but… Nate didn't even have a pair of glasses he could take off or hair he could let down. There was no magic wand to wave that could put him in Zach's league.

Life *wasn't* a movie.

Nate was always going to be Nate, the steady, solid, awkward captain of a hockey team, a man with more heart than talent, a guy who looked like any schlub you'd pick off of a Port Richmond street. And Zach was always going to be Zach, the handsome, charming All-Star, the kind of guy who could have anyone he wanted wrapped around his finger with a flash of his dimples.

The more Nate thought about it, the more his stomach churned, the nauseous panic he hadn't felt for some time now rising to his throat. Of course Zach didn't want to talk about it, because it had been—it had just been Zach being a nice fucking guy, or pitying Nate because he was such a fucking mess he couldn't even—didn't want to even go out and meet someone.

Nate, on the floor, thought: *goddamn, I was a pity fuck.*

Well. That was that.

Nate wasn't going to bring it up if Zach wasn't going to bring it up. He'd known he'd be risking the most important thing in his life if he went for it, and he'd gone for it anyway, fueled by alcohol and desperation and a moment where reckless bravery had won out over his own innate caution. That didn't mean he had to ruin things again. Especially when Zach, an incredibly kind person, had given him an out to save his own dignity. He wasn't going to ruin that. He wasn't going to seem pathetic and desperate, even if he *was.*

Nate sat up and scrubbed his hand over his face. He really wanted to smoke, but he didn't have the ready-made excuse of his Rumspringa week, and he kept himself strictly under control otherwise. He'd hit the gym instead and maybe if he worked himself to exhaustion, he wouldn't keep thinking about Zach's hands. Zach's mouth. Zach's eyes.

Wouldn't keep thinking about the way Zach's voice had sounded when he'd said *come here, baby.*

It didn't get any better at the gym, because as he changed, he looked down and saw the line of bruises Zach had left on his neck and hip and thigh, and he had to take a minute to compose himself, think particularly unsexy thoughts, and *then* put his shorts on.

Lifting didn't really help either, because he just thought about all the times he and Zach had gone to this gym together and the way he'd tried not to look too long at Zach's straining muscles, at the sweat shining along the line of his back, and hadn't even really given much of a thought about *why* he couldn't bring himself to look.

Nate's head was a maelstrom of feelings he couldn't really identify. He probably should have talked to someone about it, but who the hell would he even have talked to? He couldn't talk to Zach, his usual go-to option, because Zach was the cause of his current suffering. He couldn't talk to Bee, who meant well but was about as comforting as a brick wall. He couldn't talk to Mike, who'd finally figured out his own shit, because Nate was far too fucking embarrassed thinking of the numerous talks they'd had where Nate had tried to get Mike to figure out his shit.

He had *some* pride left, even if Mike wasn't the kind of guy to say *I told you so.*

And then, a thought almost made him drop the bar on his chest. When Rachel had broken up with him in February two seasons ago and he'd asked why, she'd said *you're in love with someone else.* At first, he'd assumed that she had meant Bee, who had told him that Rachel had been very cold toward her, for no apparent reason. But that was ridiculous: Nate had never felt anything for Bee except a big-brotherly protectiveness, and Bee had been involved with Mäkelä.

For a stupid, wild second, he wondered if this was what she'd meant. If Zach was who she'd meant. Except that was idiotic, because he wasn't in *love* with Zach, he was just—they were best friends, and Zach was really, really hot; anyone would probably be knocked off their axis by hooking up with him.

Okay, so clearly, Rach wasn't right about the being in love thing, but she had definitely seen something he hadn't. He really, really wished she'd warned him, so he wouldn't have made such an ass of himself. Nate wished a lot of things, but he didn't have a time machine.

There was nothing he could do about it at this point except go home, shower, and pack his bags for the start of the Cons' next road trip. And if he spent a little longer in the shower than he normally would have that wasn't anyone's business.

One of the few things that helped him deal with anxiety was planning, but there wasn't really a way to plan for this. He had no idea what to expect when he saw Zach again. He had no idea whether he'd be able to pretend nothing had happened in front of the rest of the guys. He had no idea how he would be able to get through scheduled media appearances like the call-in they were supposed to do on *Sportsnight.*

Nate sat down on the floor again. He took a deep breath.

A second.

Then three.

None of it helped.

The more he thought about it, the more that Zach realized that the difference between Life Before the Incident and Life After the Incident was like a study in going about your business as usual and then a study in slowly having your skin peeled off. Little things he normally wouldn't have given a second thought to suddenly seemed completely insurmountable.

For example, as they were heading to the airport, he

thought about how he always sat next to Nate on the plane. It was just how things went. No one else ever took his seat, even when ideal seating arrangements were in short supply. But now he felt like—okay, he had to think about this logically.

So the thing about Zach, the thing he knew was nothing to be proud of but did nothing to change, was that he didn't really *think* about things. Other people considered consequences and made plans. Zach went for it and dealt with the consequences later. Generally, because he was hot and could fool people into being charmed by either his smile, his dimples, or his abs, the consequences were never that bad.

The worst thing that had ever happened to him was getting traded to Philadelphia, and that had also turned out to be the best thing that had ever happened to him, so major points to Before Zach for *that* particular fuckup.

But the point was that he wasn't used to *thinking*. He wasn't used to *worrying*.

Now he was going over it in his head—like, would Nate be weirded out if Zach sat next to him? Would it be worse if he didn't sit next to him? Would that jog his memory about what had happened the night they went out together? Zach touched Nate all the time; it was second nature at this point. At first Nate had been weird about it, almost skittish, but eventually, he'd learned to lean into it. If Zach stopped now that would be weird, right? But if he didn't stop now, would Nate realize something was wrong?

Would it be worse to accidentally remind Nate what had happened and ruin their friendship, or to keep silent and torture himself the way he was doing right now?

Was this what Nate felt like all the time? Zach couldn't imagine it. It was exhausting.

"You okay, Reedsy?" Netty asked, as they crossed the tarmac to the stairs that would take them up to the plane.

"Huh?" Zach asked, head whipping around. "I'm great, bro. Why wouldn't I be okay? What's up?"

Netty grinned, except it was more of a baring of his tooth gap. "You jumpy."

"Nah," Zach said, waving his hand dismissively.

"All right," Netty said, although he didn't sound convinced.

"Just wanna win these next few, you know?"

"All right," Netty said again, although he still didn't sound convinced.

In the end, Zach took his usual seat next to Nate, because he was a fool. They were flying to Tampa for the first stop on the trip, and the flight was only three hours, but he was still a fool. He'd either have to pass out in self-defense or keep up the kind of idiotic conversation that usually came so easily to him, but that with this newfound *thinking about things* was really *hard*.

"Buddy," he said, as he slid into the seat. There were a million things he wanted to say, and he couldn't say any of them.

Nate looked up and half smiled and Zach was definitely an idiot. "Ready for the road?"

"I just wanna win one, you know? Three in a row feels...bad."

"You weren't here for the worst of our seasons," Nate said, leaning back in his seat and closing his eyes. "There was one time we lost thirteen in a row."

Zach had never experienced quite that level of failure

in his life, but he knew better than to say it. "Don't worry. I won't let it get that bad again, okay?"

"Got your personal guarantee for that one, huh?" Nate asked. His eyes were still closed, but the smile still tipped the corner of his mouth up.

"Hell yeah, Cap. And listen, if we lose, you get the forfeit."

"Deal."

They bumped fists on it. The forfeits were usually practical—Zach had made Nate do all of his laundry for a week once—or silly, like the time Nate had made Zach sing an embarrassing song at karaoke with the team, except the joke was on him because Zach never got embarrassed. But now his brain was taking it all kinds of other places. Things Nate could do for him with his mouth, places he could let Zach touch that he'd never touched before… He had to stop thinking about that. He couldn't think about that on the plane, with all of their teammates playing cards or dozing around them.

Eventually, he did drift off, and only woke up when the plane was starting to descend. Nate was still asleep, his head pillowed on Zach's shoulder. Zach wisely resisted the urge to push the hair away from his face, or do anything along those lines, because he was *overthinking things* these days. Instead, he said, "Hey, buddy. Time to get up."

Nate recoiled like Zach had slapped him, like as soon as he realized where he was, he regretted it. "Sorry, I—sorry."

Zach stifled a sigh. "It's cool. You weren't drooling on me or anything."

"That's not what I—" Nate's face was hard to read sometimes. Not that it wasn't full of emotion—it was just that sometimes he had so many of them it was impossible to figure out *what* was going on back there. "Okay."

Ugh. Like having your *skin* peeled off.

Zach actually couldn't wait for the game to start, just so he'd have an excuse to maybe...hit someone. That would be good. Even if they didn't win.

Nate took a minute out of warmups and before the game to speak to Sally and Zach, his only alternate captains following Bouchard's abrupt retirement last year. He didn't really know what he wanted to say. He usually preferred to lead by example, if possible, but sometimes you had to use your words. The problem was that Nate was very bad at using his words.

Usually it helped to have Zach watching him when he spoke. Instead of worrying about how he looked or sounded, he focused on Zach's familiar face and familiar smile, and everything was easier. But today it just made him feel weird and shivery, like his skin was too tight. And Zach wasn't even smiling; his face looked tense and nervous, the same way Nate felt.

"We gotta win this one, boys," he said, finally. The rest of the team was already on the ice, skating, stretching, taking practice shots on Mack. "I know you guys always do what you can, but we really—we need to step it up. If you see something sloppy, let the guy know on the bench after. We can't afford any stupid mistakes tonight."

Tampa was a perennial contender for the Cup, although they hadn't won it within the last decade. A streak of bad luck in the playoffs had kept it out of their grasp. Nate knew that feeling all too well recently. Still, the Mariners were a tight, aggressive team, and it would take some effort to avoid a fourth loss. The crowd here wasn't as loud as in some barns, but they were intense, and the arena had kind of a weird vibe, particularly because they usually stopped before puck drop to honor veterans or police officers or something. It was uncomfortable.

"Aye aye, Captain," Zach said, flipping him a joking salute.

"Take this seriously, Zachary," Sally said, before Nate had to.

Zach looked pleadingly at Nate, like, *can you believe this guy?*

"I, uh, I'm sure he's taking it seriously, Sally."

Sally's ice-blue eyes reflected no expression, but it was clear exactly what he thought regardless.

Zach took the face-off and won it. And the game was on.

It felt good to just play hockey again. The last day and a half Nate had been on fire with the kind of nervous energy that only a game could burn away, and it had been a thousand times worse because he'd been alone in his own head. There was sometimes barely time to think on the ice, and when there was, he had to direct all his attention to the game at hand.

On the bench you had to watch for when your line was up so you wouldn't leave Mäkelä in the lurch on a change, and on the ice you had a hundred things to occupy you. Nate had always pushed himself hard, even though the shifts were short, and the pain was especially welcome today.

It didn't hurt that their line was really firing on all cylinders, having one of those days where everything was clicking. Passes sauced cross-ice with no interference, and Bee scored about six minutes into the first period with a beautiful wrist shot above the Tampa goaltender's left shoulder. Nate grabbed her up in a hug, even though she was almost as tall as he was, and Zach crashed into both of them a second later, almost knocking him off his feet.

It wasn't that the game was easy. The Mariners had last change, and somehow the fourth line ended up on the ice against the first, and a bad turnover led to a 3-on-1 that Mäkelä couldn't stop, no matter how desperately he dove for it.

Nate had to take an interview in between the periods, something he always hated doing. For a while the beats had actually stopped asking for him because he'd given such bad answers, and that had been a relief, but then his agent had told him to knock it the fuck off and it had all started up again.

"After losing three you've been on fire today," Maria, one of the Cons' media panelists, was saying. "Is there any internal pressure to really win this one?"

This was part of the reason he hated the interviews so much—the questions they were asked always led to stupid answers. What was he going to say? *Nah, we're ready to tank it for the number one draft pick next year and completely throw out all of the progress we've made?* Instead Nate stammered something about how he always put a lot of internal pressure on himself, even more than he did on the team, but she was already moving on to the next question.

"And your chemistry with your line mates, especially with Zach Reed—how would you describe that?"

"I, uh, we, uh, you know, we've, uh, played for three seasons together now, you, um, you kind of get to know the guys, figure out where they're gonna be—it's, uh..."

"And you two are almost always together—you even bought houses around the corner from each other. Does that contribute at all?"

Nate could feel his face getting hot, the sweat beading even thicker on his forehead as he managed to grunt out one-syllable answers and a mumbled "I don't know."

Mercifully, she cut him off, because they only had so much time allotted, and he'd filled most of it with *uh*. He slunk away, his face a brilliant red that had nothing to do with the imprint of the helmet on his forehead.

"Real eloquent," Zach whispered to him from where he'd been watching in the wings.

"Shut up, please."

Zach's entire face crinkled up into that horrible, infectious smile. "Dude, no, you gotta go with either *shut up*, or *be quiet, please*, commit to like…one attitude."

"Shut up, please," he managed, because he was already smiling back helplessly, and it didn't help at all.

"Aww," Zach said, patting him on the arm. "It's okay. At least you didn't say anything about getting the puck to the net."

Nate thought about all of the times he had said exactly that and sighed. "I hate interviews."

"You did fine, I was just giving you a hard time."

Nate's mouth opened and closed. "I—yeah."

Zach's face was completely innocent. "C'mon, Cap, period's gonna start soon. I'm *ready*."

It was a chippy game, the score seesawing back and forth fast enough to give anyone whiplash. He knew plus/minus was a stupid stat, but he was *tanking* it today. It didn't matter: in the end, thanks to Netty's hard work during the third in the neutral zone, Zach was able to slip through some open ice as the lines were changing to score the game-winning goal and get them the two points right before regulation ran out.

Nate barely realized what he was doing but opened his arms as he saw Zach skating right at him. The weight of his body crashed into Nate's, and he swung him around, on reflex.

"Nice fucking *work*."

Zach didn't say anything at first, just pulled back far enough so that Nate could see him grinning. "See? I was taking it seriously."

"Never doubted you for a minute."

The next game was in Sunrise in two days, but because they were on the road the team was staying in Tampa that night and practicing the next morning. That was, at least, the reasoning behind going out after the win. The team wanted to celebrate, and it wouldn't be at the expense of game play. Zach wanted to keep the winning streak going because they sure as hell weren't going to make the playoffs, let alone win the Cup, if they kept up like they'd been going.

But there wasn't any harm in team bonding. At least that was what Zach kept telling himself. He wasn't drinking as much during the season as he'd been the year that he got traded, and he was definitely staying away from the rest of it, but he still liked—you know. Letting loose. There was a lot on his shoulders these days and it wasn't like he was getting photographed doing anything stupid, except maybe sometimes singing karaoke at Ray's. So as he finished up in the shower and got his shit together, that's where he was planning to go.

That was a nasty goal, buddy, Jammer had texted him.

Zach texted him a thumbs-up emoji. not doing too

bad yourself this season huh? Jammer led the Royal's defensemen in both goals and points, which was an enviable status to have; Zach usually trailed Bee and Nate, because a lot of times it was easier to score as a winger, but he didn't mind, as long as the line was putting up the points.

Helps 2b inspired bro. U should try it.

i don't understand poetry and i do NOT want to understand it

Lmao. It's not that deep, nothing to do w/ poetry.

sure buddy, guess it's got everything 2 do w/ hot poets

Doesn't hurt.

Zach slid the phone back into his pocket and decided he wasn't going to ask about that further. The visitors' locker room was starting to clear out by now, and the Cons' group chat buzzed with chirps and plans. They'd let Netty take the lead because not only did he have an inborn talent for finding the best dive bars, but as with many of the cities they went to, he had a vast network of friends or relatives, either blood or by marriage, ready to either host them or let them know where the best places to party happened to be.

So by the time Zach made his way onto the road, Netty had already scoped out a spot with cheap drinks and was well on his own way to sloshed by the time the rest of the team showed up. Zach slid onto a barstool next to him. He accepted a shot of something clear that burned on the way down and a pat on the back that almost knocked him off the stool and onto the floor. Netty knew his own strength; he just didn't care.

"Drink more," Netty said severely, and so Zach did.

The nagging little voice in the back of his head told him it was a bad idea. That he wasn't really drinking to celebrate. Zach attempted to drown the voice out with vodka, which worked, for a time. He was starting to feel it when he saw Nate and Sally come in, and the voice said, *yeah, that's why you're drinking.*

Zach thought: *shut up.*

The night went by. Mike was on his phone for most of it, probably texting Garcia, and Bee and Mäkelä were huddled in one of the corners—it seemed like she was passionately explaining something to him, her hands moving to emphasize her points. He had that small, fond half smile on his face that only seemed to show up around her, and Zach felt, for a strange, jealous moment, a twinge in his chest.

He wasn't *avoiding* Nate, exactly; he was just...keeping his distance. He was doing the right thing, being smart about it. He kept an eye on Nate, of course. It was just what he did, particularly because even around the team Nate was sometimes too introverted and shy and would try to sneak out too early. He seemed to be doing all right tonight, though. Lindy was taking it upon himself to make sure Nate was drunk enough to enjoy it, so Zach relaxed and went back to drinking and, you know.

Just keeping an eye on him.

At some point he got up to go to the bathroom. Alone, he closed his eyes, felt the piss and some of the tension flow out of him. Breathed a sigh of relief that it was almost over without incident.

As he was washing his hands, the door opened. Zach glanced up to catch sight of Nate in the mirror. Face flushed, the way it got when he was either embarrassed or drunk enough to forget some of his usual anxiety. He swayed a little and Zach fought the urge to go over there and slide his shoulder under Nate's arm, the way he always did when they were out and one of them was a little worse for the wear.

"Uh, hey," Nate mumbled, unable to quite meet Zach's eyes. "Dude, are you—avoiding me? I thought after the game that… I don't know…"

"No!" Zach definitely sounded way too fucking cheerful on that one, but it was out before he could stop it. That fake-bright, shiny smile of self-defense. "I, uh, no, I'm not avoiding you."

"Okay, because you kind of—the entire night, you've been avoiding me."

"No, I was just, the boys are all here, and I've just been talking to Netty."

Nate took a step forward, into Zach's personal space. That was usually a Zach move, and he didn't really appreciate it being turned on him like that, especially when it made him feel so off balance. But then Nate's teeth were pressing against his lower lip and Zach got distracted.

"It's just I really don't want you to feel like—you can't—around me?"

"Nate, for being the smart one in this friendship, you're kinda regressing here."

One second Nate was staring at him with something like frustration or maybe stomach pain, and the next he'd lurched forward and shoved Zach back against the sink. Nate's hands were on his face and Nate's tongue was in his mouth.

Oh, we're doing this, huh, Zach thought, for a second, and *I was fucking trying*, and *I guess this is what's going on in there when he drinks*, and then *oh, this is a bad idea*, before his brain shut off and his dick took over.

For someone without a lot of experience kissing different people, Nate had certainly picked up quickly enough on what Zach liked, or maybe it didn't matter, because what Zach really liked was kissing Nate.

Nate had no technique at all, but there was something stupid vulnerable and enthusiastic in the way he did everything, the way his eyes immediately closed, the way he immediately opened his mouth under the press of Zach's tongue, the way Zach could feel his abs tremble and the sharp intake of his breath when Zach took the lead and twisted his fingers in Nate's hair, that was hotter than almost anything he could have imagined on his own.

The noise of the door behind him startled him into action; he pushed Nate, stumbling, away. The two of them whirled like guilty children to face Netty.

Netty turned his blank shark eyes from one to the other, raised his eyebrows, and said, "All okay in here, boys?"

Nate made a noise that sounded a little like he'd choked on his own tongue, so Zach, who was still drunk enough that his voice was thick and foggy when he spoke, said, "Just taking a piss, and *the* piss. Or I was. I'm done now. Come on, Cap," and grabbed Nate by the shirt and dragged him out of the bathroom.

"Oh, god," Nate was muttering to himself once they were safely in the hallway, "what the fuck was I thinking? I'm sorry, I'm so sorry, I don't know why I did that."

"Hey," Zach said, fighting the urge to press his hand over Nate's mouth to shut him up, because basically they were in public, which was something *he had better fucking remember*, "it's cool, chill out, it's cool, it's just not—it's just—uhhh...do you wanna...get out of here?"

"I'm sorry, I—what?" Nate's eyes were a darker blue than Zach had ever seen them, his mouth hanging open like Zach had just slapped him.

Zach wanted to kiss him again.

Maybe it was alcoholic courage; maybe it was the fact that it was easier to slip back into his old habits of not considering the consequences. He still had his hand pressed against Nate's chest. Nate's heart thudded under his fingers through the thin dress shirt; he could almost hear it in his ears. He'd done this before and kept it bros, so there was really no reason he couldn't have *this* and keep it bros. Like, he was still tier one with Jammer after all of those years of on-and-off hooking up when they were single and bored.

There was absolutely nothing that could go wrong.

"I said, do you wanna get out of here?"

Nate swallowed hard and Zach thought about how if they were back at his hotel room, he could have put his teeth against Nate's Adam's apple and felt the swallow under his tongue.

"I... Okay."

"Yeah?"

"Zach—"

"Just follow my lead, okay?"

It was like watching another Zach doing it. Dragging Nate out of the bathroom hallway, casually lurching from one teammate to the other as he grabbed their suit jackets and said his goodbyes and apologies, "oh yeah, Cap's tired, gotta get him back to the hotel," pounding everyone on the back.

He didn't feel like he was back inside his own body until they were in the cab, and then he almost wished he wasn't. The stupid sense of anticipation made everything feel charged with electricity, hypersensitive. Each time Nate's knee knocked against his, he had to fight the urge to put his hand on Nate's thigh. The cab driver must have thought both of them were crazy, the way they were completely silent, the way they couldn't even bear to look at each other, the way they couldn't stop touching each other even in the dumbest, smallest ways.

Somehow, he dragged Nate through the lobby and into the elevator. There were cameras, so he didn't kiss him, even though he couldn't think about doing anything else. Instead he slanted a glance sideways to make sure Nate was still, like, doing okay. Just in case Nate had decided to have a delayed freak-out about the entire thing.

Nate wasn't freaking out, but he was brilliant red from his face down to his throat, and his hands were curled in fists, bitten-down fingernails digging into his palms.

"Hey," Zach said. He was surprised by how soft his voice sounded. This was a weird fucking night. A weird fucking year. "We don't have to—"

Nate licked his lips and couldn't quite look Zach in the eye. Then he realized he was looking at Zach's dick and looked up at the ceiling. "I…really want to."

Little Zach made a valiant twitch at that, and Zach thought, *don't look a gift bro in the mouth.* But he kind of knew where Nate was coming from. The first time it had happened it had been kind of inevitable, maybe, but a surprise all the same. Things had escalated quickly.

But this was a conscious decision, even if both of them had gotten drunk first. Steps had to be taken to get there.

It was probably a lot, particularly for someone who'd never really done casual hookups before.

"Okay, I just want you to know, buddy, you're really important to me, I don't want you to be uncomf—"

Nate cut him off with his mouth, which, okay, not what Zach was expecting at all. He made a muffled noise of surprise, but then the elevator chimed and Nate pulled away again, face an even deeper red.

"Sorry. Sorry. Sorry."

"Jesus Christ, stop apologizing and get in here," Zach said, dragging him down the hall by a handful of shirt. Nate dutifully followed, and then dutifully waited while Zach fumbled in his pocket for the room key.

Once they were inside and the door was safely shut behind them, Zach finally felt like he could just *look* at Nate, the agonized hesitation on his face and the tension in every muscle in his body.

Nate stared at him just as intently at first, then eventually, he swallowed self-consciously and said, "What?"

"I just—come *here*," Zach said, and Nate took one step forward, and then two. Zach closed the distance between them and leaned up to kiss him.

It was a different kind of kiss than they'd shared in the bathroom.

This was slow and deliberate, teeth dragging along Nate's bottom lip, tongue teasing his mouth open. Zach didn't want to rush it this time. He wanted—he *wanted* so many things. He wanted to know everything about Nate's body. All of the places to touch him, all of the sensitive, hidden parts of him. He wanted to catalog every single noise he made.

He *wanted* to take him apart.

Nate was breathing raggedly, frozen under Zach's

mouth and hands, but when Zach started walking him backward toward the bed, he went willingly enough. When his calves hit the mattress, he let Zach push him down, scooted backward on his elbows so that Zach could look at him. Zach didn't know what *he* looked like, but evidently, something in his face was weird enough that Nate had to look away.

Zach straddled him, a little shock up his spine when he felt Nate's dick pressed against him and rolled his hips into it. "Yeah," he said, even though Nate hadn't said anything at all, and leaned down to kiss him again.

It had been a really long time since he'd wanted to spend hours making out with anyone, but he honestly thought he could do it with Nate, who was so fucking keyed up that every drag of Zach's fingers, every touch of his hand, seemed to make him shiver. If he was being honest with himself, Zach wasn't any better.

There was something about Nate—his best fucking friend, the person who probably knew him the best of anyone in his life at this point—completely losing it underneath him that was just, like… Zach was pretty jaded about a lot of things, but this felt new and overwhelming, and he didn't entirely know how to deal with it.

He actually lost track of time, focused only on Nate's mouth, the sounds he made when Zach's hands explored his body, the way his legs tightened around Zach's hips when it seemed like he might pull away even when he wasn't trying to end things, just undress Nate.

"Baby," Zach said, finally, as he propped himself up on his hands, and he could feel Nate's dick jerk in response. Nate looked fucked up, and it was all because of him. His mouth was red and swollen and his hair was a mess and his eyes weren't focusing properly. It was fucking something, all right. “Baby,” he tried again, rewarded with a small noise in response, “Let me take these off, okay?”

“Yeah,” Nate agreed breathlessly. “Okay, oh…”

They were both naked now. The thing about Nate that drove Zach absolutely insane was that Nate really didn’t seem to have any idea how hot he was. He was always kind of awkward in the locker room, turning away from cameras and anyone who looked at him for too long, even though he had basically a perfect body for hockey or, well, anything else.

Zach by this point had memorized every inch of him, every stupid scar he’d picked up from errant skates and sticks and hits and surgeries, every freckle in unexpected places, every thick line of muscle on his hips or thighs, his solid barrel torso. And that wasn’t even going into his stupid fucking face, which Zach loved and hated looking at in almost equal measure most days, because he knew he always looked like a dumbstruck fool when he did.

Nate was squirming now, probably embarrassed by how intently Zach was staring at him. But, like, Zach didn’t really know how often this was going to happen, and he was determined to remember every single second of the time he had. Zach reached out and caught one of Nate’s wrists, pinned it down on the bed at the same time he trapped one of Nate’s thighs beneath his knee. Nate was so still then, his chest heaving, and Zach said and thought exactly the same thing.

“Jesus, fuck.”

“What do you…?”

“You just, I’m going to do it for you this time, okay?”

“I, uh—okay. Oh, god.”

Zach had taken advantage of the moment of stillness to scramble his way down Nate's body and slide his fingers around Nate's dick. Later on he'd remember the rest of it in an almost dreamlike way, little screenshots of sense memory. The way Nate's head slammed back against the bed when Zach took him in his mouth. The bitten-off noises Nate tried to stifle but couldn't. How responsive he was to the smallest, lightest touches. It was almost too much, and despite his best intentions part of Zach's brain blocked out too many of the little details. The way Nate tasted, the way he felt pressed against the back of Zach's throat, the way his thighs clenched almost painfully around Zach's head when he came.

The way he lay there, panting, trying to recover, his eyelashes wet and clumpy looking against his cheeks, and Zach felt a weird sensation in his chest, almost physical pain.

Which, by the way, what the fuck?

It took Nate a few minutes to regain control of himself and struggle into a sitting position. His eyes were that dark fucking blue again, and for once he didn't look nervous, just intent, like he knew what he wanted, and what he wanted was Zach.

It was a lot.

"Okay, let me." Nate's hands were big and warm and all-encompassing and when he wrapped his fingers around Zach, it was like—

It was like someone had punched him. Just the warmth of Nate's hand, and everything else preceding it, built up in him without an outlet, and he was coming, his head buried in the crook of Nate's neck. And it was intense too, wrung out of him, the kind of orgasm that left you boneless and incoherent afterward.

Nate, thank god, didn't fucking say anything. The last time Zach had felt that humiliated, he had been about twelve years old, had just touched a tit for the first time, and come in his pants. This was honestly worse, considering how much time had gone by, how much experience he'd had since.

"I—uh—that's—" he gasped, finally. "That's—never happened to me before. I mean—like—as an adult, I just—I—never—"

Nate stared at him, hand still wrapped around Zach's dick. There was come all over his fist, rapidly drying, tacky to touch. Objectively, it was gross. Subjectively, it was so fucking hot. Nate's thumb brushed over the head of Zach's dick and Zach shuddered convulsively. It was too much, he was too sensitive, but he didn't really want Nate to stop.

"Oh my god."

"Um," Nate said, and took his hand away.

"It's just," Zach was still saying desperately, like if he explained enough, Nate wouldn't find this whole thing as pathetic as it was. "I was really—I didn't—I wanted this to be—"

"I, uh… It's cool, Zach."

Zach looked away from him because it was too much, and at the clock, because it was right there, and saw that it was almost three in the morning. They really *had* just been making out for hours. What the fuck was *happening* to him? "I—uh—should probably go back to my room. You know. For tomorrow morning."

"Yeah," Nate said. His face was unreadable. "It's late."

"I—uh—good game," Zach said, "really good game, buddy," and fled.

Good game? Seriously, what the fuck was happening to him?

He was not at all sure he wanted to find out.

Nate stared at the door for the second time that week, and thought, *okay, no more drinking.*

He forced himself to his feet and stumbled into the bathroom to get a glass of water from the sink and realized that they had both forgotten that they'd been in *Zach's hotel room*. Zach's bathroom kit was sitting on the sink, messily spilling over onto the counter. Nate looked at it for a moment, sighed, poured himself the water, and drank it.

He had no idea when Zach was going to figure it out and come back, or whether he'd just crash with someone else, but Nate didn't know if he wanted to stick around to find out. He'd gone and fucked things up again, when he'd really been trying to be the responsible one. It was just like every careful plan went out the window when he was around Zach lately, even though he'd gone into the bar bathroom intending to ask a question and only ask a question.

That was one thing he knew for sure: he *really* couldn't be here when Zach realized. He didn't want to provide an explanation as to why he was still hanging around the hotel room. What if Zach was so weirded out by the whole thing that he'd run away, and *then* he came back to find Nate sitting there like he was hoping to go again? How disgusted and scornful he'd be... Nate could already feel his ears turning red, the burning heat of the deep-seated humiliation rising to the surface as quickly as always. His stomach churned, the old, familiar nausea.

So instead of staying, Nate got dressed, stumbled toward the door, and shut it behind him. He went back to his own hotel room. But he didn't get anything approaching a good night's sleep. It took him a long time, tossing and turning and replaying the best blowjob of his life over and over again in his head. The way Zach had been so keyed up by going down on him that he'd come just from Nate's lightest touch.

In retrospect it was probably pretty ridiculous he'd thought he was straight.

On the plane to Miami, though, Zach flopped into the seat next to him like nothing had happened. At least at first. He wasn't wearing the same clothes he'd been wearing last night, so clearly, he'd figured it out, or at least worked up the courage to go back to his room. Where Nate hadn't been. He grinned a little sheepishly at Nate, and asked, "Sleep well, Cap?"

Nate choked on the water he'd been in the process of drinking, swallowed hard, and lied, "Uh, sure. Yeah."

"Okay, good," Zach said, and then slouched down into the seat, stretched out his legs, and closed his eyes, leaving Nate seething in the thin line between the frustrated desire to shake him, and the desire to kiss his eyelid. Because *that* was an extremely normal thought to have.

Jesus Christ, his brain was not doing him any favors this week.

They beat the Barracuda. The Florida team was finally coming out of a rebuild, starting to look like a dangerous group. Especially in transition. Still, tonight, it wasn't even close. Nate had a hat trick, and the final score was 7-1. Complete and utter domination. It had only been two games, but it felt like they were playing like themselves again, finally.

After last night, and with another game in Raleigh the next day, no one was going out, which was perfectly fine with Nate. He ran on autopilot in the locker room for postgame interviews, exhausted from the game and his mind a thousand miles away. One of the reporters noticed.

"Nate, you've just won two games and had your fourth career hat trick, and yet you don't seem satisfied—can you elaborate on that?"

Nate mumbled something about how he was always looking to the next game, and the goal this year was the Cup, but it was only about a quarter of the truth.

Later that night, safely in his own hotel room, Nate half listened to the news on the TV in the background while he flipped through the Google Doc he and Bee kept updated for the rest of the team, with notes on their upcoming opponents. Some of it was from the coaching staff, some of it was Bee's insane well of hockey minutiae, and some of it was Nate's contributions. He wasn't sure how many on the team actually utilized it on a day-to-day basis, but he pretty reliably saw Mäkelä, Mike, and Sally's names pop up at the top, so that was something, anyway.

It wasn't always necessary, but he liked to have the knowledge fresh in his head. Knowledge and planning were the best ways to manage anxiety, and he had certainly been incredibly fucking anxious the last couple of weeks. He tried not to think about the Zach thing too much, but it was almost impossible *not* to think about it.

Sex, his brain supplied helpfully, *not the Zach thing. It was sex, and you don't want to think about sex with Zach. Because you had sex with Zach. Twice. You started it. Twice. It was really good sex too, not like the last time you tried it.*

Nate looked at the document again and said, out loud, "Carolina. You are playing the Carolina Oaks tomorrow. They're probably going to fire their head coach midseason. It's a mess down there."

Someone knocked on his door.

Nate set his phone down and went to answer it. He didn't really think about the fact that he was only wearing boxers, because it was probably one of the guys from the team, so it wasn't like they hadn't seen it before. He'd been trying to get better about letting people look at him and not being fucked up about it, trying not to think of his body as something he hated, but rather something that he had to use for his job. And as he'd settled into the captain role, he'd gotten into the habit of talking to anyone who needed to come in and talk. He wasn't always very good at it, but it had definitely gotten less awkward than it had been his first season, and he thought he'd helped some of the rookies, at least. It was important to have a welcoming environment where people could feel like their voices mattered.

And, you know. That shit.

He opened the door, and Zach looked up at him, the bright, megawatt smile on full display. It wasn't his crooked smile, the one Nate particularly loved and the one that lit up his entire face. It was the one that didn't quite reach his eyes. The one he used for the media. Nate was instantly suspicious because usually a smile *that* wide either meant that Zach had fucked something up or was intending to fuck something up.

Usually, Nate wasn't on the receiving end of that particular smile. It was unnerving.

"Can I come in?" Zach asked. He wore a pair of gray sweatpants and the Agalloch T-shirt he'd stolen from Nate's room at his parents' house in their first season after Mom's Chanukah party. He'd never given it back and Nate, once he'd discovered where it had gone, had never asked.

"Yes," Nate replied, automatically, and took a step backward. It was weird how sex had changed things. Normally, Zach would have already been hanging out in his room, or Nate would have been in Zach's room, because even on the road they spent most of their time together. It was the longest he'd been alone during a regular season in a long time, and he knew exactly how sad that sounded even just in his own head.

He took another step back, and Zach took a step forward, completely negating his efforts.

"Hey, buddy." Zach's eyes were fixed solely on his face and that was probably a good thing. Normally, Nate would have felt self-conscious but for some reason he couldn't look away to worry about it.

"Uh...hey. What's up?"

"I was thinking," Zach said, and grinned at him. This was a more regular Zach grin, one of the ones where Nate knew he was making fun of himself. "Yeah, I know, bad idea, but I was thinking..."

Nate's normal reaction when Zach said something self-deprecating about his own intelligence was to cuff him on the arm and tell him to knock it the fuck off, but his mouth was too dry to say anything.

"So—I'm just gonna come out and say it. We hooked up twice, and we won twice, right?" He waited expectantly, and when Nate finally nodded, slowly, he beamed. "So it's obviously good luck, right? Like a pregame ritual."

"Uh..."

The smile didn't falter, exactly, but Zach hesitated a second. "Uh, and if it's good luck, we should keep doing it, right? Like...why mess with success?"

Nate felt a little like he was listening to another language, one that was almost adjacent to English but somehow didn't make any sense. "You want to keep hooking up with me before games...for good luck?"

"Ferda, dude. And it makes perfect sense, right? We snapped our losing streak after the first time, and I blew you last night and we won and you got a hatty tonight, so I'd say that's, like, a pretty good sample size so far, right?"

Nate stared at him, trying to see whether Zach was fucking with him. After the way things had ended last night, he *had* to be fucking with him. But Zach stared back, all wide brown eyes and completely guileless smile, and it was clear that he was actually being serious.

Of course, it did make sense.

The first two times had been a drunken mistake on Nate's part. Well, not a mistake, but definitely a drunken lowering of his inhibitions. But there had to have been some kind of reason Zach would want to do this with *him*, when he could have had anyone. And they were both completely sober this time, which was...a step. And hockey players *were* superstitious as hell.

The more he thought about it, the more it actually did make sense, even if it was a bizarre kind of sense.

He wasn't sure how it made him feel.

Nate supposed it was good to be needed.

Still, it didn't feel that great.

"So what do you say?" Zach pressed on, arms crossed over his chest. He looked nervous, although Nate had no idea why he would. It was just Nate. And he doubted Zach was rejected by anyone very often, let alone in times when the success of the team was riding on it.

"I mean—if you really think it would help."

"'Course I do," Zach said, like he was offended Nate would even question him. "You're my good luck charm. So we're good?"

"Uh...yeah. We're good."

"Sick," Zach said, and extended his fist for Nate to bump.

Nate obliged with their secret handshake, warily, but before he could ask *are you* really *sure about this?* or anything like it, Zach was kissing him, sloppy and enthusiastic, and Nate was a weak and helpless bastard who couldn't help giving in.

When they finally pulled apart for air, Nate must have looked about as confused as he felt, because Zach said, "Cap, come on, we're playing Carolina tomorrow."

"Oh—you want to—now?"

"You got other pressing business?" Zach said. His voice had dropped a little, a husky tease, and his thumb traced a line over Nate's stomach and hooked into the waistband of his boxers for a second before dipping lower. "I can leave..."

"I—uh—oh, god. No. Please don't."

And then Zach was kissing him again, and Nate let himself have this, however stupid it was to do it.

Later on, lying on his back and trying to catch his breath, Nate was pretty sure he had beard burn on one of his thighs. It was marginally uncomfortable, but he had the unaccountable urge to press his fingers against it. He could still taste Zach in his mouth, and it should have been gross, but it wasn't. Nate stared at the ceiling and thought, *god damn.*

Next to him, Zach sighed, happily, and rolled over on his side, propped up on his elbow. He looked down at Nate. His face was mostly in shadow, the only illumination in the room flashes of headlights on the highway through the window. Nate was struck again by the fact that there were objectively better-looking people out there, probably. Someone somewhere was probably more handsome than Zach. There were individual things about Zach that were weird looking or didn't quite add up, like his sharp little canines and crooked smile and broken nose, but also, Zach's face was almost painful to look at sometimes, he was so beautiful to Nate.

So he looked away.

"Hey," Zach was saying, with a little yawn. "It's late."

"So you have to go?"

"Well, I thought maybe I could crash with you tonight?"

Like we used to, before all of this. He didn't say it, but Nate thought it.

Zach was looking at him still, that weird expression that Nate couldn't quite figure out. "It *is* late, and I'm fuckin' wiped."

"Sure," Nate said, even though he didn't really understand how it figured into Zach's pregame ritual. He had also really kind of missed it. "I mean…it's a king, there's enough room. If you want to."

"Thanks," Zach said, flopping back down against the pillow and turning on his side. Nate stared at the line of his back, the shift of the muscle there as he wriggled around to get himself comfortable. "'Night, bro. We're gonna kill it tomorrow."

Nate didn't say anything, but thought, *well, now I have to win*, and *Nate, you fucking idiot*. Neither were particularly comforting thoughts, but thankfully, he wasn't awake for long after that.

It's just Mom's annual Chanukah party, Nate told himself, for the fifty-millionth time.

There was absolutely no reason for his chest to constrict every time he thought about it. There was no reason for sweat to prickle on his forehead and back and in his armpits every time he thought about it. Not for the last time, Nate wondered why the fuck he couldn't just be normal about anything, but the fact was: he wasn't normal about anything, and he never had been. And he just had to get on with his life.

He'd been playing with the Cons for seven years now, and his parents had thrown the party every season. Even though it wasn't a *major* holiday, his mom liked to give the players who didn't go home—either because they didn't get along with their families, or it was too far to fly for just a few days—a holiday experience with a family. The implication, of course, was that Nate's family was the team's family too.

It was kind of weird, on one level: both of Nate's parents had worked long hours when he was a kid, and sometimes it felt like they barely knew each other. They hadn't had elaborate holiday parties *then*. The team got a whole side of his parents that he'd never gotten to experience, and he couldn't even begrudge them it, because they were his brothers. And sister.

He didn't even mind the parties. Not really.

Everyone generally behaved, although there was at least one year where someone got a little too drunk and pissed in the neighbors' potted stoop plants and Nate had had to send them some expensive gift baskets from DiBruno Brothers as an apology.

And it had been two years now since the last Chanukah with Rachel, the one where he'd fallen asleep on the couch in between her and Zach. Nate had woken up to find she'd already gone home. That had been the first night he and Zach had shared a bed after they'd stumbled upstairs and squeezed into Nate's childhood twin. Nate had woken up draped over Zach's entire body the next morning. It should have been awkward, but somehow, it wasn't.

He'd thought about that night for a long time after. Never let himself think about it fully, just turned the image over and over in his head, Zach's uncertain smile and sleepy brown eyes. Should have known that he was a goner from that moment on. Had probably been a goner even before that.

Regardless of what had happened in the past, there was no reason to be nervous about the Chanukah party.

But he was.

Like he usually did, Nate went over early to help Mom with the cooking. She always went overboard, even considering that she was feeding half a team of hockey players. All of the classics: brisket, kugel, potato latkes, homemade sufganiyot. Some more adventurous stuff like a walnut and pomegranate chicken, and then some dishes that she insisted were "for the goyim." A lot of chips and dip. He'd never been able to get a clear answer out of her about what made that goyische. The one that both fascinated and disgusted Nate was the broccoli casserole: she had sworn him to secrecy about the ingredients, but it involved several different kinds of soups named after creamed vegetables and bricks of chopped frozen broccoli.

She started cooking several weeks in advance and freezing things in trays, but there was still a shitload of work to do the day of. And that was where Nate came in—quite literally, through the unlocked door.

The house hadn't changed at all since he'd moved out. It was an old-school Philly row home, and his parents had never bothered to renovate it. It was a straight-through from the door through the living room, which was still full of the same threadbare, overstuffed furniture that had been there when he was a kid, the same pictures hanging on the walls, back to the tiny dining table and behind it the kitchen.

She'd filled every spare inch of shelf with tchotchkes, little gifts people had given her, things she'd collected on their few family vacations, random family heirlooms from the old country. The house was a time capsule in a lot of ways, but what century you were in was anyone's best guess, at least until you saw the giant TV screen Nate had bought them when he'd signed his last contract, the only gift they'd ever accepted from him.

The walls were paneled with dark wood and hung with hundreds of pictures, old family photos from Russia and Germany, relatives Nate couldn't have even named if you'd asked him. Pictures of Zayde as a young boy, before the Nazis had come to power. Pictures of Bubbe and Zayde after they'd come to America, wearing the correct clothes but somehow still not fitting in. Pictures of Nate's parents, at their wedding and after; his dad at the shipyard and his mom smiling behind the wheel of her bus.

Even worse, baby photos from the time Nate had been born through the present day. You could chart his progression from gigantic baby to apple-cheeked toddler to awkward teenager to professional hockey player in the space of about two feet of wall. His draft portrait was the crown jewel: long, greasy flow, puffy face covered in red splotchy acne, braces, and all.

Nate *hated* looking at them.

He'd once asked his mom to take some of them down, or at least put them in a less prominent place, but she'd stared at him like he was crazy. "But we *love* you," she'd said. "We're *proud* of you."

And that was the worst part: they did; they were.

There was noise from the kitchen: pots and pans banging around, a knife, his mom muttering curses to herself as she went. Absolutely nothing had changed.

"Hey, Mom," Nate called.

"Ah, Nathaniel! Come in, come in. Work to be done."

"Like always," Nate said, unable to keep the wry tone from his voice. If she picked up on it, she ignored it, the same way she always ignored everything he said that she didn't like.

It was nice to settle back into helping her, even though it was a tight fit in the kitchen. Mom was a big woman too, almost six feet tall even in her house slippers, and the kitchen wasn't built for two people their size. It was a dance as intricate as anything on the ice, knowing where not to be at the appropriate time.

"Where's Dad?"

"He ran out to the beer distributor. He should be back soon."

"I could've picked it up for you—"

"Nonsense! Nonsense, we're perfectly capable of affording a few cases of beer for your friends."

There was no use arguing, so he didn't.

"How're the boys?" Mom asked a little later. "You never update me anymore."

"Sorry, Mom. I've just been really busy." It wasn't entirely a lie, even if the reasons he was busy weren't any reasons he could talk to her about.

Despite his hesitance she peppered him with questions about everyone on the team: Mom not only had the entire roster memorized, she remembered their spouses and girlfriends, their favorite foods, the things they were interested in, and in some cases, their stats. Nate tried to limit the information he gave her. Leah Singer meant well, but when she was interested in some aspect of your life, she could be a *lot*.

"And Zachary? Is he seeing anyone?"

"No, Mom," Nate said, looking down at the onions he was slicing for the salad. He wiped his eyes with the back of his hand and hoped his face wasn't too red.

"It's so strange," Mom mused, as she ladled some of the dips into bowls, "he's such a handsome, charming young man, you wouldn't think he'd have any problems finding someone."

Nate, who couldn't trust himself to say anything, didn't. And then he didn't have to, because the front door opened again and Zach said, "Hello?"

"Zachary!" Mom exclaimed, delighted. "You're early."

"I thought I'd come by and help set up," Zach said, with the brilliant smile that always won Nate's parents over, from the first day he'd shown up on their doorstep with a bouquet of flowers. He looked more at ease today than he had back then, overdressed and fidgety.

"That's *so* kind of you," Mom said, beaming. "Come in, come in. Have a snack while you work."

"Thank you, Mrs. Singer," Zach said, helping himself to some of the carrot sticks and ranch dip she shoved at him. The quickest way to her heart was to let her feed you, and Zach had figured that out early.

"You totally didn't have to do this," Nate said, as they were setting up the card table and chairs in the living room.

"I know," Zach said, grinning sideways at him. "But I know how much work it is, and I'm gonna be here later anyway, so I figured, why not. Don't tell me you aren't happy to see me."

That would have been a lie, so Nate just shrugged, and went to one of the junk drawers to search for a shim to steady the wobbly leg of the card table.

"You know," Zach said, a little later, while they were ferrying the food out from the kitchen, "Gags texted me earlier."

"Really? About what?"

"He was kind of freaking out about the party."

"Huh? Why? It's just my parents."

"Well, yeah, but it's one of his first big things as a member of the team. He wanted to make a good impression and I guess he was kind of worrying he wouldn't."

"What'd you tell him?"

"Just that your parents are kinda intense, but super nice. All he has to worry about is being himself. And not to wear dress shoes," Zach said, with an impish smile, like he too was remembering his first time showing up on Nate's parents' doorsteps in shoes that pinched his toes all night.

By the time the rest of the team started trickling in, the two of them had made sure everything was set up to Mom's liking: the table with its paper tablecloth that she'd insist on folding up and reusing next year, the mismatched hot plates holding all of the food, the cooler stuffed with ice and cans and bottles, extra chairs wherever they'd fit. They didn't have a tree for obvious reasons, but there was a designated area of the steps upstairs for the gift exchanges.

As far as evenings went, it was a pretty chill one; whenever he made the rounds to make sure things were going okay and his mom wasn't terrifying any rookies, everything was as he expected. Bee rolling her eyes a little while Mäkelä and Socks earnestly debated the relative merits of True pads versus Bauer; Netty in the kitchen eating a heroic amount of potato latkes and sour cream; Mike tagging along while Mom showed off her spice drawer to Danny Garcia; Sally in the corner discussing chess strategy with Nate's dad, a murderously intent gleam in his eye. They'd had a "game" going for the last three years, updated mostly at the holiday parties and occasionally by text.

A few minutes later, Nate noticed that Mom had cornered Gags by the sink. He was in the process of washing his hands but seemed drunk enough that he had gotten distracted by her questions—was he eating enough, how was he sleeping at night, were the boys treating him okay—that the water streamed over his still hands.

"Mom," Nate said, turning the tap off, "what'd I tell you about going easy on the kids?"

"I'm just making sure," she said with a sniff. "I did the same for you when you were his age."

Nate had remembered that one, all right: the intense humiliation of his mom asking Logan Beaulieu, the Cons' longtime captain and probably a future Hall of Famer, whether her son had settled in okay.

"Mmm," he said noncommittally, and took Gags by the shoulder. "Come on, Gags, you should maybe eat a little more dinner. Don't want to drink too much on an empty stomach."

"Oh, yeah," Gags agreed. His eyes were a little glassy, his face flushed and his hairline damp. "Everything looks really good, I just didn't—you know."

Nate patted him on the shoulder. "Yeah, I know. They're intense but they mean well. You just have to know how to escape."

"Or have someone to rescue you," Zach said, handing Gags a plate. "Don't worry, bud. We gotcha."

"Thanks," Gags said fervently. "Like, for everything, you know, this year so far, the team has been—you've been—just, you know. Thanks."

"Don't mention it?" Nate said, blinking.

"Go on," Zach said. "Go hang with the guys. If you need someone to run interference, just grab Mike, he's intimidating enough."

"Thanks," Gags mumbled again, melting back into the crowd with the plate piled high with brisket and chicken still in his hands.

"Going pretty well, I'd say," Zach said, nudging Nate in the side. "You were worrying for nothing."

"I always worry."

"For nothing, though."

Nate wanted to say *not for nothing.* He wanted to ask Zach whether he remembered that first Chanukah party, whether he remembered waking up in Nate's bed, whether he ever thought about the fact that he'd stolen one of Nate's favorite T-shirts and Nate had just let it go, whether he realized he was still wearing it sometimes.

He didn't say any of those things.

CHAPTER SEVEN

January

Every New Year's before he'd come to Philadelphia, Zach had steadfastly avoided making resolutions. It felt corny and cheesy and unnecessary, and he was *so* bad at them anyway.

And even if he wasn't bad at them, like, what was he going to resolve to do except be the best at what he did? And he did that anyway, just by existing. At least that's how it had been before. Now it was different. He'd had the goal set from the beginning of the summer—win Nate a Cup—and he was actively working on getting there. Solely based on the team's results so far, it was looking achievable. There wasn't anything else he could think of that he wanted or needed.

They played at home on New Year's Eve against the Anaheim Arsenal, a matinee game, which meant they'd have time to go out after. Anaheim was another team that had been perennially at the bottom of the standings for a long time, but they had never drafted a game changer like Bee and were still stuck in mediocrity. That didn't mean the game didn't have personal stakes: Zach had been working on a grudge against one of Anaheim's forwards, Jones, a guy who'd high-sticked him last season and had gotten away with it.

Zach wasn't a very physical player—he left that to Mike, or even Bee, to some extent—but for this asshole? He was willing to make an exception.

They started the game with the right momentum. Netty set up Gags for a ridiculous kind of goal, something that shouldn't have even gone in in a beer league game. A trickler right through the Anaheim goalie's fivehole. And then it was on, a rough ride until the end. It was like the Arsenal felt as though they had to make up for the initial weak start however they could, but they were never able to get back into it. It was one of those games where Zach skated circles around all of the opposing forwards and d-men, coasting easily on his edges.

And of course, the kind of game where your opponent felt like they had to start shit to get back into it. It started about halfway through the second, when the Cons were up 4-2. First it was just some cross-checks to the back when he was too close to the crease. That was something he could shrug off. But when the sticks started slipping higher and higher, he turned.

"Fuck off," he said to Jones.

"You fuck off!"

Zach considered his options, but the play was moving again before he could say anything else, and he was chasing the puck back into the neutral zone. He remembered in the seasons before he'd gotten there how Philly had always played a dump-and-chase style but hadn't been anywhere near fast enough to complete the chase part of the equation. It had been pretty fun to play against them, because it was always a massacre. But now *he* was Philly, and he was the one streaking after the puck.

Zach was fast enough.

But then, as he was heading toward the bench at the end of his shift, he saw Jones slam his stick into the back of Nate's neck, the wince of pain that crumpled Nate's face up. Before Zach could even really think about it, he had taken a few quick strides to get over there and break it up.

"Hey!" he said, grabbing Jones by the back of the jersey and yanking him away, "the fuck do you think you're doing?"

"What the fuck do *you* think you're doing, Reed, you fucking pussy—"

Zach thought about saying something like *hands off the captain* but what came out instead was, "Do you want to go?"

"You want to fight *me*?"

Instead of answering, Zach threw his gloves down on the ice and, after a moment, Jones followed.

He'd never fought before. He'd almost gotten into one last year, with Danny Garcia—funnily enough, also for a hit on Nate—before Mike had pulled him off. He tried to remember what Mike had taught him about fights. To keep your thumb out of your fist. That the most important thing was balance, and that if you could grab the other guy's jersey you already had an advantage. He did manage to get his fingers into the neck of Jones's jersey, but Jones was bigger, so all that ended up doing was putting Zach firmly into punching range. He got a few punches of his own in—the jarring ache of his knuckles against Jones's jaw told him that much for sure—but he was at a disadvantage.

Jones's fist slamming resoundingly into his lip and the salty tang of blood in his mouth made that much clear. Zach hung in there as best he could, but once there was a little puddle of red on the ice, rapidly freezing over, the refs split them up.

Even though he'd clearly, convincingly lost that fight, Zach accepted the stick taps from his teammates. In this case, it was the thought that counted, more so than the results.

He took the five-minute fighting major, knowing that it was probably only sheer luck that the ref had caught the cross-check before it happened so he didn't get an instigator call. Some players liked to jaw in the penalty box, but Zach was still too furious to even think of something to say. It was a weird feeling: he wasn't the kind of guy who *got* angry. Even Jones saying shit like, "I knew you couldn't fight, you hit like a girl," didn't really faze him now.

Jones slamming his stick against Nate's neck, though…

The Arsenal brought it within a one goal game while he was still in the box, after a miscommunication between Mike and Gags led to the puck bouncing right onto the stick of one of Arsenal's forwards, waiting on Mäkelä's blindside. He hadn't had a chance. The Cons managed to close it out, although it was a tense final period, scoreless.

In the locker room afterward, Nate touched Zach's wrist briefly with two fingers. "Hey," he said. "You didn't have to do that for me. I was fine."

"I know I didn't, I—" Zach stopped. He couldn't really explain to Nate why he'd done it. "I just wasn't even thinking about it. Fuck, Cap. I'm sorry they scored on that one."

"It's okay," Nate said mildly. "We still won. Not so sure about that fight for you, though."

"I really sucked, huh?" Zach asked, grinning, then winced. The smile pulled at his split lip, and he raised his fingers to touch it. It was going to be fat as hell for a week at least, probably.

Nate stared at his hand, like he wanted to touch it too. "Let's just say you have other skills."

"You wanna tell me about them later?"

Nate's face immediately flushed red, and he looked down. "Not *here*," he whispered.

"Sorry, sorry."

"It's fine, I just—I just—yeah."

Zach took pity on him and went back to stripping out of his nasty, soaking pads.

After the postgame routine of shower and cooldown and media availability and meal, everyone went home to go and change and sleep it off before heading out for the night. Nate and Zach went back to Zach's place, because he had to feed Dolly and Hank, and then just ended up crashing there.

Zach's house wasn't as nicely decorated as Nate's, mostly because he'd had to do it all on his own. Rachel had picked out, like, coordinating pillows for Nate's couch. On the other hand, Zach had finally bought actual dining room furniture in lieu of the Ping-Pong table he'd been using after moving in. So he was moved in enough, and the bed was big enough for both of them.

It wasn't a very long nap, but it was enough that both of them woke up with enough energy to get through a holiday night. By the time the team met up again, they ended up barhopping in Fishtown. Fishtown was the trendier version of his own neighborhood of Port Richmond, the old-school brick row homes mixed in with the kind of new construction that had ugly corrugated metal siding instead, or huge buildings made entirely of glass. It was one of Zach's favorite neighborhoods in the entire city;

there was always some new spot opening up to check out and it wasn't too far from home. It was a pretty chill New Year's as far as they went; everyone was tired from the game.

Zach took a second to check on Gags, who had really taken the fuckup with Mike pretty hard. He was alone in the corner, clutching his empty pint glass like if he squeezed it hard enough, he could somehow purge all of the shit in his body that had led him to make a mistake. Like it was something he could purge.

"You gotta just let those things go, Gags," Zach said, and ordered them both another beer.

"Let it go?" Gags asked. "Reedsy, I could've *lost us the game.*"

"Well, yeah. But also, Mike was involved in that play. And also, Mäkelä didn't make the save. It's never *just* your fault. Sure, you might fuck up, but there are five other guys on the ice besides you who fucked up too. And we all learn how to put it away and move on to the next one."

Gags took a large gulp of the beer and wiped his mouth and the foam on his upper lip away with the back of one hand. He was really trying for facial hair, but he'd mostly managed a horrible little mustache spread sparsely across his pale skin. "*How* do you learn it, though?"

"I don't know how to give you specifics," Zach admitted. "It's just, like, you know. The more games you play, the more mistakes pile up. And the good stuff too. But at a certain point it's all kind of a blur. It just helps to focus on the game at hand, and then after that's over, just on preparing for the next game."

"If you say so," Gags said doubtfully.

"Come on!" Zach clapped Gags on the shoulder and the beer he was holding sloshed dangerously at the rim of the pint glass. "It's New Year's, bud, and we actually pulled out the win. You don't need to be beating yourself up about this. Go have fun with your friends. Bells is looking a bit overwhelmed there."

They both turned to look: there was Belsky, in the corner, talking to two women who were probably at least five years older than him, the kind of Brooklyn transplant hipster moms who went to yoga classes in the morning and were *really* enjoying having a babysitter for the holiday. Belsky was a handsome kid, big and muscular and sharp-featured, but for all of his size, he looked like a deer in the headlights.

Gags laughed, and Zach gave him a little swat on the arm again. "Go on."

He watched Gags's back as he wove his way through the crowd, frowning a little.

"Hey," Nate mumbled in his ear, halfway through the night. The rest of the guys didn't notice. They were too busy at the bar, or drinking, or pursuing some of the very pretty girls who'd come out in their fancy New Year's dresses. "Do you wanna get out of here?"

Zach thought about it. He thought about how even last year, he probably would've been chasing after the woman in the shimmery gold dress, the one who looked like little bits of twinkly fringe all sewn together, who slipped between them with a murmured apology on her way to the bar. He would have been distracted by literally the shiniest thing in the room.

This year it wasn't even a question where he was going and who he was going with. If this was what growing up felt like, he didn't mind in the least.

Zach said, "Sure."

It didn't take them long to walk back to Nate's house

from Fishtown; the night air was chilly and crisp and Zach was only wearing his thin sweater, but he didn't feel cold at all. He wasn't even really that drunk, just a little tipsy. Tipsy enough to bump his shoulder companionably against Nate's as they walked, tipsy enough to feel the warm satisfaction of having Nate all to himself.

Once they got back to Nate's house, they went up to the roof deck, sprawled themselves out on Nate's comfortable outdoor couch, with its deep pillows that he conscientiously brought inside when he wasn't sitting on them—the kind of tiny detail that made Zach's chest squeeze when he thought about it too long. They sat in silence for a long time, watching the explosions above them. He glanced sideways at Nate's handsome face in profile, turned up to the sky, the warmth of the gas firepit glowing between them.

One of the most beautiful things about New Year's in Philly was that somehow, even though they technically weren't legal, everyone had fireworks going off in their backyard. It was frustrating, as a dog owner, because the barking went pretty much nonstop during it. But you couldn't deny that it was a sight to see. No matter which direction you turned your head, something was exploding. Chaotic and untimed, flowering bursts of pink and blue and green, streaks of red and yellow and orange. Sparkling white snowfalls. In the distance you could hear people cheering and the crackle and hiss of the rockets going off.

It wasn't anything like where he'd grown up, but lately, it seemed more and more like home.

At midnight, when the screams and gunshots and fireworks really went over the top, Zach leaned over on a brazen impulse and kissed Nate firmly on the mouth, ignoring the pain in his lip. It was risky: there were neighbors on the roof decks around them, none of whom were looking at them; there were windows, none of which he could see beyond.

But there was Nate, flushed face and wide blue eyes, and there was the New Year, and the knowledge of the promise he'd made.

"What was that for?" Nate asked, after Zach had pulled away.

"Happy New Year, dummy," Zach said, fingers on his knee.

"Well, yeah," Nate said, and licked his lip.

He asked, even though he already knew the answer. "You wanna go in to celebrate?"

Nate was smiling. He was smiling at Zach, and Zach thought his chest might burst. "Of course."

Nate tried not to think about how easy it was to adjust to the new parameters of things with Zach. It was easy in some ways, but not in others. He still felt self-conscious whenever he got naked, at least until Zach distracted him.

And it was still a game thing, but also, it wasn't.

If it was *just* a game thing, then they wouldn't have spent New Year's together. If it was just a game thing, Zach probably wouldn't keep crashing in Nate's hotel room after they'd hooked up. If it was just a game thing, Zach would probably be weird about it when Nate woke up pressed naked against his back, face tucked into the space between his neck and shoulder. If it was just a game thing, he wouldn't roll over, laughing, and breathe his disgusting morning breath in Nate's face, and kiss him anyway.

But if it wasn't just a game thing Nate didn't know what it was.

Maybe this was just what happened when you had a thing going with someone you knew as well as he knew Zach. Maybe this was just what happened when you had a really good hockey buddy, when you had an intense friendship like the kind you had in juniors and instead of things ending when you got drafted, it just kept…going. It was easy to mix up what parts of your life were what.

"Hey," Zach said, on one of those days where the morning breath was vile but neither of them was in a rush to get out of bed and brush their teeth. They were in Philly the day after the last game, and after a morning skate, they were flying to Dallas later that day. Zach's hair was messy; he hadn't really cut it after the playoffs like he usually did, and it was still long enough to tie up in a weird-looking hipstery topknot. Nate knew this because he'd pulled the topknot out the night before. "We've been playing some pretty great fucking hockey, dude."

"We have," Nate agreed. He felt unusually cautious, like if he said the wrong thing, something unexpectedly bad would happen. Or he didn't want to say too much, reveal too much.

Zach seemed equally cautious, which was unusual. He looked, searching, into Nate's face. "It's good, I guess. That's what I wanted to say. It feels like everything's finally clicking."

"Coach just had to give you the A," Nate said, poking him in the stomach. There wasn't much to poke; even this early in the season Zach didn't have one damned extra ounce of fat to cushion the muscle. "That lit a fire under your ass."

Zach snorted, swatted his hand away. "Yeah, it was all the A, buddy."

"Well, you wear it well, anyway. And we *are* playing some damn good hockey."

"Thanks to your fearless leadership, Cap."

"Asshole," Nate muttered, but it was as affectionate as Zach's teasing.

The truth was, it was a factor.

Nate always had a running checklist of captain shit he had to take care of scrolling through the back of his head. When he'd first gotten the C, it had been mostly a feeling of dread that had consumed him, and the dread of course remained with him each time they didn't win the Cup, but it had been tempered with the knowledge and weight of responsibility. He still felt sick about it sometimes, but mostly, he was too busy to be anxious. There were rookies to corral, coaches to finesse, and egos to soothe, and players having personal crises to nudge in the right direction.

Some of the worst offenders from last season seemed to have gotten their shit together. For example, Mike, who'd been on the third pair or a healthy scratch for good portions of his first season and a bruised, scrappy mess for half of his second, had suddenly turned his game around. It wasn't just the game, though. He'd moved to Princeton—it was almost in between Philly and Newark, even though Garcia's commute was probably worse—and seemed suspiciously even-keeled these days.

And in more unlikely ways.

Jonathan Bouchard's player assistance stint and his residential stay in a substance abuse program hadn't really worked out while he was playing. He'd come home, and then gone right back in. He'd eventually just retired, which ultimately seemed like the best thing for him. Nate still heard from him fairly regularly—he'd been one of the guys who had eased Nate's transition from the minors to the big show, even if he'd made some poor decisions with Hill in Bee's rookie year. But he'd apologized to her, and she'd forgiven him, which was all that mattered to Nate. Bouchard spent a lot of time fishing in Kenora with his dog in tow.

Nate wouldn't have exactly classed himself as an *offender* per se, because as always, he was managing his goddamn anxiety and he was doing it with the kind of determined focus eighteen-year-old Nate would literally have killed to possess. Really, he was doing fantastically. There was absolutely no reason to feel off-kilter all the time, like he'd inadvertently done or said the wrong thing, or that he just wanted to crawl out of his skin.

So this wasn't exactly a banner season for him, personally.

It wasn't really a surprise that he turned to the things that were most able to pull him out of a funk, and also not really a surprise that because most of those things involved hanging out with Zach, it both worked and made him feel approximately fifty times stranger.

Normally, food was one of the things that made him feel more like himself. When he was on the road and had time, he liked to check out what each city had to offer, within certain nutritional limits, obviously. Nate was still careful about his weight and what he put in his body, but there was an entire world of food out there that fit the bill. He'd had some terrible meals—things he was convinced he could have done better himself—and some fantastic experiences. Usually he'd drag along whoever happened to be around. This time it happened to be Zach, who he found on his way out of the plane.

"Come try this sushi place with me once we land in

Dallas," Nate said, the morning before they left for the road trip. It wasn't really a question; he didn't expect Zach to say no, but he also didn't want to ask.

"Sure," Zach agreed, easily, like he always did, and something inside Nate relaxed.

"Cool," he said. "It's all hand rolls, some sashimi, but the fish looks really good."

"I trust you, bud."

It was a good choice. Inside, it looked about how he'd expected it to look, all dark wood and dim lighting. Trendy. It was a pretty casual place and there was only counter seating, so everyone was kind of crushed together. Zach sat next to him and let Nate do the ordering, but since the menu was so selective, he basically just got a little bit of everything, and they split it. Zach wasn't a particularly adventurous eater, but he tried everything, accompanied by some of the several varieties of sake on tap.

Their conversation was low, heads together, because it was such a small space. Zach's thigh pressed against his and Nate tried not to think about exactly how the muscle felt under his hands. He knew his face was kind of red, and he wasn't sure if it was the thought of it, the sake, or both.

Zach looked away when his phone buzzed, and then he grinned. "Dude, look. The dog sitter just sent me this picture of Hank and Dolly."

Nate looked at the picture. He'd been with Zach when he'd adopted Hank that first season in Philadelphia—at the time, Hank had been a bony, ravenous mutt, a former stray with an excess of energy and a tendency to destroy pieces of furniture. Now he had a little belly, mellowed out a lot in his old age, and was quite content to be bossed around by Dolly, a Great Dane who was undoubtedly the ruler of the Reed household. In the picture, the gigantic Dolly lay on top of the long-suffering Hank, licking his ear.

"You miss them when we're on the road?"

"Of course," Zach said, looking down at the picture. "They're like my kids, you know?"

Nate didn't, but he nodded anyway. "I, uh, feel that way about the rookies sometimes. Except we're on the road with them all the time, I know, I just meant—like my kids, so…"

Laughter exploded from Zach's mouth, a little too loud for even the buzz of the restaurant, the sort of uncontrollable glee that always made Nate smile, helplessly, in response. "Don't let them hear that comparison. Don't know if they'd find it as flattering as you meant it."

"I just meant—they're like my kids, not that they're like your dogs—"

"Remember how upset you got that they called you Dad?"

"That was a long time ago."

"Yeah…a lot of shit's happened since then, huh." Zach kept looking at him sideways, like he was trying to figure something out, which was weird because Nate was an open book.

"Yeah, uh. It's been good, though. You know?"

"Yeah," Zach said, and patted his knee.

With the meal winding down, Nate was kind of drunk, very full, and warmly content. He grabbed the check before Zach could look at it when it was brought over. "No, man, I dragged you out, so I'm gonna cover it."

Zach gave him one of those weird, searching looks again, but it smoothed out into a very Zach smile. "All right. Well, thanks, buddy. I…had a really nice time."

"Sure," Nate replied, feeling again like they might have been having separate conversations. "Me too."

"You got dinner, so let me get the cab, all right?"

"All right," Nate said, unable to suppress his yawn.

Zach patted his knee again, proprietary and affectionate. "Can't keep you out too late, old man. You need your beauty sleep, I bet."

"I'm not *old*, asshole."

The companionable bickering continued as Nate slipped his card back into his wallet, and out onto the street. And if he went back to Zach's hotel room after, that was just what they'd been doing recently.

Zach might have been an idiot, but also, his gamble had worked out better than he'd had any suspicion it would, so probably he was an idiot with occasional flashes of brilliance. Nate would have been furious to hear him say that, though, so he just thought it to himself, sometimes, when he had a spare minute. It wasn't like he had many of those these days.

There was hockey, which as always consumed his life during the season, particularly once he had gotten the A.

And there was Nate.

They were winning consistently—ten in a row—and it wasn't just because they were playing bad teams. There were a few gimmes sprinkled in there, but they were just playing really damn well. Since Bee had been added to their line in the middle of Zach's first season, things had been magic, but even then, regression could hit at any time. Sometimes the scoring chances just didn't finish. There'd been a long stretch of games in the beginning of the season when Bee particularly seemed snakebitten, shots flying wide or, even worse, hitting the posts.

But when it clicked, it clicked.

And the Nate thing was…going. Zach still had to resist the urge to grin like an idiot at nothing whenever he thought about it, because it was the first time in a really long time he'd been consistently messing around with someone he liked as much as he liked Nate.

Once they'd gotten over the initial awkwardness of the first couple of times—was this a mistake? was he gonna be weird about it in the morning?—it turned out that it was surprisingly easy to sleep with your best friend, particularly when you had a ready-made excuse. And it didn't hurt that for someone who was relatively inexperienced when it came to sex stuff, Nate was pretty open to instruction.

He was *really* open to instruction. Zach had definitely lost track of what he was doing in practice, thinking about the way Nate's eyes would narrow in concentration after asking, *does this feel good?* Of course he'd turn that stupidly intense focus he used on everything else toward sex too. It wasn't a *surprise*. It was just a lot, sometimes.

Sometimes it felt like something Zach shouldn't be able to see, or experience.

Something that had been given to him when he didn't deserve it.

But Zach wasn't even being weird about it, like, at all. He was completely chill and normal about the entire thing, totally cool as a cucumber, keeping things light and breezy, and no one on the team had noticed anything different because even before the season, he spent all of his time hanging out at Nate's anyway. There were some occasional weird moments—like Nate taking him out to dinner that one time in Dallas, which had felt so much like a date but which wasn't a *date*—where he didn't know exactly how to categorize things. But because he was being super chill about it, he let them go.

Of course, he had to navigate how he was going to handle the whole thing when they inevitably lost a game, which they did shortly after he had that thought: the first game of a back-to-back, one in Philly and the second one in Minnesota. Those games were always the hardest anyway, because you had to play, deal with the frustration of losing, do media, shower, and then immediately get onto the plane for a three-hour flight. And you know you could sleep on the flight, but when you had to get up to get to the hotel after anyway, it wasn't a good sleep.

Nate was always quiet and miserable after a loss, even if it was one that didn't matter so much. The Western Conference was a shit show, and so even if they'd lost to a bad team, it wasn't the end of the world. Zach usually tried to cheer him up, but today, he was also a little hesitant. He didn't want to break the thing they had going, but the unspoken excuse was that it was to keep winning, and now that they weren't winning, he didn't know if Nate was going to be weird about it.

But he didn't want to *stop*.

So he leaned sideways and whispered to Nate, "Come up to my room once you get settled?"

Nate blinked slowly at him. He was exhausted, dark circles under his eyes and the corners of his mouth turned down. He looked awful. He looked like Zach had felt after Montreal had traded him, but it didn't make any sense because it was *only* one game.

Nate glanced around the plane, but almost everyone else had already changed into sweats and were either sleeping or had headphones on in an attempt to *go* to sleep. He lowered his voice, and it was rough and scratchy. "Uh, we lost, though."

"We weren't gonna win *forever.* That doesn't mean we shouldn't—you know. It's been—working, mostly. Why mess with it?"

Nate was looking at him, that steady look that made Zach feel like squirming in his seat. "Uh...okay. If you're sure."

"Buddy. Dude. I'm sure." Zach extended his fist, and Nate reluctantly did the handshake. "We're not gonna slump again, I promise."

"Okay," Nate said, and for the briefest of seconds, the corners of his mouth tipped up again. "If you *promise.*"

Nate would do that to him sometimes and had been doing it since their first season together. Zach would make a half-joking, half-ridiculous threat or vow and Nate would respond in a way that would almost be flirty if Nate had been a flirty kind of person, which he was absolutely not. It had fucked with Zach's head then and he hated to admit it was no different now that things had gotten physical.

It was mostly because Nate didn't seem to realize what he was doing and the effect it had, whereas if Zach had said something like that, it would have been accompanied by the kind of smile that used to get him into almost anyone's pants. It just wasn't fair that someone who didn't seem to even be aware of his own power could have that kind of effect on anyone.

He half dozed on the rest of the flight, too nervous thinking about the rest of the night to actually let himself sleep. It didn't help that Netty snored like a rumbling avalanche and the plane was full of the rest of the team sounds, rustling as guys adjusted in their seats, low conversations between the night owls. And behind all of that the hum of the engines.

Nate, next to him, frowned while watching silent replays of the game on his tablet, leaning sideways far enough that his shoulder was pressed against Zach's.

Zach took his bags up to his hotel room and set them down. There was an optional skate tomorrow at eleven a.m., but the optional skates weren't optional for anyone and least of all him. Even if there hadn't been a practice, Zach knew he shouldn't stay up much later than this, but he pushed the comforter aside and sat down on the bed anyway, and he knew he was going to be waiting.

It wasn't long, though, before there was a knock at the door.

He almost got tangled in the sheets trying to get to his feet but caught himself before he tripped and fell. By the time he got to the door to open it, he'd collected himself enough to pull off a pretty smooth "Hey" when he smiled up at Nate.

"Hey," Nate said, but he wasn't smiling. He looked like he was—not about to cry, but like he was really upset. That was bad. Nate shouldn't be upset. Ever.

Zach pulled him into the room by the waistband of his pants, and Nate let him do it. Nate let Zach reach up and take his chin in his hand, forcing him to look Zach in the eye. "What's wrong?"

"It's just—I don't know, Zach. It just—it really sucks losing."

"I told you," Zach said, his thumb tracing the line of Nate's cheekbone, a stupid gesture that had already happened before he could stop himself. "Even if we lost this one, this season's going to be different than last season. You know New Zach always keeps his promises, right?"

Nate made a noise that was almost a laugh but sounded more like a pained wheeze. "You kept one of them, at least."

"Gimme a chance, baby, I'll keep more of them," Zach said, but before he could say anything else, Nate had leaned down to kiss him.

His mouth was warm and soft, but the stubble of his beard scraped against Zach's lip. He was always kind of intense about it, but there was something different about the way he was kissing Zach now, almost desperate. His hands were everywhere at once, like he was trying to distract Zach from something, like he didn't want him to—what? Say anything else? Zach liked talking during sex, like he liked talking any other time, running his mouth, letting any stupid thing that came to mind fly out of it. It was mostly nonsense, but usually Nate seemed pretty into it too, so. This was weird.

"Hey," Zach said, pulling back. "Hey, chill out. What's up?"

"I was thinking there's..." Nate sat down on the bed, and Zach followed him, straddling his thighs and pinning him down so he couldn't fidget and couldn't escape. Nate looked up, and his teeth were digging into his lower lip again, the way they did when he was on the verge of saying something he thought was a bad idea, and Zach fought the urge to bite it for him. "So we've been fooling around and I know we have a game tomorrow, but I just, I feel like shit and I was doing some research..."

Zach's eyebrows shot up. *"Research?"*

Nate might have been fully clothed, but the way the flush had started at the tips of his ears, Zach knew it wouldn't be long before it spread down his neck and chest. He couldn't quite meet Zach's eyes, even though

Zach was in his lap, and their faces were so close together that Zach could see the little tear in his lip where he'd bitten it. "Yeah, uh, research. I was thinking, there's other things we could do, if you, if you wanted to."

"Yeah?" Zach felt he had an idea of where this was going, but he couldn't tell if he didn't want to jinx it or if it was just a really bad idea. "What kinds of things?"

"I'm fucking embarrassed enough already, do you have to make me say it?"

"Are you *sweating*?" He couldn't quite hide the delight in his voice, because it was certainly a goddamn ego boost when a guy wanted to fuck you so badly that his face was red and little beads of moisture had broken out on his temples, but then he also kind of felt bad, because, well. Nate was suffering.

But Nate was suffering because of *him*. And that felt amazing.

Nate didn't answer, just exhaled sharply and muttered, "Look, it's stupid, I know, but I wanted… I thought I wanted to try it. And if we lost and we didn't keep going…"

There were all kinds of things that he could imagine doing with Nate, all kinds of things they hadn't gotten a chance to do yet, and for a second, thinking about ending things now that they'd just gotten started felt like a slap in the face. But he didn't have to worry about that, because Nate was here, and Nate was asking him for at least some of it.

There were things happening inside Zach that had nothing to do boners, and it was weird. It was like having butterflies in his stomach and being on a roller coaster all at once, that intense combination of surprise and giddy anticipation he'd had on his draft day, nervous and so fucking excited all at the same time. He wanted to tell Nate, *you make me feel like a teenager again*, but there wasn't a good way to say that without it sounding stupid. It was weird thinking about how jaded he'd become over the last decade or so, without even realizing it, and how different this was. It wasn't unwelcome, it was just weird.

Things were weird.

That was the new normal, things being weird, and he didn't even *care*.

He was probably grinning like an idiot, but they were both idiots, so that didn't matter. Zach shifted his hips so that his dick ground against Nate's, rewarded by the sharp exhale of breath in response.

"Buddy, if you wanted to fuck me, you could've just asked." He'd meant it to be joking and jaunty, but it came out stupid soft and quiet.

Nate's face flushed an even deeper red, and he swallowed again. "Um, actually…at least this time I thought maybe you could fuck me. Because, I, uh. I don't really know what I'm doing."

There wasn't anything to say in response to that, because Zach didn't want to risk *are you sure?* or *but we have a game tomorrow and I'm pretty sure you've never*, because Nate's entire body was tense and folded into itself, nervous, like he was expecting Zach to—what? As if he could have ever said no.

"Hey, look at me."

Nate did. His eyes were huge and dark, and his face was still that brilliant red, and Zach wanted to kiss him right then. Okay, maybe he wasn't doing such a great job at being chill about it. Whatever. It was fine. It wasn't like this was going to screw anything up.

Nate was still watching him, though, so Zach said,

"Whatever you want, baby," and pressed his fingers against Nate's lower lip.

"I want this," Nate said into his hand. His voice was rough, but there wasn't a hesitation or a stammer there. His breath was hot on Zach's fingers. "I want you."

Zach put his hand on Nate's chest and pushed him down into the rumpled covers, leaned over him and just looked for a minute, partially to rein himself in, partially because he really did love looking at Nate. Nate didn't seem to like that much, squirming a little underneath him, and Zach was maybe a bit mad with power, but he said, "C'mon, chill out," and Nate stilled under his hands.

The first part of it, he knew really well at this point. It might have only been a month and change of whatever they were doing, but you didn't play on the same line with a guy for two years and *not* pick up on his cues. He thought about all of the interviews where someone had asked him about chemistry and wanted to laugh, because chemistry was the way that he could almost seem to read Nate's mind sometimes, particularly when they were in the process of getting naked.

He knew the places Nate liked to be touched and the places Nate didn't even know he liked to be touched. Zach used to think of it like a game. Press button A, get reaction B, move on to outcome C. And it was like the way he'd fucked evolved to maximize the efficiency of orgasms. But with Nate he just wanted to slow everything down and listen to every single noise and memorize every drop of sweat and half-pained twist of his mouth.

So he did.

And then for a little longer.

And a little longer.

By that time, Nate was a mess underneath him, straining up against the weight of Zach's body pinning him down, and Zach was achingly hard already. "Are you sure you wanna…?"

"Zach, please, *yes*."

Sometimes he thought about what it would sound like if Nate called him anything except his own name, but the way he said *Zach* like that, like Zach had ripped the word right out of his throat, almost made up for the fact that Nate was just as awkward with terms of affection as he was with everything else.

"Hang on, I gotta get the stuff." Zach pulled away and stumbled out of the bed toward his bags, and behind him, Nate propped himself up on his elbows to watch.

He'd only been sleeping with Nate recently but also, he just, you know, liked to be prepared. You got caught in one or two unfortunate situations as a kid and you learned your lesson pretty quick. He fumbled for the condoms and lube and found them quickly enough.

He fell right back into bed, his hand resting on Nate's hip. "It's gonna be good, okay?"

Nate half smiled, lopsided and uncertain, and said, "I know it will. I trust you."

The *fuck* escaped before Zach could stop it, but it made Nate laugh, so that was fine.

Nate wasn't laughing when Zach took him in hand, fingers tightening around his dick in a long, slow tease. And he wasn't laughing when Zach leaned down to press his mouth against Nate's hip, the muscle of his abdomen, his inner thigh. Zach lived for those sounds, the harsh pant of Nate's breath, the way he held himself back so carefully, still so self-conscious even when he wanted Zach *so* badly.

He wanted to do everything at once, everything *now*,

but he had to slow this down. He wanted this to be—he didn't know what he wanted it to be. He only knew it had to be *special.*

"What are you looking at?"

"You," Zach said, quite honestly. "I'm just thinking about all the things I wanna do to you."

"I..." Nate swallowed off whatever he was going to say. "I can't stand waiting, Zach, I'm gonna fucking, I don't even know."

Zach knew his grin was broad and stupid but he couldn't stop himself. It was really fucking weird, the immense, swelling affection in his chest jostling for place with the fact that he was so turned on he could barely think. And while he was a dude whose strong point was definitely not thinking, that wasn't a great situation to be in. So he stopped thinking and went on instinct.

"Do you want me to tell you all the things I'm gonna do?"

Nate made a choked-off noise in his throat, and Zach, mouth pressed against his hip, looked up at him. Nate kept opening and closing his eyes, like he couldn't bear to look away, but also, he couldn't bear to see it, or hear it.

But he didn't say no, so Zach took that as a cue to continue narrating as he went, although sometimes it was hard to get the words out because he kept getting distracted by the sudden need to tease him, by the way Nate didn't seem to know whether to twist with discomfort when Zach was like, *I'm going to make you feel so good when I finger you open* or gasp when Zach slid his lips around Nate's dick.

"God," Nate was saying, "are you trying to—what are you—" Zach contemplated answering him immediately, but pressed his tongue down instead, and Nate said, *"Please."*

By the time he took a break to fumble for the lube and open it, Nate was just sort of lying there, shaking and taking short, ragged breaths that sounded like they pained him. Zach knew how he felt. He wasn't really touching himself, but taking the time to do this to Nate had really done it. Everything in him felt drawn up and on edge, tense and ready to break.

"Good?" Zach asked.

Nate couldn't answer at first, and finally managed, "Uh."

"Good," Zach agreed, and watched him carefully. He ran a finger down Nate's thigh, leaving a wet trail behind it. "I promise, baby, it's gonna be good."

"And you…always keep your promises, huh?"

Zach didn't answer, just said, "I'm gonna do it."

At first he just teased, something they'd done before, Zach's finger circling Nate's hole, a steady rub. When Nate had relaxed a little, he slowly pushed his finger in. Nate dug his teeth into his lower lip. Zach knew it didn't hurt, but it was a strange feeling if you weren't used to it. He exhaled sharply. Nate still looked kind of uncomfortable, awkward until Zach's finger, stroking carefully, started to slowly unwind him.

"Oh—that feels—that feels really—"

That was encouraging, so Zach kept doing it, watching, fascinated at the way Nate's expression was so unguarded now, unable to control himself, the way he felt stretched around Zach's fingers. It was too much, really, so he leaned down and swallowed all of the gasps and exclamations into his own mouth.

Nate kissed him back, sloppy and desperate, and Zach pulled back far enough to murmur, "Okay, it's good?" and Nate said, "Yes, okay, please—"

He lost track of the time because he was so focused on the way Nate was moving under him. The way Nate was half-brokenly asking for things he didn't even know how to phrase, a mess of *please* and *more*. The way Zach was trying to keep himself in control, to make this *good*, but he was rapidly losing it himself because some part of his shitty brain had been thinking about this for three years and now that it was actually happening it was overwhelming to the point where if he didn't occasionally stop to get a hold of himself, he might have actually just come and ruined everything.

"I'm going to—can I fuck you—"

Nate's eyes opened and they were so fucking stupid blue and the expression in them was so much that Zach couldn't look away. His blond hair was darker with sweat and his face was flushed and his lip was bleeding a little where he'd bitten it, but Nate looked at him like he was the only thing in the entire fucking world that mattered, and Zach was actually kind of speechless for a second.

Nate said, "How do I do this?"

Zach got his shit together, pulled himself back. "Uh, probably easier if you get on your hands and knees." Easier, and also he didn't entirely trust himself to do this face-to-face and not fuck things up beyond repair.

It took Nate a minute to collect his gross motor skills and sit up, but he went over onto his knees easily, without arguing. Zach just looked down at him, the broad expanse of his back, muscle shifting as he tensed in anticipation. God, it was something.

Nate heard it when Zach ripped open the condom packet, flinched a little, but he kept his head down, like if he looked it might be too much to bear.

Zach did it slowly, but he did it. There was the initial

resistance, but when Nate relaxed, it—it felt—it *was* almost too much to bear, the noise Nate made almost ended him. Zach asked, "Is this okay?"

"It's fine, it's just, you, a lot, it's a lot."

"I'm going to move."

"I can handle it, please—"

So Zach moved.

Slowly at first, rocking himself deeper, greedily reacting to the way Nate gasped each time, the way he moaned when Zach hit a particularly sensitive spot. He felt so fucking good. Not just the way he was clenched around Zach, but how his body felt with Zach's draped over it, strong enough to support both of their weight even now, when his eyes were screwed shut and his face was buried in a pillow. The slick sweat slippery between them, the way Nate's hands scrabbled to try to catch Zach's in his own. When Nate started to push back into him, Zach, panting, stopped holding back. It was too much, not enough, agony stretching this out. Something had to give, and that something was Zach.

If Zach had lost control of himself, Nate wasn't much better. Nate, his captain, usually so careful, so anxious and buttoned-up, completely falling apart underneath him. He was loud. Zach thought maybe this was what winning the Cup would feel like.

Oh, Jesus, Nate was *really* loud.

"Shh, shh," Zach gasped, remembering too damn late that there were other guys from the team staying on the floor, "baby, we gotta be quiet, we can't—"

"*I* can't. Please, oh, god…"

"Let me, let me."

"Anything, anything…"

Nate made a wounded noise when Zach started jerking

him off, overstimulated and oversensitive, his head twisting back to try for a kiss. It was an awkward angle and mostly their teeth bumped together. Zach's head was ringing when, with a ragged gasp, Nate's head dropped again and he convulsed and came.

It was almost enough to push Zach over the edge himself, but he made a valiant effort to hold on for those last few thrusts, until Nate's pained whine and white-knuckled fists were the cue it was too much.

"You feel—so—fucking—shit, baby, I'm just—"

Zach pressed his face against Nate's back and shivered. It was one of those orgasms with aftershocks. The kind of thing he'd want to write a song about if he had any kind of musical talent whatsoever. As it was, he kind of lost his balance and shoved Nate down flat against the bed, still shaking his way through it and making some noises that, if he was at all capable of self-reflection or shame, would have been *really* humiliating.

"Ow," Nate rasped. He didn't try to push Zach away. He was still taking these gasping, heaving breaths that Zach could feel like they were his own.

"Sorry," Zach managed, once he remembered how to speak. It probably took him a few minutes longer than it should have. Gingerly, he pulled out, flopping over onto his side and pulling the condom off. He should get up and throw it in the trash can. He should get up and wash himself off. Be a gentleman and wash Nate off. There were a lot of things he should have done, but Nate was looking at him. He still looked tired, dark smudges under his eyes, but he was grinning, wide and loopy and unselfconscious, and Zach leaned forward to kiss the stupid smile off his face.

"You good?"

"Uh…" Nate closed his eyes. He was still smiling, despite Zach's best efforts. "I feel…uh. Um."

"Full sentences, Nate. C'mon, I believe in you. I know you got it in you."

"Uh… That's not what I had. In me."

"Did you just make a *joke*?" Zach demanded, delighted.

Instead of responding, Nate ducked his head and half head-butted, half pressed himself into Zach's chest. Which, okay. Reflexively, Zach put his arm over Nate's side and pulled him in closer.

"You wanna—" he started, before realizing that Nate's eyes were closed, and he was asleep. And, okay, now he really couldn't move. He dropped the tied-off condom on the floor. It was gross, and they would both definitely regret it in the morning, but he stroked one hand along Nate's hip and then smoothed the hair out of his face and figured there were worse things he could do than to just fall asleep now.

This was absolutely fine, though.

He was making good and healthy decisions with his life.

Absolutely nothing wrong with any of it.

In the morning, he pushed Nate into the shower and blew him there before they had to rush to morning skate, where Nate was slow and awkward on the ice to the point that Netty started teasing him about a lower body injury and Coach told him to sit it out, and there was nothing wrong with that either.

Nothing wrong at all.

This was fine and Zach was fine.

Nate tried not to think about what he'd asked for and what he'd done, but essentially that just ensured that he thought about it all the fucking time. The elephant in the room. He'd thought about it a lot before he did it too, and he wasn't *ashamed* of—well. Of wanting to get fucked. It was just there had been a lot of recalibrating in his head, about what he knew about himself and what he wanted.

He hadn't known what to expect. It wasn't like it hurt. It had been awkward at first, and kind of uncomfortable. And then it had been really good, good enough that he couldn't even really be all that embarrassed by the fact that he'd completely lost his shit. It had been kind of a comfort that Zach, however experienced he might have been, had seemed just as fucked up by it. It had been…really good.

At least until he'd tried to skate afterward and realized that maybe he hadn't thought the entire plan through. He made it through the game against the Northern Lights, but it wasn't exactly a comfortable way to play. He wondered if it got easier the more you did it and then thought, *don't put the cart before the horse, you dumb bastard.*

That lingering, nagging fear remained. That Zach would suddenly realize that whatever they were doing had nothing to do with the fact that they were winning hockey games, that there was an expiration date he was unaware of when Zach would realize or remember how far out of Nate's league he was…that was what had driven him to take the risk of asking in the first place. On the one hand, he couldn't regret that he'd done it. And on the other hand, it had made things so infinitely more complicated that Nate's head felt it was spinning whenever he tried to parse out what he thought and felt about it.

It was easier to try not to think about it, even if it wasn't easy to *actually* not think about it.

When they got back to Philly from the Midwest, usually the guys were kind of glad to get a break from each other. Nate and Zach had always been the exception, always living out of each other's pockets, but Nate nudged Zach's shoulder as they got off the plane, shook his head a little to say *no, I'm going home alone today*, and that was that. At this point, Zach just got it, even without words.

And that left Nate, on his own again to try to get his head together.

In between games and travel, there were sometimes a day or two off that Nate usually used for errands. He knew a lot of the guys had people to clean their houses for them or used meal services, but he had been raised by a bus driver and a longshoreman and couldn't bring himself to do it. So his days off were spent grocery shopping, cooking, and cleaning. It wasn't exactly restful, but it was relaxing. And it saved him the awkwardness of feeling guilty about paying someone else to do his own damn chores for him.

Nate browsed his way through the aisles at the Pennsylvania Avenue Whole Foods and found himself stopping in the aisle with organic dog food and other pet supplies. He remembered Zach telling him how much he missed Hank and Dolly when he was on the road. But sometimes when they were at home, Zach spent just as much time at Nate's house as he did at his own place. Sometimes Zach brought the dogs, but they usually had to either go back for dinner or he'd just have to leave and come over without them.

Almost without thinking about it Nate picked out some bowls and threw them in his cart along with a bag of dry food. Was that what the dogs ate? Who knew? It was a stupid impulse, and he didn't want to think about it too much.

It was actually a good day. The kind of day where once

he got home and had made sure the house wasn't falling apart, he was able to spend a good couple of hours marinating chicken or preparing the ingredients for the kind of indulgent winter dinner that he would carefully portion control. And he needed the kind of project that was going to occupy at least three hours of his evening.

what do you even do on days off anymore, Zach texted him, while Nate was chopping an onion. im bored asf.

Nate washed his hands before picking up the phone. Clean the house, groceries, cook, he replied. You should try it some time.

effort tho

Nate thought about how before he'd bullied Zach into buying furniture, Zach's house had been completely bare of anywhere to sit or eat except for a Ping-Pong table that did double duty for dining, a mattress in his room, and a couch for video games. He snorted, then scraped the onions up onto the flat of the knife blade and dumped them into a waiting prep bowl. He considered his next response for a couple of seconds before finally taking the plunge.

You could come over for dinner if you wanted to. I'm cooking.

hell yeah, nate dinner

It'll be done in a couple hours but let yourself in whenever. Since Zach had just shown up on his doorstep in July, they'd stopped pretending that he didn't have a standing invite and the door code. You can bring the dogs if you want to.

And then he went back to food prep and didn't really think about it further, or at least told himself he wouldn't.

Zach showed up right about when Nate was ready to start cooking in earnest, the dogs in tow. They immediately made themselves at home on one of the couches, snuffling and drooling, and Nate thought, briefly, *god, Rachel would die* before remembering that it didn't matter how expensive the couches were anymore if he didn't, personally, give a shit that they were covered in dog hair.

Zach ambled over to the kitchen to see what he was doing. He wore a hoodie that was at least two sizes too big for him, soft and thinned with age, the sleeves long enough that he could tuck his thumbs into it. It was kind of cute, Nate thought, and sighed to himself as soon as he did.

"What're you making?" Zach asked.

"Coq au vin, a porkless version," Nate said and when Zach seemed absolutely delighted by this news, added, "It's French for *rooster*, not whatever you were thinking."

"Cock—" Zach started, saw Nate's stare of long-suffering misery, and grinned. "Aw, buddy, I'm just fucking with you. I'm sure it's gonna be really good."

"I fried some extra chicken in the duck fat for the dogs, if that's cool."

"Ohhh, I really shouldn't… Hank's gotta lose a few pounds…but, *ugh*, fine, they'll love it. Hey, Dolly, Hank," he called, and immediately the two of them slid off the couch and pounded over, twining around his legs while he scratched them on the head. "Uncle Nate's got a treat for you, babies."

Nate held some of the chicken pieces out in his hand, and the dogs eagerly accepted it. Dolly took her time eating, rolling the morsels around in her mouth, while

Hank scarfed his down immediately and then looked up mournfully at Nate, begging for more.

"Stop faking," Zach told him severely, even while he scratched Hank behind his gigantic, floppy ears. "We know you're not starving. I just fed you a few hours ago."

"Oh, uh, about that," Nate said, before he could forget. "I got dog bowls and food and stuff. So you don't have to leave them at home anymore if you don't want to."

Zach's head jerked up. He looked at Nate like he didn't know exactly what to say, and his eyes were suspiciously shiny. Finally, he ran his hand through his hair, pushing it out of his face, and said, "Thanks. You super didn't have to, you know?"

"I know, I just thought… You told me you missed them." Nate thought about adding *and I don't want you to not be here*, but that seemed wrong. It was exactly what he wanted, but it didn't seem like something he should say out loud.

"Well. Thanks." Zach was still looking at him like he also wanted to say something else, and Nate waited, but all he added was, "That was—yeah."

"Yeah, of course. Hey, make yourself comfortable, bud. We still got about two hours left to go."

Zach helped him put together the salad while the stew simmered, laughing when Nate looked horrified by the way he was butchering the tomatoes. Their shoulders knocked together. It was just nice. They didn't even talk about much, just stupid shit about the team and games and an upcoming trip to Montreal, some obedience training Zach had been doing with the dogs, how Zach's sisters' hockey games had been going, but it was the kind of easy conversation that had drawn him to Zach in the first place. He was just easy to talk to and Nate forgot his own awkwardness.

By the time he was ladling out the stew onto chickpea bowtie noodles, the house smelled warm and inviting, and the dogs were asleep on the couch again, and it was pretty close to an ideal kind of an evening.

Zach was making a steady headway on the wine Nate had pulled down from one of the pantry shelves; he wasn't drunk, exactly, but his body language was relaxed and loose. His mouth was stained a little too red and his elbows were propped up on the kitchen island as he leaned into it, and Nate thought *oh no.*

When Zach tried the chicken, he made a noise low in his throat that was kind of obscene and Nate thought: *oh* no.

"Jesus, baby," Zach murmured, and a shiver ran down Nate's spine. "This is next-level."

He didn't know what to say, really—could feel his ears burning. He had always liked cooking for people, especially for Zach. There was always something satisfying about someone enjoying a meal you'd made for them with your own hands. This was a level beyond that. Something about the way Zach's entire body shuddered when he took a bite, the heat in his voice. The tension strung between them, even across the kitchen island.

Zach's red mouth, parted a little, the way his eyes were focused so sharply on Nate, like he knew exactly what he wanted from him. It felt distinctly bedroom and Nate didn't know how to react, off-kilter and suddenly kind of hard.

"It's, uh, just chicken stew," Nate said, tongue thick and awkward. "It's not really that complicated."

"Mmm, sure," Zach said, and took another bite. "Shit. This is so fucking good."

"Thank you, I, uh… I really like when you like it."

Zach didn't say anything, just *looked* at him, and Nate concentrated on eating his goddamn dinner, even though his whole body was burning up from the inside out.

By the end of the dinner they were both full and kind of tipsy and Zach had pushed Nate down onto one of the kitchen stools and shoved his way in between Nate's legs, the warm length of his body pressed against Nate's chest. Zach's hand tangled in the neck of Nate's sweater, pulling his head down. It wasn't quite a kiss, but Zach's mouth was so close that Nate could feel it when Zach's lips moved, feel Zach's beard soft against his chin. He smelled like wine and coq au vin.

"Let's go upstairs, huh?"

"But the dishes?" Nate managed. Zach's other hand palmed his dick through his pants so it wasn't like he could *hide* it.

"I'll help you do 'em tomorrow," Zach said, smiling against Nate's mouth. "Don't have to go home right away anymore, you know?"

And Nate, who at the heart of things was weak as hell, gave in.

New Zach did keep his promises, after all.

When he finally went home the next afternoon, the dishes were clean, but Nate was left alone to think about how severely all of this had confused him. How he had been thrown into a tailspin. It was partially his own fault. In high school, even though he'd played junior hockey, he'd been an awkward nerd who'd mostly kept to himself and a few male friends who were equally as awkward.

He'd spent a lot of time in the offseason smoking pot and playing D&D and going to metal shows.

When Rachel had decided that she wanted to date him, she'd had to ask him out in increasingly obvious ways, and even when he'd finally realized what was happening, he'd stammered his way through the acceptance, and he'd almost said *no* out of terrified reflex, not entirely able to believe that someone like Rachel would be interested in dating someone like *him*. Rachel had been smart and beautiful and built like a sparrow, all delicate bones and sharp features. Next to her, Nate had looked and felt like a looming monster.

They'd lost their virginity to each other, a few months later; it had been just about as awkward a first time as you could imagine. He had been so anxious about everything, about hurting her, about the way he looked naked, that he'd actually cried and couldn't finish. They'd kept trying and, eventually, gotten the hang of it.

He remembered those first few months with a weird, painful nostalgia. The sneaking around to see each other, because their parents would have been horrified they weren't actually studying. The weird combination of intense teenaged hormones driving them on. The legitimate tenderness between them, before everything had gone wrong.

He didn't have much to compare it to. For over a decade, Rachel was the only body he knew as well as his own. Things had been fraught and miserable toward the end of their relationship, but even when Rach hadn't seemed to want to be around him, he hadn't ever thought he'd sleep with anyone else.

He thought again about the woman he'd picked up in a bar last year. It had been…bad. He'd mostly done it because he'd felt like he should, because he'd been in denial about a lot of other stupid things. He hadn't really been able to get it up. He'd been so self-conscious about the way he looked, about the way the girl was looking at him. Every time she'd tried to say something nice or complimentary or sexy, it made him feel worse and worse. He'd finally had to tune her out, had to force himself to think about other things just to get hard enough to fuck. In the end it had been mechanical and depressing and he'd absolutely felt like shit afterward. He'd gone home and thrown up and thought maybe he was just meant to be alone.

He hadn't tried it again.

The pain of losing Rachel was a dull ache these days, whenever he did think about it. And he thought about it less and less, if he was being honest. But the fact was that he didn't really have any conception of normal dating or sex the same way most of his peers did. He had the wild teenaged years with Rachel, the old-married-couple years with Rachel, and the estranged misery with Rachel. He'd gotten used to life on the road with a fiancée who rarely traveled with him, and the fact that they'd slept together infrequently at best.

He'd gotten really used to his hand.

He didn't really know what to make of the fact that the more sex he had the more he wanted to have it, and that Zach seemed to be just as into it. It was good, obviously; it *felt* really good. But some part of him was waiting for the other shoe to drop.

It couldn't possibly be this easy. Could it?

He really needed to stop fucking thinking about it.

Even browsing through various social media apps

didn't distract him. He caught himself at it, scrolling mindlessly without actually seeing anything.

At least until Bee texted him, privately, and not on the group chat, and then she had his full attention.

Cap? I have a question for you.

Yes?

When we next go to Montreal the PR team wants to film a mini doc about my brothers and me.

Oh...no.

I told them I would do it because I feel like I cannot say no, but I am not happy about it.

I'm sorry, Bee.

He knew how she felt about her brothers—a sibling rivalry cranked up to one hundred because all of them were insanely successful. The twins had a Cup, but the Cons and Bee were knocking on that door. She had a Rookie of the Year Award, and they had between them a Scoring Champion Award and a Defensive Forward of the Year Award. They were the Morin twins, but she was Beatrice Morin, the first woman to play in the men's league, and she had been, undeniably, a revelation.

He also knew how Zach felt about her brothers, which was, *god, they're the most insufferable fucking* pricks, *Nate, you would not fucking believe it, the stories I could tell you.* He didn't say any of that.

Bee said, Sakari's going to be there, but they wanted

to know if you'd come and meet my parents too. And I could use all the moral support I can get.

Of course, he responded immediately, Anything for my liney.

He realized, slightly too late, that it would require being *on camera* again, and sighed. Well, he was in for it now.

Merci, Cap. I owe you one.

No you don't.

:-) Bee said, typing out the entire smiley.

Stop doing that. It's creepy when you do it.

He could almost hear her laughing when she said, Got it.

Zach always had mixed feelings about going back to Montreal. It was weird, and bittersweet, and all of that other shit. It was like seeing an ex-friend-with-benefits and realizing that even though she was still super hot, you didn't want to fuck her anymore.

The worst of the sting of the trade—the *betrayal*—had faded, but it was a city that still held a lot of memories, good and bad. In a lot of ways, Zach had grown up there. One of his best bros in the entire world still lived there. But the further he was removed from it, and the more he thought about it, the less he liked the person he'd been there.

He remembered a conversation he'd had with Dad, when they'd gone home to Vancouver to play the Vanguard. Dad had looked at him sideways and said, *what-*

ever you were doing in Montreal—that wasn't you. Zach had known then that it *was* him, that part of who he was had been a fuckup. The rejection had felt a little like being slapped in the face. He'd insisted, weakly, that he'd been doing okay. Dad had looked at him, for a very long moment, almost sad. *You were playing excellent fucking hockey, but I don't think you were doing okay. You never sounded very happy when we talked to you. You always sounded exhausted.* And since then, his parents had never stopped treating him like he was three steps away from a rehab facility.

He had weird, complicated feelings about Montreal, but he also felt things that weren't complicated at all, like his need to show everyone on that fucking team exactly what they'd passed up on. Like his need to prove all of them wrong. That, at least, was understandable. That was, like, a pretty normal emotion to have, he felt. But it also made him fidgety as hell and nervous every time they played the Royal again.

Bro, Jammer texted him that morning, as the plane landed. U got an hour 2 get coffee?

always have time for u, homie

Meet me at Olympico? We can talk and walk.

yeah!

It was weird how he still remembered exactly how to get around the city, even though it had been over two years since he'd lived there. He still remembered where the house he'd planned to purchase was, but it didn't hurt quite as badly knowing he would never live there. He was around the corner from Nate now, anyway, and that was way better than any white-painted reno in Westmount.

Jammer waited for him outside the café, wrapped up in a gray peacoat and a green-and-purple paisley scarf that Zach immediately tugged out of the coat's neck.

"The fuck is this?"

"Diya bought it for me," Jammer said. He rarely smiled, but the corner of his eyes crinkled a little. He knew it was hideous and didn't care. Jammer looked good, in that sturdy Mack Truck way of his. Dead-eyed as always, but content.

"So you let your girlfriend dress you now, huh?" Zach demanded, as they went in to order. "What happened to *I dress how I want and fuck the PR department*?"

It was cold enough that a hot beverage would be welcome, and ordering coffee would at least distract him from thinking about the fact that Nate had also bought him a scarf as part of his Chanukah present last year and he was wearing it. Nate had better taste than Jammer's girlfriend, though.

Jammer shrugged it off. "Makes her happy to see it, bro, it's worth it."

"I wanna hear about dating a poet," Zach said, "in one sec." He smiled brightly at the barista, and she smiled back, reflexively. "Un quatre espresso, s'il vous plaît."

"Dude," Jammer said disapprovingly, and sighed.

"It's a game day!"

"You're gonna be too wired to nap."

Zach rolled his shoulders in a shrug and rolled his eyes to show Jammer just what he thought about that, paid for his and Jammer's orders, and after the coffee was ready, took it outside. "So you look good, Jams. Shit going okay?"

"Yeah, man," he said, blowing on the espresso to cool it. "We've been playing pretty good, and Diya's... Man, I just really like her a whole fucking lot, you know?"

Zach, who knew that blowing on espresso was the coward's way out, took a gulp and the top layer of skin on his tongue off. "Yeah? It's not weird? She seems kinda... intense."

"She is, and it's great. But she's brilliant, Reedsy. She was in marketing before this, and she's brilliant at what she does, really. An entire fucking career on haiku and stick figures, and people eat it up."

"I guess it's kinda admirable," Zach said doubtfully. "But I'm glad you're happy. If anyone deserves it, it's you."

"Thanks, buddy," Jammer said, and smiled for real this time.

Across the street, someone stopped and took a picture of them with a cell phone, and Zach sighed. Somehow, even though he'd lived here almost his entire life, he had almost forgotten how weird it was being a hockey player in Canada. Philly was a hockey town, but no one approached them for pictures or bothered them about it the same way they did back at home.

Jammer was saying, "So how've you been, bud? Haven't heard from you much recently."

Zach took another gulp of his espresso and burned the roof of his mouth this time. He ignored Jammer's disapproving glance and said, "Uh...good. Busy. Good."

"Uh-huh."

"Uh, it's just been a weird couple months, you know?"

Jammer groaned, and said, "Oh, Jesus, tell me you didn't."

"I don't know what you're talking about."

"Really?"

Zach didn't answer, because he'd already been figured out. They walked in silence for a little while. It really was a beautiful city, and he was again struck by memories as he walked. The place he used to get bagels, a restaurant he and Jammer used to go to all the time when they were treating themselves, the bar whose bathroom he'd done a line in for the first time the summer before his rookie season started, one of the parks he'd thrown up in after they'd won the Cup.

"I don't wanna pry, but I also just wanna make sure you're not getting into something you're not prepared for. I've been really proud of how you've gotten your shit together in Philly, you know?"

Zach snorted and took another stubborn gulp of espresso. "Thanks, Mom. But it's not *like* that."

"So how is it?"

Zach thought about it for a minute and said, slowly, "It's kind of like… I dunno. How do you know when you're, like, dating someone?"

Jammer's eyes went a little wider. "You don't know?"

"I've never…really dated anyone before, so…no?"

He'd had girlfriends, kind of, in high school. Girls he'd been fucking who'd gotten excited about making things official but, after he gave in, quickly got tired of the fact that he was always busy with hockey, and probably also that he'd had the emotional maturity of a potato. Nothing that had lasted more than a couple of weeks.

He'd almost had a boyfriend, once, but Dylan had understandably not hung around long after it became clear that hockey was always going to come first and there was no chance that Zach was going to be public about that before the draft. Or even probably any time after it. And there had been Alison, last year, but that had been a concentrated attempt to stop thinking about his romantically unavailable best friend all of the goddamn time. He felt kind of bad about those last two, really. Neither Dylan nor Alison had really deserved the way he had treated them.

Still, pretty much anyone Zach had ever dated had eventually realized there wasn't a whole lot going on in his head besides hockey, or that he was an idiot, and that was usually the end of things. He'd never really wanted anything more than that, so it hadn't hurt his feelings too much when it had happened. It was inevitable: people loved Zach when they first met him, but then they realized that he wasn't what they wanted, that there wasn't much beyond the surface. It was fine, that was just how things were. But also, he felt like his pool of experience had made things kind of muddy.

"Oh, *buddy*. I mean...you know. Are you going out on dates? Are things exclusive? Have you talked about it?"

"I think it's kinda dating, though? Maybe it didn't start like that and yeah, we always spent a shitload of time together, but I'm pretty sure there's...not anyone else. And he took me out to dinner. It *felt* like a date. Like, sharing food, knees touching and shit. It felt...kind of romantic, bro. And he got bowls for my fucking dogs so I don't have to leave them at home when I stay over."

Jammer glanced sideways at him. His eyes were annoyingly kind. "I just wanna make sure you know what you're doing, Zachary."

"Of course I know what I'm doing," Zach lied.

"Uh-huh."

"I mean, what could go wrong? Like, each year I've been here we've been playing better but we're on fucking fire right now, different than any other year, and the only thing that's really different is sex. Oh my god, Jams, what if my dick was the only thing we needed to win the Cup this entire time?"

Instead of answering the question directly, Jammer patted him on the back, a little condescendingly, and said, "That's a nice scarf, Zachary."

Zach glared at him. "You don't have any faith in me, but I'm gonna surprise you."

"I have a lot of faith in you. That's partially why I'm kinda worried about this."

Zach, rather than answering, gulped down the remainder of his espresso and considered how he was going to board Jammer without getting a penalty later. And then, as they walked and caught up on the rest of the Royal, he thought about Dallas and how weird it had felt, in a good way. To be out on a date with Nate Singer. Even if no one had said the word, he'd been out on a date with Nate Singer.

Granted, maybe it was his dick that would get them to the finals, but also… His brain kept turning over the details, the way his stomach flipped when Nate did shit like cook for him, specifically for him. He could do romance, right? He'd never tried it before, but he'd never had to try it before. And Nate was absolutely worth it. They just had to beat Montreal tonight, show the asshole twins who the best damn team on the East Coast was, and then he'd figure this out.

Not understanding something had never stopped him before, and it wasn't about to stop him now.

Nate, Bee, and Mäkelä took a cab from the airport to Bee's parents' house in Côte-des-Neiges. He almost chickened out, told her he wasn't feeling well, anything to get out of having to be in front of cameras when he didn't have to. But once he caught her eye outside the plane and saw the hopeful, nervous look on her face, he couldn't have done it and lived with himself, particularly after they caught sight of the camera crew waiting by the baggage claim. If they all hustled a little faster to get into the cab, who could really blame them?

The ride itself wasn't particularly comfortable either. Mäkelä and Bee were settled in the back, and Nate could only look at them from the corner of his eye. And all three were taciturn, at best. It was a silent ride, for the most part.

"Nervous, mussuka?" Mäkelä asked, breaking the silence.

"No," Bee said, but Nate knew she was lying.

"It'll be fine," Mäkelä said, to which Bee only muttered darkly, "Calisse, it'll be fine."

At least it was a short ride, only half an hour in traffic, before they were pulling into the neighborhood where Bee grew up. It was a pleasant-looking area, with more green lawns and trees then he'd been expecting. Bee's house was a modest brick affair hidden behind towering rhododendron bushes. A stone path led from the street to the front steps, and the camera crew followed along behind them as they went. Bee let herself in with a key she still had on her keyring, and Nate and Mäkelä trailed after her.

Inside, the house wasn't exactly what he had expected. It was warm and cozy, with a lot of plants hanging in the windows and arranged on shelves, the kind of lived-in clutter that came along with people who had priorities other than cleaning. It made him itch, just a little bit, with the urge to neaten it up. Bee's parents and brothers were already there, sitting around the kitchen table and having tea.

He'd met her parents before. Her mother had Bee's height, a tall, striking woman with eyes that bored right through you and skin a few shades darker than Bee's, and her father a bit shorter, a bit older, a bit plumper, with flyaway sandy-gray hair. He had a ruddy face and rosy cheeks that reminded Nate a little bit of a Christmas elf. And he'd met the twins, of course, on the ice and off. They looked a lot like Bee: all three of them were tall, strapping individuals. Except where Bee was serious and contained, the twins were always smiling the kind of smiles that instinctively put Nate on edge. It was weird, because Zach smiled just as much, and he was just as cocky, but it was different.

"Welcome to the homestead," Bee's mother said, dryly, in English. He'd been around Canadians often enough to peg her as Nova Scotian, which was unusual, given Bee's hometown and heavy Quebecois lilt.

"Thank you for having us," Nate said, shaking her parents' hands, and then the twins'. Both of them did the thing where they squeezed too hard in an effort to prove something, and he just sighed and let them crush his fingers, because really, he had nothing to say that could be settled here rather than on the ice.

The actual documentary proved to be just as insufferable. The twins took over the conversation, their competitive jabs *just* on the right side of rude, just enough plausible deniability that Bee didn't say anything back because if she did, she would have looked like *she* was the one being weird about it. She looked at them sideways with a withering stare that Nate imagined the camera couldn't miss. Watching her dealing with her brothers, for once in his life, he didn't feel any regret that he was an only child. And he felt only admiration for her, again.

"Marde," Bee said, when they were alone on the back porch.

Mäkelä was inside, helping Bee's parents with dinner, and the camera crew had shooed Nate away despite the fact that he'd asked to help. The captain and the star player's parents didn't make for juicy television quite the same way her boyfriend would.

"I'm sure they are fine with their team members, but Jesus Christ, sometimes I wish I could punch one of them. Both of them."

"You're doing a great job. You didn't even punch either of them once."

She exhaled sharply through her noise, as disdainful a noise as he'd ever heard her make. "If I punched them, that would just give them what they want. Attention, and to be the victim."

"I still don't think I could have that kind of restraint."

Bee patted him on the arm. The sun was setting in the distance and bathed the neighborhood, with its pleasant little brick houses, with a warm red glow. He nursed a Dieu du Ciel Mrs. Morin had shoved into their hands before they'd left the kitchen.

"If *you* grew up with them, you would." She snorted. "And you have plenty of restraint. For example. You have been wanting to ask me a question for the last hour and a half, but you haven't asked it."

"It's not really my day for questions."

"Mon capitaine..." Her eyebrow was eloquent.

Nate looked down at the small back yard of Bee's parents' house. Her father had planted a vegetable garden in the back. Across the street a group of children was playing football in the cul-de-sac, pretending they weren't spying on the news crew. His hands felt clammy and the words caught on his tongue.

"Whatever it is, it bothers you."

He blew out a short breath. "How do you know what's normal—a normal amount of times to, uh, have sex with someone? Who you're fucking?"

Bee choked on her beer.

Nate clapped her on the back. "I'm sorry, I didn't mean to make you do that."

"That is not what I was expecting," she said, once she had managed to swallow.

"This was a stupid idea," Nate mumbled. He could feel the tips of his ears burning.

"Um, I don't know if it is stupid so much as unexpected?"

"Just forget I said anything, please."

"Unfortunately, I cannot. Ever."

Nate looked down at the beer and wondered why the earth could not swallow him whole.

Bee glanced sideways at him, and her usually stoic face flickered with something that might have been pity. "You are *serious*."

"I just, I never really, uh, dated anyone besides Rachel, and..."

"I think...as long as you are happy, any amount of times is normal?" She paused. "Unless you are asking specifically how often Sakari and I..."

"No!" Nate exclaimed hastily. "No, I definitely don't want to, oh, this is coming out all wrong."

"Okay. Just as long as we are clear." Bee's mouth tilted up in a wry smile. "It is not like you to be tangled in a knot about someone, though."

"It's, uh…been a weird year."

"I guess all I have to say is that when things are good and right, you do not get tired of them. Of that person." She patted him on the shoulder. "But think about it. I have to go back inside."

He probably should have just dropped it there, but the problem that Nate had sometimes, when he got a thought in his head, was that he worried it over and over like a dog at a bone. It felt like he was physically incapable of letting it go sometimes. So even though he should have dropped it there, he asked a few of the other guys.

The rest of his research was almost as disastrous. Netty was less poetic than Bee had been. First he howled with laughter and slapped Nate on the back until *he* choked on his drink. Then, he said, "About time you fuck around, Cap!"

"I, uh—it's not like I *haven't*—"

"Yeah, yeah," Netty said, waving his hand dismissively. "How much is *normal*? Like, you not doing it enough?"

"Uh…not exactly…" Nate said, thinking of all of the times he had thought, *okay, we probably shouldn't do it tonight*, and completely lost control of himself anyway.

"Too much?" Netty stared at him. "Cap, you *okay*?"

"I'm fine, I just…"

"No such thing as *too much*, bro. I mean, you been wasting all this time, no wonder you're so horny."

Nate choked on a drink for the second time that night, and once Netty had pounded him on the back so hard that Nate was fairly sure he'd left a bruise, said, "I'm *not* horny, Netty."

"It's okay," Netty said, aiming his gap-toothed grin at Nate. This must have been what small prey animals felt like, staring down the maw of a wolf. "Your secret safe with me."

Before the game, he and Sally sat next to each other on the benches, watching the rest of the team warm up by playing elimination soccer. Nate's head hadn't been in it at all, and he'd been knocked out far earlier than he normally would have been. Sally's face was, as always, a bit like a statute carved out of marble, imperious and just as expressionless.

"With regard to your question," Sally said, breaking the silence, and Nate winced.

"I regret ever asking, Sally," Nate said, pleading without pleading to avoid taking the conversation any further.

"I think I have a different perspective than most of the boys, so you may take or leave my thoughts as you will."

Nate glanced sideways at Sally, but there was no sign of mockery on his face. He was equanimous as always, as calm as an iced-over lake. "I always appreciate your words of wisdom."

"In my view, sex is immaterial."

"I'm sorry, what?"

"Hear me out, please," Sally said, holding up one hand. "I don't know if you know, but Kaisa and I were an… arranged marriage, of sorts."

"You were? I didn't think that was common in Finland."

"It isn't. But ours was an unusual situation. Our families were bitter rivals. No, not like that. It was all business. Luxury cabinetry. Much more cutthroat than you might expect, many years of corporate sabotage and strife. When her family had a daughter and mine a son, we were essentially promised to each other from birth."

Nate thought about Sally and Kaisa, equally calm,

equally aristocratic, both with their aquiline features and ice-blue eyes, and tried to square that with the Finnish cabinet wars he was currently picturing in his head. "That can't have been pleasant for you."

"It was not, at first. We both did our duty, and agreed to the match, but there was no trust, of course. You cannot hate someone's family for so long and feel comfortable in a marriage bed with them. And without that—without trust—it is nothing."

"So you…?"

"Trust came, eventually," Sally said, and shrugged. "With time, and effort. But we did not consummate our marriage for almost a year."

Nate stared at him.

"It was worth waiting." For a second, the barest hint of a smile flickered over his face, like a sheet of ice sheering off a berg. "And that is my point. Now, after the merger, you can find Salonen-Heikkilä cabinets all over Finland. Don't worry about what is normal. Because there is nothing of the sort. What matters is trust."

"Uh…wow. I don't know what to say, Sally. Thank you." Nate thought, *it's like having your own personal Yoda sometimes*, except without the war crimes. And trust? He caught himself flushing, again, remembering how Zach had said *it's gonna be good, okay*, and his first thought had been *I know, I trust you*. He didn't want to think about that now.

"Whatever is going on in your personal life, Cap, I trust that you know what you're doing, my friend," Sally said, and patted him on the shoulder.

"I wish I had your confidence in me," Nate muttered, but by then, it was time to play hockey, and that, at least, he knew how to do.

CHAPTER EIGHT

February

On the brief flight to Ottawa, Zach realized that it was already February. And not only was Valentine's Day coming up, he had no idea how to be romantic or what romance actually was. And Valentine's Day was pretty much the most romantic day of the year, right? It was Zach's responsibility to figure out something *good.* So he googled it on his phone, which he had to angle carefully away from Nate so he wouldn't see it. The search bar autofilled *how to romance a man* and Zach shrugged and went with it.

He read, *to romance a man, try leaving him a cute note somewhere he'll easily see it, but not too easily. You can surprise him with a special date. Consider cooking his favorite meal to share. Be creative!*

Zach considered this. It made sense, actually, and seemed like things he could do. Well, notes, anyway—he couldn't cook to save his fucking life, but that didn't mean he couldn't try. Nate seemed like the kind of guy who would appreciate effort. Zach bookmarked the page and looked at another list, because Nate deserved thoroughly researched romance, and promptly began feeling discouraged.

1. Get handsy, the list said. He frowned. He already did that. That wasn't, like, romantic or anything. That was Nate having an amazing body and an ass that didn't quit and the fact that Zach was horny as fuck about all of it.

The list suggested changing your usual outfits, but Nate only noticed what Zach was wearing if it was something really out of character. Maybe that was the point of the suggestion, but it didn't matter. If Zach took *that* advice, he'd only ever get chirped for it, and that seemed self-defeating.

Number three wasn't any better, because it suggested sending him out with "the guys." Zach frowned more deeply. At this rate, he was going to get wrinkles. He wouldn't be able to do that one either, since he and Nate went out with the boys all the time anyway. And he didn't think Nate would appreciate it if Zach stayed home.

Sneaking in a flirty note, complimenting him, making him laugh, or having a "special experience" also didn't seem super helpful. *Switch up sex*, the list suggested, complete with a flirty winking emoji. At this point, Zach felt like his eyebrows had become surgically attached together. He was great at making Nate laugh, but the rest of it...well, they switched the sex up often enough already, he thought. But maybe there was something more he could do?

Nate looked sideways at him. "What are you reading?"

"Nothing. I can't read," Zach said, immediately, setting his phone down on his thigh. "C'mon, Cap, you know this."

"Zach, I thought we'd agreed you wouldn't say shit like that about yourself."

Zach locked the phone and thought to himself that these lists probably weren't written with guys like Nate in mind, guys who turned bright red if there was even a hint you were gonna say something nice to them, guys who were so fucking sincere that even three years after they had first met, Nate still got upset whenever Zach admitted to being stupid. It was cute. And Nate's confidence in him was inspiring as all hell and it was one of the reasons he was head over fucking heels for the guy, but despite Nate's admirable but misguided beliefs, Zach knew he was, absolutely, a grade A moron.

Only a grade A moron would be trying to figure out how to write a flirty note to a dude whose asshole he'd enthusiastically eaten out the night before.

Zach turned his most twinkling smile on Nate and said, "Don't worry your pretty little head about it, Cap."

Nate flushed, though his voice was steady. "You know that's exactly the kind of thing that's going to make me worry. You do know that, right?"

Zach really wanted to kiss him, right then and there, but they were surrounded by their teammates and Mike was watching them with one of his thoughtful, unreadable expressions that made Zach feel like he'd given away too much, just by existing, just by his face.

So instead, he burrowed more deeply into the seat. "You worry about everything, but you absolutely don't have to worry about me. I got you."

"Uh-huh," Nate replied, but he didn't sound at all convinced.

Thankfully, it was a short flight.

There was something weird going on with Zach, but Nate couldn't figure out what the hell it was. The flight from Montreal was weird: Zach seemed especially cagey. At the best of times, Zach was terrible at lying, so the fact that he was obviously trying to hide something made Nate feel a) worried and b) suspicious. After all of the terrible, embarrassing things that Zach had gleefully told Nate over the years without a hint of shame, something Zach felt he had to hide must have been really bad.

If not something bad, then something really big.

Then, when Nate was at home unpacking his bags, he found a Post-it note stuck to the plastic hotel bag filled with dirty laundry. It had something that might have been a drawing of the eggplant emoji, although he couldn't tell because it was drawn so badly, and it said, in Zach's messy, enthusiastic handwriting, *u have a gr8 ass.*

Nate stared at it, then set it down on the floor and texted Zach, Are you okay?

im great, why?

Nate thought about what he would say, and finally said, Did you leave a note in my bags?

;) Zach responded.

Nate sighed. Zach was his best friend and had been for the last three years, but sometimes, he didn't understand the guy at all.

Things just got weirder from there. After he put his clothes into the washing machine and lay down for a brief nap, he woke up to find he'd missed a few calls. One was from Bee thanking him for participating in the documentary, one was from his mom inviting him over for dinner, but one was from Zach, and he'd left a voice mail, which was so odd in itself that Nate had a sense of foreboding settle in his stomach.

"Hey bud," voice mail–Zach said. It sounded like there was something clattering in the background. If Nate didn't know Zach better, he would have thought it was a pot on the stove. "If you're around tonight, you wanna come over for dinner? Like six-ish." An intense beeping sound, like the fire alarm was going off. "Oh, fuck, I gotta go. See you!"

Nate tried to call him back, but Zach didn't pick up. He sat there for a minute, staring at the phone and trying to figure out what the hell was going on, but he had absolutely no idea. Then he got distracted because Gags had called with an urgent question about what he should do if his hookup had taken pictures and he didn't realize it until later, and by the time he was finished putting out that particular fire, it was almost six o'clock.

He couldn't leave Zach hanging, so he got dressed and walked the block and a half to Zach's place and let himself in. Since he'd bought the house, and with some pushing from Nate, he'd slowly furnished it so it actually felt like a home. At the very least, if people came over, there were actual places to sit that weren't cases of beer or milk crates or beanbag chairs.

Hank and Dolly came bounding up to him, barking, and Nate realized the house smelled like smoke. He bent down to scratch both dogs behind the ears, and called, "Uh, Zach? Everything okay here?"

Zach emerged from the kitchen, wearing an apron that said *KISS THE CHEF* splattered with red stuff that Nate really hoped was tomato. He had flour in his hair and a sheepish smile on his face. "Uh, hey! You came!"

"I apparently had to make sure you hadn't burned the house down, dude."

"Oh, uh, yeah, I had a little…sauce…mishap."

"You're *cooking*?"

"I, uh, tried to make you homemade pasta," Zach said,

and the dogs ran to him, trying to lick the splattered food from the apron.

"I'm—I'm not following?"

"Well, I dunno, you always cook for me, so I figured I should try. Um, unfortunately, I forgot that I was heating up some oil in the pan while I was trying to cut the onions, and uh… I kind of melted the pan a little. Anyway, it was only a little fire. Nate, stop staring at me like that."

"I mean…thank you?" Nate said carefully. "I appreciate it, but you know I like cooking for you, you don't need to do all of that."

"I know you do, but I *wanted to*, okay?" Zach sounded weirdly frustrated, like Nate wasn't getting something he was trying to convey. "Ugh, this is coming out all fucking wrong. I wanted you to—I wanted to—well, fuck, it doesn't matter anyway, because it didn't come out."

Nate realized he was still staring. "Well…thanks."

Zach ripped the apron off and threw it on the ground, where Hank and Dolly promptly began fighting over it and licking at the food stains. "It doesn't matter, anyway. The pasta is like, I don't know what I did wrong, but the dough's like trying to roll out a rock and I don't have another pan, so. I ordered from three different places you like in case you're not in the mood for something."

Before Nate realized what he was doing, he had stood again and crossed the room, and his hand was in Zach's hair, brushing the flour out. Zach looked up at him, and Nate felt dizzy for a moment, a swoop in the very pit of his stomach.

"You really didn't have to do any of this, Zach."

"Stop fuckin' *saying* that," Zach mumbled into his chest. "I *wanted* to do something for you."

"Zach, you do—" Nate couldn't think of a way to say,

you do so much for me just by being here that didn't sound slightly insane, so instead he rested his head on top of Zach's floury hair and said, "Come on, buddy, I'll help you clean up the kitchen."

Zach realized, after his first failed attempts, that Nate was impervious to being swept off his feet. Part of this was Zach's fault, given disasters like his attempt at homemade pasta, or his attempt to take Nate on a date in the middle of their West Coast road trip.

He'd tried to pick out a restaurant as smoothly as Nate had taken him out for sushi that one time in Dallas, but he'd gotten overwhelmed picking things out, got in his own head about whether or not Nate was going to like the dinner and ended up being a little too stiff and serious. It was just a regular American bar with slightly fancier food, but it was *awkward*.

To the point where Nate had leaned over the table and repeated, "Dude, seriously, are you okay?"

"I'm fine," Zach said, except he wasn't fine, because trying to give Nate the kind of *romance* that he deserved was rapidly becoming a disaster.

Nate seemed equally impervious to small gifts Zach got him, or at least, he seemed pleased with the new skate sharpener and pan ("It's a really nice pan, but don't you need one for your house instead? Maybe you should keep it, buddy?") but no more than he normally would have.

Zach was running rapidly through the list of things he'd made that didn't seem completely outlandish to do for Nate. Pretty much the only thing left was *switch up sex!*

That was going to be difficult too because, he thought a little smugly, they already switched it up pretty often. Not to brag—well, kind of to brag—but usually by this time in a thing, Zach found himself getting bored fucking the same person. Every time he fucked Nate, though, it was like he was learning something new about himself. If this was what dating did for your sex life, he was kind of sorry he hadn't done it before.

But this was about Nate, and what he deserved, not about Zach.

They were in Denver, and they'd won in overtime. The team had gone out afterward, but Zach and Nate had left early to head back to the hotel, a little drunk, buzzing on the win more than the beer.

Zach had been thinking about it, how exactly he was going to blow Nate's mind *and* show him that he was worthy of *romance*. He wasn't going to do anything like hundreds of candles, because he'd tried that once for a girl he'd been really into in juniors, but they'd just set off the hotel room sprinkler and Zach had gotten in so, so much trouble with his billet and with the league.

The thing was, he knew Nate really fucking well by this point. Nate, who by outward appearances at least assumed the authority of the captaincy like it was the most natural thing in the world to him but agonized over every word and decision he made. He was tired all of the time, because of their schedule, but also because constantly thinking that many thoughts was exhausting.

Zach had figured out pretty much the first year they'd known each other that Nate liked not having to make the decisions, liked giving up the control of a situation sometimes, which suited Zach just fine. He hadn't really taken advantage of it before, but he thought maybe...there was something to be said for it.

Nate looked sideways at him as they walked down the hall to Zach's hotel room.

"What?" Zach asked, completely normally.

"You've been acting really weird…what are you up to?"

"I can't try to do nice things for you without having other motives, Nate? My feelings are hurt," Zach said, turning the puppy dog eyes on him.

Nate looked down, as if he wanted to say something else, but thought better of it. "You're just—you're making me really nervous."

"Yeah, but you kinda like it, don't you?"

He was rewarded by a flush that started at the tips of Nate's ears and worked its way down. His eyes were dark and intent. "Zach…"

"Hey," Zach said, sliding the key card into the door, "just trust me, okay, baby? We're gonna have fun—it's going to be good."

There was something complicated happening on Nate's face that Zach couldn't figure out. He opened his mouth like he was going to say something but choked it back instead. Finally, he swallowed hard and said, "You know I do. Trust you."

"Okay," Zach said, and flashed what he hoped was an encouraging smile at Nate as they went into the hotel room together. It probably had slightly too many teeth in it. "Then just let me lead."

"Okay." Nate swallowed again, still prctty skittish. No matter how nervous he was, though, he was still so easy for Zach.

Zach kept smiling at him and moved forward. "I'm gonna undress you. Don't help me, you have to let me do everything."

"I *have* to?"

Zach placed his hand over Nate's mouth and said, "Shh. You said you were gonna trust me, okay?"

"I said I *do* trust you…not that I'm gonna…"

He could feel Nate's lips open and close against his hand, could see Nate's throat bob, and he couldn't entirely keep that stupid shit-eating grin off of his face. His attempts at romance might have gone to shit, but there was one thing Zach knew how to do, and, well. He was gonna fucking do it.

Nate stood very still, except when Zach went to tug the sweater and shirt he was wearing up over his head, and then he let his arms go up with it. Zach wondered if he would ever really get tired of looking at Nate like that, even though he'd memorized every line of his body by now. It was probably because even now, even after everything, Nate flinched a little, like he was embarrassed by the way Zach was looking at him. Which was kind of too intense, probably.

And they hadn't even gotten to his pants yet.

Nate just watched him with that same stare the whole time he did it, like he was afraid to miss any little movement Zach made. Zach was careful to touch him as he did it, just here and there, to remind him what they were doing. Some people probably would've been mouthing off by now, but Nate knew him, and Nate was willing to be patient.

Nate *trusted* him.

Zach wasn't sure if anyone had ever trusted him like that before and he had to swallow hard to get control of himself, had to force himself to focus. This wasn't about him; this was about sweeping Nate off his feet.

When Nate was completely naked and Zach was still wearing everything, Zach stood back to admire his handiwork: Nate, blushing and clearly kind of excited by it despite his own tendency toward nerves. Zach very carefully didn't touch him again when he said, "Go lie down on the bed."

Nate looked at him again, teeth worrying his lower lip. "Are you going to fuck me?"

"Soon, bud. No need to rush things, huh?"

"Well, we do have an early flight…" Nate started to say, but the words died in his mouth when Zach stepped forward and took Nate's dick in his hand.

"I'm not gonna do that again if you keep talking," Zach whispered in Nate's ear.

Nate swallowed, hard, and said, "What's—" but stopped immediately when Zach took his hand away.

"Get on the bed, eh?"

Nate went, and Zach admired the view. He thought about making a teasing remark, the kind of gentle shit-talking that usually made Nate laugh and forget to be self-conscious, but this wasn't that kind of night. He watched his best friend push the comforter and sheets back and lie down on the bed, his body a beacon in the middle of all that white sheet.

When he was feeling sentimental, Zach thought of all of the people who never knew what Nate looked like like this. And all of the people who would never know. It was something only *he* got to see now, and he felt the weird, fierce possessiveness that always gripped him when that thought flitted its way through his head. Jesus, he had to focus, or this was gonna go about as well as the last of the multiple times Zach had tried to take him out. Which had been a success as a dinner, but a failure as, like, anything romantic. The dosa restaurant had been small and crowded and they'd ended up having to eat standing at the counter, all of the food dripping out of the edges of the dosa and into the sambar. By the end of it, Nate, laughing, had given up and asked for a fork. The food and the company were good, but it hadn't felt like when Nate had done it.

He had to stop distracting himself.

Zach didn't go to him right away, but instead fished through his bags until he found his game-day tie. Nate watched him with a combination of apprehension and what was clearly arousal against his own better judgment, and he started to lean up toward Zach when Zach straddled his thighs. The thighs that Zach had obsessed over since his first few weeks in Philly, strong and muscular and so fucking solid underneath him.

"Nuh-uh, dude. You hold still."

Nate's whole body flinched when Zach wound the tie around his eyes and knotted it in the back. He was gonna ruin it, but its sacrifice would be worth it. Nate's temples felt hot under his fingers, but he was silent, except for his breathing, really loud all of a sudden.

"Put your hands on the headboard?" Zach asked, and admired the way the muscles in Nate's arms shifted as he did it.

"Are you—"

"I'm not asking you to do anything else, okay? I just want you to let me do this. For you."

Something shivered across Nate's body and Zach could feel him, hard against Zach's thigh. Could see his fingers tighten. "Uh...okay."

The rest of it he just made up as he went along because he didn't really know what the hell he was doing anymore. Nate made it easy, though. Nate made it easy when he tried so hard not to move, to leave his hands where he'd said he'd leave them, when he was clearly anxious as fuck not to know where Zach's mouth and hands would touch him next, and he both flinched away and arched into each touch. After a while he stopped asking questions and Zach could just listen to his ragged breath, the low whine he made when Zach stopped touching him for too long, moved too slowly.

It wasn't any easier for Zach, hyperaware of the barrier of his clothes between them, the way he had to keep himself under careful control, to focus on touching Nate and Nate only, to make him feel the way he made Zach feel inside all of the fucking time. He felt a little crazy, when it came down to it, like if he didn't get this right he was maybe going to die.

When Zach rolled off of him, finally, to undress himself, Nate made a noise that cut right through him. Half protest, half cry, half groan.

Okay, maybe he was shit at math. It was just, it was a lot.

Nate felt so warm under him, and Zach had meant to keep quiet, to keep things kinda mysterious, but he couldn't shut the fuck up, actually, so he ended up telling Nate exactly what he was thinking, which was, "You're so fucking hot, I mean, you feel like a furnace, fuck, that's not what I meant, I'm just—Nate, fuck, fuck, you feel fucking good like this."

Nate didn't say anything in response, because Zach had asked him not to, but his teeth dug into his lip and every single muscle in his arm was outlined in sharp relief, and Zach thought, *hell yeah.*

When Zach went down on him, Nate made a noise that sounded like he was trying not to cry.

"Are you—fuck, Zach—how long are you going to do this?"

"I dunno," Zach said, pulling away from Nate's dick far enough to talk but not far enough that his beard wasn't tickling it, "I figured I'd just see how much you could take and go from there?"

"Oh, god," Nate groaned, but from the way he twitched in Zach's hand, he thought he was definitely on the right track.

"You're doing really fucking good, dude," Zach said, and half patted, half stroked his fingers along the inside of Nate's thigh, rewarded by another full-body shiver and groan. "You're fucking good."

By the time he was finished working Nate over, he was aching himself from the sheer force of will it took to hold himself back. He had to take a minute to collect himself, panting, sweat trickling down his temples, planning his next move as carefully as he'd consider a face-off.

"Zach, please," Nate said finally, "I can't...come on—" and Zach decided to take pity on him.

"Don't move," he said, again, and scrambled up Nate's body to kiss him. It was a sexy kiss, sure, but there was also something that would have freaked out the Zach of only a few months ago. Nate kissed back like he was drowning, like he wanted more than anything to reach out and touch Zach, but Zach had asked him not to. All of that frustrated yearning and desire was just in the way his mouth clashed against Zach's and his lips opened and yielded and Zach thought, smugly, *he likes it*.

The joke was on him because by the time he had found a condom and carefully rolled it down on Nate, stroked his lubed-up hand along after it, manfully ignoring the noises that drew out of him, he was having a hard time forming thoughts in sentences, let alone keeping his shit together. So maybe this wasn't going to go as long as he'd originally planned.

But Nate was fucking losing it, way worse than Zach was, and he thought he would maybe remember the desperation in his voice for the rest of his life, so that was fine.

This was all fine, completely normal.

Nate was a big guy, all over, and so when Zach lowered himself down it took him a minute or two to get used to it. It wasn't like he was an *amateur* or anything, it wasn't like he didn't love it, it just still took a minute, especially because he hadn't felt patient enough to really take the time he needed to prepare himself beforehand. And it didn't make it any easier when Nate was vibrating out of his skin with the need to *move* and the desperate desire not to, just to make Zach happy.

All of that muscle and energy and strength, restrained underneath him. Well. Inside of him. They lay frozen like that, Zach draped over Nate, Nate trembling under him, for long enough that Zach kind of lost track of time.

And then he got his bearings, and shifted around, and Nate cried out wordlessly, and Zach said, "Okay, baby, it's okay, I—I'm gonna—"

It was like other times they'd fucked, but it wasn't. There was something darker, more desperate about it, Nate's arms shaking with the effort to hold them up, the blindfold damp with sweat, the heat of everywhere Zach's body met Nate's. The way he could shift to get the angle just right, Nate driving into him, the way it lit him up inside.

Finally he couldn't bear it anymore and he pulled the tie up, exposing Nate's eyes.

They were so wide and so blue and so fathomless, like, Zach didn't even know, like deep open water, and he was staring up at Zach like Zach was the only person in the universe, and Zach thought, *oh no, don't say it, no.* "Nate, I—" *don't* SAY *it*, "You can take your hands down, come on, you gotta touch me," and Nate's fingers tangled in his hair, pulling him down into a messy kiss and without pulling out, rolled Zach over into the bed so that the weight of his body was heavy on top.

"What?" Nate panted, his hand wrapped around Zach's dick, so Zach could feel every callus on his palm and fingers, "What should I do?"

"Fuck me," Zach said, and dug his fingers hard into the knot of muscle at Nate's shoulder. "Hard. Harder."

Nate did what he was told, slamming his hips up against Zach's body. The sensation was insane; Zach was already teetering on the edge and the desperate force of Nate's thrusts almost ended him right there. Nate's face was crazed, flushed red, sweaty, his eyes unfocused.

"Is this—good? Am I—"

"You're good, baby," Zach said, desperately trying to regain control of the situation, even while Nate was moving, equally desperate, totally arrhythmic, even while they were both completely lost, "you're so good, you're my—fuck, you're fucking everything—"

Nate buried his face in the crook of Zach's neck where it sloped down into his shoulder, and came. And Zach, because he was fucking pathetic, didn't last even ten seconds after that, the feeling of Nate pulsing inside of him pushing him right over the edge of the cliff.

They didn't move for what seemed like a long time, long enough that Zach thought Nate might have fallen asleep.

"Buddy," he whispered, after a moment.

"Yeah?"

"Just checking to see if you're up," Zach said, nudging him with his elbow. Nate's entire body weight was still on him. It would have been uncomfortable if it wasn't so fucking comforting. People paid a lot of money for weighted blankets, but Zach was dating one.

"Yeah, I'm..." Nate propped himself up on his elbow and winced. The circulation probably still wasn't normal, and Zach felt a tiny twinge of regret. "Where the fuck did *that* come from?"

"I wanted to—do something special for you, dude, I dunno. I mean, you liked it, right?"

Nate's eyes were still wide, bemused, his eyelashes stained darker from the tears that had been leaking out of them. He looked at Zach like they were speaking different languages. Maybe they were. His fingers reached out to brush a damp curl away from Zach's forehead before he realized what he was doing and pulled them back. "I—yeah. It was something. You're—something."

Zach shoved Nate off of him and rolled into a sitting position, wincing a little. "So I've been told."

"Come on. Let's get cleaned up. We've got a six-o'clock flight tomorrow."

Zach groaned theatrically, but still had the time to slap Nate on the ass when he got out of the bed.

Some things, romance or not, would never change.

February rolled onward.

Nate and the team were playing excellent fucking hockey, still battling the Hornets for the top spot in the division. There was the historic rivalry, but there was also the fact that last season was still a painful open wound.

Nate was determined to come in first at the end of the season, no matter what happened later on in the playoffs. It was almost more important than winning the Cup would be. He was focused and determined and he wasn't letting anything or anyone get in his way.

Now that he was in his third year of doing it, being the captain was getting easier too. He was going to be thirty in a few years, and he was getting used to the weight of responsibility on his shoulders. Even when his own life was spinning off into a horrific, out-of-control car crash, he could put on a serious face and act like he had his shit together and give advice and run interference with Coach and talk to the refs. There was something vaguely gratifying about the fact that no one knew he was an absolutely fucked-up mess about almost everything involving Zach.

His personal life was another story. He woke up every day tormented by the knowledge of the eventual moment that everything was going to come crashing down, when Zach realized that Nate was this fucked up about him, about everything. When Zach realized how Nate felt about him and decided that it was too much. When Zach realized that he wasn't anything… He woke up every day with the conflicting emotion of weird, all-consuming anticipation, happy to go to work, happy to be playing well, happy to see his friends, happy to see Zach. He couldn't remember ever feeling like that, not in his entire twenty-something years of life. The conflicting emotions were exhausting.

Intense feelings of doom aside, Nate was starting to get used to whatever it was Zach was doing. Or not used to, exactly, but he let his guard down enough so that it wasn't weird when Zach kept doing things like cooking him dinner sometimes when they were home. Or at least letting Nate help him cook.

Once Zach decided he was going to do something, and put all of his considerable energy toward it, he *did* it. Nate found that he actually liked teaching him, and that although he still enjoyed cooking solo for Zach, there was something really—nice, kind of comforting—about standing side by side at the long kitchen counter on one of their few nights in Philly, with his black metal playlist in the background, laughing at Zach as tears streamed down his face while he tried to slice shallots and the dogs begged for scraps on the floor.

Rachel never wanted to learn to cook with you, his brain whispered.

Rachel was always busy.

Zach's not *busy?* his brain, which was a traitor, replied. *You know exactly how busy he is. You're both professional athletes.*

Well, it doesn't matter. I liked cooking for Rachel and I like cooking for Zach.

Yeah, but isn't it nice to share things? Share everything*? You remember how Rachel never wanted to listen to your music either, and Zach—*

Shut up, shut up, shut up.

"You okay?" Zach asked, wiping his eyes with his forearm.

"I'm fine," Nate lied.

"You sure? You looked really weird for a minute. And also, ugh, shouldn't the sous chef be the one crying over the onions?"

"You and my mom," Nate said dryly, "always trying to get me to do the dirty work."

Zach made a face at Nate over his shoulder as he turned

to scrape the shallots into a prep bowl. "Come on, your mom? Not really the comparison I'm going for, bud."

Nate wanted very badly to just say, *I wish we could date for real, instead of just for the team*, but he crushed the stupid leap in his chest and said, "Okay, well, I'll do the garlic for you."

"Yes!" Zach said, triumphant. "I hate those stupid fucking skins. All over my fingers." He mimed flicking sticky garlic off of his fingers and made a gagging noise and Nate thought, helplessly, *I like you so fucking much.*

But that was, of course, the problem. He liked Zach *so* fucking much.

There was a Southern road trip, and they cleaned up there too. It was especially satisfying to beat the Monument at home, to listen to the silence in the arena as their fair-weather fans trickled out before the bell had even rung on the third period. It wasn't quite as brutal as a West Coast trip, just solely based on the travel, but they had four games, including a back-to-back, and a matinee immediately when they came home to Philly.

Nate went home alone after they landed, intending to pass out for the few hours he had remaining before the game. He was exhausted from the games and from the travel and from worrying, again, about the expiration date on his time with Zach. He had sorted through the mail that had piled up while he was gone and was pouring himself a glass of water in the kitchen when his cell phone rang, flashing *MOM.*

"Hi, Mom."

"Hello, honey. How are you doing?"

"I'm okay, just tired. You know how the road trips go."

"I do, I do. I'm sorry to bother you, I won't keep you long from your nap."

"What's up?"

"Well, I was beginning to make my plans and preparations for vacations and such, but then I thought, well, I was just wondering whether you would be around for the summer this year."

"Uh, why wouldn't I be around for the summer? I live here."

"Well, I know, but..." Mom hesitated in a way she usually didn't. "I wasn't sure if you'd be in Vancouver instead."

"Vancouver?" Nate asked blankly. "Why would I be in Vancouver?"

"Well, you know, Zachary lives in Vancouver, and he stayed in Philly last offseason, so I wasn't sure whether his family would want him to come home?"

"What does that have to do with me?" Nate couldn't quite quell the rising feeling of panic choking his throat.

"I thought—maybe—well, silly me, I just thought maybe you two would be seeing his family this year instead, at least for a little," Mom said. Her voice was very soft and very kind and so hopeful that Nate wanted to curl up in a ball and die.

"Mom," he said, over the sound of his blood rushing in his ears like the ocean in a seashell. "*He's* going home, *I'm* not going. It's not—it's not like we're *dating*."

"Oh, I'm sorry, I just thought after I saw you at the Chanukah party—maybe—you two had figured it out."

Nate swallowed hard and rested his head against the cool metal of the fridge. His chest felt tight and twisted. It wasn't like his mom had ever implied something like this before, but it still wasn't entirely a surprise. Of course she thought they were dating, because she had always thought the world of him and couldn't understand why other people didn't see it too. *She* didn't understand the imbalance, the weird set of circumstances and delusions that had aligned to let Nate have this, at least for a time. She didn't understand the house of cards he'd built. Zach had figured it out, and Nate was…well, Nate was Nate.

"Mom, it's really not like that."

"Oh, *Nathaniel…*"

Nate thought almost savagely, hating himself, *don't fucking* pity *me, not you too, please*, and snapped, "Seriously, Mom? Can you ever mind your own business? Can we not talk about this, please? I'm going to be there. He won't."

"Nathaniel."

"Mom… I'm sorry. That was uncalled for. I didn't mean to yell, I'm just…having a rough time this year." He stared out the kitchen window at the pots that had been his herb garden. The plants had withered and died in the cold; he just hadn't had a chance to dig them out. It was so fucking stupid, but hot tears were pricking the corners of his eyes, like he was a kid who couldn't control himself anymore.

"You seemed so much happier and at ease with yourself, that's why I thought—"

Nate's eyes stung but instead, he said, "Well, it's been a weird year. I, um, don't really wanna talk about it on the phone."

"Well…whenever you're ready, honey, you know I'm here."

"I know, Mom. I do."

"Okay, well. You owe us a dinner at home soon."

"I'll be there, I promise."

"Okay, Nathaniel. I love you."

"Love you too."

When Nate hung up, he heard the door open and then close again. Shit, that meant Zach was here. He took a deep breath and wiped his eyes with the back of his hand in a desperate attempt to look like he hadn't been crying. It was probably a lost cause, anyway. He always had dark circles under his eyes, and now they were probably swollen and red. There was Zach, standing in the living room of Nate's house. It wasn't a surprise; he often came over for a pregame nap, and he had Nate's door code. He was still in his rumpled plane sweats, frowning in concern when he saw the state of Nate's facial expression.

"Baby," he said, "what's wrong?"

"Oh, nothing," Nate mumbled. "Just, you know. My mom called."

"She didn't say anything nasty, did she…?"

"No, no, she didn't mean to be a jerk or anything, it's just…sometimes she just, uh, assumes things about me, and my life. That aren't true."

Zach stepped forward and embraced him, and for a second, Nate could let his entire body relax into it. Zach's warm arms, a comfort he absolutely didn't deserve because he was such a fucking *mess*. "You can tell me about it if you want. I'm a pretty good listener, you know. There's a reason I'm a highly sought-after date."

After everything, the words lashed his skin like a scourge. Nate could feel everything inside of him wither and die, the shame of wanting so desperately to date Zach for real and knowing it could never happen. The humiliating knowledge that he was panting like a fucking dog after something he could never have. "But it's not like *we're* dating."

Zach's arms around him went still. He looked up at Nate and took a deep breath. "Yeah, probably," he said.

"But, you know. It's not really a big deal." Nate took a deep breath of his own and counted to ten. If he could just get himself back under control, if he could just act normally, he could get through the day and then things would be fine for the game later. Just thinking about being able to sleep in the bed with Zach, to have his body curled up against Nate's, was calming.

"It's not?"

"Well, no. I just have to…not take things she says so personally. Sometimes. She means well. That's the thing with her. She always means well. It's just me that's the problem."

Zach's face was doing something complicated, a flicker of some unclear emotion that he managed to tamp down. "Parents usually do, right?"

"Yeah," Nate said, and added, "Do you want to go upstairs now?"

Zach looked up at Nate, and he was smiling in a way that he usually didn't smile at Nate anymore, the fake, sparkly smile that he used for the media. "Well," he said. "You know, actually, I think I need to go home and make sure the dogs are okay, actually. I'm really tired, so I might just nap at home afterward. Don't wait up for me, okay? It's cool."

Nate frowned, trying to puzzle out the expression on Zach's face, but he couldn't. It wasn't like Zach had been there for the conversation, but he was staring at Nate like he'd never seen him before, still smiling that horrible smile. The effect was disconcerting.

"I mean, I was going to nap too—you can stay if you want to."

"Nah, bro," Zach said breezily. "I think I'm just gonna go home, buddy."

"Zach, what are you…? Are you okay?"

"Completely fine, buddy," Zach said, smiling and smiling. "Okay, I gotta go, bud. See you."

"Wait?" Nate started to say, but the door was closed again, and he was alone.

What the hell was that?

Later on, Zach would never be sure how he got through that awful, fucking horrible game.

He'd played with a broken hand before and this was worse by far.

He managed to mostly avoid Nate in the locker room, which was a feat in itself considering their stalls were next to each other and they spent almost all of their time together. He got to the rink incredibly early, even earlier then Nate usually got there, dressed and went out for the preskate. He didn't have much of a choice during the game, since they were lineys, but he tried to concentrate solely on the game and not talk too much even when Nate looked at him with those confused, wounded blue eyes.

He couldn't entirely describe how he felt. He felt numb, but also, nauseous. It was like having a stomach virus except everything stayed in. But he felt like puking.

His play had definitely suffered. He actually couldn't remember a game he'd played that was worse. His passes weren't connecting, he wasn't able to make good decisions about where he needed to be, and just…ugh.

It was as though his years of experience had completely vanished, and he had no idea what he was doing. He felt like what he imagined most people felt like as rookies, people who didn't win the Rookie of the Year Award and the Cup their first seasons.

"Mon chum, you okay?" Bee asked him during the

first intermission. They were down three goals, goals that hadn't really been Mäkelä's fault at all, but were at least partially due to Zach's sloppy turnovers. "You don't look too good."

But it's not like we're dating.

But it's not like we're dating.

But it's not like we're DATING.

BUT IT'S NOT LIKE WE'RE—

Across the hall, Nate was doing an intermission interview with the in-stadium commentator. Zach couldn't hear what he was saying, but he looked green around the red imprint the helmet had left on his forehead.

Bee took him by the shoulder and shook him. "Zachary!"

"What?"

"Get it together, man!"

"I'm sorry. I've gotta—yeah. I'm gonna get it together."

Bee was staring at him. "What the hell is going on, Zachary?"

"Something I ate."

Bee obviously didn't believe him, but she granted him some semblance of mercy and didn't question him further.

He took a deep breath, and told himself, *get it together.*

They lost 6-2.

After the game, Zach probably got out of the locker room as fast as he'd ever gotten out of it. Usually he stayed around to shoot the shit with Netty and Sally, to tease the rooks, or chat with Coach. Today he was in and out while the media were still doing postgames. Nate saw him go, and started to say something, but Zach refused to meet his eye and just...well, basically, he fled into the hallway.

Once he was back in his own car and finally had a

moment to himself, he slammed his forehead against the edge of the steering wheel. *"Fuck."*

He didn't really know what to do, or what he was feeling. There was a lot of stuff going on in there, and it was hard to pick out one thing. Mostly he felt fucking stupid and really fucking sad, sad like he couldn't ever remember feeling before. He'd had breakups before but nothing serious. Sometimes he was even glad to see them go. Sometimes he was regretful, but it wasn't like anyone was ever irreplaceable. The worst part was, this wasn't even really a breakup, because he had been really fucking wrong about what they were doing.

Well.

Never let it be said that Zach wasn't a grade A moron.

Knowing that didn't make it feel any better.

He couldn't even text Jammer about it, because Jammer would have said *I told you so.*

Old Zach would have gone out and gotten obliterated on whatever he could get his hands on and probably fucked anyone who looked at him twice, and the pictures would have ended up on the internet. Old Zach would have felt like shit afterward, but it wouldn't have mattered. No matter how self-destructive that course of action happened to be, it was like throwing up after you'd gotten too drunk. The purge hurt, but you almost immediately felt so much better afterward. He'd done it after the trade. Jammer had had to scrape him up off of a bathroom floor and basically carry him home.

New Zach had dogs and rookies and responsibilities and texted Gags to tell him to make sure to drink some water and his dog sitter to ask whether she could take Hank and Dolly tonight.

Sure, she responded immediately. Everything okay?

Zach thought for a second about telling her the truth but settled for, going to be out of town last minute. He Venmo'd her a generous tip in addition to her usual fee and sat in his truck, staring at the parking lot. He should probably leave before Nate came out and saw him, but he didn't know where to go.

On autopilot, he started the engine, backed out of his spot, headed down Broad Street, and merged onto 95. He drove south for a while, then got off at a random exit near Chester, got back on northbound, and kept driving. Nate had texted him several times, and Bee, and then Mack, but he didn't look at his phone beyond glancing at the notifications. He didn't even listen to music.

Just the noise of the wind through the windows, and the other cars streaking by on the interstate.

If he stopped driving, he'd have to go home, and he'd probably have to see Nate. He didn't think he could do it. It might have been cowardly, but then, Zach was a coward.

When he saw the exits for Princeton, he merged onto Route 1. He hadn't really spent a lot of time in Princeton, but he knew there was a snooty college there.

Mike lived there.

Mike. Maybe he could...maybe he could talk to Mike. Maybe Mike would understand? He was out to the team, so it wasn't like he'd be judgmental about the gay thing, even if he might have had some ideas about fucking the team's captain, maybe Zach would talk to Mike.

Talk to Mike?

Maybe he could talk to a brick wall.

But he had nowhere else to go.

Zach found himself driving down cute little streets with well-manicured lawns and well-kept Victorian houses, until he found himself on Mike's street and outside of his house. Mike lived in a modestly sized single home with white shingles and a front porch with a swing and a beautiful green backyard which, *what the fuck*.

He somehow managed to find a spot to park, although it was tight. And then he sat in the truck for another half an hour, trying to decide if he should get out. It was ten o'clock by this point and he was fucking exhausted. Usually after a game, he went home, ate something, drank a shitload of water, and passed out. He hadn't eaten anything today because he thought if he did it would come right back up.

His phone was buzzing again. He turned it off.

Zach got out of the car and knocked on the door.

At first, no one answered, so he knocked again.

The door opened, and Zach withered and died in his expensive sneakers. It wasn't Mike, but Danny Garcia, former Hornet and current assistant coach for the New Jersey Scouts. He was wearing sweats, a ratty T-shirt from four teams ago, house slippers, and an eight-o'clock shadow. He was a big man, even bigger than Nate, but even if he hadn't been, Zach would've felt very fucking small at that moment.

And it wasn't because he was standing two steps below.

"Uh…hi," he said, voice shaking, no matter how much he hated showing weakness in front of a Hornet. "Look, dude, I'm sorry to bother you so late, I just don't know what else to—can I talk to Mike?"

Garcia looked at him over the thick black rims of his glasses, with an expression that hovered between curiosity and pity, and said, "Come on in, Reed. I'll get him."

Zach followed him in, trying not to stare at either the

house or at Garcia. The entrance hallway had coatracks and a little space for shoes. Some photographs hung on the walls, and they weren't even crooked or poorly spaced. Everything was in its particular place. Garcia took him into the kitchen. It looked like it had been renovated recently, because everything was kind of new, but it was full of the kind of clutter that two busy people who weren't home often accumulated. There was a stack of wet dishes in the drying rack and a revolving spice rack Nate would have loved.

There was a whiteboard on the wall with a calendar and Zach immediately noticed that Mike's games and Garcia's games were marked off in green, days they were both home in blue, and some other dates in red that Zach wasn't sure about. The fridge was covered in mismatched magnets and pictures, of Garcia and Mike, a lot of shots of what looked like Garcia's family, and a few of Mike's. Two cats, one scruffy orange monster and one huge stately black cat, ambled through the room, as if to say, *this is our space, watch out.*

Mike sat at a small kitchen table covered in books and papers, typing something on his laptop. Garcia's computer was open across the table from him. Mike was reading some kind of textbook as he typed, and Garcia had notes from work, and the whole scene was so fucking domestic and shit that Zach wanted to cry again.

"Babe," Garcia said, rubbing Mike's shoulder, "we have a visitor."

Mike looked up and almost as quickly, stood. "Reedsy?"

"Dude, I'm… I'm really sorry to bother you this late, I just…"

"Uh, you're not bothering me," Mike said, and exchanged a glance with Garcia, who scooped up both cats in his arms and left them alone. "Do you—what the fuck, dude? You just vanished after the game, and you kinda played like shit. What the fuck is going on?"

Zach couldn't think of what to say, but he must have looked so shitty that Mike took him by the shoulder, guided him to the empty seat, and shoved him down into it.

"You gotta eat something. Here. Get your shit together while I get you some leftovers. Danny made it, and he's a great fucking cook."

"I, uh...don't really feel like eating."

"You're gonna fucking eat," Mike said, so firmly that the protest died in Zach's mouth. "And then you're gonna tell me what the fuck is wrong."

While Mike poked around in the fridge, Zach looked down at his laptop. It was some kind of composition assignment, and he asked, dazed, "Wait, are you doing *school*?"

Mike looked over his shoulder and his lip curled up in something that was almost a sneer or almost a smile. "Community college. Don't tell anyone on the team, okay? I got a reputation to uphold."

"Does *Bee* know?" Zach asked, distracted.

"Well, of course she does, but she's the only one. And you, now. But. Come on, we're not here to talk about me." He put a plate in front of Zach. It was a salad, but it was full of chickpeas and chicken and nuts and a ton of other roasted vegetables in some kind of spiced yogurt dressing. It smelled amazing. It was the kind of thing Nate would have cooked, and Zach felt that stinging in his eyes again.

"I don't know where to start. I just...couldn't be at home."

"Well, you can crash in our guest room if you gotta. Danny's heading out tomorrow morning, but I'll be home, so you won't have to leave super early."

Zach wanted to say *thank you* but instead put his head down in his arms on the table. He couldn't look up to see any judgment on Mike's face, and that was kind of Mike's default facial expression. "I've done something really fucking stupid, Mike. Like stupid even for me. So fucking, fucking stupid." Mike didn't say anything, but waited for him to go on, and after a few seconds of awkward, deafening silence, it was like the floodgates had opened and he couldn't stop them. "I kind of fell in love with someone, and I thought he felt the same way, but I was wrong, Mike. I was really fucking wrong and I… I don't…know what to…"

"Oh, *fucking Christ*," Mike said faintly. "Him? Is this your first—"

"What? No! I mean I've *fucked* guys; I've fucked a lot of guys before." Mike's face was doing something complicated and horrified across the table. "But this was different, I fucking love him, Mike, I really fucking love him, and he *doesn't*—"

He was vaguely aware that his voice was halting and ugly with barely choked-back tears. If he'd had any amount of self-control left he would've been super fucking embarrassed, but as it was, the only thing he could see was the dark crook of his elbow, and if he was actually crying, no one could see anything except his shoulders heaving. He could feel Mike's hand on his back, a comforting, solid presence, and that somehow made it worse, because *Nate* usually—

Nate wasn't here, though.

Why the fuck was Zach surprised, really? This was

how things always ended. Like, he was a good-looking guy, he was a lot of fun, but he wasn't the kind of person you *dated.* He wasn't the kind of person people liked to spend years dating. And that was fine, it was just how things were, he'd accepted that. He'd just thought, he'd just felt so *sure*, that the thing with Nate was different.

Oh, fuck.

He was definitely crying.

"Whoa, buddy. Um. Well. I—fuck."

"I'm sorry, I didn't mean to fucking drop this on you and ruin your fucking, your fucking night, I just didn't know who else to talk to." He finally looked up, and saw that Mike was staring at him.

"Zach," Mike said carefully. "Your dude…it's not…"

Zach put his head down again and could not control the hiccupping sob that escaped him.

"Oh, Jesus," Mike said, and then, "Wait, *what*? He *doesn't*?"

Zach actually felt deranged, like he was having an out-of-body experience and someone else was speaking through his mouth. "It was my first real relationship and I thought things were going well, and I was putting in the effort, it was, like, a fuckin' romance, dude, it was… it was so fucking good and then I, uh, I said something kind of stupid like a joke, and he definitely doesn't feel the same way. And now I'm gonna—not just dating, I'm gonna lose, I'm gonna lose *everything…*"

"You're *sure*? That he doesn't?"

"Mike, this is n-o-o-t helping."

"I'm sorry, I just…oh, fuck it, c'mere, buddy."

And that was how Zach found himself wrapped in Mike's wiry arms in what was, at first, an extremely awkward hug. Then Mike relaxed, and it was really nice to just have someone care enough to do that for him. That just made it worse because he thought about all of the times Nate had comforted him when he'd fucked something up, and he got choked up again. Jesus fucking Christ, thank god he hadn't had anything to drink. He could only imagine how he would have been acting. This was bad enough, and he was just delirious from grief and dehydration.

"Uh, first of all, this is like…normal. Kind of," Mike said carefully. "To feel like this, I mean."

"I never *had* feelings!" Zach wailed into his collarbone tattoos. "I mean, I never had bad feelings. Like this. It feels worse than getting traded from Montreal did, and I went on a, a, fucking two-week-long bender."

"Oh, Jesus," Mike said, again, faintly. "Well, I'm glad you came here instead."

"I just…fuck, Mike, I have to go back to…"

Mike disentangled Zach's arms with uncharacteristic gentleness. "I don't have any magic words for you, dude. It's gonna hurt, and it's gonna be really fucking bad. Probably for a while. And if this is what I thought it was then…it's not gonna be easy to get over. But you gotta do it, because we can't fuck this season up, man."

Zach laughed, although it was a choking kind of sob. "Super comforting, dude. Man. Thanks a lot."

Mike smiled at him for the briefest second. So fast you'd think you imagined it. "I'm trying my best. I mean, buddy, you came to *me* to comfort you? The fuck's wrong with you?"

Zach was laughing again, half-hysterical, half-exhausted. "Do you want the short list or the long list?" Mike patted him wordlessly on the shoulder, and Zach realized something he often forgot their first year on the team together, which was that Mike was actually a couple years older than he was. "I didn't want you to comfort me, I just thought maybe...you're an adult now, man, you've got your shit together, like, you're practically fucking married..."

"It was a rhetorical fuckin' question, bro," Mike mumbled, clearly embarrassed.

"Look at you," Zach hiccupped, "fucking college boy, pulling out your fancy college terms."

Mike dug his knuckles into Zach's head, and Zach didn't even fight back. "I *am* sorry, you know."

"Yeah," Zach said, and his voice sounded small and pitiful even to his ears, "I am too."

"C'mon. Tomorrow's another day. Eat something, drink some water, and sleep it off. You can stay as long as you want."

"Mike...thanks. Like...seriously, thank you."

"Fuck off," Mike said, refusing to meet his eyes. He slid back down into his own seat. "Let me know when you're done. I'm gonna work while you eat."

The sound of Mike typing at a steady pace lulled him into a calm almost as much as the dinner did. The food was really good, but by the time he was finished, Zach was so tired he almost fell asleep at the table. He let Mike lead him upstairs, and fell onto the guest bed, still fully clothed. When the orange cat nudged the door open and cuddled up next to him, he didn't even bother pushing it away.

He fell asleep like that, pulled into the dark by the sound of the low bass rumble of Garcia's voice the next room over.

* * *

Zach woke up feeling almost hungover, except he hadn't had anything to drink.

His phone said 9:55 a.m. and he said, *"Shit."* He almost never slept in this late, even on the team's off days. He had four missed calls from Nate to go with the text messages and finally looked at them. The first few were close together, then spaced out over the rest of the night.

Hey, where are you?

Your truck's gone.

Are you ok?

Zach?

Buddy?

The last text, sent at three in the morning, said, Seriously, Zach, I'm really worried. What's going on? Please tell me?

He swallowed hard and said, i'm fine. i just went to mike's house after the game.

The typing periods at the bottom showed up almost immediately, and Zach sighed. He didn't leave the phone open to see what Nate was typing back, because he didn't have the heart to answer it.

He found Mike downstairs in the kitchen, still working at the table, just accompanied by breakfast this time. It was weird seeing his teammate in this context, comfortable in his home, intently typing away at some kind of schoolwork.

When he'd first met Mike, his first impression had

been that the guy was a shy but intimidating asshole, which wasn't *untrue*. What he'd come to realize later was that Mike had a big fucking heart to go along with the dry sense of humor and devastating fists but made himself incredibly hard to get to know.

In retrospect, most of that made sense. But it was still a big change from the overaged rookie who'd been playing third pairing/7D and keeping secrets from the rest of the team to this guy, a pillar of the blue line and absolutely one of the guys, absentmindedly scratching a cat behind its ears in the kitchen he shared with his boyfriend.

"Uh… I want to apologize again…" Zach said, awkwardly, from the door.

"Reed, seriously, don't worry about it." Mike looked up at him, that half smile appearing briefly before it vanished again. "Been there."

Zach couldn't really picture Mike, who was probably the toughest person he knew, being anywhere near what Zach was doing last night.

His face must have reflected it, because Mike said, "If it makes you feel any better, one time a bartender cut me off. In *Boston*."

"What…the fuck?"

"Last year was a weird fucking year, dude."

Zach looked around at the kitchen again, at the pictures of Mike and Garcia on the fridge. In one of them, they were in a pool, playing with a little girl that Zach assumed was a relative of Garcia's. She rode on Mike's shoulders, hitting Garcia with a pool noodle like a jousting spear. "It seems like it worked out for you."

"Yeah, well… I dunno, man. Things change when you

don't expect them to. If you know how to ask for what you want."

He felt vaguely ill in the lowest part of his stomach, again, because there was really no way for things to change for the better for him. And there was especially no way that he could ask for what he wanted, not now. It might have been a joke, but it was close to the truth, and Nate had... Well, Zach had some small shreds of his pride left.

Mike cleared his throat. "There's coffee, and leftover eggs, if you don't mind 'em cold."

"Thanks," Zach said, and was momentarily overwhelmed with gratitude and sorrow, but after he saw Mike's face he said, "Don't worry, you're not gonna get a repeat of yesterday. I'm, uh... I'm good."

Mike's eyebrows were, at best, skeptical. "Okay."

"I am, I fucking promise. But this is... You're like, it's just blowing my mind, kind of? I had no idea, man. Your house is really nice, and you're in school, and you just seem...different."

Mike shut the laptop and shrugged. "Of course you had no idea. I mean, I got used to not sharing a lot. Because, you know."

Zach did know. There was a reason he didn't go around telling people every aspect of his business, even though he wasn't anywhere near as careful about it as he probably should have been. Mike had been even more careful, or afraid, because up until he'd sat everyone down in the locker room to tell them, Zach had had no fucking clue he was gay. "But you told everyone...?"

"Shit, I dunno. It's not like I was going to hide Danny from the fucking team. And it was kind of a relief, honestly. Like a weight off. Didn't have to hide, didn't have to lie. To them, at least, and then the rest of it, it's all on my terms if I want to do more. It was easier than I thought. No one was too shitty about it."

"I mean. Nate wouldn't have let them. Oh, *fuck*."

"Have some fucking breakfast and let's not talk about the Cap, eh?"

"Good luck," Zach muttered darkly. "I mean, *you* figured it out."

"Buddy, I hate to tell you, but if the rest of the team wasn't so fucking straight, *everyone* would've figured it out. It's not like you were really subtle."

"I was subtle!"

Mike was laughing, which was a sound Zach had only heard on a few occasions last season. More often this year. He had a really nice laugh, surprisingly warm. It made Zach want to smile too, even though he didn't really feel like smiling. "Bro. Come on. You couldn't be subtle if your life fucking *depended* on it."

"No, you're probably right. But come on, it's part of my charm."

Mike poured him a cup of coffee from the pot instead of answering. They drank the coffee in silence before Mike said, "So…what's the plan?"

"I dunno," Zach said, looking down into his cup. "I mean. I can't really stay here. The dogs would miss me. And it's not like I can avoid it forever. I gotta go home."

"You could, you know, talk about it."

"I can't fucking do *that*."

"It makes things a lot easier."

"I can't."

"Okay."

"Dude, I'm being serious."

"Okay!"

"So why can't you talk about it?"

"I just… I can't make things worse than they already are. I know if I talk to him about it I'm gonna put my fucking foot in it for sure. And it's not just me I have to worry about, Mike. It's the rest of the team."

Mike rubbed a finger against his temple. "It's probably not as bad as you're—"

"I'm just going to have to do the only thing I can do, which is pretend the last fucking three months of my life never happened." In one gulp, he downed the rest of his coffee and slammed the mug, for emphasis, down on the table.

Mike stared at him. "Zachary fucking Reed."

Zach stared back, determined, triumphant. "It's going to work. It has to. Trust me. I'm your alternate captain."

Mike continued to stare at him, but thankfully, did not add, *this is the least convincing speech I have ever heard in my life.*

Zach ate his eggs and drank the coffee Mike refilled for him, and winced, again, thinking about the way he'd acted the night before.

It wasn't completely out of his wheelhouse to lose his shit in response to some bad news. His epic bender after getting traded to Philly was still talked about in awed tones and memes on r/RoyalMontreal. But the intensity of what he knew was really grief still caught him off guard.

The more he thought about pretending the last three months of his life had never happened, the more it solidified. Because he wasn't just losing Nate romantically. He was probably going to lose his friendship too.

And Nate had been his best friend for years now.

And if he was going to admit that he was in love with his best friend, he might as well admit that he'd probably been in love with him from the very beginning.

Three fucking years. That was a lot to lose.

But he'd have to deal with it, one day at a time, because they were in the playoff hunt and they were in the Cup hunt and he didn't have any other choice.

He was going to do it.

He just had to get over Nate first.

Nate's all-consuming feelings of doom were often inaccurate and mostly driven by anxiety, but when Zach played probably the worst game he'd ever played in his entire life, disappeared afterward, and didn't answer any of Nate's calls or texts, he thought that probably this was one time he was absolutely right.

It was the first time since they'd known each other that Zach had done anything like that.

In all of this time he'd been worrying about it, he hadn't thought about how he'd actually feel when it *did* happen.

And now that it was here, he mostly just felt numb acceptance. Maybe the rest of it would hit later, but he'd spent so much time thinking *guys like you don't* get *to have things like this* that when he actually lost it, it just felt like the universe aligning back into the way that it was supposed to be. The way that it always did if he felt too happy, too optimistic, too excited about anything. It was the same thing as making the playoffs, only to get knocked out of them in the first or second round.

For the briefest moment he thought that maybe, maybe he was overreacting, maybe this wasn't the end of things after all, but when Zach didn't respond to *are you coming home?* even though he'd read it, Nate realized that whatever had happened wasn't just his imagination.

On autopilot, Nate went about his day without Zach, who was in Princeton at Mike's house.

It wasn't until now that Nate realized how much of his time he actually spent with Zach on a day-to-day basis. Even before Nate's spectacularly bad judgment in December, they'd gone to the gym together, carpooled to practices and games together, and spent a good portion of their nongame time just hanging around at either Zach's place or Nate's place or in hotel rooms.

It was the first time in a long time that he'd been alone.

He didn't want to bother Zach too much, because if Zach wanted space, then Nate would have to just respect that. It didn't make him feel better, but he didn't want to be a shitty friend, so. That was that.

So Nate did what he normally did when he felt like shit, which was throw himself back into work. He went to the gym and he did his usual workout twice, he called Coach Ford to discuss some issues they had been having with Belsky and Gags on neutral zone turnovers. He sharpened his skates himself on the machine at the rink, except that just made him think about Zach giving him the little skate sharpener, which made him feel off-kilter and out of sorts.

He cooked an entire week's worth of meals to put in the freezer for when he got home from road trips.

He went to his parents' house and cleaned the entirety of their small concrete backyard, sweeping and scrubbing the detritus that built up in heavy layers during the year. Trash that had blown in from the street, droppings from the crepe myrtle that was the bane of Nate's existence. He power-washed the brick-walled front of their house.

By the time it was dark and he was preparing for the game tomorrow, he had almost kept himself busy enough that he hadn't thought about it much at all. He lowered his aching body into his bed, which suddenly felt extremely large, and thought about how he hadn't heard from Zach at all that day, and wondered if he was still at Mike's or whether he'd gone home to the dogs or whether—

Stop it, his brain said.

Oh, now *you have a fucking opinion?*

You should've said something to him before this. Now it's too late.

Shut up.

It's too late, because you're a coward.

There were only so many times you could tell your brain to shut up before it became an exercise in futility.

Nate didn't sleep well that night.

The next day, he dressed for morning skate with that same feeling of dread. This was something he couldn't avoid, but if he got there first, before anyone else, then maybe he could just get out onto the ice without having to say anything to Zach.

Unfortunately, although he did beat Zach to the rink, he didn't beat Mike, who gave him a very long, very blank look and said, "Morning, Cap."

"Morning, Mike." His mouth felt very dry.

"Long night? You look tired."

"I, uh, never really sleep that well after a loss like that."

"Yeah," Mike said, his arms folded over his chest. "Me neither."

"Uh...is Zach okay?"

"Yeah."

"Yeah?"

"You should ask him yourself," Mike said, with a withering tone that made the tips of Nate's ears go red.

"I mean... I can't," Nate said, before he could stop himself.

"Jesus Christ, Cap." Mike shook his head and skated away from the wall without another word.

The practice didn't go much better than that. Coach wasn't exactly bag skating them, but he was going through the drills at a punishing speed he hadn't employed since the first year they were trying to adopt the system. Nate, who hadn't slept much the night before, struggled trying not to look too long at Zach, who wasn't in any better form than he'd been at the game.

"Reed!" Coach snapped. "Get your head together!"

"Sorry, Coach!"

"Do 'em again. Perfectly this time."

While they were watching the second group run through the drills, he stood next to Bee and kept half an eye on Zach, who was a little farther down the rink, talking to Mike. Bee and Mike kept exchanging little glances that made him wonder how much they'd guessed, or whether they'd talked about it.

Or whether they'd—*shut up*, Nate said to himself, for the umpteenth time that day.

After the next round of drills, Nate was sweating, not from the exertion. He stood next to Zach, who looked as casual and breezy as he ever looked.

“Uh, hey,” Nate said, softly enough that no one else could hear him.

“Oh, hey, Cap,” Zach said brightly. He was smiling his media smile again, empty and bland. There was absolutely no expression in his eyes. “How’s it going?”

Nate stared at him and Zach stared back. The smile never wavered. The sweat dripped down the back of his neck, his ears hot. He wanted desperately to say something, but he couldn’t think of what to say. He always had trouble thinking of the right words, but he never did around Zach. Not anymore. Not until today. All around them, the ambient noise of practice, usually comforting, felt overwhelming.

What came out of Nate’s mouth was: “Are we okay?”

“Peachy.”

“Are you…sure?”

“Why wouldn’t we be okay?” Zach asked. Smiling, and smiling, and smiling.

After the practice, Nate went home alone. He looked at his phone, but Zach hadn’t texted him. He knew, deep in the pit of his stomach, that things were over, that for whatever reason, it wasn’t ever going to be the same again.

When Zayde had died, Nate hadn’t known how to feel. It had been a hollow kind of pain, knowing that he should cry, but not being able to make himself do it. He so often felt overwhelmed by anxiety and emotions on a day-to-day basis, but there, in the biggest loss of his life so far, he had just felt numb and frozen. That had made him feel like shit too, like he’d somehow loved Zayde less than he thought he had. It was the same when Rachel had left. He’d basically just bag-skated himself at practice, pushing himself physically until his body did the work of feeling like shit for him.

He was numb and frozen now. He couldn't *afford* to fall apart. There was an entire team and an entire city that was counting on him. Just because he'd fucked things up with his best friend didn't change any of it.

Nate set the phone down, took a deep breath, and went to clean his bathrooms.

V.
SPRING

CHAPTER NINE

March

It was hard to think about how Old Zach would have handled this, because he was such a different person now that it was almost unimaginable. Like, yeah, sure, he'd never had a real relationship before Nate—this hadn't been a real relationship either, he had to remind himself—so he didn't know how a breakup would have gone. But he knew how he handled almost everything else back then, and that was: drown it in alcohol or other chemicals. It was easy not to care about your coach being pissed at you when you knew you were just going to get fucked up later and have an absolutely insane time partying. Or at least you were until the party wasn't fun anymore.

Zach was still deeply embarrassed by the two-week-long mess after getting traded. That one had ended with Jammer dragging him bodily out of a club and throwing him, fully clothed, into a cold shower to sober him up. Even if he'd wanted to, he couldn't afford to do anything like that now.

Usually when he was upset about something, he went to Nate and let himself be distracted that way. They'd spent a lot of time like that their first year, when the Cons were on the cusp of being good but weren't quite contenders yet, when they'd both had their shit to work through.

But now he didn't have Nate.

He did have his dogs. He took them for long walks in Fairmount Park, he spoiled them rotten with treats and grooming and new toys, and that filled up some of the time. He went out a few times for dinner with Mike after games, which was a surprising friendship he'd never really thought would develop given how prickly Mike had always been, but which he found he enjoyed a lot. It turned out that now that he'd settled down, Mike had a lot of thoughts about a lot of different things, and he was actually a pretty funny guy.

And then there was Gags.

He was doing okay on the ice. Cote hadn't cut his ice time in a while, and he was pretty solidly a consistent presence on the wing of the third line. But Zach couldn't shake the feeling that there was something else going on with him. He watched Gags carefully at the team dinners after games, but he seemed just fine there, eating as much as anyone could ask for, laughing along at jokes, chirping the other guys, the life of the party. He always had dark circles under his eyes, though, like he'd been in a fight and was getting over a black eye, even though he hadn't.

"You think Gags is good?" Zach asked Mike as they were getting ready for the game.

Mike was one of those guys who could tape his stick with his eyes closed, rotating it without looking like he had the entire rhythm memorized. Zach's question threw him off, tape uneven, and he muttered a curse. "I don't know. You think something's up?"

Zach shrugged. "Just a feeling. He looks really tired."

Mike glanced sideways to watch Gags, who was tap-ing his socks. "I dunno. The league's really an adjustment from minors, you know? We're getting toward the end of the season. Could just be that—tired."

"Yeah," Zach said. But he didn't feel convinced.

"I mean, he could have shit going on you don't know about," Mike said, shaking his head. "I sure did my rookie year."

"Yeah?"

"Dude. I was *completely* in the closet, and I felt like shit about it and my spot on the team. I'd only ever hook up on the road and then I'd, you know. Beat myself up about it after. I couldn't even tell Bee about it. It was…a pretty bad time."

Zach stared at him. "I had no idea."

"Well, yeah, that's the point," Mike said. He shrugged. "Just saying, everyone's got their shit. Some of us are better at hiding it than others."

Zach thought about Mike's rookie year, the dead-eyed way he'd thrown himself into fights, the way he had seemed to relish them, even or especially when he was getting the shit kicked out of him. "Or maybe sometimes we're just really bad at recognizing it."

Mike shot him a glance sideways, his dark eyes dancing with laughter. "And now he gets it."

"Do you think I should talk to him?"

"That's your call, bud. You know him better than I do." He frowned, watching Gags and Belsky, sitting next to each other in their stalls, both looking at the same iPhone screen. "I can tell you that if someone had tried to talk to *me* my rookie year, I probably would've bitten their fucking head off."

"Gags doesn't seem like that kind of guy," Zach said doubtfully. "But maybe I'll wait and see."

"It's good you noticed, though. But you just gotta trust your gut."

Zach laughed, too loud in the locker room. It felt a little wheezy toward the end. "Bro, my gut is the fucking worst. It's *always* wrong."

Mike rolled his eyes. "So do the opposite. I don't know. I'm going to community college, I'm not fuckin' Yoda."

"No," Zach agreed. He ran his hand through his hair. He didn't know what to do about Gags the same way he didn't know what to do about the rest of his life. He didn't want to push where it wasn't wanted, and he didn't want to let something slip. He'd just have to wait and see.

Sometimes, Nate thought about texting Rachel and asking her how the hell she had figured him out. What she had seen that he hadn't, when she had noticed it, why she hadn't told him anything. Maybe it was a completely fruitless worry. Even if she had told him, it wouldn't have made anything easier in the end, because he probably wouldn't have been ready to accept that what he felt about Zach was anything except a really intense friendship, the kind that wasn't at all unusual in hockey.

He still had her number, but there wasn't anything to be gained from reaching out to her. They had broken up amicably enough, considering the length of their relationship and the way it had ended. It had been icy, but amicable. Still, they hadn't spoken since she'd packed her bags except to arrange details about things like utility transfers and when she needed to come to pick up the rest of her stuff. He wondered what she would do if he reached out to ask *when did you realize?*

But it was ultimately a useless endeavor. Nate had fucked everything up, somehow, and he didn't know how to fix it and probably never would. He'd fucked things up with Rachel and now he'd fucked things up with Zach, and that was just his own fault, for being shit at relationships, for being so deeply in his own head that he couldn't see what was going on in front of him until it was too late. That was the thing about Nate: he always fucked things up.

That was a sobering thought that stuck with him as he went through the motions of his daily routine. He went to the rink, and he came home. He worked with the coaching staff to discuss things they needed to implement with the forwards' d-zone coverage. He talked at length with Belsky about adjusting to the grind of the season and the importance of not pushing through things when you weren't feeling it, that it was okay to take a maintenance day if he needed it.

"Uhh, okay," Belsky said, looking at him like he was crazy after Nate brought it up. "I'm not injured, my wrist is just a little sore. I'm managing it."

"I'm serious," Nate said. They were sitting on the bench at the practice facility, watching the defensemen working through a small-ice drill. "I know the general league isn't always like that, but here we don't want you playing through shit if you have something going on."

Belsky laughed. He had a pleasant laugh, an unusually deep voice for a relatively young guy, booming and carrying. "Okay, Dad."

Nate sighed. He'd gotten used to the rookies calling him Dad, even if he didn't really like to hear it. It was a good thing they trusted him as a captain, but he wasn't even technically in his late twenties yet, and it made him feel so fucking old. And then it made him feel like shit, because if he was a real father figure for them, shouldn't he have figured out his shit by now, instead of imploding his personal life around his own head?

Because he was really imploding his personal life around his own head.

He had to sort things into life before Zach and life with Zach and life after Zach, and if he was being honest, life after Zach was pretty bad. Every time he came home to his empty house, devoid of Zach or the noise of the dogs, he was reminded of how he'd fucked things up. Every time he went to practice and couldn't joke around with Zach during the little pauses between drills, he was reminded of how he'd fucked things up. He'd squirt the water from the bottle into his mouth and think about how Zach used to tease him when he did it. And it was even worse when he was playing.

The thing about having linemates was that by the end of the season, you should have developed chemistry. The key to a successful line was knowing how the other guys would think, being able to anticipate where they would be. When you played together long enough, it was automatic, about as close to a psychic link as you could get without being an X-Man or something. It was fucking weird that he could still do that with Zach, but he couldn't talk to him off of the ice, couldn't spend any time with him, couldn't talk to him about his concerns about the team or the fact that he thought maybe Belsky was hiding an injury and the training staff hadn't picked up on it.

They were on a weird kind of road trip, first to Carolina and then to Pittsburgh, where they would be playing their perennial rival and the defending Cup champions. Zach usually sat next to him during road travel, but today, he passed right by and went to the back of the plane, where he settled into a group of four seats turned to face each other with Bee, Mike, and Netty. He didn't look Nate's way.

Nate ended up sitting alone, which was fine. It gave him time to update the Google Doc with his scouting reports for the Oaks, who had been having some issues with goalie injuries, and his notes on the Hornets' defensive depth—they had lost Garcia in the offseason, of course, but had picked up another veteran right-shot defenseman in free agency before the season started. All in all it was a wash, particularly considering they'd had the short offseason post-Cup hangover that a lot of teams had had, but by this time in the season it had evened out. Toward the end of an eighty-two-game year, everyone was starting to get banged up.

Everyone was exhausted.

Nate felt exhausted too, heading out onto the ice to play another game at Zach's side without being able to actually talk to him outside of the usual shorthand of yelling shit like *off* or *got time* or *one on.* Every warmup was torture; they used to mess around during those too, flipping pucks at each other, pushing and shoving behind Mäkelä's net, squirting each other with water or Gatorade.

Sally's line took the opening face-off because his winger, Ben Meyer, was from Raleigh, and the coaching staff were kind enough to give a little nod to him on a homecoming game.

So Nate watched the first shift from the bench, fingers white-knuckled around his stick. Mäkelä froze the puck and the whistle blew; Nate jumped over the boards to take the defensive zone draw with Zach and Bee. It was Zach's weak side, technically, but he'd been practicing taking those draws on the backhand—so it wasn't even really his weak side anymore. And it had the added benefit of the curve facing the way you wanted to dig the puck.

Nate sighed when he saw him settle into the familiar posture. It meant the puck would probably get shoved back Nate's way, but also just served as another stupid reminder of why he was so fond of Zach. All of the small details of the game that he studied, that he tinkered with. For someone who was constantly making jokes about how dumb he was, Zach was a *smart* hockey player. He had good hockey IQ, but he also read a lot, watched a lot, stole a lot of things from other guys. He'd noticed one of the centers on the Mariners doing it and had been intrigued enough to practice.

The ref dropped the puck, and Zach was already moving. The key to the face-offs was muscling in early, but not early enough that you'd get thrown out of the circle. Zach had the puck on the curve of his stick before the Oaks center could react, and whipped it back to Nate, who was in the process of using his shoulder to shove the winger he was covering out of the way and gain possession. The way the three of them still moved as a unit, Bee higher up the ice to accept the stretch pass, Zach streaking down the middle to follow, all of it was the same as it always was.

Nate was able to turn off his brain for a little, concentrate only on the game. Moving his feet. Getting pucks to the net. Toward the end of the first, the Cons were up 2-1, a close enough game that they had to be careful but a lead nevertheless. One of the Oaks' forwards—Armstrong?—tried to slam him into the boards as they battled for the puck, but Nate probably had twenty pounds on the guy. So he didn't go anywhere, barely even got knocked an inch sideways. His first mistake there was probably laughing, but he couldn't help it. It was always funny when a guy just bounced off of him.

Armstrong's face went red and he snapped, "Shut the fuck up, Singer, it's not my fault your fat ass ain't easy to move," while he put his shoulder into Nate's side.

The thing was that Nate was used to hearing trash talk on the ice. He was used to being called a woman, a pussy, various and less creative slurs about his sexuality that had been the norm for guys trying to get a rise out of you from mites onward. He'd been called the k-word, once, and that had been the only time he'd ever even considered fighting. Logan Beaulieu had gotten there first, and he hadn't had to make the choice for himself.

He was used to all of that, as shitty as it was.

Still, this time…the words got under his skin.

On the bench, instead of paying attention to the ice and the line changes, he thought about dropping in the draft rankings because there were concerns about his *conditioning*. He thought about feeling tongue-tied and awkward in locker rooms from the time he was ten and aware that he was so much bigger than everyone else there. He thought about the way Rachel had looked at him, sharp and knowing, the first time he'd taken his shirt off, like everything about him suddenly made sense. He thought about feeling like it was too good to be true when Zach was actually interested in hooking up with him—even though he didn't look like he had looked as a teenager anymore, they were in such different leagues. He thought about how Zach had abruptly decided he wasn't interested in hooking up with Nate anymore and he didn't even know why and—

"Cap?" Bee asked. "What's wrong?"

There wasn't a whole lot of time to talk on the bench

and this wasn't something he wanted to talk about on or off of it. "Armstrong was chirping me a bit," he said. "I should just let it go. Sometimes it's easier than others."

Bee's face instantly darkened. "He didn't—"

"No, not anything like that," Nate said hastily, because he didn't want her fighting.

Bee was unfortunately used to dealing with that shit too. The team stuck up for her whenever they could, but she could also take care of herself. The worst of it had happened in her rookie season, before the rest of the league had learned that not only could she *play*, she would put her fist into your teeth if she had to. And that she had an entire team of guys behind her who'd do the same.

Those same guys, and Bee, would have stuck up for him too. But it was just chirping, it wasn't even a nasty one as far as those things went. It wasn't even that bad. It wasn't worth getting anyone hurt over. It just happened to be the particular knife that slipped perfectly between Nate's ribs.

"Well, if he does," Bee said, patting his glove with hers, "you let me know."

"Thanks, Bee."

She followed up with him after the game too, trailing after him after they had finished with the showers and the media availabilities and the cooldown and the quick meal. She was still munching on a granola bar, a weirdly childlike gesture, and he thought how it was easy to forget sometimes that she was still only in her early twenties.

"It's not like you to get so rattled about some chirps," she said, when he didn't say anything but just let her follow along.

"I've been, uh…having kind of a rough few months. Things kind of stick when they shouldn't, you know?"

"Um, about that."

Nate wished that the parking lot was closer because he knew what was coming and he didn't want to deal with it. He didn't say *what about it*. He didn't say anything.

Bee didn't give him the reprieve he'd been looking for. "I mean, are things okay? With you and Zachary? You've always been so close and if you had a falling-out for whatever reason, I think...well, I think it is important to the team that we actually face it and talk about it. Because you two are very important to the team. And also to me."

Nate wanted to wither into nothing. Curl up and die. Go sprinting down the hallway and leave her in the dust. Anything would be better than Bee's earnest face and concerned looks. Instead, he said, "Uh, Bee, I can't really, I... Things are...complicated."

"Try me," Bee said bluntly.

For a second Nate thought about just blurting it all out, telling her all of his secrets. Even though he'd figured out things about his sexuality that hadn't made any sense before, it wasn't like he'd actually *told* anyone. On top of everything else, holding that in had been weirdly and uncharacteristically lonely. The only person who knew was Zach, and that was the whole can of worms. It would have been nice to tell Bee, who he trusted not to be a dick about it, considering she was best friends with Mike and had been the first person *he'd* come out to. But it wasn't just Nate's own secrets that were at stake here. It was Zach's too.

"Bee, I just can't," he said, hating himself for not being able to be brave and do it.

"Mon capitaine, we won this game, but our line is *not* working the same way. And if we are going to win the

Cup this year, then we have to be operating at top capacity. Can you just tell me what the *hell* is going on? It really isn't like the two of you to have a fight."

They'd never had a fight—not a real one, anyway—since Zach had gotten traded to Philly and Nate had gotten to know him. He'd been reserved and a bit standoffish at first, taking everything the wrong way, but Nate had won him over, somehow, and then the real Zach had started to emerge. And since then, they'd had periods of awkwardness, like when Zach had had that girlfriend last year, but never anything like this.

"We're not fighting," Nate said. It was a terrible lie and Bee clearly didn't believe him, but he was saved by the fact that the rest of the team was starting to trickle out of the visitors' locker room and head down the hallway toward them. Already he could hear the whoops of laughter as Netty had Gags in a headlock, the protests as Gags flailed his arms, trying to get a blow in.

"Okay," Bee said, "but you know, if you want to talk. I am here."

Nate thought for a second about telling her the truth. *I fell in love with Zach and then I fucking ruined it somehow, because I ruin everything I touch.* He thought about the rest of the team hearing it.

He said, "Yeah. Thank you. I'll take you up on it."

CHAPTER TEN

April

Nate should have been satisfied.

The Cons finished the season with the lead in the division and a momentum that they would desperately need to keep going. The Hornets had struggled enough in the post-Cup season that they had the wildcard spot, which meant that for the third year in a row, the Cons would have to get through them to make it to the Cup.

There were a few other surprises: the Boston Beacons had missed the playoffs for the first time in almost a decade after suddenly taking a leap off of a cliff around the middle of the season and finishing below .500, again for the first time in a decade. The Scouts, on the other hand, had made the playoffs for the first time in a few seasons thanks to stellar goaltending and a strong defensive performance.

In the first round, the Cons would be playing the first wildcard, the New York Railers, which always promised to be an unpleasant grind. The Railers counted on smothering you with defense, but they had hot and cold streaks with scoring. Especially if they were on a cold streak, it was a winnable series. He should have been satisfied.

He should have been satisfied, but of course he would never be fully satisfied until they won the Cup. Two seasons ago had been the heady, overwhelming euphoria of making the playoffs for the first time in years, last year had been the heartbreak of missing it when they had been *so* fucking close, and this year...what was this year? He was afraid to try to look into the future, like that might jinx it, somehow.

But no matter what *actually* happened, Nate was keenly aware that this year was the prove-it year. Gordon Smith, the Cons' general manager, had walked it back after last year. Given them all another chance. Despite the second-round exit, there hadn't been any major trades. The core was still there, and it was only guys on expiring contracts who didn't fit the timeline and hadn't been producing as expected that had gone in free agency. Nate and Zach and Bee, Mike and Lindy and Graham, all of them were still here. Mäkelä and Socks were still here. They had the chance to do it as a group.

If they *could* do it as a group.

It somehow didn't feel like a group anymore, not when there was still the gaping distance between him and Zach, not when the rest of the team was still dancing awkwardly around it, like Sally's kid had spilled Legos all over the floor.

Sometimes Nate thought the guilt was actually going to eat him alive, that they had this chance and that he had ruined it. The group was still a group, but it wasn't the same at all, and he didn't know how to fix it. It was *his* job as the captain to hold the team together, to motivate them and keep them going, but all he had done was to act selfishly to get things he'd wanted, things he'd *known* were a terrible idea but had wanted too much to think with his head.

If the team didn't make it through the playoffs, it would be all his fault.

So no. Nate couldn't be satisfied.

He went to the rink and he talked to the coaches and he made sure the rookies were doing the things they needed to do the same way he always had. But it was all empty. It didn't mean anything. He knew he was a fraud; he knew he had fucked up, and he couldn't fix it.

"Singer," Coach said, after practice.

"Yes, Coach?" Nate asked, unsure.

"Can we talk in my office?"

"Uhh...sure?"

"Great," Coach said. He wasn't smiling.

The coach's office was just like any other room in the Frank. He'd chosen it for its proximity to the dressing room and the players, and it was clear that he'd been very utilitarian about that choice. It still had the kind of cinderblock walls, painted white, that gave it an institutional feel, like a hospital or a prison. Rather than personal decorations, the room was filled instead with notes and books and as many whiteboards as the walls could hold. All of them were covered in diagrams, notes, and the depth charts. Cote's desk itself felt almost like an afterthought, buried in the corner out of sight.

Although Cote shut the door behind him, he didn't go to sit down at his desk. He paced around the middle of the room instead, arms folded over his chest. He was a handsome man in his late forties, but when he was frowning at Nate like that, he looked years older.

"Uh," Nate said after a minute, "Coach, do you want to tell me what this is about?"

"I was going to ask you the same damn question," Coach said, brusquely. He didn't sound mad, just disappointed. "What the hell's been going on out there?"

"I don't understand," Nate said, even though he knew all too well.

"You're playing like shit, to put it bluntly. And the room is fucking rotten."

Nate opened and closed his mouth and wondered whether everyone had figured it out. Whether he was that fucking obvious. Nate respected the coach, of course. Cote was the one who had decided that Nate had it within him to be the captain. But their relationship had never been like that: they weren't *friends*. This wasn't something he could confide in him.

"Uhhh… I don't understand," he said, finally.

"Whatever issue you and Reed are having, I need you to get the fuck over it. We're starting the first round of the playoffs this week and I can't afford to have my leadership group fractured like this. You're hurting the *team*."

The guilt was overwhelming, nauseous and sick. A confirmation of all of the worst things he'd suspected about himself. "I know," he said quietly. "I'm sorry."

"Look. We're all adults here. I know you have experience mediating conflicts between team members. It was a damn good job you did here your first year when Morin was having trouble. But I need you to figure this the fuck out, Singer. This isn't the kind of team we can take into the playoffs. It's just not going to work."

"I understand," Nate said, swallowing down bile. "I'll fix it."

"See that you do."

His mom called on his way out into the hall. Nate frowned at the phone and double-clicked the button on the side to send it straight to voice mail.

It didn't make him feel any better.

Zach remembered what it had been like his first year in Philly, when they'd made the playoffs for the first time in five years and then promptly shit the bed because Bee and Mäkelä had broken up and both of them were suffering. He almost wanted to laugh hysterically because here he was, two seasons later, and he was going to end up dooming the team exactly the same way, without even meaning to. He was truly trying to keep it the fuck together, because the playoffs were so long if you were able to make a deep run, but he couldn't.

His stall was still next to Nate's, and since they'd broken up, every time after a game, every time they changed, he regretted that placement. He tried not to look at Nate's familiar body, the way he knew Nate's abdominal muscles would clench and shiver under his hands, or how soft the hair on his powerful thighs actually was. Nate never looked at him during those times and Zach knew the silence was probably as loud as a scream to the rest of the team.

He should probably start trying to pretend that things were fine. He should probably go back to making jokes with Nate the way he used to, tease him until he turned red and couldn't meet Zach's eye. But he couldn't. They'd just dropped the first game of the first round by a disappointing score of 2-1, and every time he thought about it, he knew it was his fault.

This close to Nate it felt like all of the hair on the back of his arms was standing up, electrified by the proximity, a magnetic current running between them. Nate, who studiously refused to look at him while the reporters went around the room for the scrum. They were converged around Netty now, on the opposite side of the round of stalls.

"Can we—at least pretend things are normal?" Zach said, before he could stop himself. He'd managed to keep it quiet, at least, so only Nate could hear. "In front of everyone else?"

Nate lifted his head slowly and stared at him. His eyes were that fathomless blue that used to remind Zach of the ocean in Tulum but now just looked cloudy, shadowed by the dark circles under his eyes.

"If that's what you want," Nate said, after a moment.

"It's just, it's just been really tough. To make things go right around here. When we aren't even talking," Zach found himself babbling, even while his brain was screaming *shut the fuck up, you fucking idiot* at him. Nate was looking at him still, with that sad, serious expression on his face. There was absolutely no way this could end in anything that wasn't disaster. But the playoffs were here, and they had already lost a game and he had to *try*.

"I… We can try. At practice. But Zach, I just… I can't," Nate said. He was looking at his feet again, bruised where he'd blocked a bad shot with his skate and more than visible through the slides he was wearing. He swayed a little in place, like his body wanted to magnetically orient itself toward Zach's, before he caught himself and pulled back. "I'm not good at pretending."

"I'm not either, but…we can't do to the team what

Bee and Mäkelä did my first season here, Nate. I won't be responsible for that."

Whatever Nate had been about to say was lost when they both noticed that the beat reporters had finished up with Netty and were turning toward their end of the half circle of stalls. Nate swallowed any words that might have been on his tongue and looked at them like he was about to face a gallows and executioner.

Pretty much any other time, Zach would have stayed with him, backed him up without thinking about it. Now his instinct was to melt into the shadows and flee. It was a cowardly fucking feeling, and he kind of hated himself for it. That was something that Old Zach would've done, caring more about himself than about his teammate. His brother.

With a huge sigh, Zach took one step to the side so the bright lights from the cameras weren't shining right in his face and waited, just in case Nate needed the assist.

Nate's eyes darted sideways to look at him, just for a second, registering that he hadn't left after all. A tight smile creased his mouth before it disappeared. And then he turned back to the beats, like Zach wasn't even there, and they just—had to go on like that.

Nate hadn't known how to react when Zach had asked him to just pretend, at least when they were at the rink. He hadn't lied when he had said that he wasn't any good at pretending. He was probably the worst person ever when it came to pretending things were normal. Maybe it was anxiety, but also, maybe he was just that obvious about his feelings.

The thing was that Zach was *right*. Coach was *right*. They were hurting the team by acting like this, and if he could have been a less selfish, braver person, he would have been able to get his shit together and just pretend. But he was himself, and he was a fucking mess.

The first round of the playoffs started. They scraped together a win against the Railers in Long Island, and if they could manage another one, they would keep the home ice advantage for the series. But it hadn't been a win that felt *good.* It wasn't *easy.* The plentiful offense that had carried them through large parts of the season was worn down by the Railers' neutral zone trap, by the clutch and grab of the playoffs. There was a time when the Cons had been known as the Broad Street Bullies, but that time was many decades in the past. They were still a weird, scrappy underdog team, but they'd lost a lot of height and a lot of weight and sheer nastiness in the process.

Gags, for example, was getting absolutely bullied out there. The bigger Railers' defensemen were targeting him on every shift, and he didn't have an answer for it except popping right back up and back checking furiously to recover the puck. It happened: it was one of the rites of passage for younger players. He had been on the ice for both of the goals against, but that wasn't anything to be ashamed of. Again: a rookie rite of passage. But Gags was… Nate didn't know how to describe it except that it felt off.

Gags was as full of nervous energy as he usually was, but he seemed too twitchy, laughing too loud. He kept touching one of the bruises on his arms, like he was surprised it was there, and when Netty tried to sling an arm around him in commiseration, Gags wrenched out of the embrace and said, "I'm gonna go back to my room."

Nate checked in on him in the hotel after they took the bus back. He was rooming with Belsky, who Nate had run into heading downstairs to buy a late-night snack from the concierge. That was good: he wanted to talk to Gags alone. When he knocked, he could hear something drop, like Gags had hit something or thrown it against the wall. Or maybe fallen off the bed. Some scrambling.

"Uhhh, one sec!" Gags said, coughing.

"It's just me," Nate said. "Singer."

"I know, I'm coming, just—"

The door opened. The hotel room looked like any other rookie's room, and Nate smiled to see it. Gags's stuff was strewn all over the place like his suitcase had exploded on the hotel desk, while Belsky's was all neatly folded and in separate little dividers inside the case itself, his dirty laundry separated out into a bag. Both of their beds had the rumpled, disarrayed look that hotel beds got when hockey players came home from the rink at weird times to nap and missed the housekeeping schedules. All of that was normal.

Gags, on the other hand, looked kind of ill, his pupils huge and his face flushed and sweaty. "What's up, Cap?"

"I just…wanted to check on you and make sure things were going okay," Nate said. It was hilarious, really, that he was doing this. He wondered who captained the captain, who would come to *him* and check in on him to make sure he was sleeping and wasn't moping around after his center.

"Why wouldn't everything be okay?" Gags asked. He sat down on the bed, mock-casually.

"Uh, you were just taking kind of a beating out there, and I just wanted to make sure you weren't beating yourself up in here."

"I'm fine, Cap," Gags said. He looked like shit, really: he had a black eye, but the rest of his face was gaunt and shadowed, like he hadn't been sleeping enough. His mouth was turned down at the corner and his eyes, pupils aside, were kind of bloodshot. He was fidgeting still, his leg bouncing nervously up and down so much that the TV, loose in its moorings where it was screwed into the bureau, rattled a little as he did it.

"You seem a bit jumpy?" Nate said, arms crossed over his chest. He felt like bouncing his leg too. He wasn't good at this shit, even though he felt obligated to try. "I just wanted to tell you that what's going on out there—getting targeted, getting knocked down—it's not your fault. You've been playing really well and it's a testament to that that the other team is going after you specifically like that. No one blamed you for that goal, you know?"

"Um. I mean, I know," Gags said, and swiped his hands through his sweaty hair.

He sniffed, like his nose was running and he was trying to suck it in. His eyes darted toward the door, as if he was half expecting Belsky to walk back through it. He was clearly hiding something and for a moment, Nate wondered if he'd, like, interrupted something he hadn't been supposed to, if Belsky and Gags—but that was an insane way to think. Just because *he* hadn't had any self-control around his teammate didn't mean that anyone else was like that. Statistically it was almost impossible.

"I won't keep you any longer," he said, feeling the red flush starting to rise up his neck and the sweat prickle at the back of it. "I just wanted to check in and let you know that no one is expecting anything more from you than you're already giving."

Gags's face softened almost imperceptibly. "Thanks,

Cap. I really—I appreciate all of your little chats, you know? But I'm fine. *Really.*"

"Okay," Nate said, trying not to sound too doubtful.

"Good night," said Gags, and rubbed his eyes.

Nate walked down the hall to his own room, alone, feeling once again like he was missing something really *fucking* important.

The Cons managed to grind out win after win against the Railers, although the series ended up closer than Zach would have liked. Bee had scored a few clutch goals. Sally had been playing his shutdown role to perfection, frustrating even the largest of the Railers' forwards. But it still took them to six games to clinch it. And after that, they would play the Carolina Oaks, and then there were the Conference finals, and then, if they had managed to get through it, the Cup finals. He couldn't afford to be tired, despite the brutal, bone-crushing pace of playing against one of the oldest and toughest teams in their division.

They had a few days off to recover, and Zach should have been using it to recover. Somehow, he just couldn't fucking sleep.

It was funny, like breaking up with Nate had just popped the seal off all of Zach's bad memories of Montreal. It was funny mostly because at the time he'd been there, he hadn't even had any idea that they'd be bad memories. As far as Zach had been concerned, at least at first, he'd been having the time of his life, playing hockey and partying it up and getting his dick wet every chance he could. It had been like a buffet: everyone was eager to line up to give him what he wanted, whether that was access to the best dance clubs, the most exclusive bars, the best drugs, or a warm bed or cold bar bathroom or wherever it happened to be.

Zach had been so young that staying out all night and then waking up early to go to practice hadn't made a dent in his quality of play, or so he'd thought. By the end of his time there it had started to feel like a bubble, expanding further and further until the skin was so thin it would burst. Until it finally had.

That had been a rude fucking wakeup call and he had struggled to get his shit together in the offseason so he could show up at training camp with the Cons and prove Rejean Poulin, the general manager of the Montreal Royal, *wrong*. He felt he'd done a decent job of that, but it had been an unpleasant few months, constantly second-guessing everything he'd done and every decision he'd made. It had really been Nate's friendship that had helped ease him onto the team for real, helped cement him as an integral part of the roster and make him feel less like a cast-off fuckup and more like…well, like a real person.

But without Nate, Zach woke up from dreams that he would have enjoyed all those years ago but now felt a little more like nightmares. Sweaty encounters in dim bar bathrooms. Not the rush of coke so much as the drawn-out energy and joy of being around his friends. Wasted and pushing his way out of the sunroof of a rental car. A sloppy blowjob, the wet mouth of a girl whose face he couldn't even remember. Now when he realized what his subconscious was doing, he woke up feeling wrung-out and guilty, like he was betraying his current self by remembering what his past self had done.

He didn't have any choice but to shake it off, try to concentrate on the task at hand. They had to win the game in Philly to keep the home ice advantage, and they couldn't afford to go out in the first round or second round again. The "rebuild" was way ahead of schedule, so maybe Gordon Smith wouldn't blow everything up immediately the same way he would have if they had been trying and failing for a decade.

But he didn't want to find out.

He had all of this shit knocking around in his head all of the time now, and he wondered how Nate had dealt with it all of those years. They'd talked about it before, the way his anxiety worked, the way his brain was constantly yelling at him with all kinds of doom and gloom. Zach had only been experiencing that for a few weeks—not that it was anxiety, but the general inability to shut off his own brain when he wanted to—and he felt like shit. The fact that Nate performed at the level he had all of these years...it was kind of mind-boggling.

Zach suited up for the first game against the Oaks, thinking about how he had practically begged Nate to just pretend that things were normal. That had been going great too, by the way. Even now he had to shrink his own body into itself because knowing Nate was a few inches away, half naked and getting ready to play, made the hair on his arms stand on end. It was a stupid thing to ask, the kind of wishful thinking that didn't mean shit in the real world.

He frowned, watching Gags and Belsky across the circle. Gags was really looking rough these days, the dark circles under his eyes practically caving in. He sniffed and wiped his hand across his nose, his leg jiggling, bouncing up and down nervously, and something in Zach's head clicked into place, and he thought, *oh*, shit.

That's what Zach had looked like toward the end of his time in Montreal.

"Hey, Gags," Zach said, while the rest of the guys were still getting ready. "Come out in the hallway with me?"

"Huh?" Gags asked, blinking. "Why?"

"Just want to chat about something, okay?"

Although he looked both terrified and suspicious, all at the same time, Gags complied. They went out into the hall, the lope of skates on the dressing room floor and then the rubber-lined halls. Gags shot a glance sideways at him but didn't say anything immediately.

"So we've talked before," Zach said.

"Yeah," Gags agreed.

"And did Nate talk to you before?"

"Yeah. And I said—"

"And you said everything's fine, right?"

"Because it is," Gags said, his chin jutting out stubbornly.

"Well, I'm just going to make some suggestions. And you can tell me if I'm wrong," Zach said, taking a deep breath. A few seasons ago he never would have trusted himself to handle anything like this. He still didn't really trust himself to handle anything like this, but Gags was *their* rookie, and he needed to do things that scared the shit out of him occasionally if the team was going to be successful. "I think maybe you're, um…more than a little nervous. When it comes to like, playing the games, the social stuff."

Gags stared at him, dark brown eyes wide, before he got himself back under control and shuttered the expression down protectively. "I—"

"Nah. Just let me keep going. That's not really unusual."

"I just...when I think about how much is riding on this, and maybe getting sent down, and now it's the playoffs, I get like... I can't *sleep* at night sometimes. My brain just doesn't shut up ever."

Zach exhaled. "And, uh, maybe we could talk about the ways you're finding to shut it up."

Gags flushed red almost immediately. "I don't know what you're talking about."

"Uh-huh," Zach said, and then shrugged. "Look, I'm not trying to judge you or anything. In some ways I *was* you, my first couple of seasons. For different reasons, but I was, uhhh...well, you know why I got traded. I thought I had control over things I didn't actually have any control over, and it bit me in the ass *hard*."

"I don't..." Gags said, but he couldn't meet Zach's eye.

"I know the coke sniffle. Again. From personal experience. And if it's at the rink, like...you know that's serious. We have some talking to do outside of the rink."

For a second he wondered whether Gags was going to bolt, then and there. There wasn't anywhere to go, really. They both had to get ready for the game, and it wasn't like it wouldn't be incredibly noticeable if a guy in full hockey gear went clattering down the aisles and rows of seats in the rink.

"Like I said, Gags. Not judging. Just... I've been there, and it's not any fucking fun."

Gags exhaled another breath. His messy red hair flipped up, briefly, with the force of it. "It's just—I can only get my brain to shut up sometimes. And to get myself tired enough to sleep eventually or, like. To play. I need my brain to shut up."

Zach reached out to gently brush his thumb against

Gags's cheekbone, right below the deep shadows beneath his eyes. "From where I'm standing, it doesn't really look like you're getting any sleep to begin with."

Gags looked down at his skates. There was a long pause. Finally, he said, "No."

"Bud, you could've talked to me any time, you know?"

"I was just… I'm just a rookie. I can be sent down any time. I didn't want to fuck up my career if I said something I shouldn't—"

"The team isn't like that. *I'm* not like that. We just wanna make sure you're okay, buddy."

"What are you going to tell Coach?"

"I'm not. Not right now, anyway. I think you should talk to Cap after the game when we can get a chance. And then we can figure out what would be the best way to go from here. Does that sound fair?"

Gags frowned, his mouth turning down a little, like he was thinking through his options. Something softened in his face again. "Yeah. You know, Bells told me I shouldn't worry about talking to you guys, about making it worse, but…"

"Yeah, well, next time? Listen to your buddy, you dumb fuck." He punched Gags in the shoulder, and together, they walked back into the locker room.

CHAPTER ELEVEN

May

They won the first game against the Oaks, and it wasn't particularly close. Nate wasn't sure what had happened, but it was like things that hadn't been clicking suddenly settled into place. The Oaks were a fast team, but if you rattled them, the defense kind of fell apart. They had one top pair guy that anchored everything, but beyond him, it was easy to poke holes in the coverage, to find the open ice and get the greasy goals netfront, the kind of goals that had been Nate's bread and butter for years.

Gags still played like he had a monkey on his back waving a paw in his eyes to distract him, but the third line didn't sink them, even if their possession stats were so far underwater that they would have needed a James Cameron expedition to dredge them up. Overall the team played well enough that Nate was somewhat surprised when, after the game, before he could head back to his car, Zach came walking briskly up to him, Gags in tow.

"Can I help you guys?" Nate asked.

"Gags wants to talk," Zach said firmly, while Gags looked at the ground and couldn't meet his eye.

Nate blinked at them, surprised. He briefly ran through his conversation with Gags in the hotel room, how determined he was at insisting that he was fine. Clearly Zach had been able to get through to him in a way that Nate hadn't. That was the thing about Zach—they complemented each other. Or they had. "Yeah, of course."

"We should probably do this away from the rest of the team," Zach said, and Gags looked down at his feet, looking like a guilty child.

"Okay," Nate said, and glanced around. It would be difficult with everyone still going about their post-game routines, particularly since the routines involved the locker room, the main equipment storage and preparation area as the equipment managers rushed to get things put away and cleaned and Carolina's equipment managers were rushing their boxes out to the bus, some of the warm-up rooms, and even the conference room where the nutritionists provided a postgame meal for anyone who wanted it.

He couldn't just kick anyone *out*; that would be too obvious.

"Follow me," Nate said, after a pause. He took them to Coach Cote's office, which was dark and empty. The coaching staff must have been in the video room, going over footage from the game like they didn't have the entirety of the next day to do it.

When Gags and Zach came in after, Nate took a deep breath and locked the door. He gestured for Gags to take a seat in one of the two chairs that faced Cote's desk, but after the kid slumped down in it and Zach sat in the other one, Nate had a moment's sweaty panic wondering where *he* was going to sit. He didn't want to sit in Coach's chair, because that would seem like he was taking a position of authority he didn't actually intend to assume; he didn't want to sit on the desk because he didn't want to be too intimidating looming over poor Gags in the seat.

Eventually he settled for pacing around, never staying in one place for too long, which wasn't an ideal solution at all, but also meant that his leg wouldn't be jiggling up and down while they talked. Gags was doing the jiggling for him, and Nate felt a momentary rush of sympathy. "Okay. So. Do you guys wanna tell me what's going on?"

It wasn't what he was expecting.

Sure, he had noticed that Gags was probably having some issues with anxiety—Nate knew enough to recognize *that*. He'd recognized that Gags seemed to drink a little too much when they went out with the team. But he had no idea how much Gags was relying on drinking and how much he was relying on more illegal drugs. It wasn't like cocaine was uncommon in the league, but most of the guys who did it used it in a social, party kind of situation. Not coming to the rink high. Gags kept insisting that it wasn't an addiction issue, he could stop whenever he wanted. It was just dealing with the pressure was so fucking hard, he couldn't handle another way of managing.

Nate didn't know whether he believed that. They'd heard the same from Bouchard, one of the forwards that had been an alternate captain Bee's first season with the team. He'd made a lot of promises that he hadn't been able to keep. And here was Gags, fifteen years younger than Bouchard had been, saying the same words with manic sincerity.

Nate's stomach sank, the sick feeling that always lurked there lurching back into full nausea. This was so far beyond his pay grade that he didn't even know how he was going to begin to handle it.

He thought, briefly, of his weekends alone in between the seasons, the reset and recharge. He thought about Gags. He felt sick, again. Just because he had it under better control during the season didn't make it any different, really, when it came down to it.

But Gags was still talking: "And like, I know I shouldn't be doing that, but it's just so fucking hard to come to the rink every day and constantly worrying about my spot on the team and whether I'm playing well and whether they're going to send me down to the minors and now that we're in the playoffs and we're so far into things, it's like…even worse, somehow, you know—"

"Gags, I know *exactly* what you're talking about."

"How?" Gags demanded. His face, shadowed in the dim light of the room, was twisted up like he was in actual physical pain.

"Not all of it. I mean, like…the anxiety part. The self-doubt. I've had to deal with some form of it my entire life, basically? Like since elementary school at least it's always been like my brain doesn't shut the fuck up about anything, and if I listen to it, it's just…it's hard to keep going when your own brain is constantly telling you what a screwup you are. I used to throw up before games pretty much every time."

"You did? How do you *deal* with it?"

"I just kind of force myself to do it."

"You've just been raw-dogging this for *twenty-seven years*?"

"Uh, I wouldn't exactly put it like that…"

"But like… Singer, you're the captain. You're one of the star players. How the fuck did you get here?"

"Like I said. It's not easy. It fucking sucks sometimes. But I just have to put my head down and deal with it. But *you* don't have to do that."

"No?" Gags asked, voice so dry that you could have scraped your skin on it like sandpaper. He shrugged and flicked shaggy orange bangs away from his eyes. His hair had been growing out into a pretty intense playoff mullet, and it was dampened darker with sweat.

"No," Nate said. And as he said it, he felt, weirdly, confident about the words coming out of his mouth. "We're not going to go to Coach about this, like Zach said. At least not right away. I want you to contact the players' association tonight and see whether we can like. Get you set up with a therapist. You're gonna cut it out with the substance use during the playoffs. If either Zach or I have a *hint* that this is going on, especially at the rink, we aren't going to give you the benefit of the doubt anymore."

While he was talking, Gags's chin set mulishly, but he didn't argue. Zach, in the chair next to him, nodded in agreement, his arms crossed over his chest. Nate couldn't tell what was going on in his head. It was weird, being in a situation where even a few months ago, they would have been on the same page and dealing with it together. And they still *were* on the same page, but at a weird distance where he couldn't actually talk to Zach about how worried he was, about whether Zach thought he had done the right thing.

He couldn't talk to him about anything.

Somehow, Nate kept going. "I trust that you wanna do the right thing for you and the right thing for the team. So I'm trusting you not to do this. We're not going to be following you around every second holding your hand.

But I want you to make the call tonight, and I want you to start working. *Tonight.* Do you understand me?"

Nate held out his phone and Gags, begrudgingly, took it. "Yes, Cap."

"Okay," Nate said. "Let's get it handled. Because we have a round to win before the Conference finals, and you're a big fucking part of that, buddy."

Nate felt exhausted by the end of it even though there was at least one more round to play—they had the Eastern Conference finals waiting for them before they could even sniff the Cup finals. He suspected that it was going to be Tampa in the Conference final again, based on the way that the Mariners had been playing all year. And maybe Vegas in the West, if they made it to the finals. But he'd never been good at predicting things that way.

They swept the Oaks in the second round in four games, but there was no real joy in it. Nate felt like there were definitely going to be some major changes down in Carolina in the next season, even though they'd beaten the Hornets to get there. It wasn't the same as beating a team that had really made them work for it. Still: it wasn't really his problem, when it came down to it. He had the Conference finals to look forward to.

Gags had seemed to be keeping it together, whenever Nate or Zach checked in with him, and that was good. It was also the only time that Nate ever talked to Zach anymore, mostly in passing or by short text messages confined solely to conversations about the rookie. It felt, a little bit, like having 50/50 custody in a nasty divorce, but he didn't have the time to think about it very much, because they only had a few days' respite before the Conference finals began.

This was the furthest he'd ever been in the playoffs by far.

Since Nate had been a roster player for the Cons, they'd been a bottom-feeding team. There had been the rebuild. It had been shorter than anyone had expected, mostly thanks to Bee, but they had still failed to make it out of the second round each season since they'd had her.

And now Nate was in the Conference finals, and the whole team was relying on him to lead them to the end. Nate spent the whole year pretending to be a different person than he was, but now he had to do it with all the amps turned to eleven.

They lost the first game against the Mariners, which felt like a bad omen. Tampa had always been tough to play against, fast and aggressive and just toeing the line of dirty. The fourth line had been the only one to crack the problem of the Mariners' goalie, and unfortunately, it just wasn't enough.

One game wasn't the end of the world, but Nate was superstitious at the best of times and an anxious mess at the worst of times. It was hard to feel very confident about getting to the finals when he was still having trouble sleeping, when he'd wake up in the middle of the night and turn over, half expecting to feel Zach in the bed next to him. When they'd still been involved, it had been shockingly easy to fall back asleep if he woke up in the middle of the night. Something about Zach's solid, warm body made it easy. And now, well.

Nate woke up every day with dark circles under his eyes just as bad as Gags's, and a feeling of dread knitted around his damn bones.

The second game was a shit show from the start too. The Mariners came out with cannons blazing, and defensive breakdowns and unfortunately timed screens in front of Mäkelä resulted in two goals against before they even got to the halfway mark of the first period. In other years, that would have been a death knell: there would be no way they could come back. Now the Cons were still in it, but that didn't mean that it was easy to claw back a victory against one of the toughest teams in the league.

The second period started just as bad, chippier and chippier after Bee put one past the Mariners' goalie, high glove side, and then Mike, who had joined in the rush and was coasting by a passing lane where no one expected to see him, managed a chip-in shot from a rebound. Nate was used to getting cross-checked in the kidneys in the playoffs; it hurt every time. Cameron had been one of the major offenders before he got traded, but the rest of the Tampa team played on that edge too. It was one of the few times he was relieved to be as large as he was, because he was able to shrug off a lot of things that someone smaller might not have.

Someone like Zach, Nate realized, as he turned toward the bench at the end of his shift to get ready for the change. He looked up just in time to see Zach, who had just passed the puck to Lindy, go careening toward the ice as one of the Mariners' defensemen clipped him in the mouth with the blade of his stick as he was changing direction in pursuit of the puck.

Everything after that happened in a matter of seconds. Nate saw Zach, on his knees, shaking his head like he was trying to clear it, slow to get up. He spat some blood onto the ice. The Tampa defenseman—Leo Cohen, Nate saw now—smirked and said, "Sorry, gotta keep your head up, Reed." It had happened right in front of the referee, but this was the playoffs, and apparently there wasn't going to be a call. And then one of the forwards skating by said, "Come on, get up, you fuckin' diver, you already won the Oscar for this one," and Cohen laughed.

Before Nate could think about what he was doing, his gloves were on the ground, and he was charging forward. He had never fought before. Had never *seriously* considered fighting before. But right now, he was not thinking. It was like seeing Zach on the ground and Cohen laughing had just snapped some thin, fraying rope he hadn't even realized was at the point of breaking.

He could see Cohen's face, his eyes widening, like he was shocked that Nate was even considering this. But once he saw that they were on a collision course and the only option to avoid it was to surrender before the fight had even started, he dropped his gloves too.

Nate immediately realized that he had no clue what he was doing. Cohen was smaller than he was, but not by much. He was maybe six feet if you were being generous, barely 190 pounds soaking wet. That didn't mean he didn't fight like he was Nate's size. Nate whaled away with his fists, which connected hard against Cohen's cheekbone and nose. Blindly, Nate realized that Cohen was hitting him too, but he couldn't feel it at all. He had the advantage of height and reach at least, even if he was flailing and awkward.

By the time the ref and linesmen separated them, Nate realized that his nose was gushing blood and he was probably sporting the beginnings of a black eye. Cohen, somehow, didn't look much better. That was fairly impressive considering Nate had thrown himself into the fight with his eyes closed and hoped for the best.

Everything in his head was all mixed up. He couldn't believe he'd done that. It wasn't even like he'd lost his temper, it was just—something he'd had to do. And strangely, for once, he didn't feel nervous or anxious or anything. He felt strangely, deeply calm, like gears that had been grinding against each other, jammed with debris, were suddenly moving smoothly again. He could hear, across the ice, his teammates smacking their sticks against the boards.

"Are you okay?" he managed to yell to Zach, as he was escorted to the box.

"Fine," Zach said. He had managed to haul himself to his feet, and he spat out some more blood, wiped his mouth on the back of his glove. "Just a high stick."

Looking at him, in that moment, Nate knew two things.

First: they were going to win the game.

Second: they needed to talk.

Before he could do any of that he needed to sit for five minutes for the penalty. He didn't get the instigator because even though the original high stick hadn't been called, the ref who'd given him his penalty had seen it and apparently factored that in. So it would be regular old five-on-five hockey for the next five minutes and until the stoppage of play, and Nate had to watch, agonized and hopeful, while his team went on without him.

It was a weird experience, sitting there that long, especially in the Conference finals like this. Nate had been a Sportsmanship Award finalist almost every year he'd played, and he was pretty sure that this was his first major penalty.

It was like the team had seen what had happened and they were determined not to lose it for him. Even though the lines had been messed up by his absence, Sally managed to put them ahead by one, breaking the defender's ankles as he maneuvered toward the goal. In the box, Nate was on his feet yelling; he could already picture the announcers laughing about it. Sally had talent and Sally had positioning, but he wasn't exactly known for his wheels.

At the intermission, Nate checked in on Zach, who hadn't had to go through protocol but had a pretty nasty scab forming on his lip. They didn't actually say anything, but there was a strange look on Zach's face when he saw him, like he was trying to puzzle something out about Nate. He was still watching when Netty burst into the locker room and grabbed Nate's head to noogie him, yelling about the fight, but whatever Zach was thinking, he kept it to himself. Somehow, the team managed to hold on until the last few seconds. It was a narrow win at 3-2, but Nate was satisfied.

And then, after, he managed to make it through the postgame interviews and the shower, even though his head was turning over what he was going to say like a tumbler. As if it was a rough rock he could polish. There was nothing he could say to make this better, nothing he could say to really fix it. But he was going to have to try.

By the time he managed to get Zach alone, it was almost two and a half hours after the game, and both of them were exhausted. Zach, at least, didn't immediately make an excuse and hightail it out of the locker room when Nate said, "Zach?"

Instead, he just looked again, quiet and measuring. "What?"

"Come home with me?" Nate asked. "I, uh, I think maybe we need to talk about some things." Even after the shower, his hands were so fucking sweaty, and he felt like his heart was going to jump right out of his throat. He had no idea what he would do if Zach said no.

Zach looked at him, soft brown eyes a little wary, a little fond. "Okay," he said, finally.

Nate exhaled. "Okay."

Zach wasn't sure what to expect on the ride back to Nate's house. They'd made the same drive together so many other times before, but they hadn't had the same history in between them, and they didn't have the same baggage there was now.

He wanted to say something: *was this ever anything to you? Did this mean the same thing to you that it did to me?* But he couldn't. Part of him couldn't bear to be wrong about what he had suspected it meant to Nate, and part of him hoped so much it hurt, like someone had wrapped cold fingers around his heart and squeezed.

He didn't press Nate any further, even though he desperately wanted to. There was no rushing Nate if he was worrying about something. Zach's head buzzed with thoughts, that he was glad he'd asked his dog sitter to take Hank and Dolly, that he couldn't believe that this was happening after he'd resigned himself to being miserable in Philly for the rest of his contract.

Inside, the house seemed especially quiet, like the room itself was waiting for them to figure it out. It looked exactly the way he had left it. If he had been expecting to see signs of inner turmoil, that wasn't the way Nate dealt with things. Everything was still in its place, squeaky clean. He wondered if Nate had been using cleaning and organizing as a distraction and felt, once again, that overwhelming, awful fondness.

For a few long seconds they stood in the doorway awkwardly. Zach didn't know what to say and he assumed Nate didn't either.

Nate ran a hand through his hair and said, "Will you sit down?"

Zach sat on the couch and waited. It wasn't a very comfortable couch, all things considered. The pillows were *way* too stiff. The armrests were too low to actually comfortably rest your arm, let alone your head, if you were lying down. Rachel had picked it out, Zach knew.

Nate sat down on the other end of the couch, his hands clenched into fists, white-knuckled over his thighs. Just a few months ago, Zach would have gone over there and unclenched them, run his own fingers over Nate's knuckles until he relaxed. Now he pressed them flat on his own thighs, so he wouldn't do something stupid before he figured out what the hell was going on.

"Look, I…" Nate started. He was chewing on his lip. "I just don't know what happened, with us. I don't know why things suddenly ended the way they did, I don't know what I did, but after everything with Gags and actually doing team stuff together again and… I wanted to say that I'm *sorry*. I'm so fucking sorry, Zach, and I just, I don't want to go on like this anymore. I miss you so much. I miss *us* so much. You're like the most important person in my life and it's killing me not to—"

"You *don't* know what you did?" Zach blinked. He felt weirdly hollowed out, like someone had scooped out all of his insides with one of those melon ballers. "Do you, uh, not remember saying that it wasn't like we were dating? Because I heard that loud and clear. And I can get the idea. I know I'm not the kind of guy you date, but… Whatever you heard about me. I kind of still have my pride."

Nate stared at him. Zach stared back.

"Oh my god," Nate said, finally. "Oh, *fuck*."

"Nate, what…?"

"You thought I meant that I didn't feel…?"

"Uh, yeah…?"

"I'm so fucking sorry, Zach. That's not how I meant it at all."

Zach felt light-headed, like this was all happening in some kind of alternate reality. "It seemed pretty clear to me."

"It's just…you know how I get about stuff. Right? Uh, you know how I worry and…?"

"Yeah?"

"Well, I was just thinking this whole time that I was too lucky for getting to have you as my friend, and then when everything changed, I didn't think you could, you know. Feel the same way about me, even if we were fucking around."

He'd rarely seen Nate look like that, so downcast, so quiet and despairing. The last time had probably been after they'd been knocked out of the playoffs by Pittsburgh.

"Because I'm not… I'm just *me*. And you're you. You're so out of my league, you have to know it, right? And then Mom thought we were dating, and I was so up in my own head about it, worrying about when shit was going to come crashing down on me, when you were going to realize that you could do better, when everything was going to end…and then it did. I was waiting for it to happen, and it happened. And that seemed like the right thing to have happened. The thing that *should* have happened."

Zach stared at him. "Nate, you fucking *idiot*."

"What?"

"I know you get anxious, we've been friends for how long now, of course I know that, but Nate, it's *me*. You don't have to be anxious about *me*. You're the most important person in the world to me too. I thought that was obvious? I thought you knew?"

Nate looked up at him. His eyes were so fucking sad. Red-rimmed. Dark circles under them. He had been suffering just as much as Zach had been suffering, but somehow worse, because he'd known that he was the one who had done it. "But that's the thing about the way my brain works. It doesn't matter. Like, I know. But I don't *know*."

Zach shifted forward on the couch, sliding his hand over Nate's knee. "So you *did* think we were dating?"

"I wasn't sure what to think. I was so afraid to talk to you about it because I didn't want to fuck up our friendship, I didn't want to fuck up what we had… I just—I was just so happy that things were going the way they were going, and I just wanted it to be real so fucking badly. But it wasn't real, it was just a good luck charm."

"It was always real for me. Nate, it was *always* real for me."

"Then why didn't you just say something?"

"I don't know, it's just…if you were scared, can you imagine how I felt? I've never even had a relationship before. People don't *want* to date me. I'm great to fuck around and have fun with, but people don't like to hang around. And I wasn't sure if you were…sure about things. I didn't want to stop, but I was just, I was scared. And it was completely stupid, the good luck thing, but it was less fucking terrifying than actually talking to you about it."

"I…" He slipped his fingers over Zach's. They were shaking. "I just really couldn't believe someone like you could want someone like me."

"Baby, what the fuck are you *talking* about?"

"It's just…you're so fucking hot, Zach, and you've always been the best at everything you do. You were a top five draft pick and you have a Cup and I'm just some guy, just some guy from Philly who worked hard and managed to stick it out out of sheer stubbornness and I'm a fucking mess like… I'm just not in the same league as you. I never was."

Zach stared at him, and said, again, "You said that before, out of my league, but what the *fuck are you talking about*?"

"What?"

"Dude. I've been a fuckup for so long because of all of that. Because I could get away with it, because I was good at hockey and good-looking and people just let me do whatever the hell I wanted to do, and I was a fucking *nightmare*. It wasn't until coming here, until meeting *you*, that I really had the chance to be better. To do better. That I even *wanted* to do better."

"That was all you, Zach."

"Listen, shut up. It doesn't matter. The point is that I wanted to be better because of this team. Because of you. Because of what you meant to me. No one ever believed in me like you did right from the beginning. *No one.* I wanted to earn that trust."

"You did—"

"I know, I know. I know I did. But Jesus, Nate, you have no fucking clue, do you?" Zach had his hands in his hair now, on reflex, so frustrated at his inability to get the words out that he was tugging at it.

Nate's teeth pressed into his lower lip, the little gesture he always did when he was nervous. "About what?"

"Like how special you are. How important to the team you are, to me, like—how fucking *hot* you are."

Nate was shaking his head, like he didn't believe it, like he didn't want to hear it.

"Dude, yes. I don't care what the scouts said your draft year or what you looked like in high school. I would've fallen in love with you even then, if I knew you."

Nate's blue eyes opened wide, a shocked look. "In love?"

It was stupid. Zach had been terrified to even talk to him for so long and the words had just come out without any self-control whatsoever. But Nate didn't seem upset by it. On the contrary. His hands were shaking where they rested on his thighs. Zach took the plunge.

"In love. Probably since the beginning."

Nate took a deep breath of his own. "Me…me too. I mean, I love you too."

Zach felt almost light-headed for a second, the relief of knowing that weight was off of his shoulders forever. "And now…?"

"Now…what?" Nate asked. There was that little hesitation that he always had in his voice when he wanted Zach to keep going but was embarrassed to ask for it.

"And now?" Zach swallowed. His fingers tightened on Nate's knee. "I mean, I can tell you more, but I think… maybe we should go upstairs, huh?"

"I—yeah."

He followed behind Nate, still not quite able to believe that this was happening. Nate's broad back, his shoulders, and his *ass* and his thighs and all of the parts of him that Zach had gotten to know so intimately and thought he'd never be able to actually touch again. They were all still tucked away safely under Nate's clothes, but he could practically feel them under his palms even so. Some things had burned themselves into his muscle memory.

It had been a few months since he'd been in Nate's bedroom, but it hadn't changed at all either. Even now, Nate had still been carefully keeping everything clean and his laundry folded and put away, and Zach was filled with a stupid surge of affection for his dumb, responsibility-driven captain, carefully KonMari folding his own underwear even though he made six and a half million dollars a year.

Nate turned to look at him. His face was so open and raw that Zach almost wanted to look away. Except he couldn't look away, even if he'd wanted to. When Nate looked like that, it was mesmerizing. "I never thought we'd be able to do this again."

Zach took a step forward and held out his hands. Nate's fingers were warm and clammy in his. "You did it. You were the one who was fucking brave enough to take the chance."

Before he could even think about it, they were kissing, and it was like the months they'd been apart melted away under the heat of Nate's mouth, the way he completely fell apart when he was touching Zach. He had his hands on either side of Zach's face, holding him in place, but his mouth was soft and giving. It was a hungry kiss but a sweet one, all of the frustrated longing he'd felt evaporating like fog on a window with the sun.

Zach nipped at Nate's lower lip when he pulled away. "You're not out of my league."

"Okay," Nate said, flushing, as Zach walked him back toward the bed.

"You're *not*."

"Okay," Nate said, again, when Zach pushed him down

into a sitting position on it. His thighs fell apart obligingly to let Zach into his space, to grip the muscle there and squeeze it as he knelt on the floor in front of him. He wasn't really agreeing, he was just saying it so Zach would stop talking.

But he kept throwing these little glances up from the corner of his eyes and Zach knew. Zach knew *him*. "How can I convince you that you're—just, just, everything to me?"

"I don't..." Nate started, then stopped when Zach leaned up to press another kiss against his mouth.

"I think," Zach said, hands twisted in the hem of Nate's T-shirt, "maybe you don't do any talking during this one. I think maybe, actually, you're not allowed to talk at all. You just have to listen to me, okay?"

"Uh," Nate started, the words muffled when Zach pressed one hand over Nate's mouth. "Okay," he finished, his voice distorted by Zach's palm.

He'd had dreams like this, during the time they were apart, of Nate in his bed again, of Nate letting him strip away his clothes. He took his time, pulling the shirt up first, exposing Nate's broad shoulders and chest and thick torso. He ran his hands down Nate's body, his pectoral first, fingers scraping against the soft hair of his chest, his abs, his hips. Nate already felt hot and feverish. All of that emotion and energy bottled up inside of him at all times exploding outward.

"Baby," he said, "you really don't know how fucking hot you are?" Nate looked like he was about to protest and Zach, a little bit of a smirk he wasn't quite able to bite back down, said, "We agreed you weren't gonna say anything."

"You *told* me I had to listen to you." He shot a look up at Zach through his eyelashes, almost sly.

Zach couldn't help it; he laughed. "I think I remember you saying *okay*, actually. So you don't want me to—because I can stop, any time, you just have to say the words, eh?"

Nate looked up at him again and Zach thought about the first time he had comforted Nate after a bad loss, making him laugh until he was smiling, easy and open, and how heady it had felt to have the force of his attention turned on you. Three years later and nothing had changed, nothing at all. Nate looked at him like the sun was revolving around his stupid head and Zach was fucking putty in his hands.

"Okay," Nate said, very quietly.

Zach knew he wasn't the smartest guy in the world, and he knew that he wasn't very good with words. But this wasn't about smarts or about words—this was about Nate, and how Zach had spent the last three years desperately trying not to fall in love with him and somehow doing it anyway. When he thought about it that way, it was easy to tell Nate everything. The words came out of his mouth without any thought, about the way he dreamed about the feeling of Nate's muscles under his hands when he was holding himself back, about the way Nate's mouth looked when it was open and gasping, the way his eyes were like all kinds of ocean depths and—

Nate, shifting restlessly under Zach's hands, stopped. He was still flushed pink, the prettiest blush Zach had ever seen, but his mouth was tilted up in that smile that made everything easier. "Wow, Zach, missed your calling with poetry, huh?"

Zach wrapped his hand around Nate's dick and got a gasping little whine for his trouble. "I can ask Jammer's girlfriend for advice. But that's—you're not meant to be talking right now, baby."

"I'm not talking," Nate mumbled, but he shut his mouth when Zach pressed two fingers against his lips, eyebrows raised. Almost like he couldn't believe he was doing it, he flicked his tongue against the pads of Zach's fingers, and Zach could feel his heart jumping in his chest like a jackhammer, like it was going to try, at any second, to burst its way through.

"Just let me tell you how fucking hot you are," Zach said. It took him a while, because he was trying to suck Nate's dick while he did it. He had to dip his mouth down, work his lips along the length of it. Pull back. "I had dreams about your fucking thighs, baby, even before I could ever think about touching you." Back down again, while Nate twisted under the ministrations, while he gasped and panted and desperately tried not to talk. "Your torso. The way it feels under me. It's fucking insane, the things your body *does* to me."

Nate stared at the ceiling, like he couldn't bear to look at Zach at all. He probably couldn't. He was sweating, with the intensity of the moment, with the way Zach was touching him, blond hair damp and messy where Zach had pulled his head around. His eyes were huge and dark, the blue lost in the pupil, like Zach was already transporting him to some other fucking universe.

"It's not just your body," Zach gasped. His voice was a little wrecked already, not that Nate had been pushing it. Zach had, too eager to suck him down. "Your fucking face, Nate. I could stare into your eyes for fucking hours."

Nate closed them, just then, too embarrassed to even risk it. His face was so fucking red, the blush all the way down his throat and chest. Zach stopped sucking him off, shifted up his body so he could press kisses along the edges of it, against his pecs, the hollow of his throat while he slipped his hand around Nate's dick instead. When Zach licked him there, he could taste the salt of sweat against Nate's clean skin, a salt like the tears that had pricked at the corners of his eyes, still screwed shut.

"Look at me," Zach mumbled, "come on, please."

Nate did what he asked, but it was a slow opening, eyes heavy-lidded. For a second, Zach thought he was going to say something, but he didn't: he just reached one hand up, fingers gentle against Zach's cheek. And somehow that gesture said everything that words never could. Zach turned his hand into Nate's palm and for a second, he felt like *he* was going to cry.

Afterward, he could never be quite sure how he managed it, keeping up that constant narrative about all of the things he loved about Nate and touching him at the same time. Nate's drive to succeed. The way Nate took care of the team, the way he did the little things for all of them because he loved the boys so fucking much. The way he never wanted the attention or glory for himself, the way he only wanted to make everyone else around him better. It was a weird kind of feedback loop, telling Nate those things, touching him, watching him falling apart underneath it, and losing control of himself at the same time. Like saying everything he'd been holding back for three seasons had unleashed something inside of him, a waterfall of words that would keep falling and falling and falling.

He looked down at Nate, spread out under him, and was seized by such an intense feeling he almost got choked up, everything he wanted to say caught in his throat. Instead of trying to get it out, he pressed his tongue against the bottom of Nate's dick instead, slid his mouth down around it. The noise *that* got him was worth it. He looked up at

Nate, his hands twisted in the sheets, sweat beading his forehead. He was trying desperately not to say anything, but instead he was just making noises, muffled and inhuman. It was almost too much.

By the time Zach had clambered on top of him and sank down, they were both almost beyond words, but somehow, he kept managing to gasp out ragged sentence fragments, how good Nate felt inside of him, how perfect he was, how they fit together, on the ice, off the ice, in bed, all of it, like Nate was made especially for him—

Nate made a pained noise and came, eyes screwed shut, fingers digging into the muscle of Zach's back. Zach sat, frozen on top of him, staring down. He was trembling on the edge of an orgasm himself, just wasn't quite there. Reached down to take himself in hand, stroking faster and faster as he gasped, "Do you believe me now? Do you?"

"Yes," Nate said, "yes, yes—" He closed his eyes when Zach came in streaks all over his chest. While Zach was still shuddering through it, he opened them again. His pupils were huge and his eyes were dark and he looked up at Zach like he was the only thing in the entire world that Nate cared about right in that moment.

Zach, still trying to collect his scrambled brain, dragged one finger down the mess. It was rapidly getting cold and sticky. They'd have to take a shower soon. He didn't give one single shit about any of those things. Zach leaned forward to kiss him again, mess and all.

Nate still couldn't believe that what was happening was actually real. That he had had the courage to say any of that; that Zach had actually listened to him; that they had actually managed to work it out. He was still floating on the endorphins from a ridiculous orgasm, from the relief of having Zach back in his life for good. Zach's come on his chest was getting tacky and disgusting, but Nate didn't want to push him away long enough to clean up.

He wasn't sure if he could push him away even if he'd wanted to. His whole body still felt shaky and unsteady, like a newborn colt stumbling around the green. It had been—a lot, hearing everything that Zach thought about him. Everything that Zach felt about him. It had been embarrassing and wonderful and horrible all at once. Part of him felt like he could float on that high for the rest of his life and part of him, somehow, still didn't believe it.

"You really believe me?" Zach asked again. Nate looked up at him. He was handsome as always, even though he looked exhausted and silly with his sex-drunk smile and messy hair. And his expression, fond but worried, like even after all of the begging and stupid shit that had come out of Nate's mouth in the heat of the moment, he still—

The thing was. Deep down, Nate still didn't—couldn't—believe it. It was easier to bear, now, but when it came down to it nothing had really changed. The mess in his head was exactly the same, the nasty voice just as loud. He looked up at Zach and said, "Baby, I need so much fucking therapy."

"Uhh, yeah," Zach agreed, and somehow, they were both laughing, Nate on the edge of hysteria.

"I'm going to do it," he said, gasping. "I'm going to do it. After we get done with this playoff run. I'm going to be better. For you. But also for me."

Zach rolled off of him, and they lay side by side in the bed, looking at it each other. "Nate. Whatever you want to do. I'm gonna be here for it."

"I know," Nate said, and couldn't keep the dumb smile off of his face. "I believe you."

They beat the Mariners in six games. It took blood and sweat and tears to do it, but they did it. Zach, who usually wasn't a very physical player, took *immense* joy in smashing Leo Cohen into the boards during the last game, like it was a bookend on the series, a signature for them to remember him by. He tried not to look too smug in the handshake line, even though it was difficult when he met Cohen's eyes and saw how fucking furious he still looked. It didn't matter what Cohen or any of the Mariners thought, though.

The Cons had won.

Zach had been there before. He'd won the Cup in Montreal his rookie year, and that had set him on the trajectory that had almost destroyed his career. He remembered the locker room in Montreal the day they made it to the finals, the way he'd been drenched in beer, looking around at all of his older teammates: the captain, Matthew Safaryan; the Morin twins; Saarinen and Kapadia and Grenier. Making it to the finals was a huge deal no matter what team you were on. The Royal had won it all once before, before he'd even been drafted, in a Cinderella run.

All of those guys had known that it wasn't guaranteed: they'd suffered through two rebuilds.

Zach hadn't known. He'd been young and stupid and part of him had felt like that was what it was going to be like every season after that, triumphant and screaming and joyful.

It wasn't until now, seeing the faces of his teammates on the Cons, the way Nate's entire demeanor changed, his smile huge and his eyes shining, that he realized that the struggle was part of what made the reward sweeter. That he realized what it meant to win with guys you loved.

They hadn't won it all yet, of course. Anything could happen when they played Vegas in the finals. But somehow, Zach just had the gut feeling that it was all going to work itself out.

He checked in with Gags and Belsky after. Both of them were still drenched from the celebration, looking a bit like bedraggled stray dogs. Gags still looked tired but some of the shadows below his eyes had smoothed themselves out. Probably winning helped a little with that, although both Nate and Zach sure as fuck knew that even winning couldn't cure an anxiety disorder.

"You boys good?" he asked, voice low and barely audible under the din of the rest of the team, still yelling. Sometimes the team would post victory videos on the official Twitter, but there were too many dicks and too many loud curses to allow for that, even if they did some careful editing.

Gags and Belsky exchanged a glance, and Gags looked up at him. "Uh, yeah. I mean, it's still kinda tough, but like… I'm working on it. The dude I'm talking to is pretty flexible about times. And I can do it on Zoom, basically."

"Cool," Zach said, and then, even though he knew it was cheesy as fuck, "I'm really proud of you, kid. And you too, Bells. It's not every day you get to make a run like this as a rookie. And not screw it up after."

"I already screwed up plenty beforehand," Gags muttered.

"Bro," Zach said, patting him on the shoulder. "You gotta talk to your dude about that, like, immediately after you shower," and was rewarded when both Gags and Belsky started cracking up. Zach beamed at them, and with an ironic little salute, went to go get cleaned up himself.

Under the hot spray in the shower, staring a little dreamily at Nate's broad back, his skin flushed red from the heat, Zach thought about how far he'd come since he'd gotten drafted, since he'd screwed everything up in Montreal, since he'd gotten traded and thought his life was over. The life he'd built here with Nate, the team of guys they'd helped mentor. The team they'd helped drag, kicking and screaming, to within seven games of the Cup.

It was weird as hell. But damn, it felt fucking *good.*

And going home with Nate after the game felt even better.

On the flight out to Vegas, Nate tried listening to a guided meditation on Spotify, but all it did was make him more anxious, more aware of his body and how amped up he was to play in the first Cup finals of his entire playing career. He turned it off and slipped his headphones back down around his neck.

"You good?" Zach asked sleepily, next to him.

"Yeah, it's just, uh. I was trying something new, and it really wasn't for me. Don't worry about it."

Zach blinked at him, then shook his head. "We gotta get you some earbuds," he said, tugging at the headband. "Into the twenty-first century."

"Earbuds offer an inferior auditory experience," Nate started to protest, particularly because this was a conversation they had had a million times over the last three seasons, before he realized that Zach was just giving him a hard time. All of the muscles that had been tensed up relaxed suddenly, because this was familiar, this was something he could use to distract himself. For a second, he was so grateful that Zach was there with him for this that he got a little choked up.

"Dude, seriously, you good?" Zach asked him, again.

"Yeah, it's just... I don't know. When I first got drafted and the Cons sucked so bad for so long, I thought I was going to end up like Logan too. That I'd get traded or let go in free agency before I ever had a chance to win something here. And now it's here and I almost *can't* believe it."

Zach reached over and pinched Nate's thigh through the leg of his pants, smirking a little. "Well, I just pinched you, and we are still on a plane to Vegas to play in the Cup finals, so—it's real, bud."

"You might have to pinch me again."

Zach laughed, his eyes crinkling almost shut, and said, "Probably not in public, eh?"

The games themselves came fast and hard. Vegas was a tough team: they had a stacked center line, a huge defensive corps, and very good possession numbers. The Cons were definitely the underdogs by any metric: their regular season record wasn't as good, the betting lines weren't in their favor, and Moneypuck had given them a 41% chance of winning the series. That percentage dropped down to 30% after the Cons lost the first two games.

After that second loss, Nate did something he usually hated doing, which was to give a short speech in the locker room.

"Boys," he said, "the bounces didn't go our way tonight, but now isn't the time to despair. It's not the time to give up. Teams have come back from 3-0 deficits before, but I don't want to have to play with our backs against the wall like that." Somehow, it was easier to talk now without stammering, looking out at all of the teammates who had made this possible. Zach and Bee, his lineys. Mike, who'd grown up so much in a few seasons with the team. Gags and Belsky rising to the occasion. Mäkelä, playing out of his mind. Netty and Sally, dependable as always. He could still feel his face turning red, but it was easy to pretend that that was just exertion from the game. "I know we have something special here this season, with all of you. This isn't the way it was meant to go. Let's put these games behind us and come back to a fresh start in Philly in front of our home crowd. We've got this. I really do believe in you. Let's fucking *go*."

He turned away from the applause and hoots and *whoo*s, and took a deep breath, his heart pounding in his ears and sweat prickling the back of his neck. He thought about Gags starting therapy. He thought about telling someone all of the shit that knocked around the back of his head at the worst possible times. He thought about a lot of things, and somehow, it didn't feel as daunting as it used to feel. He had already pushed through so fucking much to get to this point that doing something so terrifying seemed almost easy.

The game in Philly was like starting all over again. The fans at the Frank had always been intense: it was routinely voted one of opposing teams' least favorite places to play for a reason. The fans were loud and they were rude and some of the sarcastic cheers they could come up with were absolutely devastating. There was probably nothing worse than flubbing a play at a crucial moment and then coming face to face with a drunk guy from South

Philly, dressed up as Ben Franklin, pretending to moon you through the glass.

Philly hadn't seen a Cup final since 1975, the last time the Cons had won it. They'd made it to the Eastern Conference finals a few times over the almost fifty years since the last time the Cup had come home, but those appearances were few and far between, and had always ended in heartbreak.

So to say that they were intense when the Cons came home to play was something of an understatement. With that kind of support it was easy to rally, it was easy to come back and win it. Vegas's goalie might have been having an off night, but the Cons steamrolled them to the tune of 5-1, and for a second, Nate allowed himself to hope. They won the next game in Philly too, the series tied 2-2, and the excitement was beginning to reach a fever pitch.

Vegas came back to steal the fifth game, but this time, the mood in the locker room wasn't grim. Nate didn't know how to describe the way the guys had reacted: it was like everyone knew, deep down, that they were going to do it. There were the game-day jitters, of course; there were the nerves. But no one looked despondent. As they packed up their shit and headed back to the hotel to sleep it off for the sixth game, Nate felt…okay.

The Cons squeaked out a victory in the sixth game.

Their fate would be decided, at home, in game seven.

VI.
SUMMER

CHAPTER TWELVE

June

On the morning of the seventh and last game of the Cup finals, Nate woke up before his alarm, the same way he always did on days when he was worrying about something and felt like he was going to throw up. He'd been here before, in a way. The elimination game. They'd been playing the elimination game for most of the series, in a way. He'd never gotten this far in his life before, of course. But he knew the feeling of dread, of knowing that if he fucked it up again, that was it. All of the work he'd put in during the long eighty-two-game season would end up, once again, being for nothing.

But he hadn't been here before. When he opened his eyes, the cold clammy sweat of anxiety still clinging to him, Zach was there, a warm and solid presence, even in sleep. His mouth was hanging open and his eyes were closed, but when Nate shifted to take some of the pressure off of his arm, they opened, slowly. It took him a second to orient himself, but when he did, he smiled. "Morning, baby."

"Hey," Nate said, heart thumping in his chest.

"Let me guess," Zach said with a yawn. He pressed

one finger against Nate's sternum. "You...are freaking out."

"It *is* the Cup final," Nate admitted. "An elimination game."

"It's going to be fine."

"How do you *know*?"

"I mean, I don't *know*, but... I do." Zach stretched lazily; even though he was kind of freaking out internally, Nate's brain took one long pause to admire the picture it made, the sun diffused through the curtains on Zach's skin and tattoos, the way you could see every single muscle as he moved. "This is our year. I just have a feeling."

"You have a *feeling*," Nate repeated.

"Yeah," Zach said, rolling over on top of him and pinning his arms down. "You know, just a gut feeling."

Somehow, it was easier to forget his worries, get out of his own head, when Zach was kissing him, morning breath and all, when Zach's body was warm and heavy on top of his own. Maybe, Nate thought hazily, this was the secret to winning the Cup the entire time. He'd just had to find someone to make out with him as a distraction. A human weighted blanket to quell his fears.

"Can I borrow your gut?" Nate said when they broke for air. "Mine is, uh. Not as confident."

Zach touched the side of Nate's face with one hand, fingers gentle against it. Nate's playoff beard had gotten a bit shaggy, but he could still feel Zach's hand hot against his skin. "If I could lend it to you I would, buddy. But in this case you just gotta trust me, okay?"

Nate looked up at him, his warm brown eyes and messy hair and lopsided smile. He could focus on Zach's familiar face. The roiling in his stomach didn't vanish, exactly, but it calmed. He thought about all of the other times this year he'd taken a leap of faith, trusting Zach to catch him. How the only time he'd fallen had been the fault of his own insecurity.

"I do. Trust you."

Zach kissed him again, brief and sweet. "We better get up. We have a Cup to win."

Later on, Nate would never really be able to remember how he got through the rest of the morning, making them breakfast, sitting in the passenger seat as Zach drove them to the rink, going through the pregame stretches and equipment checks. It was like it had all been wiped from his memory and he'd suddenly opened his eyes and here it was: he was in the tunnel, dressed for the game and watching the team go about their little rituals.

Netty and Sally had a complicated series of chest and shoulder bumps. Bee and Mike had a torturously long secret handshake, which wasn't really secret anymore. Gags practiced taking face-offs like his life depended on it, chopping the blade of his stick down against the rubber floor. Zach had his own fist bump and handshake variation with every guy on the team. Mäkelä crouched in front of them all, in position like he was challenging on a penalty shot or a breakaway, completely serene and ignoring any noise and any unwitting bumps from behind.

Nate watched all of them, filled with the kind of swelling affection he couldn't control. These were his siblings. His family. They were on the precipice of doing something great together, and all he had to do was keep himself together and play his fucking heart out. Dig down just a little deeper within himself than he'd dug before, give just that little bit extra he might have been holding back. He understood now, the way that guys could end their careers on long playoff runs, pushing through injuries they had no business playing through.

It was stupid. It was just a piece of metal. It was *just* the Cup.

Nate laughed, thinking that. *Just* the Cup. It wasn't just that: it was the hardest trophy to win in any sport, he was pretty sure. But it wasn't just about the Cup. It was about the guys, about doing it with them. Doing it for them.

Nate took a deep breath, caught Zach's eye.

Zach smiled, that lopsided, crooked smile that was just for Nate, even though they were surrounded by the rest of the team.

And just like that, Nate knew what he had to do.

The last time Zach had played in the Cup finals, he'd been a nineteen-year-old in Montreal, a little asshole hotshot with the deep-seated belief that the world had owed him everything because he was very fucking good at hockey. At the time, the Royal had been unstoppable: they'd had it all. The two-way center, the superstar defenseman, the hotshot goalie, the best checking line in hockey. They'd had scoring depth up and down the lineup. And they'd had Zach, with his stupid baby face and his scoring touch, in the middle.

It had been almost too easy. They'd swept two of their series and finished off the finals in five. He'd been out of his fucking mind with joy to win the Cup, but he hadn't really *understood* what winning meant. He hadn't understood what team meant. Guys he'd thought were his brothers, guys he thought would support him—they'd won it together and those same guys had turned their backs on him just a few months later when the latest round of pictures had ended up making the rounds on

Twitter and TikTok and Reddit and the rumors about his partying were spiraling out of control. Someone had gone to the general manager, whispered that he was a *problem* in the locker room.

And then he'd been shipped out of town. They'd all wiped their hands of him.

And now, years later, here he was again. The Cons had fought their way to these finals, clawed their way through every season and every series. They had earned every right to be here with sweat and blood. They'd left everything on the ice.

This was his *team*. This was Netty, always making him laugh, reminding him that he could still have fun, that hockey was *fun*. This was Gags finally telling him what was going on and being able to point him in the right direction. This was Mike giving him a place to stay and a sympathetic ear. This was Bee, just being Bee.

He'd earned them too.

He'd never felt so sure about winning a game, even though he couldn't have told you why. The Aces were a damn good team and had one of the best regular season records in recent history. They were a threat in every zone. And the Cons—well, they were the perennial underdog, even now that they'd managed to figure shit out. There was no reason to have felt so sure about it. But what he'd said to Nate about his gut wasn't wrong.

Somehow, he just knew.

"Hey," he said, when Nate shifted down the tunnel to stand next to him. "We're gonna have to go out soon. You wanna give the boys a little talking-to?"

Nate flushed red, immediately and suddenly, the way he always did when he was the center of attention. But he met Zach's eyes and calmed. "Yeah," he said, taking a deep breath. "Boys!"

The team stopped what they were doing as one. Their heads turned to look at him. Nate took another deep breath and said, "This is it. The end. Do or die." He paused for a second, like he was considering what to say. "We've played together as a team for almost three years now. And I just wanted to say that it has been an honor, every second. Whatever happens out there during the game, win or lose, I'm proud of all of you. But—I truly, I—this is our year. I just have a feeling."

No one applauded, but Bee leaned forward to bonk her visor against Nate's, and Zach could feel his chest swelling again. To hear his words in Nate's mouth, both giving him confidence and inspiring the guys. He knew, deep in his stomach, that he was right.

Now he just had to prove it.

When Nate skated out onto the ice for the anthem and opening face-off, he took a moment to look up at the crowd, even though he couldn't *really* see them beyond the glare of the lights. The seats were sold out, and somehow, the Frank seemed filled even beyond its regular capacity, a sea of red, white, and blue, blurring into nothing.

Even now the noise rippled around the arena, shouts of *Go Cons Go* and *fuck the Aces.* Strangely enough, it was the *fuck the Aces* chant right before the anthem that made him smile and feel more at ease. It was just such a Philly thing to do, not even letting up when Allie Martinez, the Cons' longtime anthem singer, stood at center ice, waiting patiently for all of them to calm the fuck down.

The game itself seemed to go on forever and also to take no time at all. Vegas played heavy, but that was nothing surprising. This was the playoffs: everyone played heavy. And this was game seven of the finals. So that went double. Cross-checks went uncalled, interferences were ignored. The refs usually only managed to catch the most egregious offenses because they didn't want to disrupt the flow of the game.

This was the shit Nate lived for, honestly. The punishing hits that left bruises on his body were just reminders of what he'd weathered. When he went down on one knee to block a slapshot, the sting so bad against the bone that he wasn't sure if he'd have to go down the tunnel to get a shot to get him through the rest of the game, that was just proof that he was fucking committed. Nate might have been a coward when it came to talking about his *feelings*, but when it came to sacrificing the body—he had no hesitation.

It paid off. The team were playing out of their minds today. Mäkelä was on fire, like every shot the Aces made was smothered in his chest no matter where they were shooting from, the almost telepathic positioning he had during his best games. The shots were even and despite everything, despite every effort Nate made to push his aching knee through the paces, the score still sat steady at 1-1 in the third.

No matter what he did, though, he just couldn't break through the Aces' smothering defense.

The clock was ticking down.

There were now thirty seconds left, they were setting up in the o-zone for a face-off, and as soon as the puck dropped Mäkelä would rush to the bench for the extra attacker, hoping that Vegas wouldn't risk it to do the same. They had the chance to end things here before going to overtime, or it could all go horribly wrong if the Aces managed to pull off an empty netter.

Every nerve Nate had was pulled tight and taut and he could feel the tension of the moment tingle all over his skin. Strangely enough, he wasn't anxious anymore; he usually wasn't on the ice, even in the big situations. It was like the complete lack of control he felt in his life was gone. He could concentrate only on the here and now.

The puck dropped.

Zach won the face-off clean and swept the puck back to Nate, who took a second to assess the situation. Bee had muscled one of the Aces out of the way and was in the perfect position in the slot.

Nate sauced a pass through traffic to her and then slipped around the defender covering him to follow up as what happened next seemed to unfold into slow motion. Bee settled the puck on her stick and twisted her body, her eyes on Nate, lulling the Aces' goalie into turning toward Nate in anticipation of the pass. And as he did, Bee shifted her weight and flicked a wrister up and over his shoulder.

The goal horn sounded, and Bee jumped into Nate's arms, screaming unintelligible Quebecois French curse words. There were still a few seconds left on the clock, but this was it: they had done it. Zach slammed into his back and then Mike and Lindy, a forceful pile of muscle and sweat and sheer fucking joy.

Nate could feel his heart in his throat, choking on it.

"You fucking beauty!" Mike screamed at Bee, over and over, as she accepted their hugs and adulation and glove pats on her helmet. Bee was beaming, sweaty and shining with pride and joy and the knowledge that they only had fifteen seconds of time left to kill.

"Fucking beautiful, Bee," Nate said, as they broke apart.

"Thank you, mon capitaine," she said, and bonked her helmet against his one last time.

Nate could barely think when they lined back up at center ice for the face-off. He could barely react when Zach won the face-off again, shoving it back to Bee, and she just kept the puck on her stick, playing keep away and toying with the attacking Aces until the horn sounded again to signal that the game was over.

The game was *over* and they had won.

They had won the Cup.

Nate couldn't describe what he felt in that moment. It was like everything he'd kept inside for so many years was just going to burst out of his chest like a particularly happy xenomorph. This was the thing he'd been working toward his entire life and it had actually happened. It had *actually happened* and it had happened with Zach at his side. Nate had won the Cup and he'd gotten his man and his eyes burned with tears and his head spun with all of the thoughts he couldn't even begin to organize into coherency.

The team was on the ice now and Zach was in his arms and Nate was hugging him with all of the force he could muster, a bone-crushing hug that felt like it would never end. He couldn't even be embarrassed by the tears streaming down his face, because Zach looked the same way. Zach looked… He had turned his head up to glance up at Nate, even though they were too close already. His eyes were soft and warm and fond and he was smiling so fucking widely. It took everything Nate had not to lean down and kiss him right there, in front of the crowds and the entire world watching.

"We did it for you, baby," Zach murmured in his ear, so soft that Nate almost couldn't hear it. "I got you your Cup."

"What?" Nate said. His heart was beating so violently that Zach must have been able to feel it even through their pads. It was going to escape from in between his ribs at this rate. "You what?"

"I told myself at the beginning of the season. I made a promise. I was gonna get you your Cup. And we got it."

"Zach—*Zach*," Nate said helplessly. It was almost too much to process, and for once, the emotion that swept him away was only joy, a fierce and all-encompassing joy like he'd never experienced before in his life.

"I love you, buddy," Zach said, and buried his face against Nate's chest as Nate's arms tightened even further. "After me I'm gonna give it to you. I promise. It's ours. Together."

"Okay. Okay—"

"And I love you. I *love* you, you know that?"

"Yes," Zach said, but he was laughing. Laughing and crying at the same time too, face wet with sweat and snot and tears. The most beautiful thing Nate had ever seen. "Of course I do. Never any doubt. Come on, baby. Go lift the Cup."

When Nate hoisted the Cup over his head and looked up at the screaming crowd of Philadelphia faithful, surrounded by the people he loved most in the entire world, he couldn't imagine a better feeling.

But then he handed it to Zach, looked at his shining face and gigantic smile as he raised the trophy for the second time in his life, and realized he couldn't have been more wrong.

* * *

TRACKING THE CONS:
WHERE DID CUP END UP DURING TEAM'S WILD BENDER
Posted: June 12, 2024—6:01 PM
Alice Mitchell | @alice_mitchell

Since the Cup was awarded two days ago, the Philadelphia Constitution have been partying in what can only be described as an epic fashion. They partied hard overnight at the Frank and at a private venue into the morning. And they did not stop when they were released onto a Broad Street strewn with the wreckage of the celebration and the greased poles that did nothing to prevent climbers scaling their heights.

It is evident that the alcohol has been flowing and the inhibitions have been loosened. Both the team and the Cup have been on a wild ride ever since. Follow along with our interactive map and up-to-the-minute liveblog.

5:00 p.m. The Cons reappear on Broad Street, and the Cup is paraded through the mess. Joshua Gagnon is forcibly removed from a hotel awning by security.

5:23 p.m. The team waits for the Broad Street Line, taking pictures with fans and signing autographs. During the ride, the Cup is repeatedly passed up and down the aisles.

6:08 p.m. The Cons are on South Street eating cheesesteaks at Woodrow's. At one point, the steaks were in the Cup. By now, the steaks are gone and there's definitely beer in there. If you ever wanted to do a keg stand with Zach Reed, now is the time to get yourself down to South Philly.

[An image of Zach Reed, held upside down by Nate Singer and Andrey Kuznetzov. He has his head buried in the Cup's bowl; his stained T-shirt is slipping down around his torso, and you can see every single ab in sharp relief.]

8:35 p.m. The Cons are barhopping along South Street, and making their way deeper into South Philly. Bit of a carnival atmosphere here, folks.

12:00 a.m. It's officially Thursday.

2:42 a.m. While we all know that closing time is 2:00 a.m., the Cons appear to have vanished into a club for the time being.

7:55 a.m. A party bus at 8:00 in the morning? Why not. We tracked down some Instagram stories from two lucky fans who were able to get an invite on the bus after singing the first verse of "Maamme," Finland's national anthem, at Antti Salonen. On the bus, it appears that the Cons are listening to "Tubthumping."

[Shaky video footage, filmed on someone's very old phone, of the dark interior of a party bus. Various Cons are passing around a bottle of vodka; Chumbawumba's "Tubthumping" blaring at top volume drowns out almost any other noise.]

9:30 a.m. The Cons are posing for pictures with the Rocky statue and singing "We Are the Champions." It is not evident that any of them have singing talent, but copious amounts of alcohol are likely involved. Andrey Kuznetzov has climbed the statue and is currently perched on Rocky's shoulders. Over/under on the police arriving to get him down?

9:55 a.m. The Cons are running up and down the Art Museum steps. Or at least attempting to. There've been more than a few wipeouts on the way up. "We Are the Champions" going again.

10:22 a.m. The Cons have somehow gotten hold of

trashcan lids and are "sledding" down the steps. Let's all pray there aren't any serious injuries.

10:24 a.m. Oh dear. It appears that Antti Salonen has taken a header into the ground.

10:32 a.m. *Update:* he's bleeding. But according to the thumbs-up he just gave us, he is okay.

11:10 a.m. In what is perhaps an unsurprising twist, after picking themselves up from the concrete, the Cons have crossed the Parkway and they are currently in the fountains on the Eakins Oval. Some of them are clothed. Some of them are not.

11:15 a.m. *Update:* Salonen is no longer with them.

1:00 p.m. The Cons are on Broad Street. Some of the Philadelphia Police Department public relations officers are trying to talk Andrey Kuznetzov down from the light pole. The poles had been greased in preparation for raucous celebrations, but he managed to get up there anyway and is currently perched on the crossbar. Mike Sato is throwing him cans of beer, which is he shotgunning.

11:55 p.m. Judging from several pictures and social media posts, the Cons are in Rittenhouse Square (some of them in the fountain) and a very drunk Beatrice Morin has just gotten down on one knee and proposed marriage to Sakari Mäkelä, the Cons' goalie and her boyfriend of several years.

[An image of Beatrice Morin, in the middle of Rittenhouse Square Park, wearing a very disheveled-looking button-down shirt, jacket, and tie. She is on one knee on the ground; Sakari Mäkelä looks shocked. Around them, the rest of the team are in varying states of surprise and celebration. Some of them have their fists in the air, some of them have their hands over their mouths, and Sato is in the process of quite literally jumping for joy.]

11:58 p.m. *Update:* Mäkelä said "yes!"

It is unclear where the Cup went overnight, although some of the Cons have dropped out voluntarily or, in some cases, involuntarily—Salonen apparently ended up in the emergency room at HUP getting stitches in his face after the sledding incident and his wife made him go home afterward.

8:45 a.m. It is now Wednesday morning and several of the Cons are at Central Tattoo Studio in Olde Kensington getting Cup designs inked. Judging from social media posts from the tattoo artists and spectators, some of the designs are very large and very gaudy. Mike Sato is holding Adam Belsky's hand. This looks painful.

9:30 a.m. *Update:* Belsky is eating a piece of pizza and sobbing.

10:01 a.m. *Update:* Sato is getting tattooed. We didn't think he had any space left. We're not sure where that one's going, but they had to put up a modesty curtain, so you can use your own imagination for that.

[An image of Michael Sato's hand, giving a thumbs-up, popping out from the side of a curtain. Some of his teammates are sitting just outside of curtain-view, in varying states of impressed and/or horrified.]

11:00 a.m. Barhopping on Frankford Avenue.

6:30 p.m. The Cons arrive for a team dinner at Kalaya. Whether the head chef will tolerate the boisterous singing is anyone's best guess.

9:30 p.m. The Cons are crashing a wedding at Philly Distilling. I'm not sure whether the bride or groom are really happy about this, but the Cup appears to be full of a delightful concoction of gin and cucumber.

[An image of Nathaniel Singer and Zachary Reed, both very drunk, with their arms around a woman wearing a mermaid-style wedding dress and a very bemused-looking man in a suit, presumably the groom. Both Nate and Zach are beaming. Behind them, you can see the wedding's bartender gamely ladling drinks out of the Cup.]

10:26 p.m. Round sixteen of "We Are the Champions."

3:15 a.m. Attention: it appears that the Cup is finally going home with the Cons' captain, Nate Singer.

3:16 a.m. And according to social media so, it seems, is Zach Reed.

* * * * *

ACKNOWLEDGMENTS

Once again, it takes a village to put a book out into the world.

Thank you to Deidre Knight, my agent, for your continued advice and guidance.

Thank you to the entire Carina team—Stephanie Doig, Mackenzie Walton, and everyone behind the scenes—for your hard work and polishing.

Thank you to Cait and Jo, for your early reading and encouragement; to my server buds, for advice and venting and humor.

As always, I am in your debt.

Turn the page to read an excerpt from *Home Ice Advantage* by Ari Baran, the next book in the Penalty Box series.

CHAPTER ONE

September

On the day of Ryan Sullivan's forty-fifth birthday he discovered that his wife had gotten him a divorce.

Embarrassingly, it took him until the afternoon to realize it.

He had left early in the morning to get to the game with his peewee hockey team. That kept him occupied for a few hours. It was his first coaching position and he'd been taking it *really* seriously. Sure, it was only peewee, but eleven- and twelve-year-olds were a real handful on the best of days. To make matters worse, Ryan had been mediating a season-long dispute between the parents of his 1C and the parents of a kid who thought *he* deserved to be the 1C. He'd kept their ice time pretty even, but that didn't matter to hockey parents who looked at the lines beforehand and kept track of matchups and deployments.

After the game, Paul, the father of Jaxon-the-2C, confronted Ryan outside of the locker room. Ryan had to talk the guy down, spinning a tale about PP1 time and reassuring him that really, *no one* was scouting this early, and it truly was not a knock on Jaxon's hockey skills that Wyatt had been taking more offensive-zone draws, but simply that Jaxon's defensive responsibility was stunningly well-developed for his age and—well. At least Paul hadn't punched the locker room wall this time.

Ryan had been so busy with the parents that by the time he got out to the parking lot, it was over an hour later than he normally would have been on his way home. He took a moment, alone in his car, to rub his eyes. When he was on the ice with the kids, he fucking loved every minute of it. He'd always considered himself a people person, but the parents…man, the parents were something else.

And holy shit, did Ryan know about *parents.* Ryan had four brothers who had all played pro hockey in some form or another, and their dad made Paul look like a family therapist in comparison.

By the time he had gotten out of the rink, stopped by Dunkin' to get his third cup of coffee, braved the shitty weekend traffic on the way home and narrowly avoided getting sideswiped by some asshole doing 80 mph with nowhere to go, the headache was building up behind his eyes. The news radio was still talking about the fact that yesterday the Boston Beacons, who'd already fired their general manager in the offseason, had fired their head coach in the middle of *training camp*, which didn't bode well for the season. If anything, the headache intensified.

It didn't get any better when he actually got home.

He parked in front of the house the same way he always did because the garage was where he'd set up all of his hockey equipment and the skate-sharpening machine and you could only fit Shannon's car in the other side anymore.

He keyed in the door code and the lock whirred uselessly in place.

Ryan frowned and tried it again. Another long, sad

whirr. He waited for the lock mechanism to reset before trying again, slowly this time, to make sure he hadn't typed it wrong.

The combination didn't work.

Ryan tucked his coffee into his elbow as he shifted his bag around and fished for the cell phone in his pocket. "Shannon?"

"What do you want, Ryan?"

"Did you…change the locks?"

"What do *you* think?"

"It seems kinda like you changed the locks."

"Really? Wow, look at the brain trust we got over here today."

Ryan took the phone away from his ear and stared at it. This kind of venom in Shannon's voice wasn't entirely out of the blue, but he couldn't figure out what he'd done today. "Shannon, why did you change the locks?"

"Why didn't you stay at the rink so my fucking process server could find you?"

The pieces of the puzzle fit together with the sudden clarity of figuring out the right move on the ice ahead of anyone else. Except this time, he was trailing the play. "Shannon, are you *divorcing* me?"

"No shit, Sherlock. I've only been trying to talk to you about it for the last goddamn month."

Ryan stared at the phone again. "You have?"

Shannon hung up on him.

He thought, for a second, about all of the teammates and friends he'd known who had gotten divorced and how you probably weren't supposed to lock your spouse out of the house without warning. He thought about equitable distribution and how humiliating it would feel, telling a judge, *well, she locked me out, so…*

He had never really wanted to move to New Hampshire in the first place, but it was close to Shannon's family. The thing was, he'd never even been particularly fond of the house in the first place. It felt like more work than it had been worth, the constant negotiations with Shannon about how much of his awards and medals and memorabilia he could keep anywhere except the basement. About how much space in the garage he was allowed to use up for his workshop.

Maybe…he could just let her have the house.

Every time they fought, it was a reminder that they had started dating when they were eighteen years old and had just kept going, even though it became clear, the longer things went on, that they had really different priorities.

Shannon had wanted the big house in Newfields to be close to her family. And at the time, Ryan had wanted what Shannon wanted. She'd deserved it after years of living far away from her family and friends, in the kinds of places she never would've chosen if she hadn't married a hockey player.

It wasn't until later that Ryan had realized exactly how much he hated living in New Hampshire in a house that was far too goddamn big for two people.

He called her again.

"*What*, Ryan?"

"Shannon. Just to be clear. You're really divorcing me? Really, completely, seriously divorcing me?"

"Yes, Ryan."

"But…what about all of my stuff?"

"We can figure out a time for you to come and pick it up. But I'm over this. I told you I didn't want you to start coaching. I've waited years to have a life without fucking *hockey*—"

"But that is my life, Shan. It's always been my life."

"Not like this. Not like you get. Or did you forget that I made birthday brunch reservations for today—"

"You knew I had a game!"

"You couldn't have gotten the assistant coach to do it, Ryan? It's your *forty-fifth birthday*. It's peewee fucking hockey! I'm sick of always being reminded where I stand in your priorities and how as long as it's something hockey related, I'm at the bottom! And it's clear you don't understand this at all. We don't have anything else to talk about right now. I'll text you times and dates if you want to pick up your stuff."

Ryan thought about asking her to throw down a bag of clothes to him or something, but the back of his neck felt hot and sweaty. He hadn't fought much on the ice when he was a player, but the few times he'd gotten angry enough to do it, he'd felt like this. Like a teapot whose lid was about to explode with the force of the pressure built up under it.

Instead, he said, "Okay," and hung up again.

He stood there in the driveway—not *his* driveway anymore—and looked at the house. It was an ugly McMansion, and he could admit that now that Shannon had kicked him out. He couldn't quite figure out what he was feeling. It wasn't sad and it wasn't angry. Maybe *resigned* was the closest word for it. Maybe this is what it felt like to not care about losing anymore. He'd never felt like that in his life.

Ryan walked back to the car, slung his bag of hockey gear back into it and sat down in the driver's seat. He wasn't sure how long he sat there, but it was long enough that he could see Shannon peeking out at him through the curtains, probably wondering what the hell was going on and worrying that maybe he'd try to call her again.

His phone rang, and he almost threw it across the cab. *No, Shannon, you don't have anything else you could say to me.* It wasn't Shannon's number, though. He didn't have it saved as a contact and didn't recognize it at all. It was a Boston area code, though, which didn't bode well.

"Hello?"

"Ryan Sullivan?"

"Uh, yeah? I'm Sully."

"This is Joe Conroy, the general manager of the Boston Beacons."

Ryan blinked.

Joe Conroy was a legend. Ryan had grown up wearing his jersey. Conroy had played for Boston for years. Had his jersey retired at the Spectrum. Had been hired after Boston's last general manager was unceremoniously fired in the dumpster fire of the last season. Ryan knew him socially, but not enough for a phone call like this.

"Hello?" Conroy asked, and Ryan realized he had probably been silent too long.

"Sorry. Sorry, I was just—surprised."

"Well, you're going to be a hell of a lot more surprised than that by the time we're done. Do you have some time to talk?"

When he looked up at the house, Shannon glared at him from the upstairs window. Ryan pressed the ignition and said, "All the time in the world."

The Penalty Box series is available wherever books are sold, including Harlequin.com.